D0261559

INSECURITY

Also by Matthew Lynn

The Billion-Dollar Battle
Birds of Prey

INSECURITY

MATTHEW LYNN

HEINEMANN : LONDON

First published in Great Britain 1997
by William Heinemann
an imprint of Reed International Books Ltd
Michelin House, 81 Fulham Road, London SW3 6RB
and Auckland, Melbourne, Singapore and Toronto

Copyright © Matthew Lynn 1997
The author has asserted his moral rights

The extract from 'Crazy Love' by Van Morrison is quoted
by permission from International Music Publications Ltd.

The extract from 'Watching the Detectives' by Elvis Costello
is quoted by permission from Plangent Visions Music Ltd.

A CIP catalogue record for this title
is available from the British Library

ISBN 0 434 00377 8

Typeset by Falcon Oast Graphic Art
in 12 on 14 point Times
Printed and bound by Clays Ltd, St Ives plc

To my parents

PROLOGUE

A thin bead of sweat, hot and sticky, rolled gently off the man's brow and along the edge of the gun that was wedged firmly into the folds of flesh around his throat.

Sam Draper was nervous and afraid. The burning intensity of the late afternoon sun mingled with the rising terror of the moment had soaked his shirt and skin. His lips could taste the salty liquid dripping from his forehead, and the taste was bitter and sour.

'Kneel.'

The accent was English. London, working class. The speaker was six feet or more, dressed in khaki shorts and a denim shirt, with broad shoulders and wavy blond hair. He seemed ill at ease, here in the countryside of northern Thailand. A long way from the Whitechapel snooker halls and pawn shops that might have been his more natural habitat.

'Fuck you.'

The gun wedged tighter into his neck. Draper could feel the metal stretching the membranes. Any tighter and the skin would burst. The pain was starting to sear through his muscles and up into his jaw. 'I said kneel, fuckhead.'

Draper dropped to his knees. The mud on the ground was dried and cracked, burnt out by the long summer. A crap assignment, he thought to himself. With a crap ending. It should have been a milk run. An easy way to pay the mortgage. Investigate the illegal counterfeiting of drugs on behalf of the World Pharmaceuticals Forum. Checking up on a bit of dodgy faking for a trade body. Nothing complicated. Good fees and unlimited expenses. A joy ride. Not a ride where you expected to run up against any serious gangsters. Certainly not heavy thugs from the East End.

Until now. Too bloody close, he told himself. The factory had not been that hard to find. A few discreet questions placed among the rougher trade in the Patpong bars. Put a fifteen-year-old whore in the laps of those men, swill some Carlsberg down their throats, and their tongues soon started to loosen. A joy ride. A trip up to the country, a few snaps with a zoom lens. Nothing difficult. Money in the bank.

Too close. The factory was bigger than he expected. And the security tighter. Nothing like the fake Rolex or Chanel factories he was used to investigating in South-East Asia. More sophisticated. And run by professionals.

He could see the plant now, stretching out before his eyes. A simple compound built from bamboo and corrugated iron. Inside there was a printer churning out the packaging and next to it a pill manufacturing machine. Canisters of chemicals were hung above a rotating drum. Out of it spat an endless series of perfect little round pills. Pill after pill after pill. Hundreds of them. Twenty or so Thai workers, old mostly, both men and women, collected the little packages, and put them into their boxes, neatly folding and sealing up the containers. To Draper's tutored eye, it looked like a high-quality fakery. Prozac, today, judging by the lettering. But no doubt there was a different drug every

2

few days. Thai forgery factories, he knew from experience, were masters of the art of flexible manufacturing.

'Too close,' he muttered to himself, out loud this time. Nobody listened or responded to his words. His head was spinning and his vision blurred. The sweat was dripping over his eyebrows, mixing with the blood still seeping from the cuts, clogging up his eyes. The guards had pounced on him a couple of hundred yards outside the compound. Caught him red handed with the zoom lens. A chance patrol, perhaps. More likely the area was rigged with electronic sensors. These people seemed to have plenty of money. No expense was being spared.

Four Thai guys. Youngish, mid-twenties, but experienced and tough. Trained. Two sharp blows and then they dragged him, already bruised and bleeding, into the compound. And introduced him to the Englishman.

'You might want this.'

The Englishman handed down a square, black strip of cloth, pressing it into his hand. Draper knew what it was for. A blindfold. He wiped the moisture from his eyes, and took the cloth, tying it tightly around the back of his neck. Blackness.

'Jimmy,' the Englishman shouted. 'Get the camera. Time for some snaps.'

Draper could see nothing but he heard the sound of feet scurrying across the dirt surface, and, a minute or so later, he heard the sound of a man returning. He muttered a few words in Thai that Draper could not understand.

The Englishman bent down and stuffed a small photograph, and two sheets of documentation into Draper's breast pocket, positioning them so the photo of an Oriental woman was just visible. The barrel of the gun rapped sharply against his chin. The Englishman was so close Draper could feel his warm breath on his cheek.

'Smile for the camera,' he said.

'Fuck you,' Draper repeated. It was all he could think of.

Above him he heard the click of the camera, once, then twice, then three times, and the whirring of the motor rolling on the

3

film. In the distance he could hear the clatter of the factory. Otherwise, he was surrounded by silence.

His head recoiled as he felt the gun being thrust into his ear. Beneath him he could feel his knees trembling, and in that instant he felt his hands fall forward. He was kneeling on all fours now.

'Closing time, matey,' said the Englishman. Draper could hear the camera clicking above him. And then he heard the sound of the trigger being squeezed.

ONE

The man's head was lying down in the cracked dirt. A single gun-shot wound was visible to the side of his face, and the blood, run-ning into his sweat-soaked hair, was still moist. His eyes had a sad and sorrowful look; a look of remorse and regret that his life should have been emptied by a single, callous bullet on a strip of parched wasteland. Poor guy, thought Jack, as he placed the black and white photograph carefully down on the table. Nobody wants to die. Not ever. And certainly not like that.

'Welcome back, Mr Borrodin,' said the Chairman.

Jack glanced upwards. It had been two years now since he had seen Sir Kurt Helin face to face, but the patriarch of the Kizog pharmaceuticals empire had changed little. His hair was a fraction thinner perhaps. Its shade a touch whiter maybe. And the wrinkles around his jowls had grown deeper. But the eyes were the same; dark and piercing with a sly, combative sparkle.

'Your posting? How did you find it?'

'Challenging,' Jack replied. 'Hot. Bad traffic.'

The Chairman rose up from behind his long wooden desk, walking closer to Jack. His back arched slightly, betraying his age, and there was a slight limp in his left leg. Jack could see him more closely now. He looked older. His face was tired and drained. Worse for wear.

Jack could feel the Chairman's hands patting him on the back, and he recoiled slightly from his touch. 'I won't trouble you with an old man's advice,' he said. 'Except for this. Not everyone gets this kind of a chance. But everyone should take it when they do.'

A break, thought Jack. For the past two years he had been working in the Bangkok office, a sleek air-conditioned suite in one of the downtown skyscrapers. There were only five of them there, two from head office and three drawn from other parts of Kizog's world-wide empire, plus some local support staff. The work had been difficult. Trying to recruit a salesforce, establish distribution systems, open up the market, and keep tabs on the competition. All in a country where the infrastructure to support a modern multinational business was only just emerging. It was challenging enough in itself. But most of all it was impossible to keep track of where you were in the company. There was no flow of gossip from head office. No speculation. No rumours. Precious little networking to be done. And no way of knowing where you stood in the race; a kind of career limbo. Of course, there was always the remote possibility that the results would speak for themselves. Yet somehow Jack doubted it. Results seldom spoke for themselves at Kizog. People spoke for themselves.

'I was surprised to get your call,' he said.

The Chairman's eyes opened wide. 'But why, my dear boy, why?'

'I felt I had been sidelined,' Jack replied. 'Sent out to Thailand because I wasn't going to make it back here. The Japanese have a phrase for it, don't they. The man who sits by the window.'

A broad grin creased up the lines on the Chairman's face. 'Purgatory, that's all. A boring but necessary interlude before the

6

ascent to heaven. I'm exaggerating, naturally. But head office anyway.'

'What exactly do you want me to do, sir?'

'What do *you* want to do, Jack?'

Jack eyed him closely, but beyond the outline of a small, greying man, wrinkled by age, he could see nothing of any tangible substance. The Chairman was as elusive and inscrutable as he had always been. There was the same knowing look, the same calculated air of infinite wisdom, the same casual humour, and the same veneer of warmth and concern. One of the great salesmen of all time. And still, Jack pondered, one of the most tempting men he had ever encountered.

He was, of course, a legend among the younger staffers. A myth, simultaneously inflated and ridiculed, as leaders of organisations usually were. Time forgot how long Sir Kurt had been in the company; since before Jack was born, that much was sure. A lifetime. He had started as a scientist in the early sixties, risen to be head of research and development, and moved smoothly on to become chief executive in the early seventies, before assuming the chairmanship of the company. He was, by now, the company personified. Its successes were his successes, its faults his faults; a point reinforced every year in the long essay on the state of the business and the world that prefaced the annual report.

'Nothing out of the ordinary,' Jack replied. 'To contribute to the company. And to do well personally. To get ahead.'

'That's settled then.'

Jack laughed. 'Any specific instructions, sir?'

The Chairman walked closer, standing no more than a foot from Jack. 'Be very careful,' he said. 'You know what head office can be like.' And then, his eyes moving away again, he turned to the intercom on his desk. 'Send them in,' he said.

'Be careful of what, sir?' Jack asked.

The Chairman smiled. 'Your enemies, of course.'

The door opened and two men were ushered into the office. The Chairman stood up to greet them, padding silently across the floor, softly shaking their hands. He turned and introduced them

7

to Jack. 'Herbert Strowser the third, and Dieter Schmidt, both from the secretariat of the World Pharmaceuticals Forum,' he said. 'This is Jack Borrodin, a special assistant of mine, and one of the cleverest young men in this organisation. We can trust him. He may even have a role to play in these events.'

Jack shook hands with the American and the German. Strowser was just over six feet, with greying hair, a tanned, weather-beaten complexion, and the look, Jack decided, of a man who could handle himself in a corporate struggle; Schmidt was shorter, with a squashed appearance, and eyes that darted around the room with mistrustful speed. Behind him, a secretary was bringing in a silver tray of coffee, placing it carefully down on the table. The four of them sat down on the two black sofas at the far end of the expansive office, the two sides facing each other, Jack averting his eyes. Be careful of which enemies, he wondered to himself.

'How can we help you this morning?' began the Chairman.

'These are difficult times,' said Strowser. 'As you know, Sir Kurt, counterfeit pharmaceuticals have long been a problem for our industry. In many Third World countries, racketeers and gangsters have been churning out fake copies of patented medicines to sell at a fraction of their real cost.'

'I am aware of this,' replied the Chairman softly. 'And the position of this company has always been clear. There are millions of people out there who can only afford the counterfeit medicines.'

The German replied this time. 'We now have information that counterfeiters are starting to target both the United States and Western Europe,' said Schmidt. 'One or more sophisticated counterfeiting rackets are operating on both continents with the technology and expertise to put fake drugs into the healthcare system. There have been one or two isolated incidents of this before, but usually they have been pretty amateur, a matter of faking the packaging and not much else. This is much more serious. These people know the formulations of the drugs they are copying and are turning out exact replicas. We estimate the losses to the industry could now be running as high as two billion dollars.'

Strowser and Schmidt looked to the Chairman, scanning his face for some reaction, but it was on hold, a blank screen, transmitting no signals. 'The policy of the Forum in the past has been to keep the existence of the counterfeiters secret,' continued Strowser. 'Medicine depends on confidence. If people started to lose faith in our products, then we could see some really dramatic falls in sales.'

'Keep it all covered up, eh gentlemen?' said the Chairman, the smile on his face widening as he spoke.

Strowser appeared uncomfortable with the remark. 'Most members feel an investigation contained within the industry would be the best way of dealing with this,' he answered flatly.

'You want money,' said the Chairman. 'But of course. Why didn't you say so.'

Strowser pulled a pair of pictures from his briefcase. He passed them first to the Chairman, who glanced down briefly before passing them on to Jack. Both portrayed the man lying dead in the dirt. They were the same pictures he had seen on the Chairman's desk only a few minutes earlier. For a brief moment Jack gazed again into the eyes of the victim. Why did the Chairman already have these pictures? he wondered. And why would he let me see them?

The two men turned towards Sir Kurt, waiting for a reaction. He paused, rolling his eyes towards Jack, fixing upon him a look that was both conspiratorial and knowing. Jack turned away, unsure of the correct response. 'One man working for us was close to cracking a counterfeiting ring operating out of Thailand. He died last week. Executed as soon as he was captured,' said Strowser.

The Chairman nodded, cloaking his expression in an air of gravitas. 'How much would you say this man's life was worth, Jack?'

'About £10,000.'

The Chairman turned to Strowser and Schmidt, an air of

amused sympathy playing on his face. 'The callousness of youth,' he sighed. 'They think life is cheap. When you get to my age you realise just how much it costs. Now tell me, how much do you need?'

'It is impossible to quantify the commitment, Sir Kurt, because of course we cannot be sure how long it will take to solve this problem,' said Schmidt. 'But I would estimate somewhere in the region of £250,000. From each of the major companies.'

'Kizog will make its full contribution,' said the Chairman. 'Jack here will assist your people in any way he can. I am sure you'll find him invaluable.'

The American and the German thanked the Chairman and stood up to leave. 'Our people will be in touch,' said Schmidt, shaking Jack by the hand.

Jack nodded and said nothing, watching them carefully as they departed from the office. 'I'm a little confused, sir,' he said soon after the two men had departed.

The Chairman nodded, but remained silent. 'You described me as your special assistant,' Jack persisted.

'Good title, don't you think. Hard to pin down.'

Jack hesitated, anxious to make a good impression on the Chairman, and yet at the same time reluctant to accept any posting that was not clearly defined. 'And my tasks, exactly?' he asked.

'I'd make it up as you go along, if I were you,' the Chairman replied casually. 'All the best jobs are self-invented.'

Tara Ling clipped the plastic name-tag on to the collar of her red cardigan, pausing only momentarily to read the slogan that ran across the bottom of the visitor's pass. 'Kizog – Better Medicines for a Better World' it read, the words printed out in slanted blue lettering.

She walked across the marbled foyer and took a seat on the row of black leather sofas, below a wall of display screens. Turning upwards, her eyes scanned through the confection of good deeds written up on the wall, digesting the mixture of smiling pictures and smiling words. Happy children, black, white and yellow, held hands, whilst the blurb chirruped away about the contribution the company was making to the health of the world.

Lies, stupid lies, Tara told herself. Inside her mind she began compiling an alternative script; an internal monologue of the inequities imposed on the poor and afflicted of the world by the commercial pharmaceuticals industry. So what am I doing here? she asked herself, before her attention was snapped by the approach of a woman in her late twenties. Dr Peter Scott was ready to see her now.

Tara followed into the lift, and up to the fifth floor. Along the directors' corridor, thick carpets, soft underfoot and perfectly silent, led up to the sombre panelled doors. The opulence, the lavishness, of the decoration felt misplaced to her; it was distant from the spartan surroundings of the National Institutes of Health in Bethesda, Maryland, where she worked now.

Dr Scott's office was the third room along the corridor that twisted through the executive suites. Tara's eyes fell first on the nameplate on the open door: 'Head of Research', it said, and then on the man. It was the first time she had seen him. He was about forty-five, with thinning brown hair combed over his head, and wearing a single-breasted brown suit. There was distinctly a shift downmarket from the appearance of the surroundings to the appearance of the man, a fact which Tara found somehow re-assuring. Dr Scott shook her hand with both of his, and motioned to her to sit down. 'It was good of you to come so far to see me,' he began.

'I am not used to such corporate extravagance,' replied Tara, reflecting on the first-class air ticket that had flown her across the Atlantic, the five-star hotel room, and the chauffeur-driven car that had delivered her to the office.

'I can imagine,' Dr Scott answered, flashing what he hoped was his most welcoming smile. 'There is never much money around in the public sector.'

11

'True,' Tara replied. She paused before continuing: 'Tell me why you want me to work here?'

Dr Scott glanced down at the dossier lying open on his desk. A summary of her life was sketched in the barest detail. Born in 1964, in Vietnam, the daughter of an American serviceman and a Vietnamese woman. Left Vietnam at the age of seven for the United States. Studied biochemistry at Harvard. Very bright. And already an expert on leprosy. He glanced back up at her, admiring the silkiness of her long black hair and the soft delicacy of her Eurasian features. His eyes moved slowly, searching for a way forward, but her expression was calm and relaxed. Hire her, the Chairman had instructed. It's important.

'Most of the major companies keep close tabs on the young biochemical researchers,' he said. 'Your track record is very impressive. As good as any I've ever seen in a person your age.'

Tara shrugged, settling back in the plush, brown leather armchair, fixing a long, cool stare on the middle-aged man trying to woo her into his fold. Let him talk, she decided. See how far he is prepared to go. 'Perhaps my work is impressive because I care about what I am doing,' she said flatly. 'I am working on a disease I think is important.'

Dr Scott observed her cautiously, a smile fixed on his face, but with a sigh close to his heart. He too had been around this track many times, trying to coax brilliant young researchers out of the cloistered groves of academe and into the harder corridors of a commercial laboratory. He knew they enjoyed it; that sense of power, that flattery, that acknowledgement that they were somehow special, who could resist? But he himself found it a tiresome and trying experience.

'I hear what you are saying,' Dr Scott began. 'Of course your commitment to fresh and original science comes first. That is true for all of us. But I think you are wrong in believing that there is so strong a contradiction. At other companies perhaps. But here at Kizog we are as committed as you are to providing affordable healthcare to people all around the world. Naturally we would make it worth your while. A starting salary of say £80,000 would be no problem. That is considerably more than double what you make at the National Institutes. Then of course we could provide you with free accommodation and a car paid for by the company. And a bonus scheme . . .'

The words trailed away. Dr Scott spoke in even, measured tones, balancing his words, but he had been through this charade enough times to know that the money and the car made little impact, particularly on the women. They were not so easily seduced.

Tara shook her head softly, her hair swaying around her shoulders. 'If you have seen some of my papers, then you will know that my main work is on leprosy, and I can't imagine that is something Kizog would want to fund.'

Dr Scott held his hands up. 'I won't waste your time. And you are of course right as well. Leprosy isn't a disease we would normally research here, since even if we discovered an effective drug it would hardly be profitable. Those are the blunt realities of this industry.' He paused, leaning forward slightly on his desk, and fixing a quizzical look on Tara. 'Does Ator interest you?' he said. 'Given your work on leprosy it must do.'

'Ator?' questioned Tara. She was well aware of the virus. But she had not expected it to be raised so quickly in the conversation. Or indeed at all.

'Absolutely,' said Dr Scott. 'Now that is a disease where we may have some common ground. How many deaths does the UN say it has caused in Africa and Asia? Two hundred thousand. Now that it is spreading into the West there is no question that the industrialised nations would pay for a cure and for an inoculation programme to stamp the disease out. So it would make money and be beneficial to mankind and you wouldn't have to worry about compromising your integrity.'

'But I am not an expert in Ator,' answered Tara. 'It is so new that few people are.'

'But you are an expert in leprosy.'

Tara could feel the buds of curiosity growing within her. What

13

does he know about what happened? she wondered. And is that why I have been asked here? 'Go on.'

'Like leprosy, Ator is a disease of the central nervous system. It has rather different effects, naturally. And the body starts to decay much more quickly. But our research indicates that the two diseases are chemically very similar. At the molecular level there could be very little difference.'

'You believe that Ator is a form of leprosy?' asked Tara, the surprise evident in the tone of her voice.

'A mutation perhaps,' answered Dr Scott. 'The point is we have studied your work on leprosy, and we believe that if we combine that with our knowledge of the chemistry of the Ator virus we could be very close to a vaccine.'

'A vaccine for Ator?' questioned Tara.

Dr Scott leant back and smiled. He could detect the interest in her voice. 'It would be one of the great pharmacological break-throughs of the twentieth century,' he said, searching for the words to drive the hook deeper. 'I'm terribly excited by it. But it does require your coming to work here. You know how these companies work. Unless you are on the staff we can't share our research with you. Kizog is willing to put hundreds of millions behind this project, but obviously the information has to be pro-tected and the patent position can't be compromised.'

This was far from what she had expected, and for the moment Tara was lost for a response.

Dr Scott leant forward again, his hands inching across the desk. 'Stay for a few days and look at some of our research? I am sure it will fascinate you,' he said. 'We need you, Miss Ling.'

TWO

Dani Fuller seemed stranded somewhere in those empty years between twenty-five and thirty-five, a decade women go through where their ages are hard to pin down. She was sitting in the back of the bar, a whisky in front of her, so far hardly touched. There were a couple of cigarette butts in the ashtray already. Her long blonde hair was tied up behind her head, revealing her drawn, thin face and sharp features, and her shoulders were tensed. Her eyes were scanning the room, moving inquisitorially over each person that passed by. Jack guessed at once that she was the one – she was wearing the black suit he had been told to look out for – and nodded in her direction.

He stopped at her table, leaning over to introduce himself. No wedding ring, he noted. He ordered a bottle of Beck's from the waiter, and turned back towards her. There was a pause, lingering and slow, while both surveyed each other, casting their eyes over the person opposite. Mentally, Fuller began noting the

15

details of the man who stood before her: five feet eleven inches, black hair, swept back over his head, mid-eighties style, no more than medium build, but with solid blue eyes that expressed a sense of calm and reserve. A good and probably decent man, but hardly a fighter, she decided.

'It's good of you to meet me here this evening,' she said.

Her accent was English, but indeterminate; Jack could not locate the region or place she might have come from. There was a strength to her voice that he found surprising, however; a sense of steel underpinning her tone. It contrasted sharply with her appearance. Everything on the surface seemed archly feminine; the neat suit, with the shoulder pads and short skirt, the stiletto shoes, the jewellery, and the harshly drawn make-up. Yet everything inside, judging from her eyes and voice, was tough enough to be verging on the brutal. A very hard woman, Jack decided. And not someone to take any chances with. Not unless you had to.

He told her that the meeting was no problem, his pleasure entirely, and so on. But he knew he was lying. He was meeting her because he had to. It was an order.

He had just completed his first day back in head office. The place had a familiar feeling to it, a warmth and security that made him feel as if he had returned home. Which in a way he had. There were people he knew in the corridors. People who stopped and said hallo, and asked him how he had been whilst he was away, and who filled him in on the gossip he had missed. It was superficial chatter, meaningless and trivial, but, all the same, it was the kind of contact he had missed. And he was glad to have returned.

Nobody talked for very long. Nor, apart from a few jokes about his tan, did they ask him much about himself. No one seemed to have any idea what he was doing, and Jack didn't have much idea himself. Special assistant to the Chairman. Sir Kurt had been right. It was a good title. It sounded grand. But it certainly wasn't very specific.

He had his own office, and a secretary he shared with a

number of other people. It was on the third floor, which suggested a middle-ranking position in the corporate hierarchy, and there were two other people there who were also special assistants; one to the finance director, and one to the chief executive. Jack wasn't too sure what they did either, and didn't like to ask. The first day seemed a bit early to own up to the fact that you were entirely clueless about what your job might be. And, anyway, something would probably turn up.

A sheaf of papers had come down to his office from the Chairman. Attached was a note. 'Study the available information on counterfeiting,' it said. 'Do your own research. Meet this lady. And keep me informed.' At the bottom, there was no signature, but a simple, spidery K scrawled across the page. Jack made one call, and arranged the meeting for this evening. Dani Fuller, according to the papers, was an investigator with the Medicines Control Agency, who had been seconded to work alongside the World Pharmaceuticals Forum on counterfeiting. She was the key person in the investigation. The co-ordinator. And she wanted to meet Sir Kurt's assistant.

The briefing papers had been prepared by the Forum. A warning written across the top made it clear that only board-level executives should see the material. An advisory note suggested that it should not be passed on to non-executives. Clearly, nobody at Kizog was taking that warning too seriously. Not the Chairman anyway.

In the last two years, the document stated, counterfeit medicines had started turning up in First World countries. It cited examples of counterfeit Zantac being prescribed in the UK and Germany; of Prozac in the US and France; and of Capoten in the US and Germany. 'These fakes have been discovered purely by accident, but they appear to be of a very high quality. Both the packaging and the chemical composition of the compounds suggest they have been made with the aim of producing exact replicas of the real thing. This is a situation the industry clearly cannot tolerate. We believe it is imperative that the industry acts now. After discussions with the relevant government bodies both

17

in the US and Europe, it is proposed that the industry works alongside the detection agencies to combat the counterfeiters. Both the US Federal Government and the European Commission have agreed to co-operate. In light of the importance of the pharmaceutical industry to both the European and American economies, they have also agreed to keep the existence of the counterfeiters secret for as long as possible.'

'How much do you know about counterfeiting?' asked Fuller.

Jack shrugged. 'Not much. I have seen the briefing material supplied by the Forum.'

She took another sip on her whisky, casting a long, inquisitive look at Jack. 'Tell me your feelings about this.'

'Concerned,' answered Jack, aware that he was spinning what he believed to be the company line. 'There is a serious threat here. A threat to people's lives, but also to the profitability of the company. So you have our full commitment to whatever action is necessary. The Chairman has assured the Forum of that, and I can assure you personally.'

Fuller was still looking right through him while he spoke, the same lingering stare fixed on his face and lips. Jack sensed that she believed him even less than he believed himself. 'But your own feelings?' she asked.

'Nervous,' Jack answered. 'This is a dangerous situation that needs to be handled with great care both by me and by the company. But I'm confident also. I am sure the resources are there to cope.'

Fuller sat back in her chair, a smile playing on her face. She crossed her legs. 'Do you know much about how counterfeiting works?' she asked.

'Nothing beyond the obvious,' Jack replied.

'Let me brief you,' said Fuller, her voice suddenly acquiring a tone of authority. 'Point one. Making drugs usually isn't much harder than making candies. The counterfeiters obviously have manufacturing facilities. They may be in the Far East, perhaps in Africa and the Middle East as well. Possibly in the former Soviet Union, we're looking into that. Somewhere where they can put

18

down a small plant without attracting too much attention to themselves. Their next problem is getting hold of the formulae. There are two ways of doing that. One is to get the patent application. That will give you the details of the chemicals used in the drug. Once you have that all you need is a good biochemist to reverse engineer the thing. Another option is to tap into the knowledge within the company. Within Kizog for example there must be dozens of people who know exactly how to manufacture the company's drugs. Find one of those who is susceptible to bribery, pay him or her off, and you walk away with the formula. But cracking the right formula and then setting up the manufacturing facilities is only the beginning. The difficult part is getting the drugs into the system.'

'And that must be a lot harder, right?' said Jack. 'There are controls on the distribution of pharmaceutical drugs. You can't just wander into a pharmacist's and offer a box load of cut-price medicines. And you can't sell them at street markets either.'

'Correct,' answered Fuller. 'But because prices are different in each country, there is a trade in shipping medicines from one territory to another. Most drugs pass through many different wholesalers between leaving the manufacturer and arriving at the customer. On average it might be five wholesalers, sometimes many more.'

'That is the weak link,' said Jack.

'No question,' replied Fuller. 'They have access to formulae, access to manufacturing, and access to wholesalers at many different levels. Putting this operation together has taken a great deal of money and a great deal of organisational talent. Whoever we're dealing with, they are professionals, and very, very clever at what they do.' Fuller paused for a moment, her eyes widening as she focused more intently on Jack. 'We know a certain amount about the organisation, but all our information comes from the periphery,' she said. 'We have nothing from the heart.'

'You want an infiltrator?' asked Jack. Already he was starting to feel nervous about the direction the conversation was taking.

'Absolutely,' replied Fuller. 'We need to find somebody who is willing to go inside the organisation. To be recruited. To find out for us who they are, what they are doing, how they are doing it.'

Jack nodded, draining his beer glass. He wondered where this was leading him. 'I guess you need somebody from one of the major pharmaceutical companies,' he said. 'If you are right in supposing that they are tapping employees for information, then this organisation will be keen to recruit executives who can provide them with the information they need. That person, if he was working on our side, would be perfectly placed to discover who was really behind this thing.'

'Are you willing to go that deep?' asked Fuller.

Jack paused, deliberating over his reply, his mind calculating the consequences of what he was about to say. 'I would need to check with my superiors.'

'They promised to co-operate.'

'I know.'

'But you need to be personally committed.' She looked up at Jack once more, piercing him with a penetrating stare. 'This would need to be more than just following orders.'

His first impression was, Jack decided, probably correct, and unlikely to ever change; solid-to-the-bone boffin. Her long, black hair was neatly parted down the middle, and fell in two straight lines down the sides of her long, thin face. She was wearing steel-rimmed round spectacles, which hid her eyes, and her face was undecorated with make-up of any kind. Her body was wrapped in a shapeless white lab coat, beneath which he could see a pair of black jeans, and a pair of very sensible black shoes. There were no rings on her fingers, but there was a single, gold bracelet dangling from her left arm.

The phone call from the Chairman had taken him by surprise that morning. No sooner had he arrived at his desk, his mind still full of last night's meeting, and collected a cup of coffee than Sir Kurt was on the line. Jack glanced at his watch. It was still only ten past eight.

'I have another task for you,' he began. 'I'm sure you can be a most persuasive young man.'

Jack was unsure how to respond, and kept silent.

'I was at your age. Got a girlfriend?' he asked abruptly.

Not a great subject to get into at this time of the morning, thought Jack. And certainly not with the Chairman. 'Not now. In Thailand there was . . .'

'No conflict of interest then,' the Chairman cut in. 'Just get to know her.'

'Who?'

'Tara Ling. Young scientist. Temperamental. She doesn't like drugs companies. Worried about our ethics. Can't say I blame her myself. But she is important. We need her. She has information. Dr Scott is trying to bring her on board and he is showing her around. But like all the boffins, he is such a charmless old bastard, I wouldn't trust him to pull it off. You're the salesman. Bring her in.'

The phone went dead. Orders are orders, thought Jack, even if they don't make much sense. A quick call to Dr Scott's office had told him that Tara would meet him in the main lab building. Right now.

Neither the Chairman nor Dr Scott had mentioned that she was Oriental, or, judging by the lightness of her skin, and the roundness of her eyes, perhaps half Oriental. His two years in Thailand had taught Jack to distinguish between Asiatic races; he could tell Thais from Chinese, and reckoned he could distinguish the Japanese from the Koreans, but he could not place her. She could be from anywhere. 'You are considering joining us?' said Jack after he had introduced himself.

'Considering? Yes,' said Tara.

Her accent contained no trace of the Orient, thought Jack. Mid-Atlantic, and hard to place. Except that it was clearly Caucasian. 'I'm told you are a brilliant scientist.'

'Everyone is very flattering,' she replied.

They had started walking through the labs. The corridors stretched out before them, painted an industrial grey, and every ten yards exactly there was a solid steel door, with a window,

21

through which three scientists, each in regulation lab coats, could be seen. Most were stooping over test tubes, or peering into computers. Some of the labs had pictures on the wall; mostly *Far Side* cartoons, or Dali pictures. There were clocks everywhere, all of which were constantly referred to. For a supposedly creative part of the company, Jack reflected, it was about as industrial as it could be.

'Development,' explained Jack as they walked by. 'This is really the most intensive part of the research centre. And the most mundane. Development, as no doubt you know, is a matter of legwork.'

He found it hard to imagine that the prospect of joining the lab rats, cooped up in these cages all day with their test tubes, held much appeal. He was already wondering how to explain away his failure to bring her on board to the Chairman. Inscrutable Oriental seemed a good line. Difficult people to predict.

'You work with the Chairman, don't you?' asked Tara suddenly.

'Special assistant,' replied Jack.

'What does that mean?'

Jack paused. It was a good question. Glorified gofer didn't sound very good. Nor did errand boy. 'I work on special projects. And I keep tabs on different parts of the company's operations,' he replied. 'The eyes and ears of the Chairman,' he added, allowing a touch of pride to seep into the tone of his voice.

'And the brains?' asked Tara.

There was something about her manner which made Jack suspect she was being sarcastic; not enough to be rude, yet enough to raise his suspicions. He could feel himself becoming defensive. 'One or two of my suggestions have been implemented.'

'Such as?'

'I helped set up the company's operation in Thailand,' replied Jack.

Tara turned away, as if such matters did not interest her, and together they continued their stroll through the labs. Inwardly, she noted the expensive Boss suit, the smart watch, and the carefully shined half-brogue black shoes he was wearing; standard

22

executive armour, she decided, and he was probably a standard corporate creature, although there was something about the half-smile constantly playing on his face which suggested Jack did not take his role one hundred per cent seriously.

Tara commented on how expensive it all looked, and Jack agreed. It was a fabulous amount of money devoted to research; seven hundred million a year, almost half of it spent in this building alone, he told her.

'At the National Institutes we could probably do twice as much with only half the money.'

Jack laughed. 'The overheads are higher here.'

'Like my plane ticket, and the chauffeur,' said Tara. 'A lot of the money must be wasted. Still I suppose it prevents the profits from appearing too high.'

Sharp, thought Jack. 'True. But it is also a way of keeping the share price high. The stockmarket always figures the more you spent on research the better, and none of the analysts or fund managers would ever be able to figure out whether you were spending the money well. Everything goes into the research budget. Company jets, conferences in Hawaii, the Chairman's mistress, bribes to Italian officials. The more you spend, the happier everyone is.'

They had drifted towards the coffee area now. At the inter-sections of each of the four wings of the lab buildings there were cakes and biscuits on the tables, and newspapers and scientific journals on display next to the comfy armchairs. It was one of the Chairman's personal innovations, and taken very seriously. His idea had been to introduce some free space, like an academic common room, where scientists from different disciplines could meet and talk and swap ideas. Cross-discipline creativity, had been the phrase used at the time, which sounded to Jack like something the McKinsey people who drifted through every couple of years had come up with. For a few months it had been virtually compulsory to drop in for an hour or so a day and talk about what was on TV last night; the researchers, Jack noticed, all seemed to be keen viewers. Now it was practically empty.

23

'Have you decided?' he asked.

'Not yet.'

Jack wondered what tack to take. 'The Chairman wanted you to know that I could be your contact on the commercial side of the company. That if you have problems with the work you were doing here, we could take them directly to Sir Kurt. It is a most unusual arrangement. He must want you very much.'

'How much do you know about Ator?' asked Tara.

Jack sensed the conversation was about to wander into territory he was unfamiliar with. 'Third World virus. It is new and mysterious. A few cases are now emerging in the US and Europe,' he said vaguely.

'Would it be a priority disease for Kizog?'

'Now that it is appearing in the First World, yes, perhaps.'

'Not before?'

'Unlikely.'

'Then why has the company done so much work on it?'

'It has?' answered Jack, realising after he spoke that his tone betrayed his surprise.

'Dr Scott has been leading me through some of Kizog's research,' Tara continued. 'It is very impressive. They are quite close to a vaccine. But he believes they need access to some of the research I have done on leprosy to take them closer. That is why they want me here.'

Jack was unsure how to respond. He was intrigued by all that she was telling him, but mindful as well of his mission. 'Aren't you keen to help? I mean, apart from the money we would pay you, it would be a major scientific achievement.'

Tara cast her eyes down, lost for a moment in her own reflection. 'It would.'

'Then what is holding you back?'

'The research they have shown me is strangely incomplete,' Tara said. 'As if *they* were holding something back.'

'Until you join the staff, it is impossible for them to be entirely open with you,' he said.

Her eyes met his, and for the first time Jack could detect a

24

softening in her expression. 'Are they always honest with you?'

'So far,' replied Jack. 'It is a big and sometimes brutal organisation. But keep an eye on the rules, and things usually work out.'

'Perhaps so,' said Tara, the firmness returning to her eyes. 'And perhaps not.'

THREE

Pausing at the traffic lights Jack stuck a CD into the hi-fi on his new company BMW, one of the remastered Costello reissues; this was the soundtrack of his adolescence, and it still touched plenty of chords within him. *'They call it instant justice when it's past the legal limit,'* sang Elvis. *'Someone's scratching at the window I wonder who is it?'* Jack tapped his fingers in time to the music as he drove.

The beamer had been delivered to him just yesterday, and it still had that strangely disinfected smell of an unused machine; the faint aroma of leaked oil and burnt brake pads they acquired after a few thousand miles was still absent. If he was honest it was not his favourite car; there was too much of the yuppie-mobile about it. He would have preferred a Mazda or one of the new MGs, but the forms that came down from personnel offered only a 3-series or a Ford Scorpio. Hardly any choice at all, Jack reflected.

Who cares? he decided. Take the rough with the smooth. The car was fast, it was powerful, and, best of all, it was free; a sign that he was on his way. Another three years, he decided, perhaps four. The last reshuffle of the board had seen one of the younger guys promoted to director: Harry Smile, and he was only thirty-six then. He too, like Jack, had joined the company in his late twenties, after an MBA from INSEAD and a spell with one of the consultancies the Chairman liked to call in every year or so, followed by a posting abroad and a stint in the Chairman's office. What can stop me? Jack thought, touching his foot on the accelerator a little. A seat on the board. Plus stock options worth a minimum two hundred thousand a year. Enough to keep a family, raise children, retire before the company took too much of a toll. Enough, as well, to get out while he was still young and fit enough to enjoy the rest of his life. London, he realised, would take some time to adjust to. Thailand he had enjoyed, even though he had never quite been able to figure out why Kizog sent him there. After following his parents as the oil company shifted his father from one territory to another, entering a new international school every few years, he had felt more at home somehow in the Far East; he was used, he realised, to being a foreigner. Back here, as a native, he felt strangely dislocated. As much as he liked England and the English, for him it was a place without roots, and he regretted the fact that his parents were not here now that he had returned; his father had often spoken of retiring to the south-east of England, and Jack was still pained by the knowledge that he had not lived to make that happen. He would have liked to have had a family here with him. It would have made things easier.

Briefly, his memory touched on the death of his father two years ago. It had been sudden and unexpected, a heart attack only a few months after the posting to the Ukraine that he had expected to be his last. It had happened only a few days after Kizog told Jack they wanted him to transfer to Thailand for two years. Even now, he could still vividly recall the look on his mother's face as he told her he was leaving the country, just as she was trying to come to terms with retiring alone to the cottage they had bought together to pass their last years in. Exactly like your father, she had told him, not with bitterness but with remorse; unable to stay for long in the same place. On reflection, Jack could see now that she was probably right.

It was one of the last conversations he had with his mother, which was why, Jack reflected, he remembered it so well. She had died a year after he departed for the Far East, and the funeral had been the most miserable moment of his life so far. Her few surviving relations were there, and though they said nothing to suggest it directly, he could not help but sense their disapproval of his absence from the country during the last year of her life. Whether they really disapproved or not, he could not tell. He certainly disapproved himself, and that was what counted.

Jack was still pondering his sense of loss, contrasting it with the opportunities he could feel lay ahead, as he parked the car, and walked through the neatly trimmed lawns towards Administrative Block A, the Helin Building. I have sacrificed a lot to get where I am today in this company, he decided to himself. I should make sure I don't blow it now.

'You're late,' said Jenny, as Jack walked purposefully towards his desk.

She might have only been working with him for a few days, but the secretary was already starting to adopt an air of reassuring familiarity. 'The Chairman wants to see you at eight sharp,' she continued.

'Anyone else in yet?' asked Jack.

The secretary put a cup of freshly brewed coffee down on his desk. 'Sam and Layla are here, but they are not involved in this gig. The Chairman asked just for you.'

'Good or bad?' asked Jack.

'Sam and Layla looked quite miffed,' answered Jenny. 'That's good. But the Chairman had a particularly vague tone in his voice when I asked him what he wanted to see you about. That's bad.'

Sam and Layla, miffed, thought Jack. My two new colleagues,

28

so called. All three of them had the title 'special assistant'. The ice around the office was starting to melt, and a quick check on the fate of the earlier special assistants had revealed some interesting statistics. Of fifteen over the past seven years, three had made it on to the board. Two had dropped out somehow so they didn't count in the calculation. Another five had left of their own accord. And five were stuck in some remote outpost of the Kizog empire. His chances were good, he figured; but so were Sam's and Layla's. Particularly Layla's. There had never been a woman on the Kizog board, and, around the office, there were rumblings that accusations of sexism were starting to be an embarrassment for the company. If the Chairman was of a mind to remedy that situation, which he might be, given his hang-up about a progressive public profile for the company, then he would certainly want it to be one of his girls. And Layla was the only girl he had.

Most likely Layla has been spreading this talk about it being time for a woman on the board, thought Jack to himself. Hoping it will percolate up to the fifth floor. 'Heading up?' said Layla, poking her head around the office door.

'I was just thinking about you,' said Jack.

'Dreaming, more likely,' said Layla.

Which was true up to a point, thought Jack. With long, thick, red hair, a fine figure, and a pert face, Layla was certainly attractive, and her feline way of moving through the corridors, stalking gossip and leaving behind a trail of conjecture and rumour, had always impressed him. They had met soon after he had joined the company, when she was still working in marketing research, and had remained friendly ever since. She flirted constantly, and, at first, Jack had felt there might be something between them. Until he noticed that she flirted with everyone. Better to keep the relationship professional, he decided. We might be rivals one day.

Jack stood up and walked towards the lifts side by side with Layla. 'Seeing the Chairman as well?' he asked.

'No such luck,' replied Layla. 'Monday morning smoochies

29

with Sir Kurt Helin would really get my week off with a bang. No. I'm seeing Geoff Wheeler.'

'PR?' said Jack, his voice adopting a tone of mock disgust. 'Candyfloss, Layla. Some way from the real heart of the business, I'm afraid.'

'Too true,' said Layla. 'Although I might be able to mention the speech that CBI guy made the other day about how every Footsie company should have at least one woman on the board. All too true, I suspect. Patriarchy could be turning into a real problem for this company.' The lift door slid open, cutting the conversation short. 'Good luck,' said Layla, turning away. 'Mention that CBI speech to the Chairman will you, there's a sweetie.'

The contrast between the fifth floor of the Helin Building and the rest of the company was sudden and striking. Unlike the fiercely modern, utilitarian designs that dominated the rest of the Kizog headquarters, the fifth floor was cloaked in the style of a nineteenth-century country house. The walls were panelled in fine old wood, portraits of past chairmen were hung on the walls, there were elegant sofas and chairs sitting empty in each hall, and, next to them, bookcases crammed with old leather-bound editions of classic works.

Mrs Barnes, the Chairman's PA, was on the phone, and when she finished Jack asked if it was OK to go in now. The Chairman was busy, she told him. Wait five minutes. Jack sat down. He had prepared his ground well, he reflected to himself. He had run the lines through his mind a hundred times, tuning each one until he felt happy with it. It did no good, of course. He was still nervous.

The advice yesterday evening had been invaluable. Before leaving the office he had grabbed five minutes to re-introduce himself to Ralph Finer, the finance director. Finer was the closest he had to an ally in the company, at least among its senior figures. They had worked together before Jack was posted to Thailand, and they got on well. He suspected Finer might have played a part in his recall to head office. He certainly seemed pleased to see him, offering him a drink, and engaging him in some light-hearted banter about his time in the Far East. His manner only changed when Jack brought up the subject that was troubling him most.

Finer frowned: 'They want you to become an infiltrator in a counterfeiting racket?' he asked hesitantly. 'Does the Chairman know about this?'

Jack shook his head. 'He volunteered me to assist the Forum, but I don't imagine they told him what they wanted me for.'

'You have to be careful with Sir Kurt,' said Finer. 'There is often no way of knowing what he does and doesn't know. I find that constantly.'

Jack thought for a moment. 'Would you do it?'

'Of course not,' Finer replied instantly. 'But if it is a request from the Chairman . . .'

'What's the downside?'

'Black marks, at the very least,' said Finer with a wide smile. 'Possibly a posting to Eastern Europe.'

'That bad?' Jack asked rhetorically.

'You know how the Chairman is about loyalty,' said Finer. 'I'd get guarantees if I were you. Make absolutely sure you are protected. And make sure there is a reward. You don't want to walk away from this empty-handed. If he refuses, say no. The Ukraine isn't so bad, I hear.'

Finer patted Jack's shoulder sympathetically. 'And talk to me if you need any more advice.'

'There is one thing I need to know,' Jack said. Finer raised an eyebrow. 'Is Ator a priority for the company?'

The finance director waved his hand dismissively. 'A side issue. I wouldn't get involved in that project if I were you, whatever Sir Kurt has to say.'

'I already am marginally involved.'

Finer's eyes narrowed slightly as he looked directly at Jack. 'A mistake.' He paused before continuing. 'Listen, if anything develops on that front let me know about it. The Chairman isn't getting any younger and we could be into the endgame sooner than anyone imagines. You'll need friends at the court after the king is gone. And remember, not everything is always the way it seems.'

Jack was still pondering the significance of the remark when a barked command from Mrs Barnes snapped him from his recollections. The Chairman was ready now, she said. Jack began walking into the office. 'The boardroom,' instructed an icy voice behind him. Jack turned and began walking back along the corridor. He could see Sam Taylor, the chief executive, walking through the door. He nodded to him, and said good-morning, but Taylor merely raised his eyebrows. Jack figured that Taylor didn't know who he was.

The Chairman stood in the doorway, beckoning him forward. There was a light tap on his shoulder as he got within range, a feline stroke that made Jack feel like a house pet. 'Congratulations.'

'Thank you, sir,' said Jack. For what? he wondered.

A long, shimmering wooden table stretched through the length of the room, polished until it gleamed, and thick black leather swivel chairs were lined up alongside it. Portraits were hung along the walls. There were two of the Chairman. To the artist, at least, he had hardly aged at all during his long reign at Kizog, although here in real life he looked much older than his depiction on canvas.

The Chairman sat down. 'Miss Ling has joined us,' he continued. 'Temporarily at least. But it'll do. If she doesn't stay, we'll have squeezed her dry in a few months. She can leave then if she wants to. I'm putting her down in the files as someone you brought into the company. Scott will be annoyed, but never mind. You deserve the credit.'

Jack was unsure he had played any role, but decided that credit, no matter how little merited it might be, was always worth storing away. 'I need to talk to you about the counterfeiting issue, sir.'

'Quite so,' said the Chairman.

Jack started to explain, running through his meeting with Fuller. 'I told them I needed to check with my superiors,' he said firmly. 'I'm not convinced it is something Kizog should involve itself in.'

'Really, why?'

'If it backfires in any way, the company could be left in a very embarrassing position.'

The Chairman frowned, and Jack could feel his annoyance filtering across the table. It was uncomfortable. Not working, he thought to himself. 'Breathe a word of this to no one, but there is a major strategic initiative coming up in the next few days,' he said. 'It's vital we keep this counterfeiting business under control for the next couple of months. After that, we can drop it. But for the moment I need you to string the Forum along. Do what they ask.'

'I think I would need protection, sir.'

The Chairman nodded, a look of concern wandering across his face. 'But of course you shall have it, my dear boy. All the protection you need. The company stands right behind you. You know that.'

The Chairman sat back, folding his arms across his lap. His expression was the picture of serenity. 'Comfortable surroundings, don't you think.'

Jack nodded. He sensed that he was losing control of the conversation. 'You'd like me to proceed.'

'It's a very good life.'

His point was clearly made, and Jack already knew what was coming next. Buttons were being pressed in all the right places. The Chairman leant forward across the boardroom table, and patted Jack on the wrist. 'It's all waiting for you. I'd hate for you to disappoint me.'

A pale half-light shone down on the Kizog research library that evening, two tubes of neon casting their dim glow on the strips of grey metal shelving, the black metal desks, and the stack upon stack of thick files and dossiers. Beneath it, only half illuminated, Tara sat alone, surrounded by her files and preoccupied by her thoughts.

33

It was only a few days now since her meeting with Dr Scott, and three days since her first morning with her new company. Everything has been so rushed, she thought to herself. Too rushed to be sure if I have done the right thing.

He had impressed her, she knew that much. Not personally. He was not an impressive man; he had little presence and no bearing. And his academic record was not overwhelming; very respectable, but not in the very first division. More of a technician than a scientist. And yet . . . the amount that he knew was astonishing.

Tara was still trying to get a handle on how much information the company had already uncovered about Ator. She had suspected the laboratories here were on to something. But she had not expected to see her suspicions confirmed so dramatically or so quickly. The company would, of course, have some research underway. In the five years since the new disease had first been isolated and identified it had attracted enormous world-wide publicity; in some of the more hysterical articles it rivalled Aids as the new plague looming over the world. But nobody knew very much about it yet, or so Tara had thought.

The first day at the lab had been spent being shown around and introduced. It was a first impression, she knew, but it had not been good. The buildings were divided up into row after row of small laboratories, each with the same standardised computers and testing equipment. The scientists worked in teams of two or three, mapping out enzymes, or laboriously testing different compounds for their possible medicinal value. The structure was much the same as her old base at the National Institutes, but the spirit was different. There was none of the excitement or the camaraderie; nothing of the shared sense of a mission.

But the library had intrigued her. Not the building, or the range of papers and books stored there. That was all to be expected. But the extent of the work done by Kizog over the years on the central nervous system was more impressive than she could have hoped for. It was an arcane area, explored only sparingly by most of the commercial drugs companies. But here spread out before

34

her was some of the most detailed work she had seen on the complex biochemistry of the nervous system.

There was so much to learn. Some of it she had duplicated in her own research, but much was new to her, and threw fresh light on her understanding. It included some specific work on leprosy, mapping the series of chemical reactions by which it spread through the body. A yellow jotter at her side, Tara was working her way through the papers, her eyes burning into the mountains of papers, her hand scratching notes as she deciphered the implications of what she was looking at. She had been there for two hours already. Tiredness was starting to catch up with her after an exhausting day. She looked up for a moment, dragging her eyes from the pages, glancing around the pale room.

The Chairman was standing ten yards away, leaning against the bookshelves, his eyes cast in her direction. Tara was startled, taken aback, unsure of how to respond. She had been watched by men before, and it was not an experience she enjoyed. She glanced around, sensing that they were alone together, and then looked back towards him. 'You have been watching me,' she said.

The Chairman didn't answer. He lifted his shoulder away from the bookshelf, and sauntered towards her, a slow, sloping and deliberate walk, disfigured by his slight limp. A foot or so away from her he stopped, and rested his hand on her desk. 'I like to watch my researchers study from time to time,' he said. 'It tells you something about them, don't you think? Something about the quality of their minds, and the power of their concentration.'

Tara looked up. 'What can you tell about me?'

'Your concentration is of the highest calibre,' he replied. 'I was standing there for close on ten minutes, and you didn't notice me. Had your mind wandered from the page for even a fraction of a second you would have seen me. But no. An impressive achievement. And you are tired as well. I saw you yawn. Stressed, too, I would imagine. Concentration in those circumstances takes a mind like a laser.'

The Chairman bowed slightly, showing a degree of old-fashioned courtesy that Tara found faintly endearing. He offered

35

her his hand, and Tara shook it. 'I'm glad that you are with us,' he said.

'I'm sure you would manage without me, Sir Kurt.'

The Chairman shook his head. 'Perhaps,' he replied distantly. 'What do you think of all this?'

Tara shrugged. 'Impressive,' she said. 'There is more here on the central nervous system than I would have imagined. And much of it is of a very high standard. There are many things here that aren't in the generally available literature.'

'Perhaps the quality of science here is higher than our reputation over at the National Institutes implies,' he said, his tone inflected with a trace of irony.

'There is much more here on leprosy than I would have expected,' Tara replied. 'More original work, I mean. We have been duplicating each other. There are things I don't understand, though.'

'Surely the chemistry is straightforward enough for somebody of your expertise.'

'The chemistry is fine,' said Tara. 'But why is work being done here on leprosy? I thought it wasn't a commercial disease, not something that would interest the company.'

'We cover the ballpark,' answered the Chairman softly. 'We look at lots of things that have no immediate applications to any products. As it turns out that work might end up being very useful because of the connections with Ator. Who knows?'

Something buried inside his whisper made her suspicious. 'But why leprosy?' Tara demanded. 'There are hundreds of different diseases to work on.'

The Chairman patted her on the shoulder; his touch was cold and remote, and Tara could feel her muscles twitch under his fingers. She found his presence intriguing, but also slightly threatening. His concern seemed to mask an air of menace. 'Some researcher had a particular interest, I suppose,' he said. 'Probably a sideline.'

Tara looked at him, scrutinising his reactions. 'You did some of this work yourself,' she said. 'At least your initials are on it.'

36

'My initials?' he asked, his voice betraying his surprise.

Tara lifted one of the pages and showed it to him. The Chairman took it from her and peered at the paper, squinting to read the fine print. The look of concern vanished, its place taken by an expression of avuncular amusement. 'I signed off on everything in that department,' he replied. 'It was a matter of routine. Most of the documents I hardly looked at.'

'It looked as if you had worked on leprosy yourself,' Tara persisted.

The Chairman shook his head. 'The man who did that work has long since departed.'

Tara looked back down at her papers. 'It would have been interesting to hear your views on the disease,' she said thoughtfully.

'It is your views we want,' he replied. 'That is why you are here.'

The Chairman patted her on the shoulder once more, and turned abruptly, walking away from her desk. Tara glanced at her watch. It was just after nine. She tried to look at her papers, but found that her concentration had gone, shattered by the interruption. There was too much information coming towards her, and too little time to deal with it; she needed some space to sort through it. And some time to wonder if the Chairman had been telling her the truth; it was hard to believe he hardly looked at papers he signed. The Chairman did not strike her as a man who did anything casually. Carefully she put the papers in a neat pile, folded her notes into her attaché case, pulled on her overcoat and headed out of the buildings. There would be plenty of time for more research in the morning, she decided. And plenty of questions to be answered.

FOUR

The words glimmered up in black lettering against a shimmering blue background from the terminal on Jack's desk. 'Personnel records' it read. 'Access denied.' Jack hammered a key number into the machine. It flickered, and then sprang to life. 'Name requested: . . .'

Jack glanced up over the screen, checking there was nobody in the vicinity. 'Tara Ling' he typed. 'Secured information – access denied . . .' responded the computer. Jack pulled out his wallet, and took out a yellow Post-it note with six digits written on it. He subtracted two from each number and keyed it in backwards; the personnel department's code was a useful thing to possess, he thought to himself, and he was grateful Layla had given it to him, even though he had no idea where she had obtained it. But not something you wanted to have found on you.

The numbers disappeared into the mainframe. Within seconds, the file had appeared on the screen.

Name: Tara Ling
Sex: Female
Age: 28
Marital Status: Single
Place of birth: Vietnam
Ethnic Background: Eurasian
Education: Daytona High School, Ohio, USA; Harvard
    Medical School; National Institutes of Health
Publications: 'Leprosy – A Mechanism for Viral
    Transmission': *Journal of Tropical Diseases*, 1990;
    'Leprosy – A Genetic Analysis': *Journal of Genetic
    Disorders*, 1992; 'Leprosy – A Plausible Cure?':
    Journal of Tropical Diseases, 1994.
Status: Senior researcher
Salary: £80,000
Benefits: Car, house, BUPA membership
Contract: One year, renewable, six months' notice on
    either side.
Tasks: Secured information – not available for personnel
    files.
Hired by: Jack Borrodin, special assistant to the Chairman.
Remarks: Memo from Dr Peter Scott to Personnel. 'Ms
    Ling has been hired by Mr Borrodin to work on a
    special project he is supervising, but since she is
    operating in my department she comes under my super-
    vision on personnel matters. No attempt at integration
    into the corporate culture is to be made with this
    employee. She has been hired for a specific task and is
    unlikely to be with us for long. Any problems with her
    contract or any other matters arising should be referred
    directly and immediately to myself or the Chairman.
    Circulate her photograph to security, with the request
    that any movements by this employee around the plant
    after 6.00 p.m. be noted and reported to me within
    twenty-four hours.'

Heavy, thought Jack. Security was tight within the head office, he knew, and nowhere more so than in the laboratories; the company already knew of enough cases of industrial espionage to be aware of its competitors' attempts to penetrate its secrets. But any movements around the plant to be reported to Dr Scott? There was, he realised, much about Tara that still eluded him. Too much. Particularly as the records stated that she was working on a project he was described as supervising. What project? he wondered. Nobody told me.

Time, he decided, to discover more about Ator, and more, as well, about the researchers who had worked on the virus.

Her remark yesterday had taken him sideways. On little more than an impulse, Jack had decided to stop by the laboratories on his way out; he felt he should drop round to thank her for joining the company, and to wish her luck with her research. She had seemed pleased to see him, although surprised when he mentioned that he had been credited with bringing her into the company. 'So that is what special assistants do?' she asked.

Jack felt slightly bashful. 'I suppose I didn't have much to do with it,' he replied.

She shook her head firmly.

'I guess I owe you a favour, then,' Jack continued. 'If you ever want anything, just ask.'

Tara turned back to the lab bench, and started fiddling around with a microscope, pressing her eye firmly into the lens before replying. 'There is something you could do,' she said, without looking up.

'Of course,' said Jack.

'Some of the world's best researchers into Ator are now working in private industry,' she said. 'They are people I might be able to check ideas with, although they work at other companies so it might be delicate. You must have contacts around the industry. Perhaps you could check if they are still working on the virus, and see if you can find out anything about what they are up to.'

After saying good-night, Jack had thought little more about it.

40

Yet reading through the file, he recalled the request. A promise, he decided, was a promise.

Jack made his way down to the library. The place was almost empty at this time of the afternoon; the scientists would be back in their labs by now, and the executives were all at lunch. Just as well, Jack decided. Some privacy could be useful. Who, he asked the librarian, are the top twenty Ator researchers in the world? She seemed briefly nonplussed by the question, and Jack showed his new ID card, a freshly minted strip of electronic plastic that described him as a special assistant to the Chairman. An important project, assigned by the big man personally, he explained. 'I only have a couple of hours.'

She returned a few minutes later, holding a print-out in her hand. 'Based on the number of articles published on the virus in the medical and scientific journals, these are the top people,' she said. 'Of course, this only tells you the quantity of their work, not the quality,' she added.

Jack took the list and thanked her. Back in his office, he scanned through the names, and wondered where to start. Begin at the beginning, he told himself; check whether they are still working at the same companies. Picking up the phone he put a call through to the Bayer head offices in Germany. Speaking in English, he asked for Dr Mechal. In a meeting, his secretary explained. Could she take a message? No, Jack replied. He dialled the next number, this time calling Upjohn in America, and asking for John Talbot. He got through right away, and, on hearing the man's voice, Jack hung up.

After six more phone calls, Jack was starting to feel he was wasting his time. None of these people seemed to be going any-where, and this was telling him nothing about their research. Try one more, he told himself. The sixth name on the list was David Sunningdale. He was forty-two, and worked as a researcher at Bristol Myers-Squibb in their New Jersey lab. As far as Jack could tell he still worked there. He called the company and asked to be put through. No longer with the company, explained a receptionist. Jack said he was an old acquaintance who was trying to get in touch, and asked if he could have a new number. Sorry, not possible, replied the receptionist. Mr Sunningdale died late last year. Jack asked what happened. It was a car accident, the lady explained. Everybody at the company was very sorry.

Jack hung up.

Five more calls produced fit, healthy and living researchers, none of whom appeared to have changed jobs. He put his next call through to Alicia Thomas at the Genentech research laboratory in California. Thirty-eight years old, unmarried, and a senior researcher at the biotechnology company. She was an expert in the genetic engineering of viruses, one of the best in her field. Kizog had approached her to join them about eighteen months ago, according to a note scribbled on the list. She had turned them down.

No, sorry, the receptionist explained, it would not be possible to put his call through to Ms Thomas. Could he leave a message? Ms Thomas no longer worked with the company. Did she know where she could be contacted? No. It was not possible to divulge that information. Have a nice day. Jack tried the local paper, available on one of the US electronic databases. He keyed in her name and found two stories. The first was about Ator. It described how some cases of the virus had now been detected in the US, and some of the work Genentech was doing in locating the origins of the virus. Thomas was quoted as saying the company was making good progress. The second article was dated from last November. It described her murder. Her body had been found in her eighth-floor apartment in a downtown block about five miles from the lab. The police described it as a burglary. There was extensive damage to the apartment, a few minor items – the TV, the Apple, the hi-fi and the video – had all been taken and there were signs of a struggle. Police officials were saying that there were no suspects so far, but they were still investigating.

Jack saved the two files on to his hard disc. The body count was starting to look a little higher than he would have expected. He made four more calls. Each time he dialled the number, he found he was increasingly concerned about the person he was ringing; I hope they are there, he whispered to himself. Call number seventeen was to Basle. Hans Gerter had worked at Roche for eighteen years, all of them in the lab. He tried the company, but was told only that Herr Gerter no longer worked there. No other information was available. Typical Swiss, thought Jack. He put a call through to an acquaintance who had been working for Roche in Bangkok, but who he knew had now been transferred back to Switzerland. He asked if he could check Gerter's file. Nothing important, he said, just doing a favour for a colleague. The guy said he would call back. Jack waited, making the remaining three calls, relieved in each case to discover the person was alive and well. Yet somewhere in the back of his mind he sensed he already knew what had happened to Gerter. Dead, came the reply, only twenty minutes later. In a gas explosion at his house outside Basle. He and his wife and daughter were all killed in the blast. Jack asked if the file said anything about what Gerter had been working on in the past couple of years. No, came the answer. The files were silent on that point. Nothing at all. Most unusual. Except that he had been collaborating on a biotechnology project with Genentech.

Jack put the phone down and sat silently, motionless, behind his desk for a few moments, lost in his own thoughts. Somewhere in the pit of his stomach he could feel a knot tightening. Why had Tara wanted him to check up on these people? he wondered.

His thoughts were interrupted by a voice at the door. 'Council of war,' said Layla briskly.

He could see her red hair was wrapped up behind a hairband today, and behind her she had Sam, the third of the special assistants, in tow, trailing her like a puppy. Jack's finger flicked to the F7 button on his workstation, killing the files, and he checked the list was face down on his desk before looking up. 'Come inside,' he said.

Layla and Sam walked into the twelve feet by twelve feet office, Layla sitting down on the chair, Sam perching on the edge of the desk. 'If you check your e-mail in the next thirty seconds, you'll find you're wanted in the boardroom,' said Layla mischievously.

Jack glanced back at his screen, and, in the right-hand corner, saw a 'message pending' icon start to flash. 'Board meeting at 4.30. Special assistants required to attend,' it said.

'What's the word on the corridors?' asked Jack.

'Talk that the Chairman could be about to announce his resignation,' replied Sam.

'That old chestnut,' said Jack. 'The Chairman will be taken out of here in a box. Any other ideas?'

'Talk also of some major new strategic plan,' said Layla. 'Don't know where it comes from. Some of the old stagers just think he has a strange look in his eye.'

The door to the boardroom on the fifth floor was open by the time they arrived there at four-thirty sharp. Inside the long oval-shaped room, Sir Kurt Helin was sitting at the head of the table that stretched through its length. Sitting next to him was Ralph Finer, flanked by Sam Taylor, and Kenneth Strong, the marketing director, and alongside him, Alain Perez, chief of European operations, Bill Laidler, North America, and Frank Rodgers, Asia-Pacific. Sam Taylor sat next to the Chairman, and by his side were Dr Scott, and Geoff Wheeler, the PR man. Jack, Sam and Layla nodded to each of them, and took their seats at the far end of the table.

There was a silence, left hanging over the room for ninety seconds or so. There was a playful smile spreading across the Chairman's face, and a look of contentment in his eyes. In front of him, there was a jotter, and he was scribbling notes furiously.

The Chairman put his pen down and spread his palms flat on the table-top. He took a deep breath and composed himself. 'Don't you just love the scent of battle,' he said.

There was no response. The Chairman pushed his chair backwards, folding his hands behind his back, and began pacing around the table, looking at no one as he spoke. 'This isn't a formal board meeting but there is an issue I believe it is important we all discuss together. As all of you I am sure will be aware our results this year will not be everything we would have hoped for. Selinokose has gone off patent and sales have I understand dropped quite substantially. Turrownese is facing stiff competition and can't be expected to maintain sales for much longer. Our pipeline of new products in the last few years has not been as full as we would have liked. All in all, the company faces a difficult situation. Not an alarming situation, but one of gradual stagnation. This is dangerous. Our stock price will fall as this becomes clear, and, in time, we will become vulnerable to predators.'

He stopped, turned sharply on his heels, and looked across the boardroom table. 'Who here wants to be taken over?'

The Chairman leant forward, putting his hands on the table right next to Jack, and cast a narrow glance around the room, hunting for signs of dissent. 'We are in a state of drift. That means we are not in control of our own destiny. And this is not a situation which I as Chairman can allow to continue. We must seize the initiative, and take back control of our own future.'

The Chairman raised his left hand, a gesture those around the table recognised as a command of silence. 'The logic of our situation dictates that we must make a bold leap. I have therefore decided that we must launch a take-over bid for one of our major competitors.'

Beneath the table, Jack felt a nudge in the shins from Layla. He looked down, and saw a note in her hand. 'He's lost it,' she had written. Jack ignored it, looking back at the Chairman.

'So who's it going to be? Anyone you particularly dislike? Someone you'd like to see ground into the dust? Any particular scores to settle?'

He stood back, holding his chin with his hand, waiting for an answer. Then he chuckled. 'But seriously . . .' and he began pacing around the room again, circling the table with a gradually quickening pace. 'There have been friendly, informal conversations with some of our rivals. Those conversations have led me to conclude that there is no prospect of an agreed merger. The other option, therefore, is for us to launch a hostile take-over. Fine, fine. If that's the way they want to play it, so be it. It's worse for them and better for us. By going hostile we can choose from a greater range of targets, since there is no need to restrict ourselves to those that will come to the table willingly. I have studied the potential candidates, and I have concluded that our interests are best served by targeting the Swiss firm Ocher. It has an excellent marketing capability, a good product pipeline, but one or two well-publicised problems with its anti-depressants have I believe opened a window of vulnerability that we would be wise to exploit.'

With uncanny timing, he finished the sentence just as he reached his own chair at the head of the table. Sitting back down, he broadcast a grin across the room. 'Of course, that's just my opinion. Feel free to argue.'

There was a silence lasting seconds, perhaps minutes. Finally Laidler raised his head above the parapet. 'I think its a fine idea, sir,' he said. 'The expansion of the sales force and volumes through taking over Ocher would give us exactly the kind of muscle we need in the North American market.'

'I think it is the one strategic play that shows real vision,' said Perez.

'A bold move,' chimed Rodgers.

What a bunch of yes-men, thought Jack. They must know this is a high-risk strategy. Winning would be fine, but losing would put the company in play.

'There are arguments against, Chairman,' said Finer.

At last, someone with guts, thought Jack.

'It would be very dull if there weren't,' whispered the Chairman.

'It could be tough to make the numbers add up,' Finer said. 'Ocher made profits last year translating into sterling at about £600 million. Assuming an exit ratio of about twenty, which frankly I think we would be lucky to get away with once you add in the control premium, then you are looking at a price of around £12 billion. We don't have that kind of money in the bank. We could borrow it, but the interest charges would be crippling. The only other option is to issue our paper in exchange for theirs. But I can't see that working either. Right now Ocher stock is more highly rated than ours. Therefore we can't issue Kizog shares for Ocher shares without diluting earnings. As soon as the market realises that, which will take about five minutes, our stock price will head south, meaning we have to issue more paper, thereby increasing the dilution of earnings. End of story. The numbers don't wash.'

Finer finished his spiel and leant back in his chair. Jack glanced across at him, impressed by his performance. He turned to look at the Chairman, curious to see how the analysis had gone down. He paused, furrowing his brow, and turned to Finer with a quizzical expression on his face. 'As usual we rely on Ralph for an acute assessment of our situation,' he said.

Jack noticed the look of relief on the finance director's face; and the look of annoyance passing through the other executives. 'Obviously we are not in the right position to mount an immediate take-over of Ocher, for the reasons the finance director has most cogently explained,' the Chairman continued. 'What he forgets is that the problem only exists so long as Ocher's stock is more highly rated than ours. If our share price were higher than theirs then a paper offer for the company would in all likelihood succeed. Now, I'm sure all of us are aware that pharmaceutical stock prices move quickly in response to encouraging news from the laboratory of major new products coming through the pipeline. Dr Scott, can you help us out on this point?'

All the eyes around the board table turned to the research and development director, who so far had remained not only silent but almost motionless as well. 'Chairman?' he said.

The Chairman rapped his knuckles on the table. 'Anything major coming through the pipeline?'

'We have a whole range of products going into testing at any given time,' he started.

'Quite so,' said the Chairman. 'But I believe we may be close to discovering a vaccine for Ator.'

47

The eyes round the table remained rooted on the research director. Dr Scott hesitated, fumbling for a reply. 'It is true that we have some very promising leads that may soon turn into something solid.'

'And am I not correct in supposing that given the threat the Ator virus poses to the world, the governments of the industrialised world will pay for a global vaccination programme to eradicate this threat?'

'That would probably be a correct assumption, Chairman,' answered Dr Scott.

'Thank you. We would of course offer it to them at a minimal cost, given the gravity of the situation,' continued the Chairman. 'We would not want to risk accusations of profiteering. Even so, the vaccine should provide additional revenues of between £2 billion and £3 billion annually. Let us be optimistic then about the work of the laboratory. Assuming it is successful our story will run like this. We announce the news of the bid for Ocher, paid for in a mixture of cash and Kizog stock. At the same time we announce the news of the Ator vaccine, arguing that we need to take over another company to give us the manufacturing and marketing resources to make the most of the new product. Our stock price I feel sure will rocket on the news. That will then make the offer very attractive to Ocher's shareholders.'

The Chairman's eyes swept the table, and he raised one hand into the air. 'End of story. We win. Any disagreements?'

There were nods around the table. 'We have an agreement then,' continued the Chairman. He turned towards Dr Scott. 'You will have responsibility for ensuring that the Ator vaccine is delivered in some plausible shape for this announcement to be made.'

'How soon is that?' answered Dr Scott.

The Chairman's eyes took one last tour of the landscape, surveying the audience, scrutinising and probing as his gaze fell upon each person in turn. He waved a hand to dismiss the room. 'As soon as possible. Burn up all the rats you need.'

She was sitting alone when he found her. Leaning against the doorway, he watched her as she removed her glasses and pressed her right eye into the microscope. Her features were a picture of pure concentration as she peered down at the bacteria, her whole mind focusing on one insignificant speck of life. Perhaps not solid-to-the-bone boffin, thought Jack, as his eyes wandered across her sharply carved face; perhaps someone I might even find attractive.

He knocked gently on the side of the open door and stepped inside. The room was six feet by eight, with only one window high up in the corner, through which little natural light managed to seep. The walls were white and bare, barren of decoration of any sort, and along one side of the room ran a single stainless-steel shelf, polished until it glimmered. It struck Jack as more of a prison than an office.

On her workbench, a white mouse was scratching against the bars of its cage. Jack bent down, and the animal peered up at him, clinging to the metal with its paws. 'Very sweet,' said Jack, surprised by the effect close proximity to Tara was having on him.

'He has leprosy.'

Involuntarily, Jack stepped back, moving as far away from the cage as possible, eyeing the creature warily from a distance. 'You don't know much about disease, do you?' said Tara playfully.

Jack shook his head. 'It's hardly contagious at all,' she continued. 'Even between humans.'

'What about leper colonies?'

'They were mostly suffering from syphilis. The symptoms are pretty similar. And the colonies were as much for treatment as prevention. It is a very debilitating disease.'

'He looks OK,' said Jack hesitantly. 'No limbs falling off. Nothing like that.'

'Leprosy takes a long time to develop. Often many years. In humans anyway. The mouse I'm not so sure about. I'm watching him closely.'

49

'Well, I'm sure he's very useful.'

'He's miraculous.' Tara started to explain. 'One of the major problems with leprosy has been that you can't get the bacteria on to a lab plate. It's impossible to isolate it. That is why there has been so little progress in finding any drugs to use against it. The mouse is a real breakthrough. His leprosy mimics human leprosy. By testing compounds on the mice we can start to build a picture of which chemicals might be effective in combating the disease.'

Jack nodded. 'And Kizog developed the mouse?'

'Strange, isn't it?' replied Tara. 'For a relatively uncommercial disease. I found the files in the library, and this one I have just infected.' She walked across to the cage, and peered down at the small rodent. 'I'm keeping a close eye on him to see how he develops.'

'The mouse convinced you to stay,' said Jack, leaving the question hanging in the air.

'Among other things,' she replied vaguely.

'Despite your reservations?'

Her eyes met his. 'Did you check up on the others?'

'I ran a check on the top twenty researchers in the field,' said Jack. He passed across a sheet of paper, with the name of each of the researchers and their current whereabouts written on it. 'Three of them have died in the past year,' he continued, before adding, 'The circumstances in each case looked quite innocent.'

'You think so?' asked Tara warily. In her eyes there was a look of curiosity, but also of suspicion.

'The lady in California was obviously murdered, but it could have just been a random robbery. Otherwise, what else do we have? A road accident, and a household explosion. These things happen.'

'But a coincidence, don't you think?' said Tara.

'There must be hundreds of scientists working on Ator. Thousands even.'

'Sure,' Tara replied sarcastically.

'So we are talking about three from thousands,' Jack persisted, his voice rising as he spoke. 'A tiny percentage.'

In the background Jack could hear the mouse clawing at the bars of its cage. 'But these three were among the best,' she said quietly. 'They were so close.'

Jack leant forward. 'What were they close to, Tara?' he demanded. 'A cure?'

Tara turned away from him, and for a moment she seemed to be shaking her head. 'Perhaps. Any of them could have been close to finding a cure. Or perhaps closer to something else.'

'Like what?'

She shrugged, her brown eyes flashing up to meet his. 'To finding the truth,' she replied.

FIVE

Tara nodded to the guard, pressed the red button, and stepped inside the airlocked chamber. She stood alone, enclosed inside the tiny cubicle, feeling the air rush past her. Two minutes later, the seconds counted down on the digital screen in front of her, the green light ahead of her flashed, the door opened, and she stepped into the viral chamber.

The anti-viral suit, a silver, crinkly overall, covering her from head to toe, weighed her down, making her move slowly as she made her way through the small, airlocked laboratory. The room was pale and odourless, sickly almost. Inside the air was constantly recycled through a separate air-conditioning system, kept free from any contact with the outside world to make sure none of the germs kept here could find their way into the atmosphere outside. The airlocked door was there for the same reason. And only the anti-viral suit stood between Tara and instant contamination.

It was still and calm in here, thought Tara; isolated beyond reason. In a way she liked it; a place of perfect solitude. And yet she also recoiled from the room; its isolation was imposed and unnatural, a prison for molecules too deadly to be allowed to escape, a warehouse of plague.

To her right, along one wall, was a grey machine, vibrating steadily, humming. Inside, there was a rack of carefully stacked vials, each two inches high, each containing a light, colourless liquid. At a steady unvarying pace, the vials rotated, the liquid inside swilling back and forth, mixed into a cocktail of disease. Tara checked the timer, and flicked a switch on the side of the machine. The humming stopped, and, in a minute or so, the rotation had ceased. She reached inside and pulled out one of the vials. Cooked, she thought.

It struck her as ironic that Ator, a virus that much of the world went to great lengths to avoid any contact with, should be manu-factured here. There was something sinister about deliberately preparing so deadly a substance. Tara held the vial between her fingers, contemplating it for a moment. The enemy, she thought.

Still holding it, clutching it in her palms, she took it across to the stainless-steel workbench on the opposite side of the room, placing it carefully down in a test tube rack. The workbench was empty and spartan, a strip of sheer metal, with some metal racks, a microscope, a workstation and a washbasin. Before it, there was a high metal stool where Tara sat while she worked.

Things had moved quickly in the last week. After spending days reading her way through the research documents Kizog had filed on Ator and the workings of the central nervous system, Dr Scott had freed up this viral laboratory for her sole and personal use. Back at the National Institutes, there had been only one viral lab, and time in there had been precious. At best, she had spent a few hours a month performing experiments. Here, she had the place to herself, open twenty-four hours a day, of which she had been using about fourteen for the past week; this, she knew, was her best chance of cracking the virus, and she was determined not to waste a single moment.

She had been astounded by the amount Kizog had achieved. The store of knowledge here on the Ator virus far outstripped anything available in the academic libraries; a complete molecular map of the structure of the virus. It added up to a complete survey of the territory where a vaccine might be discovered. All it lacked was an X to mark the spot.

Dr Scott had been right, pondered Tara. Ator was clearly a close relative of leprosy. That it was a mutation of some sort seemed inevitable. Theoretically it was possible that both viruses had evolved from a common source but Ator was so new and leprosy so ancient that it seemed more plausible that the new virus had evolved from the old. That happened all the time. A virus, like any living entity, was constantly adapting to its circumstances, finding new ways to survive and flourish. From microbes to men, thought Tara. Same principle.

For a mutation, however, it was very sophisticated. Leprosy was a terrible disease but a slow one. It could incubate inside the body for up to twenty years before symptoms started becoming apparent. Ator would appear within two weeks maximum. Often much quicker. And once it started, the progress of the disease was rapid. A leper would suffer a slow and lingering death; the skin would start scaling up, slowly they would lose control and then possession of their limbs, but death could take years to catch up. Sometimes it never did. Ator was different. Within hours control of the limbs would start to vanish, turning the victim into a lifeless jelly. And death would follow within days.

Tara spread a computer print-out in front of her. Combining her work with the research done by Kizog had yielded a list of possible compounds that might act against the disease. The company, uniquely in the world so far as she knew, had managed to isolate the Ator virus, in much the same way they had done for leprosy. Nobody else had yet managed to do that, making the search for a vaccine practically pointless. Now, with the virus boiled down to a liquid in a test tube, the serious work could begin. She had already, over the past few years, identified compounds that could work as a vaccine against leprosy. Since Ator was a mutation, there was no reason why one of them might not work against the new virus. That was why they had hired her. And, to be fair to the company, it was certainly worth a shot.

It was laborious work; perspiration rather than inspiration. For the past three days she had been steadily testing, so far without success. Looking into the microscope, pulling bottles from the shelf, she concocted compound number thirty-nine on her list. Stitching the elements together, she pulled the vial towards her, and, taking care, placed it beneath a Geiger counter, testing for radioactivity. It registered. Taking the compound she had prepared, she injected the liquid into the vial. With her right hand she shook it, mixing up the two liquids.

Carefully she put it back under the Geiger counter, her eyes fixed on the dial, watching for any movement. Should the compound she had just prepared prove to have any effect on the virus, the radioactivity would fall, a simple measure of a reaction taking place between the two molecules. This time, for the thirty-ninth time in a row, nothing happened. The dial wobbled, registering a brief movement, then stabilised, back exactly where it had started. Tara carefully picked it up and put it back on the rack. Turning to the computer, she logged the information on to the screen.

'Test sample negative,' she typed. Again, she thought.

Behind her, she heard a noise. Turning, she looked to see another person standing in the airlocked doorway. Masked behind the silver anti-viral suit, she couldn't make out who it was. The green light flashed, and the man walked inside. Tara looked closely, peering into the Perspex covering his face. 'Dr Scott?' she said.

'How is it progressing, Tara?' he asked.

'Slowly,' she replied.

He rested his hand on her shoulder. 'It always is,' he said sympathetically.

'Thirty-nine tests so far with nothing to report. But it is just a matter of patience I think. We are on the right track, I'm sure of it. It is just a matter of completing the tests.'

'How many do you have on your list?' asked Dr Scott.

'The computer has listed out 1,892 variations on the basic formula I worked out,' she said. 'But who knows. We could get lucky and find it at the one thousandth attempt.'

'How long is each test taking?' asked Scott, his voice sounding worried.

Tara shrugged. 'An hour or two.'

His brow furrowed as he made the calculations. 'So it could be months.'

'Assuming I'm working fourteen hours a day, seven days a week,' replied Tara. 'Which I am.'

Dr Scott sighed, and tried to rub his chin through the anti-viral suit. He walked closer to Tara and leant over the desk, peering down at the list of formulations lying on the print-out on the desk. His mind was still full of the meeting with the Chairman yesterday, and he was painfully aware that this was taking too long. They needed a vaccine quickly.

He ran his fingers through the list, a mass of chemical symbols, his eyes squinting as he worked out the formulae. Halfway through he stopped, resting his left hand on the list. He turned to the computer, and keyed into the database. After peering into it for a few moments, he punched several keys. Tara could faintly hear the sound of the hard disc crunching its way through the calculations. Three minutes later, a list appeared. It contained eighty-six different compounds.

'Try this,' he said.

Tara looked up at him, the questioning expression on her face hidden by the mask. 'You know something?' she asked. 'Something you aren't telling me?'

Dr Scott shrugged. 'Call it a hunch,' he deadpanned. 'Remember, I have been doing this far longer than you have.'

'What did you do?' she demanded.

'I took out one of the molecules you were including. My guess is that it is active in the creation of leprosy, but not in Ator. That narrows the range of compounds considerably.'

Tara peered down at the new list. She noted the one change he had made, and shrugged. It made sense, she thought, but no more sense than the earlier list. She knew even from her limited experience that when you came this close to a discovery there was no way of knowing what would work and what wouldn't. Only trial and error. Mostly error.

Reaching back up on the shelves, she started preparing the compound. Elements were squeezed together under the microscope, shaken, and poured out into a clean vial.

Tara could feel Dr Scott behind her, watching while she worked. She turned to face him, holding the liquid in her fingers. 'Your choice, Dr Scott,' she said. 'Would you like to try it?'

He shook his head. 'This is your project, Tara.'

She took another vial of Ator from the machine, and carried it carefully over to the workbench to get another reading. Placing it under the Geiger counter, she registered the level of radioactivity, and placed it on the rack before her. Taking the vial, she mixed in the liquid, and closed the stopper. Holding it in her fingers, she looked again at Dr Scott. 'What do you think?' she asked.

'You can't tell by looking at it,' he answered. 'You never can. Test it and see.'

Tara turned back and put the compound under the Geiger counter. Her eyes locked on to the dial, heavy with anticipation. Even after countless tries she still found this moment exciting. The dial jumped, lurching suddenly forward, then it fell back again. There was no consistent reading. She took the vial from the rack, and went back to the computer, logging down another failure.

From behind she felt a padded palm pat her on the back of the neck. 'Just keep trying,' said Scott. 'You'll get there soon enough.'

SIX

The lights dimmed. In the background, Jack could hear the ripple of piano music, music he couldn't place, fading into obscurity, washed away by the babble of chatter and speculation as the journalists found their seats in the conference room of the Dorchester Hotel. Along the side of the hall, three TV crews were busy setting up their cameras and lights, trailing wires and searching for plugs.

He was standing at the back, almost too tired to pick up on what was happening around him. The last ten days had been exhausting. Ever since the Chairman had announced the take-over, the head office had been a mass of activity; teams from the two merchant banks advising on the deal had been working round the clock, firing off questions which Jack and the other two special assistants had to pick up and run with. It had been chaotic but fun. Until this morning.

He had found a note on his desk asking him to call Dani Fuller.

Reluctantly, he had put the call through. She would see him later, she told him curtly. She would decide where. It was still preying on his mind. Somehow, amid all the activity, he had managed to put her request to the back of his mind. Its return to life was unwelcome, he decided. Most unwelcome.

Up ahead, Sir Kurt Helin limped on to the stage, his head bowed and his back arched. Under his arm he was carrying a sheaf of papers, haphazardly stacked, looking as though they might fall from him at any moment. The professorial act, thought Jack; one of the many guises under which the Chairman travels, this one calculated to create an air of other-worldly distance, a careful deception, aimed at relegating his own role to one of gentle, distracted brilliance. He was followed – at a respectful distance – by Sam Taylor, Ralph Finer and Dr Peter Scott, men whose halting pace showed they were uncomfortable walking as slowly as the Chairman, yet were reluctant to move ahead of him. The Chairman sat down, poured himself a glass of water from the jug on the table, and peered hesitantly around the room, his eyes flashing from place to place. In front of him, the journalists were quieter now, the whispers down to a trickle.

'Good morning, and thank you for joining us here today,' he began. The tone was measured, stately, and the words ampli-fied, so that they echoed around the room, bouncing back a split second after they had been spoken. 'As you are no doubt already aware, the purpose of this meeting here today is to dis-cuss the offer that this company, Kizog, has just made for our Swiss rival, Ocher. Our bid is worth roughly £12 billion. Rather less this morning, considering the initial reaction of the stock-market to the announcement we have made.' The Chairman smiled, a thin, forced smile, and there was a chuckle around the room. He raised a hand. 'That is not as I would wish it to be but I am not unduly concerned because not all the relevant infor-mation has yet been released to the markets. Recent scientific developments in our research laboratories have made this offer particularly timely.'

The Chairman slipped a sideways glance towards Dr Scott, sitting a yard or so to his left. Scott had disposed of his usual brown suit and M&S tie, replacing it with a double-breasted grey suit and a club tie, one Jack couldn't recognise. Wheeler and the PR girls have been at him, he thought.

Dr Scott was ill at ease talking in public, slurring his words and stumbling his way through his sentences. He sat down through his talk, shifting in his chair, his eyes buried into the text laid out in front of him, reading each phrase carefully before pronouncing it. His expression was lost somewhere between enjoyment and denial. 'The growth rate of Ator since the virus was first identified five years ago has turned this disease into perhaps the greatest human health challenge now facing us,' he began.

Behind him, a slide flashed up on the screen. It showed a photograph of an Oriental child – Vietnamese, thought Jack, but who could tell – its limbs sagging and eyes despairing. The child was being cradled by its mother, wrapped tightly in her arms, while across the image a thick black line sloped sharply upwards. 'Projections made by the World Health Organisation, and by other respectable experts in the field, now concur that Ator is likely to become a major world-wide pandemic unless action to control the spread of the disease is taken immediately.'

Over Dr Scott's shoulder, synchronised seamlessly with his words, the screen flashed again. This time it showed a collection of newspaper and magazine headlines: 'Mystery Virus Strikes Two', 'March of the Killer Bug', 'New Plague Feared as Ator Hits Britain' and so on. Scott took a deep breath and continued. 'The challenge to the pharmaceutical industry, perhaps the greatest challenge it has ever faced, is to find a way of stopping the virus before it becomes a world-wide pandemic on the scale of the black death. At Kizog we have realised that our responsibility, whatever the potential for profit or loss, has been to find a cure for this disease. That is why we are delighted to announce that an intensive research effort by our laboratories around the world has resulted in

60

what we believe is the first safe and effective vaccine for Ator.'

He looked around the room; the pens were alert, scribbling in their thin notebooks, and the mikes had their machines held out close to catch every word. Dr Scott turned towards the Chairman; throughout the scientist's talk he had been sitting still, saying nothing, with no more than a half-smile fixed rigidly on his face. In the background, the graph lingered, hanging behind him like a dark cloud.

The Chairman nodded at Dr Scott. He peered first up at the graphs, a sense of astonishment playing on his face, and then, his expression turning to one of high seriousness, he turned to face his audience. From a distance, Jack found himself marvelling at the old man's grasp of theatre.

'And so we come to the real reason behind the take-over offer for Ocher announced this morning,' the Chairman began. 'Eradicating Ator from the world is going to be a major challenge for this company. Alone we do not believe we have the size, resources or scope to manufacture the vaccine on the scale that our estimates suggest will be needed. But by combining the resources of Ocher with our own we believe it is a feasible task.' The Chairman raised a finger towards his audience. 'I can make a promise this morning that Kizog will not attempt to profiteer from its involvement with Ator. It is not our desire or our intention to make any more than a minimum amount of money from lifting this world-wide threat. I must point out, however, that even a very slim return on a product manufactured in these volumes will still earn a satisfying return for the shareholders in the company.'

His eyes took a sweep around the hall, rooting through the assembled hacks, burrowing for any dissent, searching for any sceptics. 'This is why I believe that this merger between these two leading pharmaceutical companies is in the best interests of both their owners, the shareholders, and of the world.' Finishing, the Chairman folded his arms and rested his case.

'Terrific drama,' said Layla.

Jack turned. She had appeared at his side during the presentation, but he had not noticed her. 'I suppose so,' he answered hesitantly.

'Great opportunities,' she said playfully. 'For you in particular.'

'What have you heard?' asked Jack.

She smiled. 'Just that you are working on a crucial project,' Layla replied. 'For the Chairman. Tell me about it.'

Inwardly Jack sighed. 'I'd like to,' he replied. 'But I can't.'

Weird, thought Jack, old Wheelie's office being on the fifth floor. A flak rolling around here, up among the big wheels. It was one of the great Kizog mysteries that the corridor gossips Jack mingled with had never quite been able to crack.

Geoff Wheeler, the director of corporate communications, to give him his proper name, was into his fifties now. It showed. The hair was greying, and going fast. The lines around his face were crashing into each other, jostling for space, unsure where to go next. And the skin colour. A reddish-grey hue, only found at the back of pubs. Too much sauce, thought Jack.

He had been at the company for about twenty years now, as long as anyone could remember. Before that he was believed to have spent a few years at the *Financial Times*. He had, according to the legend anyway, been brought here personally by the Chairman; one of the very first appointments he had made. Wheelie was certainly reputed to be very close to the Chairman; the only person who could be regarded as invulnerable. There was never any gossip about Wheelie's head being about to roll. A true survivor. One of the few.

Give him this, he does a good job, thought Jack. The coverage Kizog received in the press always seemed to be very favourable. There had been the occasional bout of sniping in the business sections about the relative underperformance of its share price in the last two or three years. But the rest of the media was sweet on the company; the result of its high-profile community and charity work. Work which Wheelie made sure everybody knew about.

Inside, the publicist's success was clear. To the left of the office, a desk was stacked high with newspapers and videotapes, evidence of the coverage the Ator vaccine had generated in the twenty-four hours since its announcement. At one end of the table, Dr Peter Scott was sitting with his head bowed, a slight frown on his forehead as he examined the clippings. Next to him sat Wheeler, a cigarette dangling from his mouth, his chewed fingernails tapping the edge of the table.

Tara was sitting across from both of them. Jack's eyes fell upon her first, running along the slender curves of her body; it was the first time he had seen her without a lab coat cloaking her, and he was quietly impressed. She smiled a half-smile, a communication that while on the surface friendly was also unknowable and unreadable.

'How are you?' he asked, attempting a smile.

'So you two know each other?' interrupted Wheeler.

'I was involved in hiring Tara,' explained Jack.

'Borrodin gets around,' said the PR man. 'The eyes and ears of the Chairman. A powerful young man, or so I am told.'

'I'm very well, thank you,' said Tara, looking up at Jack, and ignoring Wheeler.

'Such modesty,' exclaimed Wheeler. 'The inventor of one of the most miraculous discoveries of the modern age, you should be on top of the world, simply on top of the world, my dear.'

'Are you involved in this one, Jack?' asked Scott.

Jack looked across at the scientist. There was a tone of suspicion in the man's voice, and an air of wariness in his eyes. Scott had a reputation for treating the Chairman's gofers with a degree of ill-disguised contempt, and Jack had learnt to handle him carefully. 'Sir Kurt asked me to come along,' he replied. 'This is clearly a very delicate time for the company.'

'The bid?' said Scott.

'Everything we do over the next few weeks will be very carefully scrutinised,' replied Jack.

Scott sighed. 'Do you think we will win?'

'Depends purely on the share price,' answered Jack authoritatively. 'It is a paper offer. If our prospects look good, better than Ocher's anyway, then shareholders will be glad to swap our shares for theirs.' Jack turned to Wheeler: 'That's why we are here, isn't it.'

'Absolutely, old boy.' The PR man picked up a pile of the papers and spread them across the desk. 'This is great,' he said. 'This is very good. There is plenty in here about the Ator vaccine. All of it positive.'

'There is nothing unusual about that,' said Scott. 'I've yet to see a medical breakthrough that got a bad press.'

'True,' said Wheeler. 'But we have to make sure it continues. Our first priority is to keep the news on Ator flowing right through the bid. We need to keep it in people's minds. That way our share price will keep climbing.'

'There is not much left to say,' interrupted Tara. 'We have the basis of a vaccine, yes. But it still has to go into development. The chances are that it will not survive. There may be side-effects. This vaccine may never even reach the market.'

Jack turned to Scott: 'What's your opinion?' he asked.

'You know the statistics as well as I do,' Scott replied. 'Only one in ten discoveries make it through all the stages of testing. Failure is the norm.'

Tara had a stern look in her eye. 'This strikes me as a very cynical exercise.'

Jack and Wheeler turned to meet her gaze. 'How so?' asked Jack.

'I am starting to understand why Sir Kurt was so keen to hire me,' she continued. 'There was always a reasonable chance that one of the compounds I had been investigating for leprosy would show laboratory effectiveness against Ator. Not certain but likely. The company knew that, and the Chairman must have known for some time he was planning to launch this bid for Ocher. Jack, how long does the bid last for?'

'Under Takeover Panel rules we have thirty days.'

Tara nodded. 'Kizog brings me in and gets a compound. It releases the details, and lifts its stock price, and launches the bid. There is no way we will know in the next thirty days whether this compound works or not. But by then of course, it doesn't matter. Kizog will have won.'

Jack listened with growing admiration. The Chairman, he knew, could be devious and cunning, but this was a strategy of such elegant manipulation, it was hard to be anything other than impressed. It was a wonderful ploy. And Tara had seen straight through it, as though it were made of glass. Jack studied her for a second. She looked somehow different from when they met the other day. More sure of herself. Less edgy. There was an anger in her eyes. An anger that rippled through her body, tensing her muscles. He could sense trouble. The Chairman wanted her to be portrayed as the inventor of this wonder cure. And there would be repercussions if she did not play along.

Try to reason with her, thought Jack. 'It is important that this take-over succeeds; otherwise we might not have the resources to make the vaccine on the scale it is needed, if it proves successful,' he began, stressing the words as he spoke. 'And there is no reason to think it will not succeed. Even if it doesn't, the company has invested a lot of credibility into coming up with a vaccine. Huge resources will be thrown into finding one that does work. Surely that is useful.'

There was no expression on Tara's face. None that he could read, anyway. 'It is not something that I would want to be involved in,' she replied stonily.

Wheeler leant across the conference table, patting her wrist with his chubby hand. She drew away quickly. 'All we want is to make sure that you get the proper public recognition for your role in the discovery. You have done important work. Historic work. You deserve the praise.'

'It doesn't interest me,' answered Tara. 'The science interests me.'

Wheeler looked puzzled. He has trouble understanding someone who does not want publicity, figured Jack. Reclusiveness

65

was alien to him. Try to reason with her, Jack reminded himself. Find her wavelength. 'If nothing else, the information we have released will spur our competitors into devoting more resources into finding their own vaccine,' said Jack.

Tara looked up at Scott, a quizzical expression in her eyes asking silently for his opinion. 'I think you should consider it,' he said. 'The commercial world is new to you. But Jack has a point.'

She nodded: 'I suppose I'm in too deep to turn back now.'

The four of them stood up to leave. Scott and Tara headed off towards the laboratory buildings. Wheeler started tapping Jack for gossip on the likely board reshuffle if the bid was successful, but Jack did not feel in the mood for office politics. He wanted to speak to Tara. He sped through the corridor and stopped by the lift, relieved that she was still there, and alone. He turned to face her and attempted eye contact, but she turned away. 'I'm not such a bad person,' he said.

'Prove it,' she answered.

'I'd like to,' he replied. 'But how?'

Tara shrugged. 'Think of something.'

'The deaths of the other scientists,' said Jack. 'Are you worried about that? That someone might come after you. Surely you don't think that.'

'I don't know what to think,' she answered sharply. 'I just know I didn't really discover that vaccine. It doesn't feel right.'

The flickering of her eyelashes betrayed her nervousness, and for a moment Jack felt instinctively protective. 'Security can be organised. Let me talk to the Chairman about it.'

Tara met his eyes, suspicion starting to drift across her face. 'Bodyguards?' she asked.

'Yes, if you like,' said Jack, wondering if he was being melodramatic.

Tara shook her head. 'No guards.'

'Why not?'

For a moment Tara seemed lost in her own thoughts, and she

hesitated, her eyes scrutinising Jack, before replying. 'Because I am worried that it starts here.'

'The take-over ploy?' Jack asked.

'No,' she replied stonily. 'It goes much deeper than that.'

SEVEN

She was sitting in a dim light, with her legs crossed, and with one black stiletto hanging off the end of her foot. The other was lying abandoned on the floor, a yard or so away from her chair, and she was leaning back, relaxed and composed, as though she owned the place.

Dani Fuller looked up at him, a slow smile playing across her lips. 'Surprised.'

Jack was too shocked to say anything. It was his flat and he certainly hadn't let her in. Nor had he given her a key. On turning the look to his apartment, he had been aware of the light inside. But it was only one or two bulbs. Perhaps he had left them on in the morning.

The sight of her sitting there, cool and in command, as though her presence was the most natural occurrence imaginable, drained him of a response. Jack could feel a fluttering in the pit of his stomach. Fear.

68

Play it cool, he told himself. 'Would you like a drink?' he asked.

Fuller stood up, straightening out her short black skirt. 'Whatever you have.'

Wandering towards the kitchen, Jack cast anxious glances around the apartment. No signs of damage. The lock did not appear to be broken. The windows weren't smashed. And though his mind was racing through the options, he could find no evidence of how she might have made her way into the flat. He made a pot of coffee, and poured out two cups, bringing them through to the sitting-room.

'Aren't you wondering what I am doing here?' she said.

'Tell me?' he asked warily.

Fuller turned away from him and sat down. 'Our investigations are making progress,' she said. 'We have made contact. Don't ask me how. For now information is best handled purely on a need-to-know basis.'

'And how much do I need to know?'

'Only this. We need your help.'

Fuller crossed her legs, revealing the outline of her thighs. They were, to Jack's eye, strong and muscular, not slim, but appealing all the same. 'These people have already learnt a little bit about you,' she said. 'The suggestion has been made that you have heavy debts. The result of some ill-judged investments in currency options. They believe that you are desperate for money.'

'Desperate enough for what?' asked Jack. 'To get involved in counterfeiting?'

'We need a way in, Jack,' said Fuller lightly. 'We know something about these people and their methods. But we have nothing in the way of concrete evidence. Nothing that will stand up in court. And nothing that will allow us to start making any arrests.'

'And you want me to provide the evidence?'

'All we need is somebody to have dealings with them who can be relied upon to give evidence.'

'Bait,' snapped Jack.

69

Fuller shrugged. She finished her coffee and stood up, standing close to Jack. 'Entrapment is the normal term,' she replied coldly. 'Can we count on you?'

Jack could feel the butterflies again, flapping inside him, creating a tensing of the muscles, and fuddling his mind. He was uncertain. The notion of dealing with criminals made him fearful; his nerves were jangling, loosening at the edges, unbalancing his judgement. He looked into her eyes. She was staring straight into him, but there was little he could read there. No guidance. 'It would be dangerous,' he said eventually. She turned away, saying nothing, avoiding his glare. 'I would need guarantees,' Jack persisted.

She turned to face him once more. 'Are you afraid?'

Was this a challenge, wondered Jack. 'I need protection.'

She smiled. 'But of course. You'll be wired. We'll follow you. Phone calls will be taped. Meetings will be videoed. We're collecting evidence, Jack.'

Tara removed the vial carefully from the rack. She marvelled at the still clarity of the liquid; here under the dim neon light, beside the cold, steel, reinforced wall, beneath the hushed whirr of the air-filter, it had a special kind of innocence and purity. Progress, she thought.

She placed the vial on the workbench in front of her, and uncorked it. The vile stench of the liquid wafted up to her nostrils, forcing her to recoil slightly. She pulled down the protective mask over her face, and tightened the bindings on her thick gloves. A mistake, she knew, to allow herself to be exposed for even a second. Her stomach felt slightly queasy. And her head was aching. Exhaustion, she thought. She was becoming careless.

Tara glanced down at the notebooks spread out in front of her. There was still much to be done. The vaccine was good, that much had been established, but it was still far from perfect. It could lodge minute particles of the disease in every cell, creating an irresistible barrier to infection, but the mechanism by which the virus was prevented from replicating itself still had to be perfected. Otherwise they risked creating as much molecular havoc as they were preventing.

Her task, she knew, was urgent. Every day the virus was still spreading, capturing another victim every eight minutes, according to the most recent World Health Organisation data Tara had seen. That was down from one every twelve minutes six months ago; the virus was becoming smarter, more cunning, leaping from carrier to carrier with greater agility and stealth. Tara tried to tell herself that every minute counted. Every eight minutes she delayed meant another person lost.

And yet, the truth was also important. The truth about this awful disease and where it came from. A truth, she suspected, that was as deep and mysterious as the molecule that carried the virus. And possibly as deadly.

She was, Tara realised, achingly tired. The lids of her eyes were heavy with work, and the numbers and symbols in her notepad and on the computer were swimming past her in a meaningless blur. Her appetite for further discovery was escaping from within her.

Leaving the vial exposed, she left the small, air-locked laboratory, pausing within the steel doors as the air around her was sanitised. Slowly she walked through the corridor. She glanced at her watch. It was a quarter past nine; late for a commercial laboratory, and only a handful of people were still working. Very different from the National Institutes, she thought to herself. There, nine was still early. There would be plenty of people, particularly the younger scientists, hoping that at this late hour they might find it easier to get time on the equipment, time that they could use to try out their latest ideas. There would be a sense of excitement about the place, a buzz, even in the silence, a spirit of comradeship. Here there was only the unrelenting grind of the targets. And the slow ticking of the clocks on the wall.

The coffee bar at the end of the laboratories was almost empty.

There were half a dozen of the workmen from the basement where they kept the animals; the rats, dogs and monkeys on which the products were tested. They were playing cards. This was the start of the night shift; feeding the animals, administering their drugs, watching to see if any of them died, although the video cameras and cage sensors would capture most of that. The men themselves had little to do. A few tables along a couple of scientists were drinking some coffee and talking. About what she didn't know; she did not recognise them. And through her mask, they could hardly be expected to recognise her.

The old coloured lady – Doreen she was called – sat behind the counter, her white-haired head bowed over a book. Tara asked for a coffee and a doughnut, without realising that her voice could hardly be heard through her mask. The old lady looked up at her quizzically. Tara slipped off the helmet, tucking it beneath her elbow, and repeated her order.

'You shouldn't work too hard.'

Tara smiled. She didn't particularly feel like talking, but she was acutely aware of how dismissive Orientals usually were towards blacks, even worse than whites, and she didn't want to compound the curtness of her race. 'But there is so much work to be done,' said Tara quietly.

'It will wait. Go out and enjoy yourself. Find a man.'

Tara and Doreen had spoken before, and had already established the fact that she was single; a fact of which Doreen heartily disapproved. 'Men are harder to crack than molecules,' she replied.

'Ain't that the truth.' Doreen laughed. 'And they cause more trouble, too.'

Tara smiled. 'I have enough trouble with the molecules, for now.'

'I saw the story about you in the paper.'

The paper, yes, thought Tara. It had appeared yesterday. She had featured in a panel in a long piece about Ator in the *Sunday Times*. It had described how she had played the key role in the identification of the potential vaccine, and gave a short summary of her life story. She had not met the writer, at her insistence. Wheeler had briefed him. And there were no photographs. She had insisted on that as well. 'How did I come across?'

'Too serious.'

Tara mixed some milk into the large Styrofoam cup of coffee. 'Do you know Jack Borrodin?' she asked. It was a senseless question. She knew full well that Doreen was a mine of information on everyone in the building.

'Nice-looking boy.'

'Should I trust him?' asked Tara suddenly.

'I hardly know him. Been away for a couple of years. Haven't seen him around very much.'

'Your instinct?'

'Honey, I don't trust any man,' she laughed. 'But he don't seem any worse than the rest. Better even.'

Tara smiled, took her coffee, and her doughnut, and went to sit by herself. She placed the mask on the table in front of her. The workmen glanced leeringly in her direction, saw the suit, and hurriedly looked away again. Everyone in the laboratory knew it meant she had been working with a lethal virus, and she found it a great deterrent to conversation. A useful tool when you wanted to be alone. Which Tara often did.

The coffee refreshed her, the kick of the caffeine alerting her mind, and the sugar of the doughnut seeped into her bloodstream, renewing her energy. Her curiosity was returning, yet, at the same time, wandering. Drifting away from the work she had left in the laboratory, and into new and unexplored directions. Questions occurred to her that had slumbered in the back of her mind, and, by now, were ready to get up and start walking around. Questions such as how much did these people know? And why had their investigations into the Ator vaccine been so advanced even before she arrived?

Swilling back her coffee, Tara ran her eyes around the room, and slipped the mask back over her face. She walked back along the corridor of the laboratory, but as she passed her own lab she merely glanced up at the red light over the airlocked door, a light that signalled no entry, and kept on walking. Her mind had disposed of the immediate problem. It was grappling with the underlying story. Researching. Making connections.

Dr Scott's laboratory was located at the furthest end of one of the corridors leading through the complex. She glanced briefly through the thin porthole. It was, as she would have expected, empty; it was late, and Scott did most of his work shuffling papers in his office. Nobody saw him in there very often.

She glanced down at the door. Like all the important labs and offices within Kizog it was protected by a numerical lock; every authorised employee had a key number they had to punch into the doorpad to gain access to their part of the building. Tara had never tried to break into anything before, and she could feel her pulse quicken as she contemplated the next few moments. Be strong, she told herself. And be careful.

She had already run the technique through her mind; indeed, in moments of quiet, it had been one of her main preoccupations. A friend at the National Institutes had explained how he had done this for a bet once, so she knew the theory. But the tension in her muscles told her the reality could be very different.

Taking a vial of sodium from her lab coat, she uncorked the glass container, and, checking the corridor once again, gently sprinkled a dusting of the fine yellow powder over the lock. Much of it inevitably fell on the floor, and she ground it in with her shoe. Kneeling, she put her eyes as close as possible to the lock, squinting so that she could see exactly the shapes formed by the thin film of powder. Gradually a pattern began to emerge. From the traces of the fingerprints marked out by the sodium, she could see the four digits that had been pressed into the lock: two, three, seven and nine. Now at least she knew which four numbers made up the code.

Each lock, she knew, was programmed to accept two tries. Employees might make a mistake the first time, but if they failed to get the number right on the second attempt, the door would lock solidly for the next thirty minutes, and an alarm would trigger security that a break-in was being attempted. Just punching those four numbers at random would not be good enough. She needed more information.

Recalling what she had learnt from her friend, Tara took a pair of standard lab magnifying spectacles from her pocket and began to study the fingerprints more closely. The chances were that Scott, like most people, pressed hardest on the first and third numbers. Studying the prints closely, Tara decided two and nine were heavy prints, three and seven were light prints. Making a quick mental calculation, that gave her four possible numbers: 2397, 9723, 9327, or 2793.

It had to be one of those four numbers, and with two chances, she now had a fifty per cent probability of gaining access without being detected. She also had a fifty per cent probability of being caught. Too risky, she decided.

One more clue, Tara told herself. Reason dictated that a normal person would press most heavily on the first digit, and then use a slightly lighter touch as they ran through the numbers. Squinting once again at the two heavier prints, she looked to see which had the deeper imprint. The marks were all very faint and she suspected nobody had used this lock for several days. Even so, glancing from the two to the nine, she decided the nine had the stronger print. OK, she decided. Two possible numbers: 9723 or 9327.

Drawing a deep breath, Tara allowed the oxygen to flow into her lungs, calming her and setting her mind momentarily at rest. Punching 9327 into the keypad, she looked nervously at the liquid crystal display above the box. 'Incorrect number. Access denied,' ran the message across the miniature screen. Without hesitating, Tara punched 9723 into the machine and readied herself to walk away briskly if the door did not open. In front of her, a small red light flashed up on the display. Reaching down for the handle, she turned, felt the lock give way, and the door opened before her. Exhaling, she stepped inside the room, shutting the door firmly behind her.

Scott's lab was smarter than the rest. Larger. Better equipped. There were more computers, and comfier chairs. Tara could see no sign of any experiments in progress. The workbench was clean and empty, the vials were all tucked away, and the computers were shut down. In the recess at the back of the laboratory there was a library. Tara scanned her eyes along the shelf. There were plenty of standard pharmacology and virology reference works. Tara was familiar with them all and these were not even the latest editions; looking at them, Tara was doubtful whether Scott was familiar with the current work in the field.

Lower down, stacked upon a row of metal shelves, she found a pile of ring folders and binders. More interesting, she thought to herself.

Sitting cross-legged on the floor, Tara took out the binders and began leafing through them. The pages, old now and slightly yellowed, felt musty to her touch. It was impossible to say how old they were. There were no dates on them. No clues as to when they might have been written. Just page after page of scrawled laboratory notes, written in a script that was almost indecipherable. The words were hard to make out. Tara's eyes were straining, but the jottings meant little anyway. The formulae, however, meant more. They were written in capital letters, and their meaning was immediately apparent to her. They related to leprosy and the nervous system. One formula struck her in particular. It was close to the leprosy enzyme; the structure of the molecule that carried the virus from one carrier to another. Clearly a transmission mechanism, she thought. Close to leprosy. Close, but not quite there.

The leprosy viruses, and most of the transmission mechanisms, were intimately familiar to her; she had spent most of the past few years working on them and been commended for her work. Indeed, been recruited here to teach the company about them. Shouldn't it be the other way around, she wondered? Shouldn't there be something I can tell them?

Next to the formula, in small, tightly written capital letters, were the words: 'CHECK WITH DR ZMITT'. Standard lab jottings; junior researchers would often make a note to themselves to discuss an interesting finding with a superior. But Scott

76

was a superior. He was the head of research. There was nobody with whom he could check his work. There were no dates on the papers, and no clue to when they might have been written. Nor was there any other mention of Zmitt, or who he was, or what position he might hold within the laboratory.

Clutching the sheaf of papers, Tara left the door ajar, and walked back along the corridor to the photocopier. Still wearing her mask, the veins around her temples pulsing, she leant over the machine. Clean, fresh photocopies spat out of the machine.

'Good evening, Miss Ling.'

Tara spun round. It was a security guard. She said nothing. And as she pulled the mask down tighter over her face, she watched him walk away.

The guard checked his watch. It was close to ten. He made a mental note to himself that after he finished his round he should, as instructed, file a brief report. It would state merely that he had seen Miss Ling in the laboratory late on Monday evening.

Jack sat alone, holding a whisky and soda in one hand, peering into the gloom of a half-illuminated flat. Outside, the street was quiet, and he had switched off the TV and hi-fi. With Fuller gone, he needed a moment of silence. Complete silence.

He needed, he reflected, someone to talk to; someone who was nothing to do with the company, someone he could confide in and take advice from. Someone he could trust. There was, he realised with a shudder of regret, nobody. His time abroad had put a gulf between him and his university friends, a gulf that he now found hard to bridge. And his schooling outside of Britain meant there were no old friends he could turn to. He was alone.

Riffling through the hundreds of CDs stacked in one corner of the room, he pulled out an old Marvin Gaye album and placed it into the machine; 'What's Going On', something soulful and probing to reflect his mood. Too much time abroad, he decided, as the first magnificent beats thundered through the speakers. And too much trouble with girls.

He still had difficulty understanding what had happened to both of them. Emily, the great love of his university days, had abandoned him after he moved to Thailand. And yet, in truth, he had abandoned her. He had known when he took the posting that she would not be able to join him; she was still studying for the bar, and had to remain in London. He had not realised it at the time, but he understood now it had been part of the attraction of the move; he wanted to take a break from the relationship and yet lacked the courage to tell her. And so he took himself to the other side of the world, hoping he could return to her when he came back; somewhere within him he suspected that he would never meet another woman who combined such sharp wit and intelligence with such sensitivity, and who, most of all, loved him. And after a brief break, he hoped they would get back together and marry. But, of course, she had met someone else. And so had he.

Jasmine had been different. A middle-class Thai girl, she was a world away from the bar girls most of the other Caucasian men he knew in Bangkok had hung around with. She was, like many Thai women, drop-dead beautiful, but she was also educated and cultured, contemptuous of the hordes of beer-swilling, pool-crazy girls who swanned around the city. Perhaps that was why he had loved as well as desired her. Their affair had lasted just over a year, mostly consummated in secret; it was still not considered respectable for Thai girls to be involved with white men, and she preferred to keep him hidden away. For Jack, the element of furtiveness only heightened the romance. There was an electric charge to each of their meetings; they would eat together in distant parts of town, they would take weekends away in remote beach resorts and the sense of illicit moments snatched from time made each encounter precious. Thinking back now, Jack realised she had perhaps just been waiting; hoping that he would ask her to marry him, so that they would not have to meet furtively any more. When Kizog asked him to come back to England, he had accepted immediately, and had allowed their relationship to crumble.

Well, he thought to himself, taking another sip of his drink, time perhaps, to stop running. Next time, work harder. Try to make it last. Show some commitment. And then perhaps you won't feel quite so alone.

The phone rang twice before Jack answered it, and as he walked across the room he found himself briefly hoping it might be Emily or Jasmine. Picking up the receiver, he was careful to click the switch on the tape machine Fuller had placed next to the phone. Record your calls, she had instructed. We need the evidence. 'I may be able to help you,' said a voice on the line, the words ground out in a rough East End accent. 'If you need money, that is. But I would need something from you.'

'I can give you a formula,' said Jack evenly, trying to remember the lines he had been taught. 'In exchange for payment.'

The tone of the voice on the line sounded suspicious. 'We are talking about the same thing?'

'Counterfeiting,' replied Jack. 'We are talking about counterfeiting pharmaceuticals.'

'Tomorrow night then,' said the man. 'At the Flying Scotsman. Bottom of the Caledonian Road. At eight.'

The line went dead, and Jack replaced the receiver carefully, switching off the tape machine as he did so. He walked back across the room, pouring himself another drink, and sliding a Van Morrison CD into the hi-fi. Running his eyes over the empty room, he picked up yesterday's paper, flicking casually through the pages, stopping when he reached the panel on Tara. He had read it already, but this time he stopped to read it again, slowly. The first few paragraphs, about her work in the labs, hardly interested him, but lower down was a short description of her life.

Ling was born in Saigon, then the capital of South
Vietnam, in 1964. She confesses that she knows little
about her parents; her father was an American serviceman,
one of many who fought in the war, who was killed soon
afterwards. Her mother, unable to support her, placed her
in an orphanage, and records of who she was were lost
after the war ended. In 1971 she moved to the US, under a

79

programme to bring the children of American military personnel back to the country. She was adopted by an elderly couple in Ohio, whose only son had been killed in the war, and to whom she was a surrogate grandchild. 'They were very good to me,' recalls Ling. An excellent student, Ling won a scholarship to Harvard, where she took a first degree in medicine, followed by a postgraduate degree in biochemistry. From there she worked at the National Institutes of Health, where she specialised in virology, before being hired by Kizog to work on a vaccine for Ator.

The soft beats of the music pulsed through the room. *'And when I come to her that's where I belong/Yet I'm running to her like a river's song/She give me love, love, love, love, crazy love,'* hummed the record. Jack cast the paper down, pausing only to glance at the picture of the laboratory where she worked. There was no picture of her; Tara had refused to have her photograph taken for reasons he well understood. A strange life, he reflected. And a strange way to wind up in the laboratories at Kizog. She must, he decided, be very alone.

EIGHT

Jack checked the locks on his BMW. It was a bad area. And he rated the chances of his car surviving the evening at no more than fifty-fifty.

The Flying Scotsman was a few yards from King's Cross station. The street outside was littered with human debris: tramps and crack dealers, plus a few whores, so beaten, scarred and doped it was hard to imagine anyone wanting them for nothing. Money was out of the question.

The fear was lifting from Jack now. There was a roll in his step. His adrenalin was running, coursing through his veins, pumping his emotions. It was a strangely intoxicating sensation; a sense of walking on the other side of the line. Fine, he reflected, so long as you were just visiting. A tourist. And so long as you were not planning a long stay.

He checked his pockets and glanced anxiously around the streets as he walked. According to Fuller, he would be followed.

His movements would be traced, and his words recorded. He could see nobody. Just as well, he told himself. If he could see them, then so could they.

Trust us, Fuller had told him. I hope so, thought Jack. I certainly hope so.

He ordered a beer and stood by the bar. To the back of the pub, a stripper was cavorting on a makeshift black stage, raised about a foot or so above the ground. Tina Turner's 'What's Love Got To Do With It' was playing in the background, dimly, through a badly tuned speaker system. An unoriginal choice of music, thought Jack. She was seventeen or so. Blonde, long hair, clean skin, with firm breasts, and a tattoo of a snake with a sword running through it on the inside of her right thigh.

'The thing that people don't usually realise about criminal activity is that it is best carried out right under the noses of the police.'

Jack turned to his left. He had failed to notice the man standing next to him. He was over six feet tall, with broad shoulders and wavy blond hair. He was wearing neat, black, pleated trousers, and tasselled shoes, a black polo sweater, and a black jacket. His face was rugged and tanned, and his nose was hooked; broken thought Jack. 'You are the man I am meant to be meeting,' he said. 'We spoke on the phone.'

'The very one,' the man said harshly, holding out his hand. 'Angus Shane.'

Jack shook; the grip was firm, too firm, but the squeeze was not severe. 'Take this place,' Shane continued. 'Constant police surveillance. There'll be a couple of narcs in here. I could point them out to you if you like. Outside they got video cameras tucked away in the walls, the whole works.'

'And that makes it a good place to meet?' asked Jack warily.

'You have a lot to learn Mr Borrodin. Amateurs see, they always suggest you meet someplace quiet, someplace you won't be noticed. A sleepy country pub. Or a motorway caff. Very fond of that service station just past Watford. I've noticed that. They've seen that on TV. Very dangerous. You see, you can't afford to deal with amateurs in this line. Not worth the trouble.'

Shane looked about forty to Jack. Give or take five years either way. Ex-army, perhaps. He had that look about him. Jack had noticed it with the security guards at Kizog. The soldiers were a better cut of man than the other yobs hired by the security contractors. More bearing. A greater sense of self-confidence. And a toughness that was evident in their muscles and in their eyes. 'You said on the phone that we could do some business,' said Jack.

'Perhaps we can, young man. Then again, perhaps we can't. It all depends.'

'How did you find me?'

'Contacts. We ask around. Keep our noses to the ground. It always pays. There is always someone who needs some money.'

'Money for what?' asked Jack.

'Interesting question.' Shane pulled out a packet of cigarettes – Camels – from his pocket, lighting one. He dragged on it, hard, the smoke curling up around his eyebrows. 'Forgery. Like those blokes you see selling perfume in Oxford Street. The packaging is all there. Nice bottle. Might smell like dog's vomit, but the girls can't tell the difference anyway. I've done a bit of that myself. Long time ago, mind. I've moved on. It's a nice little trade, but small time. And the coppers bother you now and again.'

'And now you forge pharmaceuticals,' said Jack.

'Much better than forging perfume,' answered Shane. 'Higher prices, for starters. The highest priced retail product there is, if you work it out on a pound per milligram basis. Cheap as well. Cheaper than scent, anyway. Cheaper than Rolexes, too. You don't have to bother with fancy packaging, bottles, none of that. Just a cheap little pill, and a small box with a brand name on it. Easy. But the best part of it is the punters never know. With perfume, the punters know it's fake. They'll buy it, but they ain't going to pay full whack. Pharmaceuticals is different. I mean you come home with your Zantac or your Zovirax, you don't know what it looks like, what it tastes like.'

'You have the formulae for these products?' asked Jack.

'Of course we do.'

'The exact formulae?' Jack persisted, aware that he was meant to be collecting evidence.

'Chemical entity, manufacturing process, the works. I'll be honest, and say that our stuff ain't quite as good as the real thing. The factories aren't up to scratch. Can't get the staff, you know. And there may be some modifications that we aren't aware of. But pretty close.'

'And you get these formulae from employees? People like me.'

'Easiest way. You could break in, steal the formula, but it's a lot of work. We aren't law-abiding citizens, you see. Amateurs, like you, don't really understand the way a criminal enterprise works. The bottom line is we don't like to work too hard for a living. Don't need the hassle. Scaling fences, dodging security guards, running away from the dogs, all that. We can do it if we have to, but to be honest for all that trouble you might as well get a job. Night work, as well. Plays havoc with your social life.'

'And it alerts the company,' said Jack. 'They will know it's been stolen.'

'You catch on quick.' Shane turned the gaze of his cool, grey eyes directly on Jack. 'You have financial problems.'

Jack paused. 'I have debts. Options. A few bad calls on the market. I lost a packet.'

'How much do you need?'

'Above a hundred thousand.'

Shane whistled. 'Serious problems. What can you give me?'

Jack paused. 'The formula for Zimetnant. The antibiotic. How much would you pay?'

Shane creased up his brow. 'If I wanted it, I'd pay you £250,000. I laundered money, of course. Untraceable. Deposited in a bank account in an offshore centre of your choice.'

'But you might not want it?'

'I don't know if I trust you.'

Jack hesitated. It had seemed to be going so well up until now. Easy. No trouble at all. But perhaps Shane was just playing him along. Perhaps he knew he was a plant. He paused, hoping to banish the fear from his eyes before continuing. 'You don't trust me?'

Shane turned to face him, leaning forward slightly. His eyes no more than a foot away from Jack, peering into his mind, fishing for signs of nerves or betrayal. 'I'm not saying I don't trust you. All I'm saying is I don't know if I trust you.'

Jack tried to compose himself. 'What proof do you need? A look at the formula?'

Shane shook his head, swaying the whole of his torso as he did so. 'No,' he answered firmly. 'I need to know you. As a man.' His arm rested lightly on Jack's shoulder. 'We'll have some fun together. A night out. Then I might know you.'

The invitation startled Jack, catching him off-guard. To refuse would seem awkward and might blow his mission. But to accept? How could he know what dangers he might be exposing himself to? 'OK,' said Jack eventually, hoping to disguise the nerves in his voice.

Shane drove a silver-grey Mercedes 500SL, a two-seater sports model, with black leather seats and a CD player. Jack noted the car, and took it as a sign that the man had money. Together they headed towards a Japanese restaurant in Hampstead, a place Shane claimed was a favourite of his; it was a tense, almost silent, drive, during which Jack was too unsure of how to handle the situation to make much conversation.

The choice of restaurant surprised Jack. Shane didn't have the look of a sushi type: more of a steak and chips and black forest gâteau sort, he thought to himself. Or biryani.

Throughout the meal, Shane talked and asked questions. About Jack's life, his parents, his family, his girlfriends, his work. And about money. Mostly about money. About how much of it there was, about how easy it was to acquire, about all the things money could do for you. And about the things people would do for money. Anything, in Shane's view. Anything you wanted. Particularly the women.

The man was an unashamed materialist. Or so Jack decided early on in the evening. But then what would you expect? He had imagined he might be probed on his loyalty to the firm, his

85

willingness to betray it, his commitment to the organisation, his desire to progress within it, and so on. But no. This was a trade. A deal. The importance of the money was the only thing that mattered to Shane; the willingness of his prey to put himself up for auction was the only question that concerned him.

'What kind of options, calls or puts?' asked Shane.

They were back in the car now. Shane had paid for the meal. He told Jack that the night was young. There was plenty for them to do. And still fun to be had. 'Puts,' answered Jack quickly.

Shane probed further. 'Equities, currencies or commodities?'

'Equities,' answered Jack.

'Which one?'

Jack paused. 'GEC November 300p puts. About six months ago. I paid 26p. The price just kept sinking. Useless. The contract expired and I recovered nothing. I lost a packet.'

Jack was feeling breathless. Extemporising, he thought. Winging it. This moment was unprepared. The line about losing money on options he knew, he had it figured, but he hadn't worked out which options and when. There was no point in pretending to have forgotten. Nobody forgot losing a hundred grand. It was the sort of thing that stuck in your mind.

Am I through? he asked himself. Or does he suspect?

He peered out of the window. They were heading east. Jack knew neither where they were, nor where they were going. Shane had not said, and he hadn't felt like asking. The journey could be taking them anywhere. Anywhere at all, thought Jack.

The buildings around Old Street, on the fringes of the City, he started to recognise. This was not a part of London he knew well, but the grim turrets of concrete, and the brick warehouses and sweatshops were familiar. Just. It was a different kind of city around here, darker, poorer and older, a world away from the bourgeois suburbs to the north and west. A rougher city, where lives were shorter and harder. The car swung into the street along Spitalfields market, the green awnings of the traders' stalls shut now, the wide road empty apart from a few trucks and cars, and, in a corner, a late-night van selling coffees and hamburgers. The homeless were lining up for a bite to eat, sitting on the steps of a church with their food. Shane slowed the car down, riding hard along the edge of the kerb. Jack glanced at his watch. Just before twelve.

He noticed the women about ten yards up the street. Two of them, one wearing a short black skirt and a white T-shirt, the other thigh-high black boots, gold shorts and a black leather jacket. Their eyes followed the car as it pulled to a stop alongside the kerb. Silently, Shane beckoned to the girl in the boots. She swaggered across, a jaunt in her step, leaning over the side of the car as the automatic window slid down. Jack could feel the cool breeze of the night air drifting through the car. Her face was no more than a few inches from his, and he could smell the perfume. Cheap. She was wearing just a black bra beneath the leather jacket, and her large breasts swung in front of him. An OK body, blonde hair, dodgy complexion, reasonable features. Nothing special.

'Business,' she said.

Shane leant across Jack to speak to her. 'Back at my place.'

'Both of you?'

Shane nodded.

'Sixty,' she said.

'Let the lady in, will you, Jack.'

Jack climbed out of the car and held the door open for her. He found he was already too numbed by the turns the night had taken to have much reaction to this latest twist. His emotions, for now, were stuck in neutral. She glanced up at him, flashing a smile. 'I could bring the other girl along if you make it a hundred.'

'You'll do,' answered Shane.

She shrugged, settling into the back seat. Shane pressed down hard on the accelerator, and the car spun away from the kerb. The three of them drove in silence, racing further east, into the murky swamp of docklands. Jack looked out of the car into the dismal streets and tried to judge whether they were being followed; Fuller had promised a private detective would be tailing him all night. There were a few cars around, but he had no way of knowing which one it might be. Or if it was there at all. Too late now, he reflected. Far too late.

The Mercedes pulled to a halt outside a warehouse. It was a large, modern conversion, next to the river. One of many converted in the last decade. Shane led the way, opening the door, through the wood-finished lobby, into the lift. The whore dragged along behind, the heels of her boots clacking on the wooden floor, hands dug deep into the pockets of her jacket, shoulders slouched. Poor posture, Jack found himself thinking. The flat was bare and minimalist. The sitting-room had stripped boards, with a balcony looking out over the river. To the side there was a steel kitchen area, and in the centre of the room a black leather and chrome sofa, with a smoked glass coffee-table next to it. Some magazines lay on it. *Autosport*, *Classic Car*, *Penthouse*. All boy's choices. At the end of the room there was a coal-effect fire, a thirty-one-inch TV, a video and a hi-fi. Not much else. An eighties leftover, thought Jack.

Shane sauntered out of the kitchen with a bottle of whisky tucked under his arm, and a tray of ice cubes. He banged the ice tray down on the coffee-table, sending the cubes flying out over the table. Picking up three tumblers, he poured a large measure of whisky into each one. 'There's ice if you want it,' he said.

The whore sat down on the sofa and took one of the Camels from the table. She was surveying the room, and there was a trace of pleasure in her eyes. Easily pleased, thought Jack. 'Which one of you wants to go first?' she said placidly. 'Or both together. We can do that. I don't mind.'

'He'll fuck you,' answered Shane. 'I'll just sit here for now'

Jack eyed her cautiously. 'What's your name?' he asked.

'Don't worry about her name,' interrupted Shane. 'It doesn't matter.'

Jack sipped on the whisky, enjoying the bitter taste of it, steeling himself. And as he did so, he could feel a tingle of excitement. There was a ruthlessness to Shane's behaviour that some part of him found appealing. A sense of pleasure taken brutally and swiftly, and without inhibition or sentiment. He had never had sex with a prostitute before; nor had he ever made love with anyone watching over him. It was, he realised, a repulsive command, designed in part, he suspected, to humiliate him. But, in the immediacy of the moment, it was also shamefully exciting.

The whore rolled her eyes towards him, the smoke from her cigarette drifting across her face. 'When you're ready, love,' she said.

Go with the flow, Jack told himself. Take the plunge. He leant over and untied the laces on his shoes, kicking the black brogues away. He placed his jacket on the floor, standing up, unbuckling his belt. Taking great care he undid both cufflinks and dropped them in his jacket pocket. He threw down his shirt, and climbed out of his trousers. Behind him he could see Shane pulling a wad of notes out. He peeled off a pair of fifties and placed them on the table. 'Make it good,' he said.

The whore put her jacket aside, and stood up, peeling off her shorts. She stood before Jack, wearing just her bra and her boots and her panties. They were black and skimpy. She reached down to her jacket and fished a condom from her pocket. Her arms reached out for him, caressing his chest, swaying her body in front of him as she did so. She rubbed her breasts into him, in a fast circling motion. And then she knelt before him, slipping on the rubber. Her tongue slipped forward, caressing him, teasing him. Her face disappeared into his groin while she sucked him noisily.

After a couple of minutes, the whore sat back down on the sofa, spreading her legs open. Jack knelt before her, and she guided him into her, raising her legs as she did so. There was a blankness to her expression, Jack noticed. An air of distance. He caught her eye, but it communicated only a servile indifference to his presence. 'Is it all right?' she asked.

'Fine,' answered Jack.

'Do you want me to talk dirty?' she asked.

Jack nodded. She writhed a little under him, bucking her hips. She rolled her head to one side, so that their eyes no longer connected. 'Fuck me,' she muttered. 'C'mon, fuck me hard.' She paused, as if wondering what to say next. 'That's it. Fill up my fanny.' Jack plunged into her while she was talking, and finished suddenly, unthinkingly. The whore stopped moaning, and reached down to guide him out of her. She felt for a tissue, and pulled the condom off, depositing the thing on the floor, leaving it lying next to the fallen ice cubes. 'All right?' she said.

'Yes, thank you,' Jack replied.

There was a formality to the situation that struck Jack as curious. He felt uncomfortable, unsure what to do or say next, ignorant of whether he should make conversation, or just let the woman lie there. Inwardly, he felt slightly ashamed of what he had just done. But then, he reflected, what choice do I have? There are worse things.

The whore looked across at Shane, still sitting, still an impassive observer on the scene. 'Do you want to go now?' she said.

Shane motioned towards the dining-table. 'Over there,' he said.

The whore walked across to the table. There was just a trace of sweat around her brow, Jack noticed. She stood still as Shane walked across the room, standing next to her, running a hand up from her boots, along her back, before cupping one of her breasts and squeezing it tight. 'Bend over,' he said.

The whore leant over the table, resting her elbows on to the glass, resting her face in her hands. She spread her legs slightly. With one hand, Shane was fondling her buttocks, then running it along her back and tousling her hair. Her expression was still empty, uninterested, her eyes staring straight forward, peering into the blank television screen.

'Stand next to her,' commanded Shane.

Unsure how to respond, Jack walked nervously towards the table, 'I might get her to take you in her mouth,' Shane continued, the edge in his voice becoming sharper. 'You might like that.'

Unlikely, thought Jack to himself. Most unlikely. The whore rolled her eyes towards his stomach, and as far as Jack could tell she didn't appear to have any opinion. Not an opinion she was able to articulate, anyway. He, however, was starting to feel more and more uncomfortable.

90

Shane's hand started to play with the whore; her expression darkened slightly as he slipped a couple of fingers inside her. 'Closing time,' he muttered softly.

With the other hand, Shane reached inside his breast pocket and pulled out a flick-knife. There was a small thud as he pressed the trigger and the thin, steel blade sprang to life. With his left hand Shane grasped a tuft of the whore's hair, yanking at it, tugging her head back in a sudden, brutal movement. A gasp came from her throat and her eyes swivelled, hoping desperately to see what was happening. She was trying to scream but no sound came out. His grip was already strangling her. Shane's right hand, armed with the knife, fell forward, and in one movement stabbed into the exposed flesh of her neck. He slashed, cutting the knife towards him, ripping through her neck as he did so. The blade sprang free from her neck, its work done.

The whore fell forward on the table, slumped. Blood was oozing from her neck, swilling out on to the table. Her body twitched, once, twice, three times, and then fell still. Her knees buckled and gave way, and slowly she fell from the table, collapsing in a quiet, lifeless heap on the floor. Blood from the table dripped down, streaking her blonde hair with purple.

Jack stood frozen to the spot, unable to move and unable to speak. The pit of his stomach was churning, and he could sense the acrid taste of vomit rising to the back of his throat. He fought it back, closing his eyes tightly, unable to look any more at the scene being played out in front of him.

His nakedness left him feeling vulnerable and exposed, and for the moment all he could think of was his own safety. Me next, he wondered. Opening his eyes, he turned back towards the sofa, reaching down for his clothes. He pulled on his trousers, searching next for his shirt and his shoes. All the time, he kept his eyes peeled on Shane. Waiting for his next move. Wondering if he would have to fight.

Shane walked to the balcony, and flung the bloodied blade far out into the river. Below, the sound of a splash echoed up to the apartment. He strode back across the room and stood close to Jack. Their eyes met. Shane pointed to the far corner of the room. 'Smile for the cameras, boy,' he said.

Jack turned to the corner but he saw nothing.

'Hidden,' said Shane. 'The whole place is wired. Everything. The whole thing is on tape.'

Jack started to speak, but he found he was mumbling. The words would hardly come. They stuck somewhere in his throat. Trapped. 'Why?' he said at last.

Shane patted him on the shoulder. 'Relax, old son. Relax.'

Jack could feel his pulse race. His mind was a shambles. 'Why?' he repeated.

'Give me the formula,' said Shane.

Jack reached into his pocket and pulled out the envelope. Shane opened it and studied the three sheets of paper. 'Looks OK,' he said. 'I'll get our chemists to check it. So long as it works out, I'll make sure you get paid.'

'Her,' said Jack. 'What was the point?'

Shane took a step forward. He was standing right next to him now, leaning, looking down. 'Trust,' he said.

Jack shook his head.

'Think about it,' Shane continued. 'How am I supposed to trust a man like you. You're soft. Weak. If the police ever come to question you about the counterfeiting operation, if they pressure you, if they beat you, you'll crack. I know you'll crack. Your sort always does.' He turned and sat down on a chair next to the whore, no more than inches from her body. 'I could threaten to kill you if you betray me, but what difference would it make? You would never quite believe me. But this way is different. If I hand this tape to the police, you will be charged with murder. You were standing next to her, and it will be impossible to tell from the film whether the knife was in your hand or mine. They'll get you as an accomplice to murder, at least. Premeditated. Worth twenty years. Can you handle that, Jack? Can you take twenty years inside? Of course not. Too soft. After the first six months you'd be trying to kill yourself. You know you can't take it. And now you know that you mustn't cross me.'

He stood up and walked across the room, leaning forward, his grey eyes slamming into Jack's face. 'You know it, don't you. In your heart. Loyalty. That is what this is all about.'

NINE

Tara checked first in *Who's Who*, but the name of Dr Zmitt was not listed, and she could feel the sense of disappointment shudder through her. The question of who this man was had been gnawing away at her since the previous evening. She had turned it over in her mind all night, the question making her restless, infuriating her. By morning it seemed like the key.

She had skipped work. That, she decided, would have to wait until she resolved this question. Taking her new company Volkswagen, she drove into the centre of London, heading for the Wellcome Institute on the Euston Road. It was the one place she could think of with a complete collection of pharmacological reference works; and the one place were she could wander around freely, with no questions asked, and no suspicions raised. Kizog was the last place where she felt like being this morning. Within its glistening compound, beneath the stretches of corridors patrolled by security cameras, and behind its computer-controlled doors, too many people seemed to be watching her. She felt as though unseen eyes and silent microchips were stalking her every movement. Here she was just another Oriental student diligently working for her degree. Anonymous. Secure.

Tara replaced the volume on the shelves, and reached for the next one. A copy of *Who Was Who*. After all, she told herself, he might well be dead. She knew nothing about him. Quickly, she turned the pages, leafing through the alphabet. She started at the back, and soon found it: 'Dr Josef Zmitt (1908–1979)'. Her eyes devoured the page: 'Dr Josef Zmitt. b. Prague 1908. Educ: University of St Charles, Prague. Moscow Academy of Natural Sciences, D.Phil, Chemistry. 1946–49. Lecturer, University of Bratislava, 1950–1962. Reader in Molecular Chemistry, University of Birmingham, 1964–1973. d.1979.'

Tara held the book in her hands, reading the short entry twice, then three times. She needed to be absolutely clear of the facts. The implications were immediately clear to her. If Zmitt had died in 1979, then the papers of Scott's she had seen the previous evening were clearly older than that. The first recorded case of Ator did not appear until the early eighties. It was not recognised as a new virus until the late eighties. And yet Kizog scientists had clearly been working closely on the structure of molecules very close to the virus several years before that. Before the virus was even known about.

She slammed the book shut and replaced it on the shelf. Her mind still bristling, she walked across to the computer terminals lined up in a row towards the back of the second floor of the library. Most of the data in the building had by now been computerised. She sat down and tapped Zmitt's name into the machine. Several seconds later the computer flashed up a list of publications. Tara scrolled downwards. About fifty were listed; relatively few for a long academic career.

Tara sighed. It looked like being a long day. Into her notebook she made a careful note of the first twenty titles. They were all published in pharmacological and chemical journals, some dating back as far as the fifties. Some were in English and some were in German; none of them appeared to be in Czech, although that was the country where he had spent the early part of his career. Carrying her notebook, she gathered the journals, some withering with age, and began to read. And as she did so, she made brief notes in the pad beside her.

The reading was slow and tedious. Many of the papers were just academic time-wasting, the sort of papers that had to be pumped out from time to time to maintain respectability within the university. They contained nothing that was either particularly new or particularly interesting. A few struck Tara as possibly novel for their day, but by now hopelessly dated. She was finding herself bored with Dr Zmitt. He appeared an undistinguished middle-ranking chemist at an undistinguished middle-ranking university.

The first paper to engage her interest was dated 1967. It was written by Zmitt, but acknowledged the research work of Dr Peter Scott, described in a footnote as a student working towards his doctorate at Oxford. So the two men knew each other back in the sixties. The article was a study of the susceptibility of the nervous system to viral attack. Tara found it intriguing. It was advanced for a piece of research that was now three decades old. How advanced? Tara racked her mind, but could not come up with an answer. The history of pharmacology had never been a subject that interested her very much.

Carefully, she reread it. The angle puzzled her. It was abstruse. Almost pointless. It went into incredible detail about the vulnerability of the nervous system to viral attack. But it said nothing about the purpose of this research. It gave away no clues as to why it might have been done, nor what its authors were searching for. And as she searched the footnotes, another strange angle became apparent; though there was clearly a lot of laboratory work leading up to this paper, there was no acknowledgement of any funding. No respectful thanks for grants or use of equipment. Nothing. Complete silence.

Tara photocopied the paper, and went back to her desk. A girl

96

sitting opposite, also Oriental, smiled at her, and Tara smiled back. She found herself glad to be back in an academic institution. It was warmer, and more open, than the closed, commercial world of the Kizog laboratories. But she had none of the time to stop and chat she might have had as an undergraduate herself. There was too much to be done.

It was evening before she had finished looking through all the papers. Most of them could just be flicked through. More academic filler. More work on vulnerabilities within the nervous system. Nothing that struck her of any great importance. By 1971 Dr Zmitt had stopped publishing entirely. By 1974 he had retired. Five years later he was dead.

She collected her notes and her photocopies and headed outside. The evening air was cool and around her commuters were still drifting into the station. Tara found her car and began driving north. Her body was drained and her mind exhausted by the day. She felt tired. Nothing about her researches had calmed her. Perhaps I am being paranoid, she told herself. Hysterical. Perhaps, she wondered. But somehow she was unconvinced.

Jack vomited into the toilet, heaving up the bowl of cereal he had forced himself to eat that morning. He dabbed his eyes, and struggled out to the basin, rubbing his face in water, and swilling out his mouth. Christ, he murmured to himself, walking out of the gents and back towards his office.

'Bad night?'

Jack glanced up. It was Layla, looking radiant in a sharp, cream two-piece suit and pearls, her face covered in a smirking grin. 'Something like that,' he muttered darkly. Layla may have looked good, but he was too busy to pay her much attention this morning.

'Out with the brilliant Oriental scientist, perhaps?' joked Layla. 'I hear you two are very close.'

'Who says that?' Jack snapped.

'A tender subject?' said Layla, backing away slightly. 'Don't worry. It's just gossip.'

Jack rubbed his brow, wondering if Layla had any aspirin, and whether he should ask for some. His mind was shot, and his stomach was still churning. He needed something to help him concentrate. 'I'm having a bad time,' he said lamely.

'OK,' replied Layla softly. She placed a binder down on his desk. 'Kizog: the Case Against' it said.

'The defence document?' asked Jack, struggling to focus on the words. 'What does it say?'

'Try reading it,' said Layla. 'There is a council of war at ten sharp. Questions will be asked.'

'Give me a break,' said Jack.

Layla moved closer, sitting on the edge of the desk. 'They say we don't make any money. Dodgy accounting. They argue that we don't have anything like the sales we claim. The numbers are massaged upwards.'

'So what?' said Jack wearily. 'Everyone does that. It helps make the profit figures look less outrageous.'

'I know. And they don't provide very much evidence. But they do say there is more to come.' She opened the slim document. 'Here: "Kizog is an edifice built on fictitious accounting. Its apparent profitability is a mystery waiting to be unravelled." '

Interesting, thought Jack. 'The Chairman won't like that,' he said flatly.

'He won't like it if we are late, either,' answered Layla breezily. 'Move.'

Jack struggled to his feet and followed her towards the lift. His limbs were still tired from last night. It must have been three or four by the time he went to bed. He had returned to his flat in a state of numbed shock; his nerves felt like they had died of fright. Sitting alone in the dark, his limbs shivered as he downed three drinks in quick succession. He drifted into the shower, and, as he stood beneath the hot jets of water, felt tears trickle down his face. For the girl or for me? he wondered.

The night wore on, but Jack could barely sleep. The pictures kept re-emerging in his mind, each with a vivid stillness, like some kind of freakish slide show. The girl on the street. Beneath him, half-naked and humiliated. Beside Shane. With the knife on her throat. The blood dripping down to the floor. And through it all one question hammered away at his dulled senses; what could I have done?

Nothing, he tried to reassure himself. Nothing at all. Talk to the Chairman, he told himself. Talk to him right away. Tell him everything . . . he promised me protection.

The meeting was held inside the boardroom. The Chairman was already sitting at one end of the table, next to Ralph Finer. To their left was David Knowlton, the head of corporate finance at Goldreich, and Simon Morrison from Whateleys, the two investment banks. Both were working on the Kizog team. With them were Anthony Donaldson, from Lansing Benham, the brokers on the deal. Each adviser had two assistants sitting next to him. Jack and Layla walked towards them and sat down. The Chairman nodded in their direction.

Sam Taylor bustled into the room looking flummoxed and slightly perplexed. His face was redder than usual, and his manner less breezy. One of life's number twos, thought Jack. 'Vicious piece of work,' Taylor said, to nobody in particular, whilst laying his own copy of the defence document down on the boardroom table.

The Chairman rapped his knuckles, bringing everybody to attention. 'May we begin,' he said. All the eyes in the room turned to face him. 'I believe we expected a vigorous response from our friends at Ocher. This is perhaps more vigorous than we expected. Simon?'

Morrison shifted uneasily in his seat. 'Sir,' he began. Jack looked across the table, struck by the slightness of the man. Morrison might be earning upwards of £1 million a year, before bonus, he thought, but he still had to quiver before the Chairman and call him 'sir'. Just like the rest of us. 'An attack on our accounting methods was to be expected. It is part of the standard bid defence. The question is whether this is just yah-boo-sucks stuff, or whether they can actually stack it up. They

99

don't stack it up here. But if they could that would be very damaging.'

'Do you believe it?' asked the Chairman quietly.

'I would never question the integrity of a client, sir,' answered Morrison, without hesitation.

Delivered with a face of granite, noticed Jack. The man earned his money.

The Chairman looked at David Knowlton. 'And you?'

'I never believe anything written by Zurich Financial. Those Swiss have the ethics of rattlesnakes. I tell you what we do. We come out and attack their accounts. Say the whole thing is totally fictitious. Say they haven't sold as much as a packet of aspirin for the last five years.' Knowlton was leaning forward now, building up steam behind his argument. But it evaporated at the end of his sentence, leaving him hanging in a silence. His eyes twitched slightly, and he slumped back in his chair, waiting for a reaction. 'We could set some of our people working on their figures,' he said eventually.

'Perhaps,' responded the Chairman quietly. 'Ralph, tell these gentlemen how seriously we should take these allegations.'

Finer was doodling on a pad on the desk. 'There may be some front-end loading,' he began. 'I would not be too surprised if some of the divisions were booking a lot of forward sales close to the year-end. Actually I know they do. That is a fairly pre-dictable result of a bonus system. As for the rest I believe there is nothing to fear from these allegations.'

'My guess is that it's just hot air,' said Morrison. 'They can spin this out until the bid lapses. This is a defence, remember. All they have to do is create a reasonable doubt in the minds of the shareholders and they will escape.'

'Quite correct,' whispered the Chairman. 'But we must not allow any doubts in the minds of the shareholders. We need this victory and we need it quickly. Time will not be generous towards us.' His eyes peeled around the room, surveying each person in turn before resting on Taylor. The chief executive was sweating slightly more now, thought Jack. He looked nervous.

'Speed,' he said. 'That is the essence of the thing.'

Shall I talk to the Chairman? wondered Jack, his mind drifting away from the conversation. Or shall I talk to the police?

'We must be more than quick,' said the Chairman. 'We must be deadly.'

'Our people are making good progress with the shareholders' register,' said Knowlton. 'We are talking to people around the clock. And I think we are making some progress.'

The Chairman waved a hand. Dismissively. 'Perhaps we should raise the offer.'

There was a silence. 'Most unusual, sir,' said Morrison.

The Chairman fixed a glare upon him. 'But of course,' he whispered. 'A deadly manœuvre is always unusual.'

There was a momentary draining of colour from the faces of the bankers. Their lips tightened, and their eyes were cast down. Nobody spoke.

If I go to the police, Jack told himself, then Shane will try to implicate me in the murder. I need the company and the Forum to prove what I was doing there.

The Chairman smiled suddenly and there was a sparkle in his eyes. 'Just a suggestion,' he said. 'We need some creative thinking around here.'

'As I said,' Morrison continued. 'Raising an offer before the first one has even lapsed would be very risky. People might assume we were desperate.'

The Chairman's fingers were sliding across the table. 'Perhaps we are.'

'But better not to let people know,' said Morrison. 'How much more were you thinking of?'

'Another £1.5 billion,' said the Chairman. 'In cash. Not in paper.'

'We have that kind of money available, sir?' asked Morrison quizzically.

'You are the bankers,' said the Chairman. 'Find the money.'

Morrison and Knowlton both nodded. In unison, Jack noticed. Neither of them looked as if he had the faintest idea where he would find the money. And they were already worrying about the kind of trouble they would get into if they did not come up with a solution. Jack sympathised. Big trouble on the horizon was always a fearful sight. The Chairman waved a hand. Taylor and Finer and the bankers and brokers all took this as their cue to leave the room, shuffling quietly towards the door. Jack and Layla were about to follow them, when they saw a long, bony finger beckoning them closer towards the head of the table. 'Stay a moment,' whispered the Chairman.

Jack's heart fluttered. Layla leapt to attention, walking purposefully towards the Chairman, pulling out the chair next to him, and placing it at a right angle to his before she sat down. She crossed her legs, allowing her skirt to ride up her legs slightly, exposing the inside of her thighs. Does the Chairman notice this? thought Jack. It was hard to believe he didn't. The girl paraded herself in front of him like a thirty-something secretary desperate to nail down a rich husband before her looks finally collapsed. Was he interested? Hard to know. Although the Chairman had harassed people in hundreds of different ways, seducing and terrorising them at the same time, and although no cruelty was too small, nor any humiliation too insignificant, there had never been any hint of sexual dalliances. As far as Jack knew he was happily married to a wife he hardly ever saw. And yet, he reflected, whether there was any interest or not hardly mattered. The mere fact that Layla could make it so clear she was happy to have her skinny young body invaded by this leathery old crocodile was enough. The Chairman would be pleased enough by the abjectness of her desire to accommodate his whims. He had already humiliated her, and that was enough. Why fuck her body, thought Jack, when he had already fucked her mind?

'Is there anything I can do for you, Chairman?' said Layla.

Speak to him now, thought Jack.

'Investigate,' the Chairman replied. 'Get close to the Zurich Financial people. I am sure you have friends there. Or you can make friends. Find out what they are thinking. And report back to me.'

'Of course, I think I know a couple of people there . . .'

'Good.' The Chairman waved his hand, cutting off her sentence. 'I'll listen to what you have to say with interest. After the weekend . . .'

His voice trailed off, and a silence hung over the room, still and ugly, as she departed. Jack stood rooted to the spot.

'Sit,' the Chairman commanded imperiously.

Jack took the chair Layla had vacated. The Chairman leant back in his chair, his arms folded across his chest, and for a moment he closed his eyes as if he was about to take a nap. He sighed, opening his eyes again, and looked around the room. 'These are busy times,' he said quietly.

Jack decided to dump his natural sense of reserve. He needed to talk seriously, not waste time with obtuse chatter. 'I witnessed a murder last night, sir,' he said.

The Chairman's interest was captured now. He leant forward, leaning his elbows on the table and resting his face in his hands. 'You know that's something I've never done. Not in real life.'

'A woman. Her throat was cut.'

'It must have been awful.'

'It was a kind of initiation, I think. The racketeer I met, the one I was supposed to collect evidence on. He wanted to be sure he could trust me. He filmed me with her and then killed her. He says he has the whole thing on tape.'

'We are dealing with dangerous people,' said the Chairman quietly.

Jack could feel himself starting to get angry. 'At the moment it appears to be just me who is dealing with them,' he said sharply.

The Chairman cast him an inquisitive look. 'Quite so,' he answered softly.

'I thought I should go straight to the police,' Jack persisted. 'I am, after all, only a witness. But if I remain silent I become an accessory.'

The Chairman shook his head. He reached out and tapped a finger on the top of Jack's hand. 'Don't do that,' he whispered.

'Wait a short while. Everything will be clear soon.'

'How long?' Jack demanded.

The Chairman stood up and patted Jack on the shoulder. 'Talk to the lady from the Forum, and follow her instructions. And don't worry. The company will look after you.'

TEN

It had been a terrible day. Truly awful. And Jack was in no mood for sitting in traffic. He had skipped the office early, ducking out before six, careful to take a winding route through the corridors, anxious to make sure no one saw him. Pathetic, he told himself. I could be on murder charges and I am worried about whether I can leave the office early. Useless behaviour. And a reminder that whatever game I am involved in, it is not one I am naturally cut out for. No stomach for it. No stomach at all.

Jack was too tired to carry on working. Too tired to carry on thinking. His mind was scrambled. The neurones were not connecting. Everything felt loose, unconnected, as if the wires had been severed. Nothing made sense.

The office had been awash with rumours, speculation and gossip. The bid for Ocher was now in full swing, and teams of people were huddled around the office fine-tuning the details of the offer. The clock was ticking. With the bid formally tabled there were now fewer than thirty days for shareholders to accept or reject the deal. Under a month. Already there was a whiff of victory in the air. A sense of expectancy. The prospect of the merger, no more than a wild pipe-dream when it had been floated, was now taking on a reality of its own. It had the feel of something that might happen. Positions were being staked. Territory surveyed. The size of the empire would double. There would be shake-ups, overhauls, restructurings. Most of all there would be opportunities. Opportunities for ambitious young executives to advance or retreat.

For most of the people around the office, this was a banquet. A time for feasting and celebration. The place was cooking, and Jack knew he should be thriving on every minute of it. A full-scale take-over bid, with all the scope for corporate intrigue and infighting it implied. What more could a boy ask for?

Peace of mind, Jack told himself. And some rest.

'What kind of job do you think I might get in the combined Kizog/Ocher conglomerate?' Layla had asked on another brief foray into his office that afternoon.

Jack had just peered up from papers he hadn't even begun to read.

'There will be task forces,' she continued, unfazed by his lack of interest. 'To determine the structure of the new corporation. That will be the place to be. Get a position on one of the task forces, and you can design your own job.'

She might well be right, thought Jack. Most probably was. Layla was a shrewd tactician of the company corridors; the perfect corporate tigress, working behind enemy lines, adopting seductive disguises, yet always masking her intentions. Normally Jack followed her advice. He enjoyed the playful cynicism of her careerism. But not today. Today was different. This was a day when his thoughts were shadowed by the realisation that he was a witness to murder. An accessory, even. An accessory before the fact; a criminal offence, carrying, no doubt, a substantial jail sentence. The thought of jail terrified Jack. A cramped cell, incarcerated with some vicious, psychotic yob, cloistered with men

106

who would hate him, hate everything about him. There would be beatings. Rape even. It was more than he could handle.

Despite the advice of the Chairman, he was still wondering whether to go to the police, but his mind was too disorganised to make any progress with the issue. In the moments when he could think straight he knew that the balance of probabilities lay on the side of lawlessness. *What could I say to the police? That I have been present at a cold-blooded, meaningless execution. By a man I was trying to sell a secret to. And, no, I don't know who she was? Or who he was? Or where the body was? Nothing.* It was not a very convincing story. In his darker moments Jack even had trouble convincing himself it was true.

He knew it was, of course. Its memory clung to his mind, inhabiting, he was sure, a corner of every brain cell. He tried to close his eyes, hoping they would disappear. But, of course, they didn't. The slides were there still. Alive in the darkness. Brightly coloured, luminous, stark and real.

Jack needed to talk, to unburden himself of the pictures, to diminish their force, diluting them through sharing the scenes with others. He had tried calling Fuller but could speak only to her answerphone; a disembodied voice, emptied of any sign of intimacy or emotion. He must have tried a dozen times. He had checked in with Finer, but the finance director was tied up at meetings with the bankers. He was ensnared in the City, and would not be returning today, his secretary said.

He even called Tara, tapping out her extension on the internal phone system, but the people in the labs said that she had not come in today. No, they did not know where she was. He looked up her home number on the personnel file he had copied on to his hard disc, but she was not there either. Just the answering machine. He did not feel like leaving a message and hung up. After all, what would he say?

Where was everyone today? Jack wondered.

As he completed the drive home, Jack could feel a sense of resentment rising within him. Others had led him here. It was not his idea. And yet here he was, alone with his predicament, shadow boxing with his conscience.

The phone rang when he entered the flat. He hurried to pick it up.

'How did it go,' said Fuller.

At last, thought Jack. 'I need to see you,' he replied instantly.

'But I'm waiting for you,' she replied.

The drive took the best part of thirty minutes; half an hour of sweat and anticipation. The radio hummed softly throughout; an aural backdrop of relentless cheer. Jack paid no attention. His mind was already drifting on a tide of contradictions and confusions.

He knew the address but he had not been there before. A mews house off Kensington High Street, a dinky little cottage, with window-boxes stacked up on the ledges, the flowers tumbling out over the pastel-shaded paintwork of the trim houses. A riot of colours. Cheaper than a hotel, she had explained, for a stay of uncertain duration.

Fuller answered the door. Their conversation on the phone had been brief and to the point. Request. Answer. Jack had not elaborated, nor even hinted at the urgency of the visit, though he suspected his voice might have betrayed the immediacy of his desire. Jack stepped inside. He didn't feel like talking, not here in the hallway, and he wanted to get a drink in his hand before he unbuttoned himself. Fuller lived in the second-floor flat, and his eyes followed her as she led him upstairs; tracing the hemline of her short, black skirt, observing the smoothness of her skin, and listening for the rustle of the fabric as her legs moved in front of him.

'You've met, haven't you,' said Fuller.

Jack froze. Before him, sitting on a black leather sofa, his feet up on the wooden coffee-table, a Camel in one hand, a glass of whisky in the other, sat Angus Shane.

Shane's eyes turned towards Jack, his look cold and threatening. 'Amateur hour,' he said. He laughed. He turned to Fuller, his look turning to a mixture of conspiracy and triumph. She laughed as well, throwing her blonde hair back, her lipstick pouting in a small, mirthless giggle.

Jack was rooted to the spot. Temporarily he was unable to move. He felt disabled. It was as if he had been disconnected from reality. Unplugged. For a moment he turned slightly, swivelling his heels, preparing to leave. But his instincts pulled him back, kept his feet on the ground, and told him to stay. Flight was impossible. There was nowhere to run to. Nobody to turn to. No place to hide.

Jack knew that now. The situation had incarcerated him. There was nothing to be done, except to drift with the tide. Like drowning, he thought to himself. After a while you stop struggling. And let the waters take you where they will. 'I think I'd better sit down,' he said. His knees, he found, felt weak, and his stomach winded, as though he had been punched. His senses were exhausted, and all that remained was a certain watchful curiosity.

'Dani works with me,' said Shane.

'I can see that,' replied Jack, his voice sounding hoarse.

'We work quite closely with some of the regulators,' Shane continued. 'Or at least with elements within the regulatory agencies. Rogue elements. And closely with certain elements within the drugs companies.'

'Rogue elements,' repeated Jack, his voice abstracted and uninterested. 'And I am to be an element within a drugs company?'

'You'll be well looked after,' answered Shane.

'But not following a path of my own choosing.'

Shane shrugged. 'Who does? And who says your choices would be so great anyway.'

'Why the charade?'

Shane looked at him closely. 'People don't always come along willingly. They have to be encouraged.'

'By force and intimidation?' asked Jack bitterly.

Shane smiled. 'I've always found it works pretty well,' he replied.

'And what is to stop me just revealing all this to the company?' said Jack. 'Going to Kizog, to the Chairman, and telling them everything?'

109

Shane shrugged, flicking the ash from his cigarette. 'I'm not bothered.'

'I think I should go now.' Jack spoke out the words slowly, looking up as he did so. His sense of freedom had diminished already; he felt as though he needed to ask permission.

Shane picked up the remote control resting on the coffee-table and pressed the button. The television sprang to life, and as the greyness faded to colour, Jack could make out the grainy, poorly lit film. He recognised himself, standing in the flat, putting his clothes back on, the woman lying on the sofa in front of him. There was no sound, but Jack could see the lips move, and he already knew what they were saying. His eyes flickered as he tried to make out the figures and their movements. He saw the woman bend over the table, and he could feel his stomach start to heave in anticipation of the next few moments. Shane had been right. From the angle of the camera, it was clear the woman had been murdered, but it was impossible to tell exactly where the blade had come from. Perhaps close analysis would reveal it was Shane who was guilty. Perhaps, and perhaps not. Right now, it was not a chance he felt like taking.

Jack turned and walked towards the door. He held the door-knob and looked back to face Shane directly. Fuller was standing right next to him, and the pair seemed well matched now. Colleagues, perfectly at ease with one another. 'Welcome aboard,' said Shane as Jack departed.

ELEVEN

Tara appeared too wrapped up in her work to notice him. She was keying data into her computer, her fingers moving deftly over the keyboard. For a moment, he remained still, observing her, soaking up her presence. There was, he realised, an air of mystery about her which made him wonder whether she was part of the enigma that was descending upon him. Which side, he found himself asking, is she on?

Turning away from her terminal, she finally noticed him, casting her eyes in his direction but remaining silent. 'I tried to reach you yesterday,' said Jack.

'Busy,' she replied. Her tone was matter-of-fact, betraying nothing. 'Research.'

'I thought we could talk,' said Jack hopefully.

She brushed away a length of hair that was lying across her face. 'Too busy,' she replied. 'Deadlines to meet.'

Jack turned to leave, a sense of disappointment overwhelming

111

him, but as he did so, he saw that she was writing. He watched her walking towards him, smiling. She stopped two inches in front of him, and pressed a Post-it note into the palm of his hand. He looked down at the scrap of yellow paper. 'Not here. We'll talk at my house tomorrow night. Come after work.' He opened his mouth, and started to speak, but she raised her fingers to his lips to quieten him. 'Not now, later,' she whispered.

Jack turned on his heels and left. She might well be right, he reflected. It might not be safe to talk in the labs. The thought made him shiver; only days ago he would have found the idea ridiculous. But now? he wondered. Who knows? So far he had trusted people. And he had been wrong to do so.

His sleep the night before had been fitful and uneven; snatches of rest interrupted by bouts of cold sweat. How long he had slept he had no idea. No more than a couple of hours. Most of the night had been spent wrestling with the mass of unanswered questions that hovered uneasily in the centre of his mind, tussling with a queue of conflicting ideas and emotions. He knew neither what was happening to him, nor why he was involved. He was beset by riddles and mysteries and, try as he might, he could not begin to unravel them.

He walked through the compound towards his office in a kind of daze. The neatly manicured lawns and the marbled foyer drifted past his eyes, not meriting a second glance. The people bustled by, carrying their briefcases and their floppy discs, but they might have been invisible for all he cared. His mind was too distracted to notice his surroundings.

Aimlessly, Jack sat down behind his desk and began scrolling through his e-mail. There was nothing that caught his eye. Work seemed somehow pointless now. Too much of a distraction. And not worth the effort. Turning to look through the plate-glass window, he allowed his eye to wander across the complex of laboratories and office buildings, each full of people, busily advancing their careers, and occasionally advancing the interests of the company. He tried to ignore the details, focusing instead on the big picture.

What am I missing? he asked himself.

Jack picked himself out of the chair, killed the computer, and headed out into the corridor. A couple of people nodded at him, but he was in no mood to stop and chat. He took the lift to the fifth floor and walked straight towards Ralph Finer's office. He would speak to the Chairman later. He needed to speak to someone he counted as an ally first.

Finer's secretary said he was busy on a call and asked Jack to wait a moment. He stood in the hallway, twisting nervously from foot to foot, trying to get his thoughts clear in his mind. Which is worse? he thought. Facing a possible murder charge? Working for Shane and his counterfeiters? Or being betrayed by the people I trusted.

As he entered the room, Finer struck Jack as looking ill-at-ease. His features were strained and haggard. Not enough sleep, perhaps. 'You look rough,' commented Jack.

'Too much work,' replied the finance director.

Jack walked closer, standing at the edge of the desk, whilst Finer rolled back in his black leather chair. He glanced down at the desk. A mass of papers were strewn everywhere, but in the centre was the Ocher defence document, with scribbles in the margin, and rows of alternative calculations at the bottom of every page.

'How's things?' Finer asked cautiously.

'Awful,' Jack replied instinctively. He had not had time to think about the answer. Already Jack had decided to be honest, to tell Finer what had happened, and to ask him his advice on what to do next. In particular, his advice on whether he should talk to the Chairman.

'Tell me about it,' said Finer sympathetically.

Jack started to explain. He told him about the meeting with Shane and about the murder of the prostitute. He ran through the discussion with the Chairman. Jack paced around the office as he spoke, the words tumbling out in a great rush, words and sentences colliding into one another. He felt gradually better as the story unfolded. These events had been tormenting his mind, and merely sharing them softened their impact. He turned, close to the desk and looked directly down at Finer. 'So you see, Fuller was working directly with Shane all along. On the surface I was working on an investigation into counterfeiting. In reality, I am being sucked into a counterfeiting ring.'

Finer leant back, his expression lost somewhere between sympathy and bafflement. 'And do you want to be sucked in?'

'Of course not,' replied Jack.

'Are you sure?' he asked slowly.

Jack shook his head. 'A criminal enterprise? It's ridiculous. Why would I not be sure?'

Finer shrugged, and his manner was somehow disinterested. 'What do you want to do now?'

'Extricate myself,' answered Jack firmly.

'Well, I am sure you have the backing of the company.'

Jack glared at the finance director. 'The company got me into this situation.'

'It is not something we would do casually.'

'Even the Chairman?'

Finer nodded. 'Even the Chairman,' he answered firmly.

'Should I speak to him?' asked Jack.

'You already have.' Jack spun on his heels. But before he moved, he already knew what he would see. The voice, a low growl, mixing threat and promises, was unmistakable. The Chairman was standing in the doorway, his arms folded on his chest, stooping slightly, a thin smile playing on his lips. He remained silent, walking forward, stopping just beside Jack, leaning against the edge of the desk. He ran a hand through his white hair. 'You have much to learn.'

Jack said nothing. For the moment he was too surprised to speak. And too unsure of what he should say. The Chairman edged forward slightly. The expression on his face was one of infinite kindness, tinged with a slight air of embarrassment, as though he had been caught out in a guilty secret. 'The finance director and the Chairman often need to speak,' he began. 'There is a speaker system connecting our offices. Ralph very kindly turned it on, so that I could hear what you were discussing.'

The Chairman leant forward, tapping Jack just below the elbow. 'I'm hurt.'

Jack recoiled slightly from his touch. He looked at the old man standing next to him, his small body tired and shrivelled, and found himself wondering once again what he should believe of him. 'That seems the least of my troubles right now,' he said.

The Chairman stood up, and walked towards the window. 'I would have thought you would have trusted me,' he said, peering out of the window, avoiding the gaze of the two other men in the room.

'I used to,' replied Jack.

'Not any more?'

'Not after what has happened.'

The Chairman began walking towards him, stopping just behind Finer and leaning on the back of his chair, looking directly at Jack. 'What do you think is really going on here?'

'Tell me!' Jack demanded.

The Chairman shook his head, a look of sorrow passing across his face. 'Too easy,' he said. 'Why do you think I asked for your help on this mission?'

Jack shrugged.

'Because you're a smart young man,' the Chairman continued.

'I don't think I have been that smart so far,' Jack replied anxiously.

'Maybe not,' replied the Chairman softly. 'So start now.'

Jack thought for a moment. 'It starts with you. You asked me to investigate.' Slowly the pieces of the puzzle were starting to come together in his mind; the picture was starting to take shape, and the jolt of recognition sent a shot of adrenalin to his head. 'There are two possibilities,' he said carefully. 'Either Fuller was deceiving you. Or she was deceiving me.'

'Which do you think is more likely, Jack?' asked the Chairman with a smile.

There was little choice but to admit it. 'Me,' Jack replied. 'You let me walk into that situation, knowing that she was working alongside the counterfeiters. So there are two more possibilities.

115

Either you are being very foolish. Or you wanted me to be captured by the counterfeiters.'

'Do you imagine I am foolish, Jack?' the Chairman said.

'Not for a moment,' replied Jack immediately.

'Then what would be my motive?'

'To enlist me in the counterfeiting ring,' announced Jack.

The Chairman shook his head. 'That would be an aim, not a motive,' he whispered.

It was, Jack suddenly realised, blindingly obvious; if he had not been so entirely unsuspecting he was sure he would have reached the answer much quicker. 'You run it, don't you,' he replied. 'The counterfeiting ring. You are in charge.'

The Chairman smiled. 'Kizog is a very diverse enterprise.'

Jack walked to the back of the office, sitting down on the black leather sofa at the far end of the room. For now he felt as if he wanted to put some distance between himself and the Chairman. Physical proximity was making him feel uncomfortable. 'It's a kind of initiation process, Jack,' said Finer. 'There are many aspects of this company that are handled very discreetly. You should be pleased, you know. You have been admitted to the upper echelons of the company. Only people who are destined to reach the very top are trusted with this information. It's a privilege.'

'What happens to me now?' asked Jack.

The Chairman walked towards him, his limp more pronounced than ever. 'You carry on working for us,' he said. 'Just at a higher level. You are still a special assistant to me, just as I explained. Your duties will become quite clear.' The Chairman shook his head, and a thin smile played across his lips. 'You are a smart young man,' he replied. 'You will soon realise where your best interests lie.'

Where should I begin? wondered Tara. She was used to investigations. The laborious and persistent business of sorting her way through hundreds, sometimes thousands of different molecules,

116

was work she was already well used to. The endless process of creating a hypothesis and then discarding it once the facts no longer fitted held no terrors for her. The disappointment and frustration of chasing dead ends would not deter her. And the thrill of finding new evidence was a sensation she had felt before.

But this was an investigation of a different sort. And she hardly knew where to start.

The train pulled into Birmingham New Street station at just after eleven that morning. Tara had taken the rest of the day off work, her second. Menstrual problems, she had told Dr Scott's secretary as she left the laboratories, confident that the research director was not the sort of man who would care to ask any further questions. She walked out of the station and into the city, the first time she had been to Birmingham. Her first impression was not favourable. The squat concrete buildings, stained and tired by the weather, shadowed the skyline, summoning up an atmosphere of drab, ungainly viciousness that seemed to suffocate the town.

At the rank, she took a taxi and asked for the University. The taxi driver tried to strike up a conversation, asking Tara where she was from, commenting on her accent, then tackling the state of the traffic and the weather, but he soon found Tara's monosyllabic answers a trial and gave up. Her mind was elsewhere, and she was happier when they could complete the rest of the journey in silence.

Tara paid the driver and walked into the University. She was dressed casually this morning, wearing black jeans, a Harvard University T-shirt and a blue jacket. Her hair was tied up behind her head, held in place with a pin. Try to look as much like a student as possible, she told herself. Inside she asked where she could find Professor Appel. The woman at the desk gave her the directions towards the biochemistry department, and Tara began walking through the corridors. The directions were not precise, and she lost her way after the first couple of courtyards. She asked her way again, eventually finding a student who knew where the department was, and within five minutes she had located the right corridor. She made her way down the long, bottle-green hallway, checking the names on the doors as she went.

The door was open, and she looked inside. It was empty. The room was typically academic; a desk and a couple of old chairs, a bookshelf running the entire length of one wall, packed tight, and stacks of folders, binders and loose papers piled high in the corners of the room. On the desk she could see an ashtray overflowing with the remains of burnt pipe tobacco. Tara checked her watch. It was eleven-thirty. There was little choice but to wait.

Fifteen minutes passed. Tara paced up and down the corridor, idly reading the notices on the walls, wondering about her line of attack. She noticed him ambling down the hall, dressed in brown slacks, plus a blue open-necked shirt, Hush Puppies and a tweed jacket. He could see her standing outside his door, and was looking at her quizzically. Definitely a student, Professor Appel decided. But he was damned if he could remember her name. Over the years he found they all looked more and more the same, particularly the Orientals. Fortunately, he found you could usually get through quite a long conversation without having the slightest idea who they were. 'Good-morning,' he said cheerfully. 'Do come in.'

Tara was slightly surprised. She couldn't recall ever having met the Professor before, and he surely could not know who she was. She followed him into the office, whilst he sat down and started filling his pipe with tobacco. 'What seems to be the problem?' he asked.

'My name is Tara Ling,' she began. 'I work at the National Institutes of Health. In America.'

'You're not a student here?'

Tara shook her head.

'Just as well,' said Appel, his expression brightening. 'You must have done well to get into the National Institutes. Where did you study?'

'Harvard,' answered Tara, wondering if he might have heard of her.

118

'Don't suppose there is much I can teach you then,' said the Professor.

'I was hoping you could help me with a research project,' said Tara. She was nervous about broaching the subject, but she was sure of her ground. Appel was fifty-eight now, and had been at the University since completing his doctorate at Cambridge in 1967, according to his entry in *Who's Who*. That meant he would have worked here alongside Zmitt for six years until he retired in 1973. 'I have been working on leprosy, and its transmission mechanism,' she began. 'I came across some papers by a former colleague of yours, Josef Zmitt. They were fascinating but strangely incomplete. If I put what he was doing together with what I have been doing, I felt, I could make some real progress in my studies.'

'Zmitt, heavens,' exclaimed Appel. 'I haven't heard that name mentioned in years. He's dead you know. Died some time in the early eighties.'

'1979,' replied Tara.

'You've obviously done your homework. I'd practically forgotten about him. He was a strange old character, kept himself to himself pretty much. He was just a Reader you know, so he didn't participate very much in the life of the University. Hard to imagine anyone being interested in his work now. There wasn't much of it, as I recall, and what there was was pretty esoteric stuff.'

'Viruses are a much bigger subject now than they were in the sixties.'

'True,' replied the Professor. 'We thought we'd beaten all the major viruses back then. Very little left that was interesting to look at. I always thought Zmitt was years behind the times, but now you mention it, perhaps he was ahead of his time after all.'

'His published work only gave glimpses of what he might have been working on,' persisted Tara. 'I thought there might be private papers he left behind, something that would give a fuller picture of where his work was taking him. Perhaps here at the University.'

119

Appel lit his pipe with an old, oil-fired lighter. 'Heavens, you came all the way from America just to look at old Zmitt's papers?'

Tara smiled. 'I happened to be in England for a conference. It probably won't be worth anything, but a small detour doesn't do any harm. Besides I haven't been to Birmingham before.'

'Don't suppose you'll come again,' Appel laughed.

Tara laughed with him. 'Would the papers still be here?'

'I'm sure the library can dig them out for you. I'll have a word with them.'

Tara thanked him. The Professor offered to take her down to the library, and stood up to leave the room. Tara followed him, and together the pair paced their way down the corridor. 'Did you know Zmitt well?' she asked.

Appel shook his head. 'He was a loner. He had an office and space in the lab and he pottered around doing bits and pieces of work. Nobody paid much attention to him.'

'He must have had a hard life,' said Tara. 'With the war and so on.'

'Was he mixed up in the war?'

'He would have been thirty-seven when the Germans invaded Czechoslovakia. Quite old.'

'True. Funny, he never talked about his past very much. Must have had some good stories. But he wasn't the sort of man to stop and chat.'

'Did he ever say anything about what he was doing in England?' asked Tara. 'After all, that was in 1964. I don't think you could just decide to get up and move from Czechoslovakia to England in those days.'

'True,' replied Appel. He look lost in thought for a moment. 'I think he did quite a bit of project work for the Ministry of Health. Reports and so on. Maybe they helped him.'

They had arrived at the entrance to the library. Professor Appel spoke with the librarian, and told Tara she would find what she needed in the archives. He wished her luck. Tara smiled, and shook his hand warmly. 'You've been really helpful,' she said.

120

'Heavens no,' replied the Professor. 'Drop round to my office if you need anything else.'

Simon Cornfield was a small, tubby man, with thinning black hair and a pale complexion. He introduced himself to Tara as the assistant head librarian. Tara explained that she wanted to look at Josef Zmitt's private research papers. Cornfield had never heard of him, and she told him when he had worked at the University. The librarian said he would look through the archives, but warned her that it might take some time.

There was a coffee room next to the library, and Tara bought herself a cup, sitting down by herself in a corner to drink it, and to mull over her progress. The room was full of students; more in here than in the library, sipping coffees, smoking cigarettes, reading the music papers, and gossiping amongst themselves. A much nicer life, she reflected to herself. She finished her first coffee, and was starting on the second when Cornfield waved to her from the library. Tara walked through. On the desk he had put a large, musty box, its lid open. Inside were a pile of papers and files. 'There are two more inside,' said the librarian.

It could take days to read through all this, thought Tara. Particularly when you weren't sure what you were looking for. She asked him if she could photocopy the documents. Of course, Cornfield replied. While he went to retrieve the other two boxes, Tara went back to the coffee room and asked a group of four students if they wanted to earn some money. They agreed to help her with the photocopying for £10 an hour each. Cash. Students, as Tara well knew, were always short of money.

Between the five of them it took an hour and a half to complete the photocopying. She settled up the bill with the librarian, and gave each of the students £20. Two of the boys helped her to carry the pile to the door, and she ordered a cab. She managed just to connect with the one-forty train back to London. It would get in just after three p.m. There might just be time to complete everything she wanted to pack into the day.

During the journey, Tara began flicking through the haul of documents. She knew it would take days of close analysis before

121

she knew whether she had anything of substance. But even a cursory glance was illuminating. Josef Zmitt, to judge by the quality of his private work, was clearly a very able scientist. Much better than his desultory academic output would suggest.

Already tired, Tara watched the rolling green countryside give way to the rougher outskirts of London. She felt drowsy, and for a few moments she leant her head against the window and drifted off to sleep. The sky overhead was grey and sullen, matching her mood. She had been pleased to find the papers, and felt sure that somewhere within the decaying pile of documents she would find answers. But now she just felt overwhelmed by the size of the task ahead.

In London Tara took a taxi straight for Kew in south London, and climbed out in Ruskin Avenue. Checking her watch she headed into the Public Records Office. The library closed at five. There was not much time.

Thirty-two years, thought Tara. Under the thirty-year rule, any documents relating to Zmitt's emigration to the UK should have been released for public inspection. Only if they touched on national security could they be held back for another twenty years. Possible, she decided. There was as yet no way of knowing with whom or on what Zmitt had worked.

Tara filled in the form, and handed it in at the desk. She had requested any Home Office files relating to Zmitt from 1963 and 1964. The clerk took the slip, and put it into the system, telling Tara to wait. She sat in the corner, patiently, casting her eye over the other researchers. They were mostly students, many of them young, presumably historians working on their doctorates. None of them paid any attention to her. Nor did she pay any attention to them. Her mind was too full of speculation and conjecture.

It was a half-hour wait. The clerk returned with a file containing three sheets of paper. Tara walked straight across to the photocopier, feeding money into the machine, and positioning the first sheet in place. She wanted to make sure she had copies before the office closed for the evening.

Tara took the file back to the clerk, and returned to her seat.

She still had a few moments before the office closed, and she picked up the first document and began to read. Across the top ran the Home Office heading, and beneath it the words 'Immigration Department'. Below was a copy of a memo received from the Ministry of Defence.

Re: Dr Josef Zmitt.
Date: 27/5/63
Recommendation: Immediate grant of citizenship.
Status: Strictly classified.

Dr Zmitt was born in Prague in 1908, and graduated in chemistry from the University there in 1928. He completed his doctorate in the same city in 1932, after filing a thesis on the genesis and transmission of viruses. Between 1932 and the German annexation of Czechoslovakia in 1938, he worked at the University as a junior lecturer in molecular chemistry. Following the annexation, he continued to work at the University, before being transferred in 1942 to the advanced research department of IG Farben, the largest of the German chemicals cartels during the Nazi regime. During that time he worked on German plans to develop biological weapons. However he has insisted in subsequent debriefing sessions that his work there was fruitless, since the German government was more interested in poison gases rather than in Dr Zmitt's speciality of viruses.

In 1944 he was allowed to return to Prague, where he remained until the liberation of the city by the Soviet Red Army. His wife and daughter had died during his absence, and Dr Zmitt worked at the University until 1946, when he moved to the Moscow Academy of Natural Sciences. The Academy in those years was primarily concerned with developing biological weaponry, and Dr Zmitt was extensively debriefed on the work he had seen in Germany during the war. He also continued his own work on viruses. In 1950 he was transferred to the University in Bratislava. He maintains that the Moscow Academy lost interest in his work on viruses. In the subsequent twelve years, Dr Zmitt continued to teach and to develop his own research projects. He maintained contact with the Moscow Academy, visiting at least once a year, and was a permanent adviser on viral transmission. In 1960 he became aware that the Academy was studying viruses with renewed vigour and his expertise was requested more frequently. He was asked to visit the Academy several times in 1960 and 1961, with some of the trips lasting several weeks. He became convinced that the Academy was by now developing a range of viral weapons.

Dr Zmitt claims that by now he was a convinced opponent of the Soviet regime, and had no wish to work on weaponry. Late in 1961, Dr Zmitt made contact with a representative of the British Embassy in Prague, and he requested political asylum in the UK. In light of his knowledge of Soviet weapons research, it was decided by the Ministry to grant this request. Dr Zmitt was not considered a high-level security priority, and his departure was managed through the Embassy. He arrived in the UK in 1963. In view of his knowledge of biological weaponry, the Ministry has resolved that it is in the national interest that he be allowed to remain permanently in the UK. Dr Zmitt has expressed a desire to give up weapons research, but has agreed as a condition of his residence in the UK that he will continue to advise the Ministry on Soviet weapons development, including regular assessments on the state of their biological capability, and contributions to our own defensive research. The Ministry will secure him a medium-level academic position and maintain low-level security surveillance. Dr Zmitt has no dependants. Immediate citizenship is recommended as a priority.

Tara neatly folded the third sheet of photocopied paper and

slipped it into her carrier bag. It was already ten past five, and the room was being cleared. She collected her bags and began to walk towards the door. She felt sorry for Zmitt. The brief documentation made it sound as if he had lived a hard and bitter life. And as she felt sorry for him, she also felt sorry for herself.

Outside, a light drizzle was falling, and it was already starting to get dark. Tara knew she had had enough for today, and she asked the minicab driver from the office opposite to drive her directly back to Hertfordshire.

Across the road, the man in the silver-grey Mercedes put down the small hand-held camcorder he had been holding in his fist, and turned the ignition, firing the car into life. It had been a long wait, and much of it had been tedious, but it had been worthwhile. She was going home and there was no need to follow her there. Nothing else was needed. Angus Shane decided he had already seen as much as he wanted to that day.

TWELVE

The corridors seemed different now. Crooked and twisted, they were no longer the straight and narrow paths Jack had once imagined them to be. Shadows seemed to fall everywhere, and he walked across their carpets with a watchful tread, eyeing every person and each machine through fresh and suspicious eyes. Do they know? he found himself asking constantly.

The office had been alive with gossip and rumours when Jack arrived at his desk at just before nine that morning. Kizog had increased its offer for Ocher, this time to £13.56 billion. The news had been released to the stock exchange at eight, and Jack had heard only the briefest report on the radio. He was anxious to learn more details. The Reuters news service on his terminal took a few moments to spring up on to the screen, and Jack scrolled hurriedly through the stories reeling across the screen. A newsflash timed at 8:02 was headlined in red, and a longer story had landed at 8:27. Jack punched it up.

Kizog increases Ocher offer to £13.56bn

In a move that took markets by surprise this morning, the British pharmaceuticals giant Kizog dramatically increased its offer for its Swiss rival Ocher from £28 per share to £31.69, an increase of 13%, taking the total value of the bid to £13.56bn.

The market had been expecting Kizog to increase its offer after the Ocher board pledged itself to fight the take-over, but had expected Kizog to wait until the first offer period expired. With the second and final offer now tabled, Kizog now has fourteen days to win the battle. Commenting on the increase, Kizog chairman Sir Kurt Helin said: 'This offer represents a full and generous price for Ocher, and underlines our commitment to building a modern and international company to capitalise on the opportunities in our industry, and in particular the opportunity offered by our new Ator vaccine.'

Analysts expressed surprise both at the size and the speed of the increase. 'This will stretch Kizog's finances to the limit,' said Roger Turnbull, pharmaceuticals analyst with James Capel, the stockbroker. A spokesman for Ocher said the board would study the increased offer before making a formal statement.

Fourteen days, thought Jack. Not long. Not long at all. Perhaps when the bid was over he could start to put this nightmare behind him. Perhaps that would be the time to make his move. Or per-haps before. It was, he decided, too soon to know.

Layla was already lolling around in the doorway, her red hair tied up in a bun, held back with a large hairpin. Does she know? wondered Jack. Was she on the inside or the outside? There was no way of knowing for sure, but he suspected not. She seemed too sure of herself, too confident, too relaxed. If she knew, surely she could not act so calmly? Or perhaps, Jack speculated, she is a tougher woman than I suspected. 'The Chairman must be in a terrible hurry,' said Jack. 'To raise the offer so quickly. We might have won anyway, at the original price.'

Layla seemed to take the remark very seriously, perching herself on the edge of Jack's desk. 'Then why would Sir Kurt do it?'

'The defence document,' replied Jack firmly. 'Perhaps it is right. Maybe we don't make anything like the money we claim we do.'

Layla shook her head. 'Unbelievable,' she said.

'Did you talk to any Zurich Financial people?' Jack inquired. 'They would know if it was for real or just rhetoric.'

Layla stood up from the desk and walked across the room. 'I couldn't get to anyone who was working directly on the defence,' she said. 'The high-level work is all being done out of Switzerland rather than London. But it does seem they think there really is something strange about our accounts. Whether it is enough to blow a hole in the take-over I don't know. I wouldn't have thought so.'

She doesn't know, realised Jack. They haven't told her.

He got up to leave, taking his jacket from the door, explaining that he had to leave for a meeting with the finance director. 'Have you sent a report to the Chairman yet?'

Layla shook her head. 'Not enough evidence.'

'I wouldn't if I were you.'

She turned to face him. 'What are you on about, Borrodin?' she demanded.

'Nothing,' Jack said, attempting a smile. 'Just be careful.'

Jack left her pondering the remark as he stepped out into the corridor. The same neat offices, behind the same neat partitions, each with another loyal employee tapping away at a keyboard, were stretched out along the passages and hallways. Where did they fit into the picture? Jack asked himself again. Surely none of them knew.

Finer would certainly have all the information. Jack had counted on him as an ally and had been rudely awoken by the meeting yesterday. Naïve, he told himself. The finance director was clearly the Chairman's man. And his loyalties were always going to be elsewhere. He could have done without the meeting this morning; there were other things to think about. But orders were orders. And if he and Tara were to have a chance, he had to play along as if he suspected nothing.

Playing dumb shouldn't be so hard, he decided. It is what I have been doing all along. Another couple of weeks won't make any difference.

Inside he could feel the anger rising; he had been loyal to this company and it had betrayed him completely. But then, he decided, it had been naïve of him to have ever trusted them. Insecurity was everywhere these days, and he was just exploring its outer edges. Welcome to the nineties, Jack decided with a wry smile.

Finer was instantly friendly when Jack walked into the room. A smug expression dropped on to his face, and he shook Jack's hand warmly, slapping him on the shoulder as he turned round. Jack took a seat and told Finer that he was feeling just fine. 'Thanks for asking.'

'I know it's been rough on you,' he said with a concerned smile.

Jack nodded. He saw no need to reply.

'It's the same for all of us. There is a moment when you cross the bridge, and it is shaky, but once you are on the other side, everything is OK again.' Again, Jack just nodded, saying nothing. 'You are dealing with this in a very mature way, ' Finer continued.

'I'm a mature person,' replied Jack. 'Perhaps that is why you chose me.'

'The Chairman and I discussed it. It was mainly his idea, but I felt I could vouch for you in terms of character.'

Well, thanks for nothing, thought Jack. That says a lot for my character. 'What am I supposed to do? I mean, my duties. I assume they have changed slightly.'

Finer said that he would move on to that later. He pulled open a drawer on his desk and pulled out a file of papers. There were a couple of things he wanted to discuss, he told Jack. Money first. The money Shane promised to give him in return for the drug.

'A promise is a promise,' replied Jack. 'Then again I don't suppose Kizog wants to pay big bucks for leaking a Kizog drug to a Kizog controlled counterfeiting ring. And I can't say I feel like arguing the point with him.'

Finer sat back in his chair with a generous smile spreading across his lips. 'Think of it as a signing-on fee,' he said. 'A sort of golden handshake.'

'Two hundred and fifty thousand?' said Jack.

'The rewards are much better once you cross over to this side.' Finer looked down at the papers on his desk. 'Obviously this money doesn't need to be declared to the Inland Revenue.' He chuckled. 'In fact, better that it isn't, don't you think?'

'Naturally,' replied Jack with a forced smile.

Finer went on to explain that the money would be paid into an offshore bank account. It was up to Jack, but he would recommend setting up an international business company in the Turks and Caicos Islands. Most discreet, he added. Jack would be the sole owner of the offshore entity, but under the local laws there was not even any need to register its shareholders. Much more secure than Switzerland these days. The money would arrive by a circuit of wire transfers, transferred from another offshore company. Nothing need be disclosed about where the money came from, nor what it was for. Once it was lodged in the account, it was up to Jack what he decided to do with it.

'The Chairman wanted me to tell you something else,' Finer continued. He paused, as if unsure how to phrase himself. 'This is just a temporary situation. It is not a permanent state of affairs. The company has some unexpected problems. Copying other companies' medicines is not a long-term policy. Simply a way of bridging some short-term cashflow difficulties. He doesn't want you to think this is something we envisage you, or indeed any of us, being involved in for very long. Once the take-over of Ocher is completed, the condition of the company should start moving back towards normality.'

'My duties,' persisted Jack. 'I still don't know what I am meant to be doing.'

'The clandestine operation has very few points of contact with the more normal operations of the company,' replied Finer. 'But there is a large amount of administration to deal with. I have been working on some of that. But with this take-over, and then with the task of integrating Kizog and Ocher, my time is really taken up. We see you moving into that role, liaising between the sides of the operation. For the meantime, you'll be working with Miss Fuller, and Mr Shane, learning some of the details of how that side of things works.'

Jack was starting to enjoy the euphemisms. The finance director was clearly uncomfortable referring to the counterfeiting ring directly; as though it left a stale taste in his mouth. 'How many people know about that side of things?' asked Jack. 'I feel I should know, otherwise I don't know who I can discuss it with.'

Finer looked troubled by the question. 'Obviously as few people as possible. There are several, but for the meantime, I'd be happier if you only discussed it with myself and the Chairman. You won't need to deal with anyone else internally, at least not for the time being.'

Jack nodded, hoping to create the impression the instructions seemed entirely normal and understandable. 'One question, if I may?' he said.

The finance director smiled his most indulgent smile. 'Of course, Jack.'

'The videotape of myself with Shane,' said Jack. 'Can I take it that was designed to make sure I went along with the company's plans for me?'

Finer shifted uncomfortably. 'Obviously the company needs guarantees,' he replied. 'These are very sensitive matters.'

Guarantees, thought Jack. Useful things to have. 'What would happen if I ignored it?'

'The Chairman has a thing about loyalty, Jack,' Finer said. 'You know how he is.'

'I understand,' replied Jack breezily.

Finer smiled. 'Good.'

He seemed relieved, thought Jack. He stood up to leave, the

two men shaking hands warmly, and he turned towards the door. He stopped at the edge of the hallway, paused, and looked back at Finer.

'None of that was really necessary,' he said. 'You guys know how I feel about this company. I would have been happy enough to work alongside you in whatever capacity you chose.'

Finer smiled. 'Then we'll get on just fine.'

'Thanks for everything, Ralph,' said Jack warmly. He turned away, and began walking down the hallway towards the lifts. Dumb enough, he thought. At least to fool that bastard. A smile started to play on his lips. I may yet have something to teach them about betrayal, he decided.

Tara shifted the lamp on her desk. The bulb shone a dim light, illuminating the stack of papers, documents and maps she had stacked on the surface. In front of her the window was open slightly, and a gentle breeze blew into the room, ruffling the papers strewn there. Through the window, with the curtains drawn, she could detect the pale shadow of the moonlight shining down on the village.

There was, she realised, a pastoral restfulness to the surroundings that was quite unlike anything she had known before. The house had a kind of cosy charm that had made her feel at home and at peace. She felt there was a neighbourhood; a neighbourhood, which she, with only a little more work, could become a part of. The man at the local shop said a cheery hallo to her now if she went in to buy something. So did the lady at the small bookshop. She suspected that they saw few Eurasians in the village, and they had barely acknowledged her existence at first. But the cleaning lady who came twice a week had told them all about her, and she felt as if she was being accepted. There was a cat – she was unsure where it came from, although the animal appeared more than well fed – who stopped by to ask for scraps of food, scraps which she gladly provided. She was starting to feel as though she belonged.

Those thoughts only occupied her mind for a few brief seconds, before her concentration turned back to the task in hand. She could not be certain, but she suspected that Jack would be along later. He had looked rattled enough yesterday morning for her to realise events were moving quickly. Tara had no way of knowing what might have happened to him, but she sensed it would be significant. Their stories were bound together, of that she was sure. There was no other rational explanation.

She wanted to be ready. Her thoughts needed to be organised, and her evidence prepared.

The documents from the World Health Organisation had been invaluable. Tara had moved the kitchen table into the study, and set up a PC next to her desk. She had arranged a modem connection to the Lexis/Nexis database, paying the signing-on fee and the twenty dollars a minute connection charge from her own pocket. It was extravagance, she knew, but what else was she to do with all the money Kizog was paying her? The WHO documents she could have found in the Kizog library. But this way she could work at home, in silence, undisturbed, and, crucially, observed by nobody. She had no doubt they would be looking closely at every move she made. And she didn't want anyone to know what she was doing.

On a yellow Post-it note stuck to the top of her computer screen, Tara had written out a message to herself in neat capitals: 'FOLLOW THE VIRUS'. Every time she sat down, it caught her eye, a reminder that spurred her on to fresh efforts. No matter how tired she might be, the message remained there, chilling and stark, chiding her to continue with her investigations.

On the table next to the PC, Tara had laid out a cheap, school-children's map of the world she had bought at the bookstore in the village. Tara loved maps. She always had done, ever since she was child, gazing wistfully at them, locating her own place in them. As she studied the WHO documents, she isolated reports of Ator, placing a mark for each outbreak. The first recorded cases, dating back to 1984, had occurred along the border between Namibia and Angola; a hospital in Osjakti, close to

133

Ruacana Falls, from where cases had spread as far south as Windhoek, and north up to Luanda. From there it had derived its name from the Portuguese word for plague, atormentor, which was what the local doctors first thought of it as. Tara marked the sites on the map. By 1986 the disease had started appearing along the borders of Burma and Thailand, reported first in Mong Loi, along the Mekong River, by the junction of Thailand, Burma and Laos. Tara marked the positions. By 1987 it was reported in Afghanistan, breaking out first in Dushambe, close to the border with Tadzhikistan. Later that year it manifested itself in Chouluteca, along the border between El Salvador and Nicaragua. In the years since, Ator began spreading out from those centres, with one or two isolated cases starting to be reported in North America and Western Europe from 1990 onwards.

Tara stood back and pondered the map. She needed not just the detail but the overall picture. And, as it had done in the past, the longer she looked at it the more mysterious it became to her. It was like assembling a jigsaw puzzle of an abstract picture; there was no way of telling how the pieces fitted together. She could see little rational explanation for the pattern spread out before her. The virus jumped from Africa to South-East Asia, to the Middle East and to Central America. Tara was aware that movements of people around the world could transmit viruses at lightning speeds, and they could also be incubated in carriers, carriers who were unaware of what they were delivering. Even so, the pattern seemed random and bizarre, drifting around the world purposelessly, without any shape or pattern to its movements. It was possible the virus was mutating from some common ancestor, and could be doing so simultaneously in different parts of the world. But even then, there would have to be some genetic differences between the regional viruses. That was not the case. Ator was genetically watertight, perfectly coded. It was one of the purest viruses she had ever studied. That it could have mutated simultaneously around the world in such a short timeframe was unthinkable.

She returned to the PC, connecting it back to the database. The

Lexis/Nexis logo flashed up on the screen. She searched through her notes for the names she had written down, the three people she knew had died whilst researching the Ator virus. The first name she tapped into the machine was David Sunningdale, the researcher at Bristol Myers-Squibb. Briefly, the small row of red lights on the modem blinked whilst the machine searched through its records. The computer spat out half a dozen papers and lectures, four of them on Ator. Tara pressed save and moved on. She tapped in the name of Alicia Thomas. The computer fetched up five papers, three on Ator, two of which were co-authored by Hans Gerter, the researcher at Roche; Genentech was majority-owned by Roche, and it was not that surprising that its scientists sometimes worked together. Tara pressed save. She tried Gerter's name by itself. Seven papers came back, the two she had already seen, plus two more on Ator. Tara pressed save and print. She got up to reload the printer. There must be a hundred pages or more here to look through, she thought to herself.

Armed with a fresh pot of coffee, Tara settled down to read. She studied the pages slowly and diligently, digesting every word, marking each part she found relevant with a blue felt-tip pen. Sunningdale had been following a similar track to the one she had been pursuing herself. He had been investigating the spread of the Ator virus in an attempt to build up a more complete picture of the transmission mechanism. His work was far more detailed than hers. It highlighted some curious aspects of the virus. One was that it transmitted relatively easily and quickly between compact population groups, but that it did not hop easily between areas; it needed close proximity to thrive. The other was that it appeared to strike particularly venomously among young males. He had illustrated these points with data on how the virus had struck most savagely at small mining communities, in factories, and in military encampments, all places where young men worked together in close proximity.

She turned to the rest of the papers, flicking through several she judged irrelevant before she came across a paper Thomas and

Gerter had written together. It had been prepared to be delivered at a symposium on Ator held in Vienna, in July 1993, but had never been formally presented; both of them had died some weeks before the symposium. A draft of their paper had nevertheless been forwarded although not published, and the database had located it in its archives. Tara began reading. It started out on conventional enough lines, recapping their earlier work, and summarising the existing literature. It then took a slight detour, discussing the genetic structure of the molecule, concentrating both on its perfection and on its lack of antecedents. Both, thought Tara, were clearly puzzled by the same questions that had long since been mystifying her. Towards the end of the paper Thomas and Gerter started to outline the conclusions they drew from their work. Tara reached for her pen, and neatly underlined the words as she read them.

> After working on the subject in depth it is our feeling that the more closely this subject is investigated the further the answer recedes into the distance. It is possible the scientists working in this field are walking along a blind alley. In the spirit of scientific enquiry we believe it is useful at this point to throw out some new and different hypotheses and test them against the available evidence. All other lines of enquiry have reached a dead end, and if nothing else we may be able to provoke some fresh thinking.

Tara knew that this was the heart of the matter, the material she needed most, and she turned the pages anxiously. It was reassuring to find other scientists thinking the same thoughts she was.

> We know that Governments in various parts of the world have been working for many years on biological weapons. Most of us here today will know colleagues who have been involved in this kind of work, or may even have been

involved in it themselves. Our contention is that if you were to design a viral molecule that could be used in a military situation, it might very well look something like Ator. The molecule certainly has the look of something that has been created in the laboratory rather than a virus that has evolved through spontaneous mutation. It has none of the obvious antecedents that are required for mutation. And it displays none of the obvious imperfections or weaknesses that would normally be associated with a recently mutated virus. It is too perfect to be true. We believe as well that a study of the most vulnerable population groups supports this hypothesis. We refer to the earlier work of David Sunningdale, which established that young males in close proximity are acutely vulnerable. The virus seems uniquely suited to military use. None of this is proof, we readily concede, but it does appear there is a strong circumstantial case to be made.

We are aware, as most of you are, that military doctrine on the use of biological and chemical weaponry is strongly influenced by the experiences of World War I. For those of you who are not up to speed on military history, we will remind you that poison gas used in that war had a tendency to drift back on to the general's own troops, making it a very counter-productive weapon. Doctrine since then has been to develop some kind of inoculation in tandem with the biological agent, simply so it can be used to attack the other side, whilst your own troops are protected. Our suspicion is that if Ator has been developed as a biological weapon, and has somehow leaked out into the general population, then the developers may also be in possession of some kind of vaccine or inoculation system. If so, we believe they should be urged to come forward. We thank you for your time, and we hope we have provoked some fresh thinking on this subject. If nothing else, if this theory can be proved wrong we will have closed down one line of plausible inquiry.

Tara sat back in her chair. Worth dying for? she thought. No. It was only a hypothesis, a theory. But worth killing for? Perhaps. If it were true.

She stood up from her desk and began rummaging through her papers. She picked up the notes she had photocopied from Dr Scott's office, and the earlier work of Josef Zmitt she had taken from the Wellcome Institute library. She laid it out on the table, and put the paper by Gerter and Thomas next to it. She knew now that the picture was starting to come together. She looked again at the papers from Scott and Zmitt, reading them closely, looking at the words and diagrams in a new light. What had previously been so mysterious suddenly became clear.

Tara sat back down at her desk. She felt slightly numb, over-whelmed by the connections she was making. The information was coming at her too quickly, and her thoughts were spinning out in a hundred different directions. She took a deep breath, a slug of coffee and tried to compose herself. Reaching to the top of the computer screen she tore off the Post-it note, and picked up her pen. Beneath the words 'FOLLOW THE VIRUS' she drew a small arrow and in neat block letters wrote a single word.

Her thoughts were interrupted by the sound of the doorbell ringing. Tara put down her papers and walked to the front door, a slight trepidation filling her as she approached it. There had been no visitors since she moved in here, and she noticed that the cottage was bare of any personal effects; only the furniture and pictures that came with the property were on view. Suddenly it didn't feel quite so homely.

She slid back the eyeglass on the door. Jack was standing out-side, the collar of his raincoat turned up around his neck. She opened the deadlock on the door and let him in. Jack walked inside, and began undoing the belt on his coat. He said hallo and she responded warmly, but there seemed to be a stiffness between them. As if he were unsure exactly why he was here, thought Tara. And indeed, she reflected, how could he know.

'Any chance of a drink?' asked Jack.

Tara shook her head. She hardly drank herself, she explained,

138

and had not bought any alcohol. There was coffee, if he wanted that. Jack accepted. They walked through the narrow, beamed hallway and into the kitchen. It was modern and functional, with pine wood covering the appliances and the cupboards. Tara emptied freshly ground coffee in the percolator, filled it with water, and waited. Jack struck her as strangely silent, as if he was in shock. He was far removed from the self-confident young executive she had first met in the Kizog laboratories only a few weeks earlier; and, she decided, he was a more plausible character for shedding that skin. 'You said yesterday you wanted to talk?'

'I know,' replied Jack hesitantly.

Tara wondered if he was having second thoughts. Perhaps she was not someone he wanted to confide in. Perhaps. But if so, why was he here? 'You aren't sure, are you?'

'Nothing seems clear any more,' Jack replied.

'I know that feeling,' she replied sympathetically.

The percolator was almost full now, and Tara pulled it out of the stand, pouring the coffee out into two large mugs. She mixed some milk and sugar into Jack's cup, but left her own black. He took the mug, cradling it between his hands, sipping on it, and remaining silent for the moment. 'You said something the other day that interested me,' Jack said eventually. 'After the meeting with the PR guy. You said your suspicions started here at Kizog. I didn't think much of it at the time. But it has stayed with me.'

Tara looked at him knowingly, her eyes widening slightly. 'So you were paying attention.'

'What did you mean?'

Tara sipped on her coffee. It was late already, and this would not be quick. But she would either tell him now, or she never would. She cast her eyes over him, wondering once more if she should trust him. The decision had already been made, yet she still wanted this last moment to reassure herself.

'Come upstairs,' she said at last. 'I'll show you.'

Jack followed her upstairs. He noticed the single bedroom to one side of the corridor, and the open door to the study next to it. They walked inside. The curtains were open, and the moonlight cast a slight glow over the village below. Jack cast his eyes over the room. He noticed the table, and the PC and the modem, and he registered the handwritten note stuck to the side of the computer. His eyes followed the map of the world spread out on the desk, with the neat marks spread out across it. And he noticed the pile of A4 pages lying next to the printer. 'Do you know where Ator comes from?' asked Tara.

Jack shrugged. 'I'd assumed it was a strange Third World disease. Perhaps of relatively recent origin, perhaps ancient. A mutation, or whatever. I am not a virologist.'

'Listen carefully,' replied Tara.

Jack did as he was told. He sat back in an armchair, drinking his cup of coffee, whilst Tara started her explanation. She delivered the talk as if it were a lecture, and Jack felt like a backward student. He had to ask her to stop and make clear the more difficult aspects of biochemistry she touched upon. She started by describing the nature of the virus, dwelling on how it was first detected. She filled in some background on how viruses normally spread around the world. And then, as she was the first to admit, she entered the realms of speculation. Conjecture followed on supposition, none of it with much in the way of solid proof to back it up. But it was, Jack had to admit, a compelling theory, made more so by the collection of scientific literature she had spread out on the desk.

When she had finished, one element of her story struck Jack as both strange and unexplained. 'I work for Kizog,' he said. 'Why would you share all this information with me?'

Tara paused. 'Another theory,' she replied.

'Tell me about it.'

'I think I first began to suspect after our meeting with Geoff Wheeler,' Tara replied. 'He said that you hired me, that you were the person who brought me into the company.'

'It's down in the files like that.'

'But you didn't really have anything to do with it, did you,' she replied, pondering the question anew while she spoke. 'Why would they do that?'

'Lots of strange things happen at Kizog,' Jack replied lightly, hoping to loosen the atmosphere, yet aware that he was likely to be unsuccessful.

'But seldom without a purpose,' Tara continued.

True, thought Jack. Very true. 'So what's the reason?' he asked.

Tara was sitting on the edge of the table now, her large brown eyes resting upon him, and she leant forward before replying. 'If they are playing games with me, then they obviously want you to be involved somehow. From that I conclude they are playing games with you as well.'

Jack knew it was true, but was still unsure how much he should tell her. 'I don't get it,' he replied. 'Why don't you just walk? Resign your job. Forget about the company. What does it matter to you?'

Tara's eyes were cast down now, scanning the floor, as if she was searching for something. 'It is too personal,' she said reluctantly.

A silence hung between them, heavy and ponderous. Jack reached across to touch the back of her hand, and for a split second felt her muscles tense, as though she were about to pull away, before she relaxed beneath the edge of his fingers. For just an instant he could feel himself drawing closer to her; the sense that she too was facing a crisis aroused a protective instinct within him. 'Tell me about it,' he said softly.

She stood up, and walked back towards the table and the computer. 'It isn't important right now,' she replied.

THIRTEEN

The drive east woke the demons in Jack's mind. With Shane sitting here at his side, the silver-grey Mercedes powering through the docklands, no more than a few miles from the scene of the crime, memories stalked him with new vigour. More than a week had passed since the event, and, inside himself, Jack could already start to feel how time was numbing his senses. Images of the girl still flashed across his mind five, perhaps six, times a day, but their ferocity was now tempered by distance and their bite was no longer so severe. Yet here, their power intensified, drawing strength from proximity, and Jack could feel himself physically recoiling from the man sitting next to him.

Maintaining a genial air through it all, he decided, was the hardest part. He knew he had to be on his guard. One slip and they would surely kill him, and that knowledge sharpened every moment of the day, keeping him in a constant state of alert.

Events had moved forward quickly since the Chairman had revealed that the counterfeiting operation was run by Kizog. The day afterwards, Shane had contacted him. Jack explained that he knew all about the links between the company and the counter-feiters, and hc was now assigned to work alongside Shane, co-ordinating between the field and head office. Shane had seemed no more than mildly pleased by his arrival. There was not much choice, he had pointed out, since he would have had to kill him if he refused. Whether he killed Jack or not didn't seem to be a matter of great importance to him, but the tone of his voice indicated that he preferred not to. One less thing to do, Jack supposed in a moment of despair.

Back in the office, Jack had been assigned the mundane task of looking at ways Kizog's and Ocher's manufacturing plants might be rationalised if the take-over went ahead; an assignment that prompted Layla to speculate he was being limbered up for a move sideways. If only she knew, he thought to himself. A move sideways would be a relief.

Most of his time was now being spent working on the details of the counterfeiting operation. Shane was teaching him about the organisation, but Jack knew that his real purpose was to dis-cover what was happening higher up the chain, to find out how all the parts of the jigsaw fitted together. Discovering the truth, he and Tara had resolved, was their only chance of escape. But that would have to come later. He could not show too much curiosity too soon. He had to tread carefully, his steps had to be watched. For now he would look, listen and learn.

The counterfeiting operation had a sophistication and com-plexity that Jack could only have dreamt of. It was, in all respects, a shadow corporation, a parasitical creature that lived under the skin of the drugs industry. Shane's tours and explan-ations about how it worked proved that. It started with the manu-facturing operations. The business had grown out of the Third World. There were secret factories located in places such as Thailand, Korea, Angola, Pakistan, and Colombia. In the last three years it had expanded dramatically into the West, and there were now factories in Europe, in Portugal, Northern Ireland, Sicily and the Slovak Republic. But manufacturing was simple. Anyone with a pill-making machine could manufacture pharmaceuticals; once you had the formula, the chemicals were easy to obtain, and the technology was not complicated.

Shane had explained how they used a ring of parallel importers. A series of wholesalers, owned or controlled by the counterfeiters, traded the drugs between different countries; a shipment could pass from Italy, to the US, to Hong Kong, to France, to Portugal. There could be ten or fifteen transactions before it reached the customer, creating a paper trail that was impossible to unravel. It was like laundering money, Jack reflected; it starts out clearly criminal, but by the time it has passed through the chain its origins had vanished. Wiped clean.

Within a few days, Jack believed he had a relatively good grasp of how the system worked. It was complex, but the essence of the system was simple. It was smuggling. The complexity was artificial, a façade, designed to confuse anyone from the outside who was trying to figure how the operation worked. If you looked at it from the inside, from the centre of the maze, the pattern was relatively simple.

Until this evening, however, the main cog in the machine had escaped him. The element of complicity by the industry was missing. By the end of the drive, Shane had taken him to the Kizog distribution centre on the Essex coast. It was a new building, constructed about three years ago, which handled warehousing and distribution for the company throughout Europe. Shane had driven right up to the main gate and flashed a card. That, by itself, had surprised Jack. He had not, for a moment, imagined Shane had security clearance for Kizog buildings. 'Easily arranged,' said Shane when Jack raised the point. 'Computers are dumb animals. They will give you anything if you tap in the right numbers. Trusting beasts. No suspicion. Computerisation has been the greatest aid to criminal activity since the invention of the gun.'

144

Jack already had clearance. As a special assistant to the Chairman, he had automatic access to all the company's operations. Together they drove through the centre until they reached the main warehouse. They stood outside the warehouse for about fifteen minutes, Shane puffing on a series of Camels, until a lorry pulled up. Shane waved to the driver. 'Good journey?'

The driver wound down the window. 'Bit of traffic in France,' he replied.

'This bloke has come from the Slovak Republic,' said Shane. 'We have a plant there, as you know.'

'So these are fakes,' said Jack carefully.

'You bet,' replied Shane. 'Now watch this.'

The gate of the warehouse rose, and the lorry drove inside. Shane and Jack followed. Inside, the lorry drove into a loading bay, and a group of warehousemen began unpacking the boxes, taking the cargo to its allotted slots in the warehouse. There must have been hundreds of boxes. Jack could only catch the markings on some of them; Zovirax, Prozac, Capoten. Some of the biggest-selling pharmaceuticals in the world.

Shane and the truck driver sat down at the computer in the docking bay. 'Give me the inventory,' Shane grumbled to the trucker. The man handed him the list, and Shane began tapping it into the computer. 'The beauty of this warehouse,' he continued, 'is that Kizog also supplies drugs wholesale to hospitals and pharmacies all round Europe from here. Makes it easier for the hospital if they buy from one supplier. So they buy from the other companies, and we slip counterfeits into the system right here.' He stood up from the computer. 'Here, you try it,' he said.

Jack sat down at the machine, tapping in details of the shipments, whilst Shane stepped back a couple of yards, telling him which keys to press, and explaining the answers to the computer's questions. 'Easy, isn't it?' said Shane. Jack nodded. 'There are about a quarter of a million pills in that truck,' he added boastfully.

'The average selling price of a drug in the UK is £15,' mused

Jack. He made a quick mental calculation in his head. 'That truck's shipment is worth £3.75 million.'

'Almost pure profit as well,' said Shane. 'Not bad for a night's work. I reckon we've earned ourselves some fun.'

Shane looked up to the far corner of the warehouse. He could just make out the security camera, glaring down at them, taping every move. He was pleased. The evening was working out very well, he thought to himself. The boy doesn't suspect a thing.

Dr Scott appeared flustered, the lines on his face creasing up, betraying the nervousness that was eating away at him. The Chairman observed him coldly. Little courage, he reflected to himself. The pressure was starting to fray his nerves, compromising his judgement and destroying his composure. Predictable, decided the Chairman. It takes a certain kind of steel to withstand this pressure, and the research director was made from a weaker alloy.

Across the office, the Chairman could see his public relations man entering the office. He stood up to greet him, shaking him warmly by the hand. It was late, and all three of them would be leaving the building soon. But not until they had finished this meeting. Geoff Wheeler stood in front of the Chairman's desk, placing two sheets of paper in front of him.

The Chairman glanced down. Over the top of the page he could see the Reuters logo. He skimmed through the story. It described how a pressure group in Germany, the European Alliance Against Biological Weapons, had called a press conference earlier that day. They had put forward the theory that Ator might have its origins in military research into biological warfare agents, perhaps carried out by one of several Third World dictatorships, and perhaps using technology exported with the complicity of the German government. It quoted the leader of

146

the pressure group as saying the evidence strengthened the case for a ban on bioengineering in Germany, and went on to quote a professor at Munich University as saying the views expressed were only those of a minority fringe organisation with little scientific credibility. He did, however, concede that relatively little was known about the origins of Ator, and no theory, no matter how weird, could be ruled out until science delivered the real answers.

The Chairman chuckled, and passed the report on to Dr Scott. 'Will this story get any coverage?' he asked, looking up at Wheeler.

The PR man shook his head. 'Reuters are carrying it, but as far as I can tell, none of the mainstream international news organisations are running with the story. We had a couple of calls about it, but I declined to comment.'

The Chairman turned to Dr Scott, who by now had finished reading the story. 'Your view?' he asked softly.

Dr Scott placed the story carefully back down on the desk. 'The Greens in Germany are always looking for any excuse to whip up public feeling against bioengineering,' he answered. 'This has the look of another publicity stunt.'

The Chairman nodded. 'No connections between these people, and any of the other scientists researching the origins of Ator.'

'Not so far as I am aware,' replied Dr Scott. 'All those inquiries were, I believe, effectively terminated. The trouble is this story will not lie down and die. Every time people start investigating the origins of the virus, a few of them are bound to start looking at the military possibilities.'

The Chairman had closed his eyes for a moment, and was sitting far back in his chair, seemingly lost in thought.

'This is the first time the theory has appeared in any of the general media, and we can't guarantee that it won't be picked up some time,' said Wheeler. 'I suspect it is just a matter of time, unless these people could be silenced as well.'

The Chairman opened his eyes again, slowly, shaking his head as he did so. 'No,' he replied. 'A pressure group is too risky. They

147

will have supporters among the public and among the politicians. The speculation has to stop soon. I think the time is approaching to explain the origins of Ator once and for all.'

Tara knew she was being watched. She could sense it. The tracking of the video cameras, mounted on every wall, was so intense, she could almost feel the video tape recording her every move. The security guards who trudged around the buildings seemed to always have a particularly beady eye open for her. And none of her colleagues she could trust. Many, and perhaps all, would no doubt be reporting back on her.

There was no hope of evading detection. Not inside this building. And since concealment was useless, she decided she might as well be brazen.

She knew that Zmitt worked on biological weapons. She knew that he had done work in the past with Dr Scott, and she knew that he had been involved with work done at Kizog. The links were there, but they were tenuous. She knew that she needed more. Most of all, she knew that time was running out.

Dr Scott's private laboratory was several hundred yards down the set of corridors. Tara left her own lab, and began walking casually through the hallways. She could feel the eyes upon her, but decided to ignore them. Dr Scott's laboratory was empty, as it always seemed to be. Punching the code into the lock, she opened the door gently and stepped inside. It looked little different from the last time she was here, and Tara would not have been surprised to learn that he had not visited it since Nothing had been disturbed. She went straight to the shelves of papers at the back of the laboratory, and began her search. Many of the files were of no interest to her; they covered reports and developments on different commercial drugs Kizog had developed over the years. It was the work on leprosy she needed. She scuttled through the pages as fast as she could. And when she found the formula that she needed, she committed it to memory.

'I thought you were unwell.'

Tara spun round. Dr Scott was standing behind her, his face slightly red, his tone harsh and unyielding.

He stepped towards her. Stay calm, Tara told herself.

'This is a private office,' said Scott.

'I know. I'm sorry,' Tara apologised, her mind searching for a plausible excuse.

'What are you looking for?' he persisted.

Dr Scott was leaning against the workbench now, his small eyes squinting closely at Tara. She could feel his gaze bearing down upon her, questioning and probing.

Tara composed herself. 'There are things I don't understand.'

'Then ask me,' he replied. 'We are all here to help.'

'The similarities between Ator and leprosy,' she began carefully. 'I was hoping some of your earlier research into the disease might be useful. We are still having trouble getting the vaccine into a stable enough condition to be used outside the laboratory. I was wondering if you might have done work on a leprosy vaccine. If so that could help.'

Tara watched him closely while she spoke, trying to judge his reaction. She was wondering if he believed her. 'We never developed a leprosy vaccine,' answered Dr Scott firmly. 'Nothing has been done on that project for years.'

Tara sensed he was backing down, unsure how to handle the situation. 'Did Josef Zmitt work on the project?'

Dr Scott seemed genuinely surprised by the question. 'You know about Zmitt?'

Tara smiled. 'I am a biochemist,' she replied, her boldness growing. 'He did some interesting work on viruses in the sixties. With you. You wrote a paper together when you were still a student.'

'Zmitt died many years ago,' answered Dr Scott nervously.

'I was just wondering if he contributed to work here?' Tara persisted.

Dr Scott shook his head. 'No, he never did.'

He's lying, thought Tara. 'His ideas on transmission mechanisms might have led somewhere if he had developed them,' she continued, trying to soften her tone.

'This isn't academia,' Dr Scott snapped. 'You should be careful about which ideas you follow up.'

FOURTEEN

The Chairman was standing in the doorway, leaning against the edge of the wall. His expression was kind and friendly, the smile benevolent and concerned. 'You are making progress?' he asked quietly.

'It's a fascinating experience, sir,' said Jack bluntly.

He rested his arms on the desk, hoping to conceal some of his work. The lines between the counterfeiters and the company were laid out in the spreadsheets. The faking of medicines was clearly a massively profitable operation, generating revenues of at least £1 billion a year. Most of that he reckoned would have to be profit. Jack hadn't seen any of the figures yet, but it was unlikely the costs were any higher than in a legitimate pharmaceutical company; he estimated the margins at around ninety per cent. Or around £900 million a year. Perhaps more.

The Chairman walked forward, standing close to Jack's desk. 'Why do you think we chose you for this task?'

'My managerial qualities, perhaps.'

The Chairman nodded. 'Quite so,' he replied. 'Your talent certainly. But something else as well. You are a loner. Your parents are both dead, you are not married.'

Disposable, thought Jack. 'That makes a difference?'

'Loyalty,' replied the Chairman. 'People without ties are always more loyal. The world is a forbidding place. They cling to organisations, because that is the only security they can find. I think that may be true in your case.'

'I have been loyal so far,' said Jack.

'Quite so,' replied the Chairman. 'Your loyalty has been exceptional. As I said, you appear to have adapted well. Surprisingly so.'

Is he suspicious, wondered Jack. Maybe I am playing too dumb. 'There is something I don't understand.'

The Chairman smiled. 'I am always here to help.'

'What is the point of the counterfeiting operation? Where does the money go?'

'I'm disappointed,' the Chairman replied. 'I would have thought you could have worked that out for yourself.'

The cat was sitting outside her kitchen door, peering up at her with hopeful eyes, and Tara decided to empty her fridge. There was not much there. Since she had moved into this house, she had been eating mostly in the canteen at the laboratories, and hadn't cooked more than a couple of times. There was some milk and some leftover scraps of chicken. She put them on separate saucers, and placed them outside, rubbing the head of the cat as she did so. Why not, she thought. I won't be needing them.

The meeting with Dr Scott last night had rattled her, leaving her nervous, and uncertain about her next move. Perhaps I went too far, she wondered to herself. Exposed myself too much. It was hard to know. But the circle would be contracting from now on. Of that she was certain.

Be prepared, she told herself. Walking upstairs, she sat down

152

at the table and began collecting together the papers strewn out in front of her. The formula she had seen in Dr Scott's office was still committed to memory, but, deciding it was better to be safe than sorry, she began writing it down in her notepad, making some notes on the side. From the bedroom she collected a black sports bag, and emptied it of the few clothes that were still inside. Dividing the papers she had into neat piles, classified according to subject, she packed them into the bag. Keep these with me, she told herself. They are too important to leave behind.

Turning to the computer, she switched the machine on, flicking the switch on the modem, and waiting whilst it brought itself to life. Patiently she watched the screen as the Internet connection sorted itself out; the modem had to dial three times, and, not for the first time, she found herself wishing the system was quicker. Using the mouse, she logged into the e-mail programme. And, pausing for only a moment whilst she decided what to say, Tara started tapping out a message to Jack. Though it surprised her slightly, she admitted to herself that she was worried about him.

The Chairman stood with his back to the office, gazing down at the complex below. Dusk was falling on a cloudless sky, and he could see the office and lab workers drifting through the compound on their way to the car-park. Good people, in the main, he reflected. People who had worked hard, and who expected their salaries and their pensions to be paid by this company for the rest of their lives. People who wouldn't know what to do with themselves if the company wasn't there any more.

Certain things, he had long since realised, just had to be done. It was for the best.

He turned around. Seated around the room were Angus Shane, Dani Fuller, Geoff Wheeler and Ralph Finer. The Chairman walked across the room, and sat down on a large black armchair next to Finer. He looked across at Fuller. 'You believe it is time to act?'

Fuller nodded. 'They are getting close,' she said. 'Tara Ling has been fishing around with the past, looking into the work of Josef Zmitt. She even asked Dr Scott about it yesterday.'

The Chairman turned towards Finer. 'And Borrodin?' he asked. 'How much does he know?'

'Probably only as much as we have fed him,' stated the finance director confidently.

'I spoke to him today,' said the Chairman. 'He seemed too calm. Is there much evidence of contact with Miss Ling?'

'He visited her house the other evening,' answered Shane roughly. 'Our man watching the place reported he stayed there about two hours. Probably shagged her.'

The Chairman smiled. 'I suspect not, somehow.'

Shane shrugged. 'Anyway we have enough.'

'We filmed him in the distribution centre?' asked the Chairman.

'We have him on film taking the shipment of counterfeiting drugs into the warehouse,' said Shane. 'I don't appear. Just him. And we have tapes of him talking about selling formulae for money. My voice is not identifiable. Just his.'

'There should be plenty to make the story stick,' interrupted Wheeler.

The Chairman looked across at his PR man. 'And Ling?'

'Plenty to make the story stick on her as well,' Wheeler replied. 'The documentary evidence is all in place.'

The Chairman sighed. 'It is a little earlier than I wanted to act.'

'Not all the variables were ever going to be entirely under our control,' said Wheeler. 'I think this is the time.'

Glancing towards the window, the Chairman noticed the first red streak of a fierce sunset. 'Very well,' he said quietly. 'Proceed.'

Jack instructed the computer to dial into his Internet connection; Tara had assured him that it was the safest way of communicating. He had his doubts, reminding her that the Internet was

154

notoriously insecure, but Tara insisted that such an anarchic and chaotic system made it extremely difficult to find anything. Jack trusted her. She was far more computer-literate than he was.

He waited a few minutes while an irritating slice of net babble downloaded itself on to his computer. There was the usual stack of files; ads for computer parts; technical problems and advice with the system; and the heap of gormless messages from anoraks. Jack brushed past it and clicked on to the e-mail function. A message was waiting for him.

To: keef@pill.demon.co.uk//from sharon@labb.demon.co.uk: Found the Zmitt files. I think I have the connection. We need to talk.

Jack clicked on to reply, and began typing: 'OK. Can you come round here tonight? Pick me up outside and we'll go somewhere else. Somewhere public, where we can be safe?' He pressed send, and watched the message disappear down through the modem. Tara's message had been sent at seven-fifteen and it was now a quarter to eight. He hoped that she was still at home, and had her machine switched on to receive the message.

There was not long to wait. Jack had wandered through to the kitchen to make himself a coffee. As he stirred the granules and the boiling water, he was wondering what the files Tara had discovered would reveal. By the time he returned, the 'message waiting' signal was flashing on his screen. Jack keyed into read, and the message flashed up on the screen.

To: keef@pill.demon.co.uk//from: dani@century. compuserve.co.uk: I don't know what you are planning or why, but it is time to move. Kizog are about to act.

Jack's heart froze. They knew his e-mail address, or at least Dani Fuller did. Perhaps they had read his conversations with Tara. In which case, he should try to warn her at once.

It was too late. The 'message pending' signal was flashing

again, and Jack pulled it up on to the screen.

> To: keef@pill.demon.co.uk//from: sharon@labb.demon.co.uk:
> Got your message. Coming right over. See you soon.

Jack walked away from the screen. He dialled Tara's number. It rang and rang, but there was no answer. He hung up. Obviously she had already left. There was nothing to be done now except to wait. She would be here soon enough.

He drank the coffee and paced nervously around the room. The importance of the message from Dani was taking time to sink in. What did she mean by saying Kizog was planning to act? And why was she contacting him with the information? A warning? If so, what was the point?

What game was she playing now?

His nerves were starting to fray. His stomach was alive with butterflies, and he could start to feel a headache pounding away at the back of his skull. Time to move, the message had said. The source was probably hostile, but that was not necessarily a reason to disregard it. Jack put on his overcoat, and checked he had his wallet and his credit cards on him. There was thirty quid in his pocket, all the cash he had on him. It would have to do.

Stepping outside into the cool night air, he looked up and down the street. He could see nothing suspicious. But then, what do I know? he reminded himself. Anything could be going on. He walked up to the end of the street, checking the main road, wondering if he could wave at Tara as she approached his flat. He had decided he would be happier if she wasn't seen there. After a couple of minutes he realised it was useless. This road was not the only way into the street. And he might miss her entirely.

Up in the distance he could see two men were standing outside his flat. Tall men, wearing slacks and sports jackets. Under the dim street-lamps they were almost indistinguishable. Probably henchmen of Shane's, thought Jack. Trouble.

They looked unthreatening. There was no menace in their

stance, nor in their expressions. But they were blocking the entrance. There was no way Jack could walk past them. He slowed slightly as he approached the entrance to the building, and the taller of the two men, edged forward slightly to confront him. 'Mr Borrodin?' he asked.

'Yes,' answered Jack, trying to pump some confidence into his voice.

'Inspector Lamming, Scotland Yard,' he said. 'This is Inspector Gilbert.'

He pulled a wallet from his pocket and flashed an identification badge in front of Jack. The second man stood to attention and did the same. Jack glanced at the badges but realised he had no idea whether they were genuine. He could not recall ever having seen a police badge before.

'Yes,' he answered cautiously. 'What do you want?'

'We need to ask you some questions,' said Lamming.

'About what?'

'About the counterfeiting of pharmaceutical products,' Lamming replied. 'We have reason to believe you may be involved in the manufacture and supply of counterfeit substances.'

Jack paused. 'What reason?' He was trying to control himself, but he could hear the fractures in his voice, and he knew he was betraying his nervousness.

'We can discuss that later,' said Lamming. 'If you would like to accompany us down towards the station.'

Jack turned and looked about himself, his eyes swivelling up and down the street. Nobody was present, but at the top of the road he could just see a car approaching. 'I'd like to call a lawyer.'

'You're not under arrest,' snapped Lamming. 'This is just questioning. You can call a lawyer if we charge you.'

The navy-blue Golf GTI was closer now, its driver slowing down as she scanned the numbers on the door, looking for Jack's apartment. 'If you come this way,' said Lamming, extending an arm towards Jack.

The tone was fierce and harsh, a voice that allowed no room

for disagreement. Jack turned on his heels. The Golf was nearing the side of the kerb, slowing down to just a few miles an hour. Unthinkingly, Jack lunged several strides towards the car. The two detectives made a grab for him, but their reach just failed to catch him. He tried the door. Unlocked. Thank God, he whispered to himself. He pulled the door open, leapt into the seat, slamming it hard behind him, pushing down the lock.

Tara turned to look at him, her expression a mixture of bemusement and bafflement. 'Jack,' she started. 'What is it?'

'Drive,' he shouted. 'Please, just drive. Drive as fast as you fucking can.'

As the wheels spun on the Tarmac Jack turned to look out of the rear window. The detectives had already started climbing into their car.

FIFTEEN

The scent of her body next to his was warm and intoxicating. Tara was lying at Jack's side, half asleep, the side of her face creased up into the pillow, her lips slightly apart, the sound of her breathing slow and steady. Her long black hair nestled up against the thick white, hotel dressing gown she had wrapped around herself. It was, Jack reflected, some time since he had slept with a woman.

Tara and he had tumbled into bed together as if it was the most natural thing in the world, but they had not made love. Since yesterday, Jack felt, they shared a bond; the comfort of refuge. They were running from the same monsters. It was intimacy of a sort, a closer intimacy than Jack had felt for a long time, but not yet sexually charged. They shared common fears, not hopes. That might come, thought Jack. Perhaps. In time.

He ran his hand along her hair and along her back. She murmured something – what, he could not hear – under her breath.

159

But otherwise she paid no attention to his caresses. Don't push it, thought Jack. Not now. Too soon and too dangerous.

Neither of them had known what to do at first. He had leapt into her car on an instinct; it was an unthinking reaction to an immediate threat. In those split seconds Jack had thought very quickly, and it was only afterwards that he rationalised and organised his decision. If the detectives wanted to talk to him about his involvement in the counterfeiting ring, if they had grounds for suspicion, their information could only have come from one place: Kizog. And if the company had talked to the police, he could be certain they would have lined up evidence and Jack would be trapped. No. He needed his own time and space to act. He would not allow Kizog to dictate events. The company was not a friendly presence in his life.

Tara had not questioned him when he asked her to drive. She had not stopped and asked for any explanation for what was happening. Her reaction, too, was instinctive and immediate. To assist. She had slammed her foot hard on the accelerator, and disappeared down the road, both of them silent, while Jack peered desperately through the back window, searching for signs of the policemen on their backs. She had been there when he needed someone. And he was grateful for that.

Neither of them had known where to go. Tara headed across the river and twisted her way through the streets of south London, until Jack assured her that they were not being followed. In truth, he was not sure, and the uncertainty worried him. He had never been followed before; never scanned the streets for someone who might be trailing him. He was not sure what to look for. Several times he was suspicious of cars that seemed to be behind them for several miles, but as they drove through empty residential streets they appeared to lose them. He scanned the skies. Helicopters, perhaps? he thought. But he could see nothing. Unless their tracking devices were very sophisticated – more sophisticated than he could imagine – they were free.

Free, but far from safe, he reflected. The instinct of the moment had told him to flee, to evade whatever questions the

160

police might have for him, but so far he had given little thought to what happened next. Keep on running? he asked himself. The adrenalin of the escape had drained now that he was clear of immediate danger, and in its place there were only questions and doubts. How far? How long? Perhaps he should turn back, talk to those men, explain himself, tell his story. Perhaps.

In time. But not now.

'Where shall we go?' Tara had asked once they were clear of the immediate threat.

'I don't know,' Jack had replied. 'Just away from here. Out of London.'

Tara turned on to the M25, and drove along until they reached the M40, heading out past Oxford, finally turning off into the Cotswolds. They drove almost in silence. Jack was preparing his thoughts, pondering his options, and wondering what they would do next. He sensed that she was doing the same. He understood that she was anxious to escape as well. There was more than just kindness to this trip; she had not just taken pity on him and decided to help him escape. Too unlikely. No. She too wanted to escape, and was glad, he sensed, of some companionship.

They had been driving for three hours and it was after eleven when Tara pulled up the car in a small town called Northleach. She parked in the square, and the pair of them climbed out. It was typical rural England. A fine old mill town, with a market square and a high street full of familiar shops. The pubs were just shutting and a few people were starting to make their way home through the dark and empty streets. It was peaceful and tranquil, a good place to relax. A good place to rearrange your priorities. 'We'll stay here,' said Tara firmly.

There was a tone in her voice that did not invite disagreement, and Jack was happy to let her take control. She walked into the single hotel in town, an eighteenth-century building with three stars, and booked a room. Jack was surprised that she booked a double, but said nothing about it as they walked upstairs. 'Get some rest,' she told him as they entered the room. 'We'll decide what to do in the morning.'

161

'I'll sleep on the floor,' Jack volunteered.

Tara shook her head. 'You need some proper rest. And you're too much of a wreck to try anything.'

They had left the conversation there. Both found they were so tired, there was little talk or speculation left in them. Just a desire to put the day behind them, to make it disappear. They lay down together, and no sooner had Jack felt the pillow on his head, and the sound of her breathing at his side, than he fell into a fitful sleep.

Jack woke first, lying in the early morning light, reviewing the events of the past few days, turning them over in his mind. They still made little sense. When Tara woke, he said good-morning with a formality that seemed forced and strained. She asked him what time it was, and he told her that it was just after eight.

They both showered, taking exaggerated care to dry and dress behind a closed bathroom door, before they went downstairs to breakfast. Jack found that his appetite had grown; a reaction to the stress, he suggested to himself. He ordered a full English breakfast, whilst Tara contented herself with a croissant and an apple and some black tea. From the lobby Jack had picked up copies of the *Telegraph* and the *FT*. He rustled through the papers, distracted briefly by the market report – Kizog was up 8p, it said, on hopes of a swift conclusion to the Ocher bid – before he found what he had feared.

The story was nestling on page five of the *Telegraph*. 'Drug Counterfeiters Sought', said the headline. Jack read intently.

Police are hunting down a ring of pharmaceutical counter-feiters who are believed to be operating throughout Europe. Officers yesterday attempted to arrest an unnamed executive of a leading British pharmaceutical company who is believed to be working with the counterfeiters, but the executive evaded capture. Police sources said last night that a nation-wide hunt was underway for the man. He is understood to be working with a researcher at the same company who may also be involved in the counterfeiting operation. Pharmaceutical counterfeiting is a growing problem in Europe. The police warn that many of the counterfeit medicines may be of substandard quality, and could pose a significant health risk to patients. Police sources said the manhunt was part of a wider European initiative to crack down on pharmaceutical counterfeiting.

Jack handed the paper to Tara. 'We're famous,' he said.

Jack ate his breakfast whilst she scanned the paper. He felt numb inside, and his appetite was already starting to disappear. The events of yesterday had faded in his mind; he had begun to wonder if it was all a mistake, something that could be talked through rationally. Now he knew there had been no mistake. They had wanted him, and they would have arrested him. A manhunt, he reflected. He was the man. Jack glanced around the breakfast room. There were two other couples, and one person sitting alone. None of them appeared to be looking at him. Why should they? They would never suspect that he was a wanted man.

'At least it doesn't mention us by name,' said Tara, putting down the paper.

She seemed, to Jack, strangely calm. 'Do we keep running?' he asked.

Tara shook her head. 'We are amateurs,' she said. 'We don't know where to run. We don't know where to hide. Sooner or later we will be caught.'

Jack noticed the look in her eye; fiery, determined, defiant. It was a transformation, different from the mood of worldly indifference he had associated with Tara up until now, and one that heightened her appeal. 'Is there still a chance?' he asked.

'What other options do we have?' replied Tara.

'None,' answered Jack.

'Then we fight back,' said Tara firmly.

Jack looked at her closely, wondering if he could find anything in her eyes. 'What was too personal to talk about earlier?' he asked slowly.

She turned her face away before replying. 'Someone I lost,' she said hesitantly.

'Who?' asked Jack, leaning forward across the table.

'A boyfriend,' she replied.

Jack had never imagined her as part of a couple, and the idea of her having a sexual history took him sideways; he was, he reflected, feeling something that could only be described as jealousy. 'Long-term or short-term?' he asked.

'Very long-term,' she replied. 'Years.'

The word captured the sadness in her eyes, and Jack realised that they had never really talked, that there had been little real intimacy between them. She started by telling him something of her childhood, about her time at Harvard, and about the young man she had met there. David was three years older than her, and studying as a postgrad medical student. They met in her first year, and by the second term they were dating regularly, a couple. They spent three years together, living in a small apartment they shared, working towards their separate degrees.

Tara had been sure that they would spend the rest of their lives together. It seemed the most natural thing in the world, and there was nothing she wanted more. And so, when he decided to spend a year after graduation working with Médicins Sans Frontières, it seemed to her a matter of little importance. They had their whole lives together. What difference did one year make?

He was posted to Angola. Tara went to visit him there once. They spent two weeks together, roaming around the South African savannah by Jeep; Angola itself was too dangerous for a vacation. That was the last she really saw of him. She had gone back and waited for him to return. In the last month of his tour she received word from the camp director that David was seriously ill. She flew at once, arriving only thirty-six hours after receiving the message. It was too late. David was not quite dead yet, but he was far beyond knowing who she was or what was happening to him. His body was almost totally paralysed, incapable of any form of movement, and strange dark spots, where the skin was rapidly peeling loose from the body, had appeared on his arms and legs and back. He seemed to have lost all feeling, the nerves inside his body seizing up, and when a finger fell loose from his hand, it was as if he had not felt it. A raging fever had left him close to deranged, and the paralysis had made it virtually impossible for him to drink, exacerbating the fever and causing him to dehydrate rapidly. The doctors had pumped him full of antibiotics but none of them seemed to have any impact. Tara spent the last few hours desperately trying to pour water into his parched throat, but it was no use. His glands were too swollen or hardened for any of the water to reach his body. It was the dehydration that finally killed him. Within twelve hours of her arrival, David was dead. Although Tara did not know it at the time, it was one of the first cases of Ator taking a Western victim.

'So you see,' Tara said, the words pronounced slowly and clearly, 'this disease is very personal to me. I was devastated by the loss. I still am, and it seemed the only thing I could do, the only thing that would keep me sane, was to spend my life finding out about Ator, discovering what caused it and how it could be cured.'

Jack had listened intently as she rushed through the story, captured by the vividness and pain of her recollections, and realising for the first time the intensity of emotion she brought to her investigations into the origins of the virus. He leant over the table and reached for her palm, surprised by the willingness with which she accepted his hand in hers. 'OK,' he said. 'We fight back.'

The meeting was just breaking up when the Chairman called Simon Morrison to one side. It had gone well. The bankers and brokers had all gathered with the key Kizog executives for a final session before everyone disappeared to the country for the weekend. The bid closed in seven days' time, and next week would be crucial. Kizog had already bought eight per cent of Ocher's stock in the market, and their share price was languishing just below the offer price. There were rumours of a counter-bid but so far no

165

sign of another offer. 'Just the usual market chatter,' said Morrison reassuringly.

Privately, the Chairman wanted to thank Morrison for all the hard work he and his team had been putting into the bid. And he wanted to warn him that there might be some rather strange reports in the papers this weekend, and to reassure him that it was nothing to worry about. 'We have everything under control,' he said quietly.

Morrison nodded and said he understood. 'I can't see much going wrong now,' he replied. 'We should be able to shake loose another seven or eight per cent of the stock next week, once our chaps start ringing round the small holders. The big fund managers here and in the States will side with us, so I think we only have to capture a few of the Swiss shareholders and it's ours.'

'It's virtually sewn up?'

'Virtually,' Morrison replied.

The Chairman thanked him, collected Ralph Finer, and strode back towards his own office. Just one more meeting, he told the finance director. And then they would be done for the week.

'Almost there, Chairman,' said Finer as they walked through the corridor.

'Almost,' replied the Chairman. 'A few more loose ends, but I think we can make it.'

'How did your conversations with the Government go?' he asked.

'Perfectly,' the Chairman replied confidently. 'They swallowed the whole story and have agreed to co-operate. Quite an achievement, don't you think?'

There was a nervous look on Finer's face. 'They can be trusted?' he asked.

The Chairman nodded. 'The Ministry of Defence is as deeply involved in everything that has happened in the past as we are,' he replied. 'And just as keen to put that episode behind them. The ministers are in the dark, of course, but their officials know what needs to be done.'

166

'We are sure?' persisted Finer.

'Of course,' answered the Chairman with a smile. 'I have made it quite clear to them. We all swim together or we all sink together. They understand.'

The finance director smiled. 'Fine,' he said confidently.

'You know,' continued the Chairman, patting his finance director on the shoulder. 'That applies to the company as well. We sink or swim together.'

Inside his office, Geoff Wheeler, Dani Fuller and Angus Shane were already waiting for them. Wheeler and Fuller stood up when the Chairman came in, but Shane remained seated, his body slunk back into the deep leather sofa. The Chairman walked over to the cabinet and pulled out a decanter of whisky. Time for a drink, he declared, pouring himself a shot and offering the decanter around. Wheeler and Shane accepted. Fuller and Finer declined.

'You saw the story about our two young friends in the paper this morning, I trust?' the Chairman said to Wheeler. The PR man nodded. 'A good journalist?'

'Very reliable,' replied Wheeler. 'Writes it straight, pretty much as it is given to him. We may use him again.'

The Chairman took the paper and passed it on to both Dani Fuller and Angus Shane. Shane took it and glanced through the story before passing it on to Fuller.

'What's the gameplan?' asked Fuller. 'With the media.'

A broad smile spread across Wheeler's puffy red cheeks. 'Deception and subterfuge,' he replied.

The Chairman smiled indulgently at his PR man. 'I think our colleagues need a little more explanation,' he said.

Wheeler swept a hand through what remained of his hair. 'The media love a good story. That is the key to dealing with the press. Journalists are often smart and dedicated people, but spin a good yarn and they are absolute suckers. They will believe anything.'

'So we spin a good yarn?' said Fuller.

'Absolutely, my dear,' replied Wheeler. 'I have arranged for a close contact of mine at the Ministry of Defence press office to leak some papers to a chap from the *Observer*, probably later on today. For some strange reason any leak from the MoD is automatically believed by the chaps in the media, and reprinted more or less verbatim. Never seems to occur to them that it might not be true.' Wheeler opened up his briefcase and pulled out a sheaf of papers. He gave one set to the Chairman and deposited the rest on the coffee-table. 'I think we should all look through this before I press the button.'

The Chairman took a sip of his drink and sat down before casting his eyes down at the document. He read slowly, drinking in the words, and a thin smile started to spread over his lips as he neared the end. Carefully, he put the document down. 'Is it credible?' he asked.

'The police have already bought it,' said Wheeler. 'We have already prepared documents, routed through the Bangkok office, showing Borrodin was first involved in counterfeiting there. We have plenty of evidence here in the UK of him handing over formulae, and, of course, infiltrating fake drugs into our warehouse. His fingerprints are everywhere.'

'And Ling?'

'We have prepared evidence that the real Tara Ling was assassinated about eight months ago by the racketeers, and replaced with this impostor, who works for them. For example, the DNA records taken of all employees at the National Institutes have been changed. That should prove pretty conclusively that she is not who she says she is.'

Finer looked doubtful. 'We need actual fingerprints.'

Wheeler fished inside his case, pulling out a photograph. He handed a copy to the Chairman, who passed it on to the other people in the room. It showed a man lying face in the dirt, blood trickling from his head. Shane took the picture, gazed down at it, and allowed a smile to spread across his lips.

'I have already seen this,' said the Chairman.

'Look closely,' replied Wheeler. 'You see something is in his breast pocket.'

Shane passed the picture back, and the Chairman squinted, trying to make out the image. 'Just,' he replied.

'The picture, of course, can be blown up,' continued Wheeler. He looked again inside his case, pulling out a negative, this time eight inches by ten. He passed it across to the Chairman. The negative had been enlarged twenty times, showing just the area around his breast pocket. This time the image was quite clear. Sticking from his pocket was a pair of documents, and a photograph. The picture was instantly recognisable to everyone in the room. Same long black hair, same eyes, same features; Tara Ling.

'The originals are being held by the Thai police, who would of course be happy to co-operate with the authorities here in Britain,' continued Wheeler. 'The documentation suggests the dead man was investigating on behalf of the World Pharmaceuticals Forum, when he discovered the links between the counterfeiters and the spread of Ator. He was looking for Miss Ling, but he knew too much, and was executed by the counterfeiters. It is plausible evidence.'

'Quite so,' said the Chairman. 'And this story can be in the papers on Sunday?'

'Certainly sir,' replied Wheeler. 'In the *Observer* on Sunday morning, followed up by the TV and radio people all day, and it will be in all the papers on Monday morning. We will have our PR agency working on it. We haven't told them the truth, of course. They don't expect it.'

'And the spin on the bid is prepared?' asked the Chairman.

'We will reveal nothing that contradicts the case for taking over Ocher,' replied Wheeler. 'The counterfeiting will be portrayed as a minor problem, which the excellence of our internal controls has uncovered. I think we can make that a plus-point for the company. And the revelations about the Ator virus will only improve our case for creating an organisation large enough to bring the vaccine to the market as rapidly as possible.'

'I see just one problem,' said Shane.

The three other people in the room turned to face him. 'Which is?' said the Chairman.

'Borrodin and Ling turn up to deny everything,' he stated bluntly.

The Chairman shook his head. 'I think we know how to cover that eventuality,' he whispered.

'There is something more to be done?' asked Fuller.

'Quite so,' replied the Chairman. 'The police are looking for them. So too are our friends at the Ministry. We have evidence against them, of course. All of you have done your work very well. But although it will be enough to explain the situation away, it might not be enough to survive a full-blown trial. Those things are very public. People have rights. Disclosure and so on. Also, I don't think our friends in government can be relied upon to support us all the way through such a thing. When the heat is turned up those people have a tendency to get out of the kitchen.'

Shane smiled. 'He wants us to kill them. The police will do that if necessary, but I wouldn't guarantee their boys can shoot straight. And the Ministry can't give an explicit order to shoot to kill. Too risky.'

'Quite so,' whispered the Chairman. 'I think that would be better for all of us, don't you. If this matter were handled primarily by company staff. People we can rely on.'

Shane squeezed his hands together. 'It only takes a couple of seconds.'

The Chairman turned away from his audience, his expression downcast. 'It is time to wipe the slate absolutely clean,' he said.

SIXTEEN

Jack sat back on the bed and buried his face in his hands. He was tired and confused. And the story Tara had just outlined to him was frightening and disturbing. He needed to rest his mind for a moment and rearrange his thoughts.

He had suspected, of course. Tara had already aired her theories, and he had felt in his heart that she might well be right. But now it all appeared inevitable; a conspiracy that was unfolding like clockwork before them. There could be no doubt.

For the first time, everything became very clear to Jack. 'We must make them pay,' he said firmly.

Tara shook her head. 'Perhaps,' she replied. 'But we must look after ourselves as well.'

After breakfast, they had gone back up to the hotel room. They had given false names at the desk, and Jack figured they could at least stay there until check-out time with little risk of detection or of questions being asked. They needed somewhere they could talk. Somewhere they could be sure their conversation would not be overheard.

Jack lay back on the bed, staring up at the ceiling, and at the single light bulb that shone dimly from the centre of the room. 'How much do we know?' he asked.

'Too much,' answered Tara. 'And not enough.'

Jack smiled. She was right, of course, he realised. 'Start at the beginning,' he said. 'Tell me everything.'

'It was an older doctor who started me on what I now realise was the right path,' Tara began. 'His name was Samuel Toboto, a Nigerian, who had been working for years in different medical camps around the African continent. He was almost sixty, with white hair, and his long exposure to every disease on the continent appeared to have left him immune to every virus and bacteria it could throw at him. It was he who sat with me through David's last hours, trying to coax some water into his body and comforting me as his life slipped away. Some hours later, having given me most of the rum that he always carried in a flask in his jacket pocket, he said something that has remained with me ever since. He said that it looked to him as if David had died of leprosy.'

Tara hesitated, running her fingers through her hair before continuing. 'I objected, of course. Leprosy takes years and years to develop, incubating in the body, and only becoming visible once it reaches its final stages. Even then, it would be still more years before the patient would die. Dr Toboto agreed. It was certainly nothing like any of the cases of leprosy he had treated before. Even so, the symptoms seemed eerily reminiscent of what was still one of the most feared diseases on the continent. It was just a hunch he had.'

Tara explained how she had thrown herself into her studies, as a way of escaping her grief. Soon afterwards she had joined the National Institutes. She specialised in viruses. In particular, she specialised in leprosy. 'There were already plenty of people around the world researching Ator,' she said sadly. 'Most were treating it as an entirely new disease, or else as some kind of mutation. I was treating it as a form of leprosy.'

'You knew all along?' asked Jack.

'That the disease was related to leprosy, yes,' replied Tara. 'Not that Kizog had anything else to do with it. But that is why I was so intrigued when Dr Scott said the company believed Ator was related to leprosy. I thought they might be taking the same path as me, and exploring whether it was some sort of mutation.'

There were two main forms of leprosy, Tara explained carefully; lepromatous and tuberculoid. Because of the symptoms she had observed in David, she assumed that it was tuberculoid that she needed to investigate, and it was that which consumed her time for the next few years. Leprosy is a cunning and elusive condition, she explained. Relatively little is known about the transmission mechanism, except that it can be communicated through both skin contact with the broken sores that appear on a leper's body and inhalation; it is breathed out through the nose. In both cases prolonged contact is usually needed for the virus to be transmitted from one person to the next.

The irony of leprosy, she went on, is that it is the body's re-action rather than the virus itself which causes the damage. After invading the body, the virus seeps into the victim's bloodstream. Body cells rush into the infected area in an attempt to seal it. This intense cellular reaction soon makes itself visible in a hardening of the skin surface above the infected area; underneath the tissues, sweat glands and nerve fibrils are thickened by the rush of cells. On the skin, a round, dry spot appears where the victim has no sense of heat, cold or touch; the senses are all gone. The cellular reaction then continues along the main trunk of the nerve, strangling it, causing a loss of all power in the infected area, since the brain can no longer transmit any signals through the nerve. Blood can no longer circulate through the area. In time, it will simply wither and die, like a dead branch on a tree, and one day it will just fall off. All of these reactions are caused by the ultimately futile attempt by the body to defend itself against the infection.

Tara finished the science lesson. She walked across the hotel

173

room, and towards the sports bag she had brought with her. It had no clothes in it. Just papers. 'I was planning to show you these when I came over,' she explained.

Jack glanced down at the sheaves of photocopied papers. There were endless series of small scribbled notes and scientific equations. It made no sense to him, but he knew at once what they were. The private research papers of Josef Zmitt. 'Do they get us any further?' Jack asked.

'Much,' Tara replied. She started to explain. The private papers had been in a terrible mess and it had taken her several days just to sort them out. There could be little doubt that leprosy had the potential at least to be a very effective battlefield weapon. The key was in its effectiveness on the nerve system. By inducing paralysis it had the ability to render men unfit for any form of combat very quickly. And unlike nerve gases it did not have be delivered by rocket or other risky means of delivery. A handful of special forces working behind enemy lines could trigger the virus. Once planted it would do all the work needed by natural processes. After the button was pressed, the rest went like clock-work.

There were two flaws. One was that leprosy worked very slowly. The time it took to damage the body was too long for any kind of military effectiveness. And the transmission mechanism was too weak. Tara started looking through the paperwork. She reached a page she wanted and pointed at a list of formulae. It meant nothing to Jack. Here, she said, is the molecular structure of tuberculoid leprosy. She turned the pages until she reached the next page she wanted. When she found it she pointed at the new formula. 'He found a way to speed it up,' she said.

'He added something to the virus?' asked Jack.

Tara shook her head, 'He subtracted from it. It's quite brilliant really.'

Jack was still confused. Tara explained that a virus is a living creature, and its instinct is to stay alive as long as possible. The last thing it wants to do is kill off the host body. As it evolved, probably thousands of years ago, it got slower and slower. That was the best way to stay alive as long as possible. Here, she said, pointing to another page, is the identification of the enzyme that governs the rate of replication; the slice of genetic code that dictates when and why it reproduces. It is programmed to move very slowly. As far as Tara knew that was the first time anyone had identified that enzyme; it was a fantastically advanced piece of research for the late sixties, less than a decade after the discovery of genetic code. 'If you could extract this one enzyme then you would have a virus that replicated itself at a dramatic rate, doubling itself at roughly twenty-four-hour intervals. The victim would not survive more than a few days.'

'Zmitt took it out?' Jack asked.

Tara shook her head. Not quite, she said. 'The technology of genetic engineering was still very primitive in those days; nothing like as advanced as it became during the eighties. Removing an enzyme is technically much simpler than inserting one, which must have been why Zmitt hit upon the route of subtraction from an already deadly virus rather than creating a new virus from scratch. It was the only scientifically feasible technique to use at the time. But all he had done so far was map out the task.'

Tara turned a few more pages. The second problem with leprosy was the slow rate of transmission. To work as an effective weapon it would have to be speeded up. Zmitt had worked his way through this problem as well. His published work had established a link between the rate of transmission and the weight and complexity of the viral molecule. Hence a condition such as the common cold was very easily transmitted because of the relative simplicity of the virus. Fortunately it also did very little harm. Leprosy, by contrast, was a complex molecule. But not all of it was necessary to trigger the rush of cells towards the invader that created the paralysis in the victim. Zmitt's reasoning, outlined in his private papers, was that as the complexity of the molecule was stripped down, so the speed and rate of transmission of the virus would increase exponentially. His task, to which he appeared to have devoted several years of research and many hours of laborious experimentation, was how to strip down

175

the molecule to a size that would speed up transmission without losing any of its deadly effectiveness.

Tara turned forward through many pages of scribbled notes and diagrams until she found what she was looking for. She handed the sheet of paper across to Jack. 'It's Ator,' she said. 'A blueprint for the molecule that causes the disease.'

'And you think that this is the blueprint that Zmitt gave to Kizog?'

'Better,' replied Tara. 'I can prove it.'

She stood up and walked back towards the sports bag, pulling out some more documentation. 'We know that Zmitt and Dr Scott worked together,' she said. 'We can prove that from the published work, and from the notes in Dr Scott's laboratory which make reference to Zmitt. All we need to know for sure is that they worked together on this.'

She handed another sheet of paper to Jack. It was clearly an internal lab record from Kizog, and it had both Dr Scott's and Sir Kurt Helin's signatures on it. Apart from that the maze of diagrams and complex chemical formulae meant nothing to Jack. He glanced up at her, his eyes asking the question.

'Zmitt did all the basic research,' said Tara, her voice cracking slightly as she spoke. 'And the Kizog laboratories did all the development. They created it. Ator is their molecule.'

Geoff Wheeler introduced Shane as a consultant to Kizog on corporate security. Inspector Gilbert eyed the man suspiciously; he was well aware there were some rough elements working in the security business, and that multinationals often had to employ people to work for them in Third World countries that they would prefer not to have had on the head office payroll. But this was not the sort of man you expected to find lurking in the head office. Still, he had been told by his superiors to co-operate with the company. And he would do as he was told.

'He has done invaluable work in investigating the conspiracy that Borrodin and Ling are mixed up in,' explained Wheeler, his hand reaching out towards Shane. 'If it were not for him I don't think we would have been in a position to stop them.'

The police inspector nodded and cleared his throat. A thin, wiry man, with a tense energy about him, Wheeler noted that he appeared uncomfortable with his surroundings. 'We are very grateful for the information you have supplied,' he began. 'It was unfortunate that our efforts to collect Mr Borrodin for questioning did not work out as we had planned.'

Shane grimaced. He knew, of course, why their efforts had failed. It had been his idea to have Fuller warn them of what was about to happen, and the trick had played out exactly as he hoped it would. After all, he reflected, the last thing they wanted was to see them captured by the police. 'We need them caught, you know,' he said.

Wheeler leant across the table. 'The company is involved in a major acquisition,' he interrupted. 'I needn't tell you that this is one of Britain's largest companies, and it is of course vital for the country that the take-over is successful. I know the Government shares our view of how important this matter is, and I trust they have made their feelings known.'

The Inspector nodded. 'We are treating it as a top priority,' he replied calmly. 'You may be certain of that.'

'All we know so far is that they escaped some time on Friday evening,' said Shane. 'It is now Saturday morning, and we have no idea of where they are.'

'They were last seen driving south through London,' said Gilbert. 'We don't know if they had a destination in mind, or whether they were just trying to shake us. I suspect the latter. Assuming they did not drive all night, they could be anywhere in the southern half of the country by now.'

'Do we know if they are still in the country?' asked Shane.

'Soon after they escaped we contacted the port inspectors with instructions to detain the pair of them on sight,' replied the Inspector. 'They could have made it down to Gatwick in an hour or so and jumped on the first flight with spare seats, but I doubt it. The police there are checking the flight details yesterday evening and can find no trace of them. Unless they had false passports and credit cards arranged, I think we can assume they are still in the country.'

Shane felt confident they would have neither false passports nor credit cards available, nor would they know where to get them. But, for the moment, he preferred to keep that information to himself. 'How soon do you think you can find them?' he asked.

'All the usual procedures are being put in place,' replied Gilbert. 'The best way to find any person is through their money. Nobody can live without money. We have alerted the banks that we want an immediate notification of any transactions they make involving plastic.'

'How quick is that?' asked Wheeler.

'Pretty fast,' replied Gilbert. 'It's basically the same system the banks use for stopping stolen cards. The list of stolen cards is transmitted constantly to all the electronic registers in the country over spare space on the BBC Ceefax system. Normally it just cancels the authorisation for the card. But at our request, it can also alert the machine to register its use by a suspect, and the retailer then knows to contact the bank. If they use a card, then we should know about it within two hours.'

'What else do you have?' asked Shane.

'They might try to withdraw cash from their bank accounts,' continued Gilbert. 'Their banks have been alerted to let us know if they do that, so again we could get a trace that way. Then there is the car. We have the registration number of the Golf they got away in, and we are alerting officers around the country to keep a watch for it. Our best hope on that front is that they trigger a speed camera. The database the cameras are connected to automatically alerts us when a suspect is photographed. That is often the best way of getting a trace. Most criminals don't pay much attention to speed limits.'

'We would like to be informed as well,' said Shane.

The Inspector frowned.

'We are very anxious to catch these people,' added Wheeler, his voice brimming with sincerity. 'We have our own resources,

178

and we should like to assist the police in any way we can.'

'A few extra men on the hunt can't hurt, can it?' said Shane.

The Inspector shook his head, recalling his explicit instructions to co-operate with the company. 'We'll let you know as soon as we have a trace on where they are,' he replied.

SEVENTEEN

Jack swept his hand across his brow and felt a trace of moisture. Sweat perhaps, he wondered. Get some guts, boy, he told himself. It's never over until it's over.

He glanced at his watch. It was a quarter to eleven. Not much longer before they would have to check out of the hotel and step back into the outside world. It was too risky to stay here. Tara was absolutely right. The game they were playing was heavy. Very heavy.

'Next Friday,' he told her. His voice was flat and calm, explaining each part of the puzzle as it fell into place in his own mind. 'The bid ends on Friday. Those are the Takeover Panel rules. If Kizog does not have a majority of acceptances from the Ocher shareholders by twelve noon on Friday, then the bid lapses.'

'That gives us six days,' said Tara.

'Do you know anyone at Ocher?' asked Jack.

180

'Not really, no,' replied Tara.

Jack paused for a moment. 'Then we will have to go through the merchant bank advising them in London,' he said. 'That's the only way it will work.' Through the fog of confusion, he believed he could see a way out. It lightened his mood, filling his mind with a sense of intellectual giddiness. 'Be patient,' he continued. 'Let me try this out on you step by step.'

'I've got all day,' answered Tara.

Jack stood up, and started pacing around the room. 'Let's identify what we know,' he began. 'I think everything has been staring us in the face all along. It is just a matter of seeing it.'

Tara nodded, and her evident enthusiasm encouraged Jack. For these few seconds, the images of arrest, trial, jails, images that had been crowding his mind, vanished, and he could think clearly. 'We know Kizog is involved in creating counterfeit drugs,' he persisted. 'We also know it is involved in creating biological weapons. In particular Ator, perhaps others. Now it is a private sector company, motivated by profit, so why would it be researching weapons? Where's the turn?'

'What's your guess?' asked Tara. 'It is known that some biochemists worked on biological weapons. But they usually worked in government laboratories.'

'Right. But this work is being done in a private company. Kizog is not a defence company, there is no division selling weapons. But there must be a profit in it somewhere.'

Tara's eyes narrowed as she focused on the question. 'So who are they working for?'

'I figure there are only three possible markets.' Jack replied. 'I suppose the old Soviet Union would have been interested. Back when that still existed. I suppose there are any number of Third World dictators who might be buyers. And then there is the West.'

'If you were approaching this as a commercial proposition, which market would you go for?' asked Tara.

Jack hesitated, considering the question carefully before he answered. 'I think I would be reluctant to do too much business

181

with the Soviet Communist Party. Too risky, and not enough money. I mean, we used to consider selling ordinary drugs in Russia, and it was never worth the hassle. There would be no way you would start making biological weapons for them. I suppose they might have paid reasonable money for weaponry. But the risk of detection would wipe out any potential return on capital to be made from the deal. The Third World is a better market. Certainly the oil-rich states. Those people would pay, and they would have the money. But it would still be very risky. It is hard to believe that the Government would be unaware for long of what you were doing. No. If you were going to do this, it would have to be for your own government. It would have to be licensed, contract work. With explicit permission. That is the only way it would stack up as a viable commercial proposition.'

'The British Government,' said Tara carefully, thinking aloud. 'That's who you think they are working for.'

Jack shrugged. 'The British, the Western alliance, who knows. I just figure they must be working for someone. A few days ago I would not have believed it possible. Now, I don't know. I'm just about ready to believe anything.'

He sat back down again, on the floor, leaning his back against the bed. Tara ruffled his hair with her hand, her fingers lingering for a moment, and her touch felt comforting. Briefly, he was deflated by the brutality of the logic he had been pursuing.

'We would need to prove that,' Tara said softly.

Jack looked across the table, peering into her eyes. The sparkle was still there. The glimmer of defiance. 'What do we still need?' he asked.

'Connections,' she replied, her voice edgy and uncertain 'We need to know the lines between the counterfeiting and the biological weapons. It must all be part of the same picture.'

True, thought Jack. 'And what do we want?'

A look of steely determination crossed Tara's face. 'To escape.'

They both paused, allowing the decision to settle in their minds. Jack knew they were taking a fearful risk. He sensed as well that the chances of success were slim. For a few grim seconds, he could feel the fear clouding his mind, blocking out all other thoughts. 'We take the information to Ocher's merchant bank,' he said eventually. 'That is the only way through. There is no point in going to the police, since we have no way of knowing who they will side with. We need a powerful ally, one that wants to see Kizog stopped, and the only candidate is Ocher.'

Jack could feel her hand reaching out, and grasping his palm. 'Until Friday,' she said.

The Chairman moved softly and silently through the corridors of the office, his feet making barely a sound as they stepped across the carpets. It was a Saturday morning, and, apart from the security guards down below, the place was almost empty; there might be a few scientists in the laboratories he supposed, but he rarely ventured into that part of the complex any more.

His work for the weekend was almost done now. Shane and Wheeler had already met with the police, and according to their reports they had agreed to inform them as soon as any trace of Ms Ling and Mr Borrodin came to light. And Wheeler had assured him that a story would be appearing in the papers the next morning revealing that they were the criminals behind both the counterfeiting racket and the creation and spread of Ator. Indeed, he told himself. My work is almost done now.

The Chairman permitted himself a leathery smile. It was, he acknowledged, something of a shame that matters had come to this. He peered down, through a plate-glass window at the end of the corridor, on to the complex below, and marvelled momentarily at the hundreds of millions tied up in investment, in research and patents and people. It was all very different when we started, he reminded himself. Momentarily, he recalled how the contract to work on biological weapons had first presented itself. His idea, he acknowledged, but not one he felt he should take any blame for. The Government needed the research. They knew, not just from the evidence Zmitt had presented, but from other sources as well, that the Soviets were dangerously ahead of the

183

West in biological weaponry. They knew they had to catch up; the virus gap had to be closed, as he himself, rather wittily he thought, had put it in one of the many memoranda he had written on the subject. And they knew as well that it had to be done secretly. The softer voices, which in a democracy always had to be given their say, would never permit open research into biological weapons. No. Operating secretly through a pharmaceutical company, with the payments never even appearing on any departmental budget, was the only way it could be done effectively. It was better even for the politicians not to know. Just a few of the senior officials at the Ministry. Men who, like him, understood the fierce realities of the world.

The Chairman turned, leaving the view of the complex behind him, and walked back along the corridor, his mind still full of reflections. The younger people could not understand how it was back then, he decided. How fearful the threat was. And how much had to be done secretly to counter it. Certainly, he conceded to himself, he was unhappy about the way things had ended up. The company, he knew, had painted itself into a corner. And it was his responsibility to find a way out. The burdens of office, he told himself with a smile.

Jack Borrodin he felt slightly sorry for. He recalled how he had spotted him some years ago as one of the new management intake, and had marked him down immediately as a likely looking prey. There were several facts in his favour. He was honest and trusting, a straightforward, deal-from-the-top-of-the-deck character, whose instinct was to believe what he was told. Both parents dead, no brothers or sisters. Perfect, he had decided. When Jack got into trouble there would be no one to help him Nor would there be anyone to grieve for him after he was gone. After all, he reflected, there is no point in creating more unhappiness than was strictly necessary. One does not, he told himself, like to think of oneself as a cruel man.

Tara Ling was another matter. The Chairman had nothing but contempt for her. Because she was Oriental, perhaps, he decided. He had never liked Orientals. Too calculating. And she was headstrong and arrogant, deluded by her own self-righteousness. Not the sort of woman he appreciated. No, he decided. The world would not be a poorer place for her absence from it.

Carefully, the Chairman turned the handle on the finance director's door, and stepped inside. He had not expected to see anyone inside and was merely completing his tour of the offices, and, on catching sight of Finer sitting at his desk, stepped back an inch. 'Just catching up on some work, Chairman,' said Finer, looking up from his computer screen.

'Quite so,' whispered the Chairman.

'Everything has been taken care of?'

'I believe so.'

Finer stood up from his chair and walked around to the front of his desk. 'I think you've done a tremendous job, sir,' he said.

The Chairman creased his lips into a thin smile. 'Nobody would know better than you how dire our figures would be looking without the extreme steps we have taken.'

'But it's complex,' said Finer. 'Can we be sure that everything will work out as we have planned?'

'One can never be sure,' the Chairman answered wearily. 'But there are only six days to go. Then all of this will be in the past.'

'And if something goes wrong?' Finer persisted. 'What then?'

The Chairman eyed him closely. 'Then we all go down together,' he smiled.

'True,' replied the finance director thoughtfully. 'We go down together.'

Jack checked his watch. It was just after twelve. He stared down at the number he had jotted down on a notepad after calling an old college acquaintance on one of the Sunday papers and took a deep breath. There was, he knew, no choice but to call. Right away. Carefully, deliberately, he punched the numbers into the keypad.

The phone rang only twice. 'Symonds,' said the voice on the other end of the line.

The tone was crisp, upper-class, public school and Oxbridge. Jack tried to recall what he knew about Julian Symonds. It wasn't much. The head of corporate finance at Zurich Financial was a respected City figure, one of the elderly grandees who had been around before Big Bang, and who had made a bundle of money when the firm he was a partner in was sold out to one of the financial conglomerates that moved into London in the late eighties. Jack was aware that he only worked on corporate defences, declining all invitations to act on behalf of hostile bidders, no matter how huge the fees might have been. He was known as a tough fighter, a man who would consider every trick, and push every tactic to its limit, if it was in the interests of his client.

'My name is Jack Borrodin,' said Jack crisply. There was a silence on the other end of the line. 'I don't believe you know me,' he added firmly.

Another pause. 'No, I don't believe I do,' replied Symonds at length.

'I work for Sir Kurt Helin,' said Jack. 'My title is special assistant to the Chairman.'

'Then I don't suppose you should be talking to me,' replied Symonds, his voice betraying surprise, but also a hint of interest.

'You may have heard of my colleague, Tara Ling. We are working together.'

'I think you should come to the point,' said Symonds firmly.

'We need your help.'

The pause was longer this time, and, though it was barely audible, Jack could hear the man sighing.

'I don't believe in dirty tricks,' said Symonds. 'I must warn you that if you are attempting to sell me information that might discredit your employers in the last few days of the bid then two things will happen. One is that I will tell you to go away. The other is that I will immediately inform your employers of your disloyalty.'

'There are things happening at Kizog that it is vital you know about. Nothing about this company or about this bid is as it appears.'

186

'How do you know that I won't immediately phone Sir Kurt to tell him that you have contacted me?' said Symonds bluntly.

'I don't,' replied Jack.

'You are taking a big chance.'

'I know,' said Jack. 'We'll risk it.'

Jack could feel his grip tightening on the receiver as he waited for the reply. 'If you'll chance it, so will I,' Symonds said. 'You have my address.'

Jack could feel the muscles in his finger start to loosen. 'Yes,' he answered.

'Six,' he said. 'I'll have about an hour free.'

EIGHTEEN

Tara came in a few minutes after he had finished talking with Symonds, and Jack greeted her with a smile, his spirits reviving at the sight of her coming through the door. He was, he realised, relieved to see her. He found that he hated being alone. Too many demons to prey upon his mind; demons which, for now, only she could banish.

He had told her about the phone call, pointing out that they had only six hours to make the appointment. No time to waste. She sat next to him on the bed, tucking up her legs beneath her. Carefully she opened up her bag and spread out a pile of notes from her purse. 'Just over £15,000, nearly all I have,' she explained. 'You must do the same. The banks are still open until lunchtime. Empty your account.'

'No credit cards?' asked Jack.

'Too easy to trace,' said Tara firmly. 'Any cash withdrawals, and any credit card transactions, will instantly reveal our location to the police and to Kizog as well. Cash is much safer. It can't be traced.'

Jack leant across and wrapped his arms around her body, cuddling her back between his palms. 'Not now,' she whispered. 'Too much to be done.'

They threw their few belongings into the one bag, and checked out of the hotel. Jack put the tab for this bill on his credit card. There was no point in worrying about being located now. The police would soon track them to this town from the cash withdrawals, and it wouldn't take them long to figure out where they had been staying. By then they would have left town.

Out on the street, in the midday sunshine, Jack explained about the car. 'We have to think of everything that might possibly reveal who and where we are,' he said. 'Better still, confuse them about where we are.'

'Fine,' answered Tara brightly. 'It's a Kizog car. Burn it.'

Jack shook his head. After withdrawing £6,000 from his account, all the cash he had, he approached a young man sitting alone on a bench on the village green. He asked him if he drove. The man said he did. Jack told him he would give him £200 to drive his car to Liverpool. There was no point in being too generous, he reasoned. He had no idea how much cash they might still need.

The man looked at him quizzically. 'Come again?' he muttered.

'You have to get this car to Liverpool, that's all. Leave it at the NCP car-park by Lime Street station and get the bus back. Six or seven hours' work. I need it there on Monday morning, but I'm spending the weekend with my girlfriend and we want to drive together.'

'How do you know I won't nick it?'

'Got some ID?' asked Jack.

The man pulled out his wallet and showed Jack a bank card with his name on it. Jack noted down the name. 'You nick it, I report you,' he said. 'Do we have a deal?'

The man nodded, stuffed the notes into his pocket and walked away, taking the keys with him. Tara and Jack located the one small second-hand car dealer on the outskirts of town. The Cortina was the cheapest vehicle on the forecourt. £350. Jack didn't bother to haggle, although he might have been able to get £50 off the price if he had tried. He counted out the notes and drove the car away. They had no insurance, but that was the least of their worries. They would probably break several more laws before the week was finished. In the meantime, they had safe transport. Jack figured it could take two or three days at least for the ownership of the car to be registered. They could use it until Tuesday, without fear of it being traced.

Jack wondered what sort of impression the car would make on Symonds. Tara was unfamiliar with the term Dagenham Dustbin, but it fitted the seventeen-year-old Ford Cortina perfectly. The underside was coated with a thick layer of rust, and the leopard-skin covers on the seats were pitted with cigarette burns. Not a classy motor, thought Jack. Not a machine to make them look like serious people in the eyes of a City merchant banker.

They drove through to Kent, taking the back roads, avoiding London. For the first hour or so they were mostly silent, both of them lost in their own thoughts, thinking through their own priorities. Jack raised the issue of money first. It had been prey-ing on his mind, gnawing inside him, and the issue, he realised, had to be confronted before they faced Symonds. 'Safety means money,' he told Tara firmly.

Though he was keeping his eyes on the road, Jack could feel an icy look descend upon him. 'For whom?' she asked.

'Say this works,' replied Jack evenly. 'We supply the inform-ation we have to Ocher and they use it to destroy Kizog. We get safe passage out of the country. What happens then? Our careers will be destroyed as well. Who knows when we work again, or for whom? This is our one shot. We either get everything right or nothing.'

'You want to demand money from Ocher?' said Tara, a tone of suspicion entering her voice. 'That makes us blackmailers.'

Jack shook his head. 'Not from Ocher,' he answered. 'From Kizog.'

'They pay us to keep quiet?' questioned Tara. 'I don't like it.'

'Much better than that,' said Jack. 'We profit from their destruction.'

Tara's eyes turned towards him across the front seat of the car. 'How?'

'When the bid is defeated, which it will be when this information comes to light, then the Kizog share price will sink like a stone. That we can be certain of. All we have to do is ask Symonds to use some of his bank's money to buy a series of put options in our name. A temporary loan, that's all. If we are successful, we collect a vast profit on the deal, and the bank gets its money back. The profits come from the speculators who are ramping the Kizog share price upwards.'

Tara sat back in her seat and said nothing. Jack had a point, she decided. They would need the money. And, so long as it was coming from Kizog, she could see no harm in it. After all, the company owed them something. 'How much money?' she said finally.

'We ask them to underwrite an options contract for two million,' answered Jack promptly, his mind racing ahead. 'My bet is that should multiply by a factor of ten or so within a day of the bid failing, clearing about twenty million in profits.'

Tara just nodded. It was getting close to six now, and they were approaching the village of Cranbrook, just outside Maidstone. Symonds had said his house was past the village, on the right, about a mile down the road from the village. They could hardly miss it; a Georgian mansion, built on two floors, with a long gravel driveway, large, well-tended grounds, a swimming-pool and tennis-courts. Jack pulled the car up alongside the gates and stopped. He climbed out, telling Tara to take the wheel and keep the engine running. 'I want to look around before we go in,' he said. 'If I am not back in five minutes, drive.'

'I'll wait,' she protested.

Jack shook his head. 'If Symonds has contacted the police and I'm arrested, I'd rather have you on the outside, collecting more evidence.'

191

Tara nodded, looked up at him, and smiled, but Jack could catch the tension in her eyes. Turning, he walked through the gates, and started up the driveway. Up ahead he could see a Jaguar and a Range Rover sitting on the gravel, but there was no sign of any other cars. Jack kept his eyes peeled for police, but he could see nothing.

He could hear the gravel crunching beneath his feet, and the door was no more than yards away now. Jack could feel his muscles tensing as he drew nearer, and his palms felt hot and sweaty. Madness, he thought for a moment. Why should Symonds have done anything other than call the police? Or even worse, contact the Chairman? There was still time to turn and drive, escape from here, and work out another plan.

He turned, casting a glance backwards at the Cortina. He saw Tara sitting at the wheel, her eyes fixed upon him, and could dimly hear the sound of the engine running. Steel yourself, he muttered to himself. If anyone is here, they will have seen you already. And the Cortina would never outrun anyone if it came to a chase.

Wiping the sweat from his palms, Jack took a deep breath, and rang the bell. The door was opened by a handsome man of about fifty-five, dressed in slacks and a polo sweater, almost six feet tall, with a square face, and silver-grey hair swept back over his head, parted at the left. 'Mr Borrodin,' he said, without offering to shake his hand.

Jack nodded. 'You'd better come inside,' the man continued.

Jack followed him through the hallway, furnished with portraits and expensive antiques, and into the sitting-room. An open log fire was burning in the grate, and a Labrador jumped up off one of the chairs to welcome Symonds into the room. Seeing no sign of anyone else in the house, Jack walked back out to the driveway and waved at Tara. In the distance, he could see her turning off the engine, and walking up the driveway. 'It looks OK,' he told her, taking her arm and leading her inside. A look of relief swept across her face, and Jack gripped her arm a little tighter.

Together they walked back into the sitting-room. Symonds returned a few moments later, holding a tumbler of iced whisky, followed by a woman with a silver tray, bearing a decanter, glasses and an ice bucket. From the pearls dangling from her neck, Jack assumed it was his wife rather than a maid. Symonds looked down at Tara, his eyes scrutinising her. 'This is most unusual,' he began. 'In all my many years of working on take-over defences I don't believe I've ever had a clandestine visit from middle-ranking executives at the aggressor company.'

'The circumstances are most unusual,' replied Jack hesitantly.

'Tell me about it,' replied Symonds, settling back into a leather armchair, fixing Jack with his steely grey eyes. 'But I won't accept any preconditions to our conversation. If you want to haggle, you can leave now. And if you tell me anything I feel may be useful, I will use it.'

Jack stared back. It was, he knew, the moment of truth; there was nothing to do now but roll the dice. Taking a deep breath, and drawing strength from Tara's presence beside him, he began. 'Kizog is not what it appears,' he started, his eyes moving past Symonds, through the french windows and on to the neatly trimmed lawn outside. 'It has been involved in two activities that are far removed from its main business. For many years it has been researching biological weapons for sale to NATO govern-ments. And it has been systematically engaged in manufacturing counterfeit pharmaceuticals.'

The tone of his delivery was dead pan yet authoritative. Jack glanced upwards at Symonds. He had certainly captured the man's interest, but so far there was no expression, no reaction, that he could read on his face. He glanced across at Tara, inviting her to take up the reins.

'You are aware of Ator?' Tara said.

'Of course,' replied Symonds.

'And of the Kizog vaccine which I am supposed to have invented?'

Symonds nodded, the expression in his eyes easing, and she felt that he would like her to continue. 'Kizog already had the vaccine and just brought me in to front their own discovery. My role was strictly for public consumption only. I didn't really do anything to create the vaccine. They handed it to me on a plate. And from the internal laboratory documents I have seen, Kizog knew about the mechanisms of the virus and about the potential for a vaccine long before the first recorded cases of the disease were registered. There is only one coherent explanation for that. Kizog created the virus as a biological weapon and created the vaccine at the same time. That is standard practice in biological warfare research, I believe.'

Symonds sat back in his chair, impassively soaking up the information.

There was a brief silence and Jack knew it was time to take up the story again. 'The counterfeiting operation is a little harder to explain,' he began. 'I was given the task of helping industry investigations into the activities of the counterfeiters. I was meant to infiltrate the counterfeiting organisation. I did so, but it soon became clear that the counterfeit trade was organised by Kizog, and I was meant to play a role in that. Now they are trying to have me arrested for being a counterfeiter myself. My role was to take the fall.'

Symonds blinked, taking a sip of his whisky. His expression was harsh and unforgiving. Jack paused, wondering if he was on shaky ground. Why should Symonds want to deal with someone who was acknowledging he was wanted by the police? He searched for a reaction but was met only with silence. 'Your defence document said Kizog's sales had been systematically inflated,' he continued. 'I think your figures were probably correct. Kizog is involved in the counterfeit drugs business, and the sales for its legitimate drugs are artificially increased so that the cash generated from the counterfeiting business can be run into the books. The cashflow and profits appear in the books as perfectly legal. It is a very neat system.'

Symonds looked at Jack, the ice in his expression starting to melt. 'You are right about the numbers. We can find no real market evidence for the sales totals Kizog are claiming. It has proved a complete mystery.'

Jack could sense that his words were being heard with some

194

sympathy, and, his confidence starting to grow, began to press into the opening. 'Aren't you puzzled as well by how Kizog can fund this bid? The cashflows are obviously tremendous. Far more than is apparent in the accounts.'

Symonds nodded. 'Why are you telling me this?' he said, leaning towards them, his expression clouding once again. 'What do you want from me?'

'Information like this would be more than enough to defeat the Kizog bid,' answered Jack firmly. 'It is in the interests of your client for all of this to be revealed, and before the bid closes. It might even be a fiduciary duty for you to act upon it.'

'And you are willing to give me this information?'

'For a price, yes,' answered Jack.

'A price,' responded Symonds, the distaste audible in his voice. 'I told you I was not interested in paying for dirt.'

Jack eyed him coldly. 'Who said we wanted your money,' he snapped.

Symonds relaxed. 'Then what do you want?'

'Help,' repeated Jack firmly. 'In two ways. We supply you with the information to prove that Kizog is a complete sham. That's our end of the deal. You use it, and you make sure that both Ocher and the Swiss government are involved in acting upon it. We need friends, powerful friends, and right now Ocher and the Swiss are the only people likely to listen to us. They get the information in return for destroying Kizog and making sure we have their protection afterwards.'

Symonds nodded.

'Next, your bank lends us £2 million, and uses it to take out a put option on Kizog stock. The loan lasts about forty-eight hours, and I expect to be charged interest on it at the usual rates for two-day money. When the bid is dropped, their share price will collapse, and we collect the profits on the deal. Your two million is returned to the bank, with interest and dealing charges deducted.'

'Two million,' said Symonds carefully, drawing out the words. 'Are you offering any collateral?'

Jack shook his head. 'What is your success fee on this defence?' he asked. 'About £100 million, more perhaps.'

'In that region,' replied Symonds cautiously.

'Let's be realistic; Ocher are going to lose this bid. You know that. Kizog have simply put up too much money. There is nothing either you or your client can do about it. If Ocher are prepared to pay you £100 million to escape from Sir Kurt, why not loan us two million? We can actually make it happen. In return for the protection and the money we will deliver proof of what we have been saying.'

Jack wondered if he had pushed too far. He had figured that a merchant banker would regard a few million as no more than a reasonable fee for several days' work. Symonds was rubbing his chin, his eyes downcast. Jack stood up, looking down at the man. 'If you want we can leave now,' he said. 'Defend your client as best you can.'

Symonds raised a hand. 'Stay,' he said.

Jack sat down again, delivering a hard look in the banker's direction. He's hooked, he thought to himself.

'You believe you can deliver conclusive proof of what you say?' asked Symonds.

'Yes,' answered Jack. 'No proof, no reward.'

'By noon on Friday,' said Symonds. 'Any later than that and it is useless to me.'

'By noon on Friday,' said Jack firmly.

Symonds stood up from his chair and walked out of the room. Tara and Jack waited in silence, unsure what was likely to happen next. Jack was pondering what their alternatives might be. If Symonds turned down this deal, he was out of options. He could hardly spend the rest of his life on the run. There would be little choice but to turn himself in, and hope for a fair trial.

Symonds walked back into the room holding a fax. He passed it down to Tara and Jack. 'I think you should see this,' he said. 'My PR man just faxed it to me. It is tomorrow morning's *Observer*. Front page.'

Jack grasped the sheet of waxy paper. The print was only just legible but the headline was clear enough: 'Revealed: Warfare and Counterfeiting scandal at Kizog'. Jack started to read the story.

Ator, the deadly Third World virus, was a biological warfare agent created by the former Soviet Union and spread throughout the world by a drugs counterfeiting ring also run out of the former Soviet Union, an investigation by the pharmaceuticals conglomerate Kizog has revealed. Tara Ling, the inventor of the Ator vaccine recently announced by Kizog, is secretly a member of a ring controlled by Russian Mafia interests that have taken control of the biological weapon. She has been working with the counterfeiters, who brought the vaccine to Kizog in an attempt to extort money from the company, alongside another Kizog executive, Jack Borrodin, who the company believes is a key figure in the western European part of the counterfeiting operation.

A spokesman for Kizog said last night that internal inquiries had uncovered the scandal, and that the company was now co-operating with the authorities. Arrest warrants have been issued for both Ling and Borrodin, who are now understood to be on the run together after an attempt to arrest Borrodin was made last week. Kizog is currently involved in a £13 billion bid for the Swiss pharmaceuticals company Ocher. A spokesman said that the revelations should have no effect on the bid. There was no material loss to the firm, and the company believes it still has legal rights to the Ator vaccine. 'This shows the excellence of our internal monitoring procedures,' said the spokesman.

The fax became too fuzzy after that, and Jack could read no further. The words blurred into one another. He handed it across to Tara, who had already been reading over his shoulder. 'Their story is a little different from yours,' said Symonds.

'They are lying,' replied Jack.

'Well, you would say that, wouldn't you?' said Symonds coldly.

Tara threw the fax down on the floor. Her eyes were alight with anger. 'Do I look like a Russian Mafioso?'

'I've never met one,' replied Symonds.

'Then call the police,' she snapped.

Symonds stood up and began pacing around the room. His head was bowed and a look of extreme concentration was written across his face. Jack knew he was trying to make a decision, and he could feel his pulse quickening. He edged forward on his chair, wondering whether this was the moment to take Tara by the arm and flee from the house. At the very least they might be able to enjoy a few days together before they were captured.

'I probably should call the police,' Symonds began carefully. 'That might be my duty as a citizen. But I must confess I find your story strangely credible. There is something very odd about the Kizog accounts. And I have a client to think about. I called Basle whilst I was out of the room, and the Ocher chairman said that we should play you along.'

Jack sat back in his chair, a sense of relief flooding through his body. He took hold of Tara's wrist, and could feel from her pulse that she was relaxing as well.

'Two conditions,' Symonds continued, turning to face them directly. 'I want conclusive proof of your story delivered to me by this Friday morning. And I want to be convinced that there has been no criminal wrongdoing on your part. Ocher will only provide money and assistance in getting you out of the country if we can be sure you are innocent. We will not help criminals.'

'Fine,' said Jack instantly.

Tara and Jack stood up to face him. Both of them shook him by the hand. 'I don't want to see you again, or hear from you again until you have the proof,' said Symonds. 'If you can't deliver, we never met.'

NINETEEN

A line of wrinkles furrowed the Chairman's brow as he put the phone down. His knuckles were tapping on the desk-top. He looked worried. Nervous even. It was not a look Shane had seen before.

His conversations with the officials at the Ministry of Defence had not gone well. Their spines were starting to loosen and their nerves were starting to buckle. Already, the story in the paper had prompted questions. Why did the Ministry not know Ator was a biological weapon? Why did it not know the Russians had lost control of their biochemical arsenals? Well, they would have to dig their own way out, the Chairman reflected. This was their project, and if any of the true facts ever emerged there would be a lot of careers destroyed apart from his own.

Bureaucrats, thought Sir Kurt contemptuously. Too little contact with the real world. Perhaps it would have been better if they had brought more people in on the operation, he reflected.

The politicians and departmental secretaries, perhaps. Then there would have been more people to co-operate with the cover-up. In the meantime, they would just have to hang together until the storm passed. 'One aspect of our policy troubles me,' said the Chairman quietly.

Shane looked up.

'I suspect that our victims may be a little more intelligent than was really necessary,' he continued. 'Stupid people are so much more reliable. You must remind me of that in future.'

'Borrodin didn't strike me as that smart,' said Shane.

'He's basically timid, and far too eager to please. Those are character flaws. But there is not much wrong with his brain. Cambridge, you know.'

'Book learning,' snorted Shane. 'No street smarts. He walked right into this thing without any sign of suspicion. Of course, I haven't really met Ling.'

'Very smart,' whispered the Chairman. 'A first-rate scientist, really first-rate. She had to be. We could never make anyone believe that some lab drone had done all this. But scientists can usually be relied upon to be very narrow-minded. Brilliant in their own field, if you put them out in the real world they go to pieces. The mad professor cliché. There is an element of truth in that.'

Shane leant forwards. 'They're in the real world now, all right.'

The Chairman looked up from his desk. 'How are our two young friends getting along?' he asked.

Shane cast his eyes down. 'For amateurs they are doing quite well,' he answered. 'After they escaped on Friday morning they drove west. Stayed in a little town overnight. The police had not planned to do anything more than pick them up for questioning so there was no reason for them to have a trail arranged. They made some payments by credit card, and that was picked up on the computers, and the information passed down to the local Bill. By the time they got there it was Saturday afternoon, but they had already moved on. It seems that they both withdrew large amounts of cash on Saturday morning. That turned up on the computers as well, and we got a report this morning, so it looks like they are aware we can track them through their credit cards. I think they are also aware we can follow the car. It was found on Sunday morning in Liverpool, abandoned. It could be that they drove it there and then caught a train. The police are checking the area, but I don't think they are there any more. They know we are looking for them and they are using their brains.'

'As I thought,' said the Chairman. 'Not stupid.'

'They did make one mistake.'

The Chairman looked up hopefully. 'Which is?'

'They used the phone in the hotel. Very stupid. They should have known we could trace those calls. It's all logged on to the computers at the local exchange. There was one call to News International. We don't know which paper, it was a call to the general switchboard. Perhaps they are hoping to sell their story. Put their side of the case through the papers.'

'I'll tell Wheeler to keep tabs, and get the injunctions ready,' said the Chairman quickly. 'Who else?'

'There was a call to Julian Symonds,' said Shane.

'The banker who is advising Ocher,' said the Chairman, his voice betraying his concern.

'We have been watching his country house, and also his office, and he has been trailed, but so far no sign of them. The phone has been tapped. But we have only been watching since this afternoon. It is possible they saw or spoke to him some time on Saturday. If so, we wouldn't know about it.'

'So we don't know where they are?'

Shane nodded. 'They'll turn up. They are making some of the right moves but they are still amateurs. The thing about being on the run is that it is very expensive. Hotel rooms, new cars all the time, new clothes, eating in restaurants, and you have to pay for everything in cash. It soon adds up. They have £21,000, in notes, that's the maximum they could withdraw. They can't survive on that for more than a month. The thing is this. You can't survive on the run very long unless you are also a robber. It's the only way to keep the cashflow going. These two aren't robbers. They don't have it in them.'

The Chairman looked at him closely. 'What would you do, if you were in their position?' he asked.

'Hit back,' answered Shane instantly. 'After all, attack is the best form of defence. They know they can't keep running for long. As you said, they aren't stupid.'

'That could be why they contacted Symonds.'

'To put a deal together. Possible. They would know things that would be very useful to Ocher.'

'They don't have proof, however,' said the Chairman. 'Ocher would only deal in proof. Speculation is no use to them.'

Shane stood up, and walked close to the desk. 'Can they get proof?' he asked.

The Chairman rubbed his brow. 'Only from the mainframe.'

Shane sat back in his chair and smiled. 'Then I don't think we have to worry about looking for them,' he said. 'They are coming to us.'

Tara's question took Jack totally by surprise. 'Why no photographs?' she said.

They were sitting in a small café on the beachfront in Eastbourne, Jack drinking coffee and Tara black tea. Through the window he could see the overcast drizzle shrouding the almost empty town, and through the light rain he could see the waves, whipped into life by the early evening wind, washing up against the sea wall. He gazed out on to the Channel. Somewhere out there, he thought. A new and very different life.

He looked down at the *Observer* story. She was right, of course, there were no photographs. But it had not struck him as particularly strange. 'None available, perhaps,' he replied. 'Or just a deadline to meet.'

Tara shook her head. 'This story obviously comes from Kizog. From that PR man, Wheeler. There is no way they could have found it out for themselves, since none of it is true. And anyway it is far too favourable to the company. So why wouldn't Wheeler supply them with photographs as well? We both know they have pictures of us on their files.'

Jack shrugged. 'Any ideas?'

'If they printed photographs of us, in the paper, alongside a story saying we were wanted by the police, then it would make things more difficult for us. Anybody might recognise us, and call the police. A policeman might spot us.'

'So they are doing us a favour?' said Jack with a wry smile.

'Most unlikely,' replied Tara. 'I think it is something else. This story they have concocted might just hold up, but it will be a lot harder to sustain if we are arrested and start telling our side of the story. We don't have proof yet, but we have a lot of circum-stantial evidence.'

Jack searched around for some plausible explanation. 'So perhaps they would prefer it if we just disappear. Into thin air. That is part of our plan, after all.'

Tara shook her head. 'Or die. I suspect that would be most convenient for them. Killed attempting to evade arrest. Then we never even get a chance to claim our innocence. In fact, it makes us look even more guilty. Looking at this from their point of view I think that would be best. That is why there are no photographs. An ordinary policeman stopping us would just place us under arrest. No. They want one of their own people to find us.'

For a moment Jack buried his face in his hands, contemplating the logic of what she had just said. He was grateful when her hand reached out across the table and touched his wrist. 'Survival is about being realistic,' she said quietly.

After the meeting with Symonds, the two of them had driven down the coast until they reached Eastbourne. Briefly, Jack had been elated by what he felt had been a successful meeting. They had allies now, and the sense of complete solitude he had felt only a few hours ago was starting to evaporate. They had a goal, and that too felt good; something to concentrate on, to take his mind away from the fate that still might lie ahead of him. Yet within hours, his sense of optimism had begun to ebb, replaced by a swell of uncertainty. The more he thought about the task

203

ahead, the more unlikely it appeared that they could gather conclusive proof. By Friday.

They had dumped the Cortina in a parking lot, leaving it unlocked, at Jack's suggestion, in the hope that it might be stolen and driven to another town; optimistic, Jack conceded, given the state of the machine. They collected their few belongings and walked through the town, checking into a small waterfront bed and breakfast, paying the forty pounds charged for the room in advance and in cash. Best to keep moving, they both agreed. At least until everything was mapped out. And they knew exactly what they were going to do next.

Tara told him to finish the coffee. 'After all, we have work to do, and not much time,' she explained.

Together they walked along the seafront, mostly in silence, and ignoring the smatter of rain falling on them. They talked a little of what they would do next, and they exchanged a few words about the future. But neither of them seemed in the mood to say very much. Of course, Jack realised. How can you talk about the future when you aren't sure if you have one?

Tara had spent the rest of Sunday afternoon shopping for make-up. When they returned to the hotel room she cut Jack's hair, leaving him with a closely cropped crew-cut that she finished off with an electric razor. Next she dyed it slightly brown. To Jack it looked awful but he didn't object. He didn't worry too much about his appearance at the best of times. And he was certainly not about to start at a time like this.

When she had finished she handed Jack the pair of scissors. 'Cut mine,' she told him firmly.

'What style?' he asked.

She smiled. 'What styles do you know?'

'I think grunge is the best I can manage,' answered Jack.

'That'll be fine,' she replied. 'I'll cut the knees off my jeans as well. At least it'll be trendy.'

Tara laughed, and Jack laughed with her, the first time, he noted, in several days. It felt good to have her companionship, and she was lightening up around him. These were shared

204

moments, precious in a strange sort of way. Jack was acutely aware there was likely to be a long jail sentence waiting for both of them. At best. Perhaps even death. He was sure that they were right, that Kizog, and the forces working with Kizog, would rather they were dead than captured. But he had not been tempted to reassess their plans for more than a moment or two. Compared with a long jail sentence for a crime of which he was entirely innocent, death did not seem so bad. So long as it was quick and painless. And this way at least they had a chance of escaping. They were taking control of their own destinies.

'Do you like it?' he asked when he had finished.

Tara went to look at her haircut in the bathroom mirror. The long, flowing, silky black hair that had been one of her best features was now lying torn and shredded on the hotel room floor. In its place was a short badly cut bob, jagged and uneven around the sides. 'Not much,' she answered.

'No dye?'

Tara shook her head. 'Orientals with blonde hair are too exceptional,' she replied. 'They stand out in the crowd. Anyway it is more important for you to disguise yourself. We all look the same to Caucasians.'

She disappeared into the bathroom, and returned some time later, showered, and wearing just shorts and a T-shirt, and climbed into bed. It was late, she told Jack, and they would have much work to do tomorrow. They needed all the rest they could get.

Jack showered, and when he came back into the room Tara was already dozing. He lay next to her on the bed, and could hear the faint sound of her breathing into the pillow, her chest moving slightly as she did so. He looked into her half-closed eyes and found a warmth that was somehow unexpected. No matter how long he searched, he had never been able to read her expressions. Her thoughts were like a closed book. Now she was starting to unravel, and he could sense her mystery evaporating. He felt closer to her than he had done to any woman for many years. Closer and more reliant. He depended on her, a new sensation for him. And he hoped she depended on him.

'Vietnam,' he whispered softly, hoping not to disturb her if she was already asleep. 'You want to go to Vietnam?'

She turned to face him. 'It's home,' she replied gently. 'At least, the only place I can think of as home.'

'When were you last there?' he asked.

'I left in 1971,' she replied. 'When I was seven. I still remember it though. I have never been back, but I have read a lot about the country. I think I would like to spend some time there.'

Jack could detect the trace of sadness in her dark eyes. 'You want us to go there together?' he asked.

She smiled at him. 'It would be a good place to start,' she answered. 'To get away from all of this. If you don't like it, you move on. Same for me.'

'We're making an OK team so far,' Jack said.

Tara looked at him closely, her eyes bright with curiosity. 'You'll come with me?' she asked.

'Why not,' answered Jack. 'I don't have any other place to go.'

She reached up and rubbed his nose. 'Sleep,' she said quietly.

Jack rolled over on his side, trying to let his exhaustion capture him. He lay close to her for warmth, and as he did so he could feel her hand reach out to touch him. His hand moved out to hold her. And wrapped in each other's bodies, they both drifted off lazily to sleep.

TWENTY

The clerk in the lobby showed little sign of interest when Tara and Jack signed themselves into the hotel as Mr and Mrs Simonson. He didn't ask for any identification, nor did he betray any surprise when Jack told him they would be paying by cash rather than card. Judging by the decaying appearance of the lobby and the faded demeanour of most of the guests, he has probably seen a good many more suspicious characters than us, Jack thought to himself.

He only showed a slight flicker of surprise when asked if the room had a direct-dial phone system. Calls were normally routed through the hotel switchboard, the clerk explained. Not good enough, Jack protested. The clerk assured him the system was very efficient, but Jack was still not satisfied. They would go elsewhere, although, he pointed out, they were prepared to pay extra for an upgraded phone connection. After checking with his manager, the clerk said it was possible, but he would have to charge an extra £25 a night for the room. 'Fine,' Jack replied. He peeled out a stack of twenties. 'We'll take it.'

They had caught the early morning train up from Eastbourne that morning, and taxied to Southampton Row, a drab street running between the British Museum and Euston Station, full of mid-market tourist hotels. Jack decided it was the best part of London in which to lose themselves. There was no point in going anywhere near his flat; that was no doubt being watched. And if they were going to disappear, the tourist districts of central London were probably the best place in the whole country. Amidst the throng of tour buses and day-trippers, they would hardly stand out, and Tara's Oriental appearance was as obscure here as it was noticeable in the country.

They could have chosen Victoria or Bayswater or Paddington, but Southampton Row had one other advantage. It was close to Tottenham Court Road, a cornucopia of shops where you could pay with cash, no questions asked, and where you could buy practically any electronic device manufactured anywhere in the world. If they were going to fight this battle, they would need plenty of electronics. All the information they needed could be accessed by modem. And Jack was certain of one thing. There was no way he wanted to go anywhere near Kizog, or run any risk of encountering Angus Shane.

Together, they walked up to the hotel room. It was on the third floor, and appeared to have been last redecorated some time in the mid-seventies. There were two armchairs, both covered with a strange orange imitation leather, and a desk, made from a wood panel resting over a metal frame. The curtains were a reddish colour, and drew back to reveal a view of another hotel 'It will do fine,' said Jack.

Tara made herself a coffee from the kettle and sachets next to the wardrobe, and sat down at the desk. There was much work to be done, converting her mass of papers and documents into a reasoned chain of evidence, strong enough to convince Ocher and their bankers of the truth of their claims. It would, she knew, take at least a day. Perhaps longer.

Jack left her there alone. He too had urgent work.

His shoulders hunched, and the collar of his coat wrapped up high around his neck, he stepped out into the street. He cast his eyes up and down the pavement, scanning the faces of the passers-by. And, his head bowed down, his gaze fixed firmly on the pavement, he walked quickly and anxiously. He hoped nobody was watching him, but he could not be certain.

Jack stopped at the first shop he came to and slipped unobtrusively inside. The store was a mass of computers, accessories, hi-fis, fax machines, a humbling array of electronics stacked high against the walls, most of it still in boxes. Jack did not stop to browse. He already knew what he wanted.

The shop assistant attempted to persuade him to survey the range, but Jack was not interested. Two laptops, with Pentium chips, colour screens, and as much hard disc space as he could have, he told the assistant. The man produced a pair of Toshibas, both with 680 megabyte drives. Fine, Jack answered. How much? £5,200 for the pair, replied the assistant. Cash? £4,900, said the assistant. Jack offered £4,700; he still had no idea how much money they would need, and there was no point in wasting it. £4,800, insisted the assistant. Fine, said Jack. And he peeled out a wad of notes, counting them over the table.

A modem was next on the list. He asked for a Hayes, the fastest they had. After a trip to the stockroom, the assistant came back with a 288. It was expensive, more than £600, but the last thing they needed was a cheap device that might break down at any moment. Jack haggled £30 from the price. Then he asked for a high-speed laser printer, offered £900 in cash, and counted out another row of notes. The shop assistant was starting to like him.

One more thing. He needed an electronic tone controller. A blue box? said the assistant with a knowing smile. Absolutely, replied Jack. Did they have any in stock? The assistant said he would have to check. He disappeared to the back room, and through a crack in the doorway Jack could glimpse him talking with another man. When he came back, the assistant explained they did have some Taiwanese devices, but they were sold for export orders only. The machines were not licensed for use in Britain. And he felt duty-bound to point out that phone phreaking was technically illegal in this country.

Jack smiled. 'It's OK, I'm a tourist,' he said. 'I won't be using it here.'

'You have your passport on you?'

Jack checked his wallet and shook his head. 'Back at the hotel. Sorry.'

The assistant looked doubtful. '£650,' he replied. 'Cash.'

This time Jack decided it was better not to haggle. 'Fine,' he replied crisply, digging into his pockets again and counting out another row of twenties.

Jack added five packets of floppy discs to the order, collected his boxes and took them outside. He stood on the edge of the kerb, looking out for a taxi. As he did so, he cast his eyes over the rubbish bin, overflowing with crisp packets and beer cans, on the side of the street. Below, lying at the edge of the gutter, he saw what he wanted. Walking across, he picked up the discarded Visa slip and tucked it in his back pocket. Now, he thought to himself, we have everything we need.

The Chairman punched four digits into the desk-top phone. Monday morning had been progressing just fine so far, he decided. The morning's papers had followed up the story of the biological weaponry, and included some generally favourable commentary on the role Kizog had played. The company's share price was down a little in early morning trading, but a quick check with the brokers and the investor relations people had established that most of the analysts were discounting the possibility the news would have any financial impact on Kizog. It was nothing shareholders need worry about, the management had everything under control, they were saying, and the origins of the Ator virus made no difference to the demand for the vaccine. Most brokers were still recommending holders of Ocher shares to accept the offer, and judging by the turnover in the stock, some

210

of the big institutional holders were starting to unload their positions.

Clockwork, thought the Chairman to himself.

He glanced upwards. David Stile, the director of information technology, was standing in the doorway. On receiving the summons to the Chairman's office, Stile had rushed straight upstairs from the third floor, and was looking slightly flustered. Sir Kurt, Stile knew, had almost no interest in computers, scarcely knowing how to turn one on himself, and very rarely requested a private audience. This must be something special, he decided, and he was already worrying if something had gone wrong with the systems.

The Chairman asked Stile, a neat, compact man of thirty-eight, to sit down on the sofa, joining him on the adjacent chair, and began talking about how they might integrate their own computer systems with those of Ocher once the take-over was complete. Relieved that nothing appeared to have gone wrong, Stile launched into a lengthy explanation of how both companies used basic UNIX systems, designed around mini supercomputers, connected into networks of office and field PCs. There were some incompatibilities in the software, he cautioned, but nothing they could not smooth out in six months or so, so long as they re-engineered the software and bought in some new kit.

'Fine, fine, I am sure you can handle it,' said the Chairman, visibly reluctant to explore the subject any further. 'There is something else I wanted to discuss with you. How secure are our computer systems?'

Stile hesitated for a moment. 'As secure as most commercial systems,' he replied carefully. 'Probably more so.'

'Not completely secure then?'

Something about his tone suggested to Stile the Chairman was not happy with his answer. 'Computer security is much like any other sort,' he began. 'If you stayed at home all day locked behind iron bars you would be one hundred per cent secure, but you wouldn't get very much done. Computers are the same. A single box accessible through just one terminal locked up and

211

protected by armed guards is secure, but not very useful. We have tried to maintain a balance between reasonable security and the advantages of connecting all our employees up to a single unified network.'

'Quite so,' replied the Chairman. 'But the bottom line is that it isn't secure. Am I right?'

'Everything is sorted into levels,' said Stile quickly. 'Low-grade information is fairly open, protected only by simple password commands. Those can be opened quite easily, not least because employees use silly passwords, like the wife's name or whatever, that are quite easy to crack. The more important the information is, the more heavily it is protected.'

The Chairman leant forward. 'How heavily?'

'Extremely heavily, sir,' answered Stile. 'I am sure it is possible for outsiders to break into the network, but that won't do them much good. All the important information is screened off behind firewalls. Those are chunks of computer code that prevent users from moving between different parts of the network. The more important the information, the more firewalls you have to move through to get to it. It should be invulnerable.'

'Should be?'

Stiles decided to correct himself. 'It is invulnerable,' he added. 'We are using the latest and most up-to-date technology available. But, it has to be admitted, computer science moves very quickly. One can never quite tell.'

'I am sure you are doing your best,' said the Chairman. 'Now, if someone from outside was trying to access our system, would we know about it?'

'Certainly. There are alarms attached to the firewalls. An attempt to break should be signalled immediately to the software managers monitoring the network.'

'And we could trap them?'

Stile shook his head. 'No, the alarms are a warning device. They are not designed to trap intruders, merely to warn them off.'

The Chairman frowned. 'So we couldn't catch them.'

212

'Not through the systems we have in place, no,' said Stile.

'It's not technically possible?' questioned the Chairman.

'It is possible to install entrapment software,' replied Stile. 'We haven't because it starts to compromise the whole network. It slows down the entire system. And makes it harder for legitimate users to get around. Up until now our focus has been on prevention, not detection.'

The Chairman leant backwards in his chair, fixing a piercing stare upon his employee. 'I want those systems installed.'

'Of course, sir. By when?'

'By yesterday,' he snapped.

Almost in silence, Tara and Jack began to unpack the equipment. They placed the two computers on the desk, next to each other. They plugged in the modem, and began hooking up the machines. Tara switched the machines on, and started checking everything was in place. So far it all seemed to work.

Jack busied himself with loading the software. Slotting in the discs, firing up the hard drives and downloading everything they needed took up more than an hour. When he had finished he checked his watch. It was almost four p.m. 'Ready to start?' he asked.

Tara nodded. Jack's arm reached out across the desk, and he squeezed the palm of her hand. 'Here we go then,' he said.

'You are sure you know how this works?' she said cautiously.

'No, I've read about it, but I have never tried it before,' Jack replied, his voice betraying his nerves. 'We'll only get one shot at this. A mistake and they'll find us.'

They had already discussed the plan in detail, and decided that despite the risks it was the best chance they had. Phone phreaking had been around since the mid-seventies, a term devised for the hundreds of different ways hackers had developed for breaking into the phone system. Usually, the hackers were trying to make free calls, sometimes just breaking into the phone company's computer systems for the simple fun of it. Tara and Jack were not interested in free calls; they did not mind paying. Nor were they were interested in looking into the British Telecom systems. There was only one aspect of phreaking that really interested them this afternoon; a technique for disguising where the phone call had come from.

Discussing the plan, they had decided they had to break into the Kizog computer system. It was the only way of gathering the information they needed. There was a chance that they could break in, take what they needed, and depart without anyone ever detecting their presence within the system. But it was a long shot. To get everything they needed, they figured they would have to stay inside the system for a decent length of time. The chances were their intrusion would be detected. And when it was, tracing the source of the call would not be difficult for anyone who had police co-operation. Such as Kizog. A simple phone trace would lead right to this hotel. Right to this room. And they were finished.

Phreaking the phones, Jack insisted, was their one chance of remaining undetected until Friday.

Jack took the phone, and pulled its socket from the wall. Carefully, he plugged the phone into the blue box controller, and then, using another lead, plugged that into the phone connection down by the skirting board.

They had talked through the technology they were using and felt that they knew how it worked. The central London area where they were staying would be using an automatic electronic exchange, meaning that calls to and from any phone in the area would be routed according to the instructions coded into a series of inaudible tone pulses the phone would transmit as it made the call. The tones would tell the system where to place the call, but they would also leave a trail, telling anyone who cared to look where the call was coming from.

Turning to the computer, Jack logged into the communications software, and set it to dial the freephone number in Holland. Next, he switched on the controller. As the phone rang, it sent a 'clear forward' tone down the line by transmitting electronic pulses at 2,400 hertz. The signal told the international call transit centre to terminate the call. But, in the split second before the exchange could do so, another signal, this time transmitted at 2,600 hertz, known in the telecoms trade as a 'seize tone', announced a request for another call. The line was then opened. The call would now be free, because the exchange would register it as a routine call between two international exchanges. But, more importantly, the source of the call had now been wiped clean. The exchange would have no idea where it was coming from. As far as the computers were concerned, it was just internal traffic, of no interest to anyone.

An icon displayed on the communications software indicated that the line was open. 'I think it's working,' whispered Jack.

Turning to the keyboard, he tapped in the number of Arbex, an Internet service provider based in Birmingham. Within a minute, he was logged on to the Net. 'Open new account,' Jack requested. He had chosen Arbex because it accepted quick connections via a modem. A page of instructions scrolled down the computer screen. Jack tapped in his name as 'KH Reid', and put down an address in Amsterdam; he didn't have an address to hand so he made one up. He filled in his e-mail address as 'ken@line', noting down the numerical IP address the computer provided him with. Lastly the machine asked for credit card details, to cover the connection charges. Jack took the Visa slip he had picked up earlier and tapped into the machine the number and expiry date of KH Reid's card. Whoever he or she was, they would, he knew, report the misuse of the card, causing the account to be closed. But that would not be until they got the statement. Which could be weeks away. And they would be long gone by then.

'Account accepted,' flashed up a message on the screen. 'Your Arbex Internet connection will be ready for use within 12 hours. Happy surfing!'

'It's working,' said Jack, allowing a smile to cross his face.

'And you are sure it is safe?' asked Tara anxiously.

'Pretty sure,' replied Jack calmly. 'We have two levels of

security here. First, we are going to get into the Kizog computer system via the Internet. On the Net, we call into the service provider, and their machine then connects into the Kizog machines. If they trace those connections, it will just lead them back to Arbex in Birmingham. Then they will have to trace back where the calls into Arbex are coming from. Because of the transformer, that will just lead them to the international exchange in Holland. It could take them weeks to find their way back to us through that maze.'

He reached across for Tara and squeezed her waist. 'We only need two or three days,' he added. 'So long as it holds until then, we'll be fine.'

TWENTY-ONE

Angus Shane introduced himself to David Stile with a firm hand-shake. Dani nodded at the man and sat down in his office. The pair needed no further introduction. The Chairman had said they were working with him on security issues, and he was to give them everything they asked for. For Stile, that was all the author-isation they needed.

The information technology director sat in a small office, partitioned by a sheet of clear glass from the open-plan office that took up a section of the third floor. Outside, groups of white-shirted programmers huddled over terminals, peering into the entrails of the system. Stile kept his jacket on throughout the day. It was, he felt, a mark of his authority.

He began by giving Shane and Fuller a short description of the computer systems at Kizog. There were mainframes, basically mini supercomputers, which were kept deep underground in the foundations of this office, plus other back-up machines kept about twenty miles away, in case a fire or an earthquake hit the site. There were more mainframes located at the Stuttgart offices, at the American headquarters in North Carolina, and at the Japanese laboratories just outside Osaka. Each set of computers recorded everything. Unless it was the end of the world, he explained, there was no way they could lose the data. Every transaction, every data entry, every e-mail message, anything entered on to a computer by any Kizog employee or consultant around the world would be logged into the machines. And kept. For ever. Hard disc capacity was so cheap these days, he continued, there was really no need ever to throw anything away.

'How far back do the records go?' asked Fuller.

'Some to the sixties,' replied Stile. 'That was when computers first started being installed into the company. Of course computers were much more expensive then, and could do much less, so much less of our work was inputted in those days. But if it was ever put into the system, it will still be there somewhere.'

'How easy is it to find?' asked Fuller.

'Depends. If you wanted to find the e-mail Joe Bloggs in marketing sent to his girlfriend in accounts last week that would be easy. Generally speaking, the further back you go in time, and the deeper you go into the more sensitive material, the harder it gets.' He pointed to the workers outside. 'A lot of our time is spent dealing with executives who have mislaid files. They send them to the wrong place by mistake, then ask us to retrieve them. It is often very hard to find something.'

'Even if you know the system?' asked Fuller.

'Obviously the more you know about the system the easier it gets. But we aren't talking about internal hacking here. We are talking about outside intruders, aren't we?'

'Can we talk in total privacy?' interrupted Shane.

'Of course,' replied Stile, eager to win their confidence.

'We believe that Ocher, or people working for them, may be trying to break into our systems,' Shane continued. 'In the hope of finding some information they can use at the last minute to defeat the bid.'

Stile felt a tingle of excitement running down his spine. This, he realised, was much more important than most of the issues that passed across his desk. He assumed an air of great importance. 'Obviously we must do everything we can to stop them,' he said.

'The new software has been installed?' asked Shane.

'We are using a Sidewinder detection system,' Stile replied. 'It is an American program, originally developed by the military, but now being made commercially available, although it is rumoured that the CIA only let it be released after they had figured a way to crack it. Anyway, it is about the best on the market. And, as requested, it is primarily about detecting attacks, rather than protecting the system from them. Our existing firewalls should do that.'

'And it is now operating.'

Stile hesitated. 'Not quite,' he replied. 'I placed the order immediately after I spoke to the Chairman yesterday. We are paying extra for immediate installation. A team of their people are working with our experts in the US office right now. Once it is installed, it will cover the whole system around the world. But it is complex software, being bolted on to what is already a complex network. Everyone is working around the clock. But when I spoke to them earlier they said they would not have it up and running for another eight or nine hours.'

That would make it Tuesday evening, thought Shane. They had no idea where Jack and Tara might be. Or how far they might have progressed. Time was getting tight, he realised. But, he told himself, if time was tight for him, it was even tighter for them. They did not have long.

'Just make it as fast as possible,' he said.

The light of dawn seeped only slowly through the one window in the hotel room. Jack woke with a start, an image of the murdered girl, her throat cut and bloody, receding in his mind as the nightmare faded. Instinctively he reached out for Tara. He felt her instantly, her warm body lying next to his. She rolled over on her side under his touch, her eyes momentarily opening and then closing again. Jack gazed down at her body, covered by the rumpled shorts and T-shirt she wore to bed, feeling the same rush of desire that was intensely familiar to him now.

He wiped the trace of moisture from his brow, wondering if those pictures would ever go away, or whether, twenty or thirty years from now, he would still wake up in the morning feverish from the same horrific scenes.

Trying to empty his mind, Jack climbed out of bed, showered and ordered breakfast from room service before waking Tara with a shake. She smiled, and rose instantly, moving into the shower without a word. By the time she had emerged, the tray of hot coffee and toast was waiting on the floor, and the computers were already humming. She poured herself a cup of coffee from the pot, and sat down next to Jack at the desk. 'Time to begin,' she said.

Jack checked first that the phreaked phone line he had set up yesterday was still open. Once that was done, he set up the communications software, instructing the machine to dial Arbex via the link to Holland. On his modem, he could see the short row of red lights flashing as the call was put through. After a minute or so the lines were all in place. The computer fed in the details of the Internet address he had created last night, and the message flashed up on the screen: 'Connection established. OK.'

'So far, so good,' whispered Jack.

At the command prompt he entered 'telnet', an Internet code for logging on to a computer system via a remote connection. Like many large companies, Kizog now allowed Internet access to its system, to enable employees in the field, or executives travelling on business or working from home, to plug into the network without having to find a dedicated line. It was a loophole Jack knew they could exploit.

He tapped in the numerical address for the Kizog network, a string of twelve numbers punctuated by full stops. A prompt for his User ID flashed up on the screen. Jack did not want to use his own login; it would be far too suspicious. Instead he used a general login for new employees, and for people who had forgotten their code. It was a very restricted password, which gave access only to limited and generally useless parts of the network. But he would worry about that next. For now the main task was just to get inside the system.

'Connection established,' flashed the computer.

'OK, we're in,' said Jack, a tone of triumph creeping into his voice.

'How far?' asked Tara anxiously.

'Just the outer ring,' replied Jack. 'The fringes of the network.'

Fortunately, thought Jack, she knew far more about computing than he did; a consequence, he guessed, of so many years spent cloistered in academia. He had explained to her that information within the Kizog network was protected by firewalls; a fact that he well knew from the many areas of the system curtained off from employees such as himself. It was Tara who had suggested that they could tunnel their way through to the information they needed.

All traffic through a computer network, she had explained, is controlled by the TCP/IP protocol, a set of communications standards originally developed by the Defence Advanced Research Projects Agency in the US but now standard throughout commercial systems. The basic building block of the protocol is the IP packet; a bundle of data that carries a thirty-two-bit source and destination address, as well as the payload of data that is being transferred, generally a few hundred bytes long. The IP address is broken down into network and host parts, each delivered in binary code. A firewall, she told him, is a piece of software that looks at both parts of the code, checks that the payload of data has come from the correct place and is travelling to a destination for which that user has authorisation. If either part is wrong, it stops the signal, dumping it into a harmless file before it can go any further. There are two ways, she continued, through a firewall. One is to establish what is known in

221

computing as transitive trust; cracking the codes for authorised users, so that the packet can pass through untouched.

Tara and Jack did not have the time to construct the complex mathematical programs needed to crack the security codes. But there was another way through: tunnelling. Essentially, Tara explained, a tunnel is a way of digging underneath a firewall, bypassing its defences, and making sure that messages pass through undetected. The trick is to bury a line of code into a longer and harmless signal. The firewall checks the message, allows it to pass, and only then is the harmless code stripped away, leaving the crucial message on the other side of the firewall.

Tara figured the Kizog system would allow information to be fed into the more secure parts of the system; the firewalls would probably be checking for attempts to login, which would allow an intruder to retrieve information. Their task, she explained, was to construct a line of code that would appear to the firewall to be a harmless delivery of information. Once on the other side, the code would be instructed to start unbundling itself, leaving just the login instruction. Once that was done, they would be through.

Jack had taken their telnet connection as far as accounts; a simple entry point where the salesmen could log in their orders from their laptops; the network would then take the order, tell distribution to dispatch the order, instruct billing to issue an invoice, and notify accounts to build the order into the accounting system. It was logical, Jack had pointed out, to assume this part of the network would link into the deeper accounting system, since the sales figures would form the core of the accounts that finally ended up in the annual report each year. 'But there is bound to be a firewall between the sales ledger and the accounts system,' he added.

Tara went to work on the system, keying in new rows of digital code in an attempt to escape the attention of the firewall. It was long and wearisome work. Hours went by. By midday, Jack ventured outside briefly, partly to catch some fresh air and to clear his mind, partly to collect some sandwiches and drinks to

222

keep them going. The streets were crowded and he passed through them unnoticed as he walked to the nearest café. He was grateful for a few moments away from the computers, yet nervous already that breaking through was taking too long.

When he returned, Tara was still sitting at the computer, her eyes squinting at the screen, her fingers running along the numbers on the keyboard, tapping new lines of code into the machine. Five times now she had tried and failed; each time she buried the second protocol into the first, the message came back on the screen 'IP protocol unresolved'. She had no choice but to try again. There were only a limited number of different gateways that could be used in a system such as this, Tara knew, and she was sure she would break through eventually.

Wearily she began tapping some new lines of code into the keyboard, trying to keep her frustration under control, and searching the recesses of her mind to find the set of binary code that would take them through to the other side. She knew they did not have much time. If they were to succeed they would have to be lucky as well as smart. Another row of digits, she told herself. Be strong.

Stile stood to attention when the Chairman and the finance director entered his office. He was not sure he could recall ever seeing the Chairman in this department before, certainly not in his own office. The importance of the task began to bear down on him once again, and in the pit of his stomach he could tell that he was nervous; there would be retribution, no doubt, if this project was not a success.

The Chairman and Finer nodded to Shane and Fuller and said hello to Stile. 'The system we asked for is in place, I hope?' he demanded.

The tone of his voice, Stile noted, was neither warm nor friendly. 'It went live about half an hour ago,' he replied. 'The team in America have been working through the night to get it up and running. According to the Sidewinder consultants, thirty hours is the fastest turnaround they have ever achieved for a system of our size and complexity.'

'Good, good,' said the Chairman. 'And have we found anything yet?'

Stile shook his head. 'The detection programme is really a vast screening device. It roots through all the work being done on the network and checks for any unusual features. If it finds anything that even closely resembles any of the techniques used by hackers, it automatically starts to investigate, and then starts tracking down the source.'

'How long will it take?' asked Finer.

'Depends on the size of the network it is checking,' Stile replied. 'We have 5,000 people connected into our network, of whom about half are logged on at any one time. Since there are roughly twenty mainstream ways of hacking into a network, it has to screen about 50,000 operations just to make a start. Then it has to start sifting through everything which appears suspicious. Even throwing massive amounts of computing power at it, it isn't that quick.'

Shane turned to Finer. 'Which part of the system do you think they will want to get into?' he asked.

Finer hesitated before answering, glancing across at the Chairman, who seemed interested in the question. 'I'd say they would be concentrating on the financial records,' he replied.

The Chairman looked directly at Stile. 'Would it make it quicker if we concentrated the search on the financial part of the network?' he asked.

Stile nodded. 'The more you define the search, the less time it takes,' he replied.

'Do it then,' he snapped.

Stile turned to his keyboard, tapping an e-mail message to his colleagues in the US, telling them to concentrate the search on the accounting systems. 'May I make a suggestion, sir?' he asked carefully.

'Of course,' replied the Chairman.

'If we are primarily worried about Ocher people stealing our

224

financial data, then we could just shut down that section of the network for a few days. That would cause a terrible backlog of work to be sorted out next week, but nothing we couldn't cope with, and it would prevent the opposition finding anything before the bid closes. I mean, you can't hack into a system when the plug has been pulled.'

The Chairman waved a hand dismissively. 'Don't you understand?' he said caustically. 'I don't really care if we stop them or not. I want them caught.'

TWENTY-TWO

Jack sat by himself on the floor of the hotel room, a stack of papers resting on his knees, each dense with numbers and notations. He grabbed at the cup of coffee lying by his side, hoping to restore some energy to his sore and aching mind. He rubbed his eyes, fighting the urge to sleep, and trying to drag his concentration back to the material in front of him. He knew he had to go on, but it had already been a long and wearying night.

Tara was asleep on the bed. They had completed the tunnel at just after six the previous evening, suddenly finding themselves through the firewall and into the main accounting databases. They now had free access to roam through the accounts, delving at will inside the financial records of the company. Only one computer could be connected at a time, and Tara had suggested they work through the night, one of them on the computer whilst the other slept, downloading as much data as they could handle, storing it away on the hard discs. Tara had worked until three in the morning while Jack slept fitfully. At three they had changed shifts, Tara taking some rest, while Jack worked his way through the mass of files on the database.

It was now six in the morning, and Jack figured he had as much material as he could cope with. Raw financial data, he suspected, would not be enough for Ocher. They needed to know how it all fitted together, what it all meant. And that demanded analysis.

There was no point in waking Tara, he realised. She knew little about accounting or finance, and most of this material would be meaningless to her, just as the scientific data had meant nothing to him without her interpretations and explanations. If they were to make anything of this material, he decided, it was up to him.

The numbers were swimming before his eyes, blurring together in a mass of lasered ink on the page. Reminding himself of how little time they had left, Jack lifted himself from the floor, and sat down in front of the second computer. He called up the spreadsheet program, and cast his eyes down the endless series of grey cells running down the screen. Keep going, he thought. You'll get there.

Jack had been working for nearly five hours by the time Tara rose from her slumber. Still half asleep, she cast her eye at the clock by the bed, and silently cursed herself for sleeping for so long. It was almost eight already. Quietly, she rose, walking to the desk, and resting her arms on the back of the chair, massaging the back of Jack's neck with her thumbs. He said nothing, certain that if he did so she would stop. 'Good-morning,' she said at last.

Jack turned to face her. Her hair was messy, her eyes drowsy, and her clothes rumpled. He smiled. In that moment, he was sure that he had never seen anyone so gentle or so appealing.

'How's it going?' she asked softly.

Jack turned back to the computer. 'I think I am almost there.'

Tara's eyes were alight with excitement. 'Tell me.'

'Over breakfast,' Jack replied. 'I'm starving.'

The Styrofoam coffee cups were piled high in the information technology department of the Kizog headquarters. One was filled with mouldy, curdled coffee, and brimming with drowned cigarette butts. As the day turned first into night, and then into morning, Shane had long since ignored the no-smoking policy enforced throughout the building and, unable to locate an ashtray, had started tipping his ash into the first thing that came to hand.

The others had all drifted away at different points of the night, catching a few hours' sleep on the sofas in some of the executive offices. Unprofessional, thought Shane to himself. Business was business, and if you had to stay up all night, so be it. When they got the trace, there would be no time to shower, have a nice breakfast, perhaps read the papers for a while. No. When they tracked their prey, they would move and move fast.

He stretched, fished another Camel from his pocket, and lit up, taking a long drag on the cigarette, enjoying the sense of the nicotine filtering through into his bloodstream. Five days now those two fuckheads had been on the run, hc thought to himself. Five days. Longer than he would have imagined. The police searches had turned up nothing. Electronic surveillance systems had been notified to pick up any traces of them, but so far they had drawn only blanks. Street patrols had been alerted to keep their eyes open for them, but could report no sightings. They had been smart. Using cash, avoiding the phones, probably staying indoors most of the time. All the basics of evading capture, they had figured them all out. But they couldn't hide for ever. Sooner or later they would have to make a break for it. Then they would be out in the open. And he would have them.

Shane tossed the end of the cigarette into the coffee cup. Patience, he told himself. They would come to him.

Out of the corner of his eye he caught sight of the 'message pending' icon flashing on the computer screen. Shane stood up, walked round the desk to the keyboard, and tapped two words into the machine: 'Read message.'

'Hacking attempt identified,' flashed up on to the screen.

'Gotcha,' Shane whispered under his breath.

He strode out into the lobby, where he found David Stile stretched out on one of the long black leather sofas, his tie loosened, and his shirt crumpled. Shaking the man vigorously, he brought him out of his slumbers. 'Wake up!' he barked. 'Your machine has found them. About bloody time too.'

Stile stood up with a jolt. He disappeared into the gents, washed his face, and, coming out, grabbed a cup of coffee from the machine in the corridor. He walked through the office, still empty at this hour of the morning apart from the cleaners doing their early rounds, and sat down behind his computer. His fingers running quickly over the keyboard, he tapped away at the machine, Shane leaning over his back, his breath reeking of nicotine and coffee.

Stile peered closely at the screen, double-checking the data, before turning to face Shane. 'It's found them all right,' he said.

The breakfast tray lay between them on the floor. Jack had taken two aspirin with his coffee and orange juice, and could feel the headache that had been throbbing for the past two hours starting to ebb. He was beginning to feel stronger, and the anticipation of a breakthrough was firing the adrenalin back through his veins.

Looking directly at Tara, Jack began to explain what his investigations over the course of the night had revealed. The financial records were complex, he said, even for someone with experience of peering into corporate accounts. He had decided that the best approach was to start with a theory, and then work backwards, searching through the database to see if he could find the evidence to back it up.

His starting point had been the Ocher defence document. It had claimed that the revenue lines in Kizog's accounts did not correspond with the sales of its drugs in the marketplace. Everyone, himself included, had dismissed it at the time as nothing more than the usual mud thrown between corporations locked into a hostile take-over battle. And yet, he pointed out, what if they were right?

Ocher would have some evidence for their claim. Market research figures would tell them roughly how much product Kizog were shifting, and their salesmen would be able to supply any other market share figures they needed. The list prices were publicly available information, and, again, the Ocher salesmen would know what sort of discounts they were offering. Multiply sales volume by price and they would have a sales figure. Ocher's people probably assumed that Kizog was inflating its figures to cover up its relative lack of success in the market. They were fiddling the books. But given what they now knew about the company there were other possibilities as well. Kizog had other sources of income, this much they knew. Sources that could not be reported in the accounts. But which would still have to find their way down to the bottom line.

Jack had started by looking at the internal revenue figures going back over twenty years. Sorting through the databases, he had been able to track two sets of revenue data, showing sales revenue and extraordinary items; data that was not published in the annual report. On the spreadsheet, he had tracked the two numbers on a graph and printed it out.

Tara took the sheet of paper, and looked closely at the three lines. The top line showed reported revenues as shown in the official accounts. Underneath were two other lines. One showed marketplace sales, growing steadily but unspectacularly through the seventies and mid-eighties, but turning down gradually from 1987 onwards. The second line, showing extraordinary items, grew rapidly through the seventies and early eighties, then started tapering off dramatically from 1990 onwards. After 1990 the sum of the two lines no longer matched the top line. 'What might the extraordinary items be?' asked Tara. 'Could they be legitimate?'

'Might be,' Jack told her. 'They could reflect disposals of assets during the year. Except that Kizog never disposed of any assets. It could be interest income. Except Kizog had no significant cash pile.'

Jack explained that he had taken a closer look at the extraordinary items. He had started out by looking through the movement of funds accounts, and then tracing those back to the billing records. He had checked the invoicing files stretching back over many years. He had looked at how Kizog billed the departments of health in each of the main European countries, and then he had sorted through the records of the government purchases of drugs in the US, mainly to the Medicaid system. Then he went back to check the figures in the market sales accounts. And then he started crunching the numbers.

'And what does all that show?' asked Tara.

'The company has been systematically overbilling the health systems throughout Europe, in Britain, Germany, Italy, the Benelux countries. Tens of millions every year from each one. And then in the US I could find nothing strange about the Medicaid billings. But I did find huge demand for Kizog drugs from the defence department, ostensibly for use by the military. Except most of those drugs were never delivered. Again, massive overbilling.'

'To all the major countries of the Western alliance,' added Tara.

Jack nodded, and looked at her closely. 'I think we have found out how Kizog was paid for its work on biological warfare. The money was funnelled into the company via the normal government reimbursements for drug purchases. Except that it wasn't drugs they were buying. It was weapons.'

Shane leant down on the desk with Fuller standing beside him now, looking down at the screen, while Stile studied the information thrown up by the program. 'What does it tell you?' he asked.

'Searching in the financial records was the right idea,' Stile replied. 'The programme has uncovered a hacking attempt in that section of the database. A tunnel. They came in right underneath the firewalls. I was always aware that it could be done, of course, but I've never seen it actually achieved before. Impressive.'

'Bollocks to that,' snapped Shane. 'How recently were they there?'

'How recently?'

Shane was starting to dislike Mr Stile. 'When where they in?'

'They're still inside,' Stile replied.

'Then find them.'

Stile turned to the keyboard and punched in a series of commands. 'This should take only a moment or two. I've told the program we are interested in this intrusion, and it is now initiating a search.'

Shane was already pacing around the room, thinking about the next steps in the plan once they located their prey.

'How long have they been in the database?' asked Fuller.

'Judging by the information here, it could have been seven or eight hours,' replied Stile.

Shane looked down at the man scornfully. 'Remind me never to buy a computer,' he said. 'These things are about as secure as Hyde Park.'

'How much information could they collect in that time?' asked Fuller.

'Depends,' said Stile. 'Assuming they are just downloading material for analysis later, and assuming they are using a very fast modem, which I think is inevitable since I doubt they are saving money on cheap equipment, they could probably be taking about a hundred megabytes of data an hour. Call that seven or eight hundred megabytes overnight, or roughly half a million pages of printed text.'

'A lot, I think, is the answer we are looking for,' said Fuller.

'Doesn't matter how much,' interrupted Shane, 'So long as we catch them. We'll get it back.'

Stile was looking back at the terminal, studying the information on the screen, a fearful look deepening on his face as he peered into the machine. 'Bad news, I'm afraid,' he said slowly. 'They didn't use a direct modem connection into the network. They came in over the Internet.'

Shane turned sharply on his heels, looking directly down at the man. His expression was fierce and unforgiving. 'What does that mean?'

Stile was starting to wonder if Shane was the sort of man who should be on the Kizog payroll, but realised there was nothing he could do about him; his authority came directly from the Chairman and to disobey was madness. 'It means the connection comes from an Internet service provider. It is their computer that is plugging into ours. The hackers will be plugged into the service provider, but it's happening at one stage removed. There is no direct connection between us and the hacker.'

Shane stuffed a cigarette into his mouth. 'You mean we can't find them.'

'It's not as bad as that,' replied Stile. 'We can find the service provider, because we have their number here. It has a Birmingham code. There won't be many service providers in that area, so you shouldn't have much trouble locating it. They will know which of their subscribers has been plugging into our network. It will all be recorded on their mainframes. Whether they will co-operate with us I don't know.'

Shane reached for the phone on the desk and keyed in four digits. It rang only twice before the Chairman picked it up. 'We need some help, boss,' said Shane. 'We located our prey hacking into the system. But they are trying to hold us up by using an Internet connection to disguise their location. You need to get the police to lean on those people at the Internet place to hand over details on which of their subscribers has been plugging into our system. Stile has the details.'

'Quite so,' replied the Chairman. 'I'll see to it immediately. How long have they been inside?'

'Overnight,' replied Shane. 'They have taken a load of gear.'

'And they are still there?'

'Still inside, yeah.'

'Does it present a problem if we stop them?' asked the Chairman.

Shane looked down at Stile and repeated the question.

'We can stop them,' replied Stile. 'But we might lose the connection into the Internet service they are using. If we really want to get our hands on these people then we need to keep them online.'

Shane relayed the answer. 'Tell Stile to let them remain in the database,' whispered the Chairman. 'I think we are very close to catching them now.'

TWENTY-THREE

Tara and Jack stood huddled together in the phone box. They had walked three or four blocks from the hotel, twisting through the backstreets, and stood outside one of the many hospitals in the area. The booth was littered with cards from hookers, and a light drizzle was falling from above them. None of the people passing by paid any attention to them, and, for the moment at least, they felt sure they were safe.

Jack fished the number from his jacket pocket, and began to dial. 'Julian Symonds, please,' he told the switchboard operator.

The call went straight through to his office. His secretary said she would see if he was available and asked who was calling. 'Jack Borrodin,' he replied crisply.

'From which company,' she asked.

'Don't worry about that. Just tell him I am on the line, and see if he takes the call.'

She returned seconds later, saying that Mr Symonds would be

happy to speak to him, and that she would put the call straight through.

'Where are you, Mr Borrodin?' Symonds asked at once. 'I had been starting to think I would never hear from you again.'

'We're still around,' Jack replied firmly.

'And how are you getting on?'

'We are nearly there,' answered Jack. 'How are your arrangements going?'

'Transport has been taken care of,' replied Symonds. 'The Chairman of Ocher has seen to that personally. A credit facility in your and Miss Ling's joint names has been established here at the bank. I have authorised it personally. You can trade up to your credit limit. Two million.'

'How do I know I can trust you?'

Symonds hesitated before answering. 'Look, we are both taking a big chance here. But it seems neither of us is in a very strong position. I am about to lose this defence. And you are about to lose your freedom. I suggest we try to get along.'

'OK,' replied Jack. 'This is the story. We have established beyond doubt that Kizog researched biological weapons and that it created Ator. We have established, beyond doubt, that it was paid for this work by the various Western governments, who reimbursed it via their health budgets. We are still a bit unclear about how the counterfeiting operation works into the picture. Now, I need you to tell me something. Do we have enough?'

Symonds sounded uncertain. 'You might do, you might not.'

'What do you mean?' asked Jack.

'We need the whole picture,' replied Symonds, his voice betraying his concern. 'Everything. The more we have, the more certain I can be that the bid can be called off, and that you can collect your money from us and be taken out of the country. Any gaps, and Kizog and their lawyers could start picking us to pieces. We have to have the whole story. With evidence.'

'OK,' said Jack. 'We are still working on it. We have until Friday, right?'

'Until Friday,' replied Symonds. 'Give me a call tomorrow and let me know how you are getting on. I will notify the Takeover Panel and the Bank of England to tell them we want a last-minute meeting. That will give us the maximum time.' He paused. 'And Mr Borrodin, good luck.'

Jack replaced the receiver. Tara took him by the hand, and together they walked silently through the streets back towards the hotel. Along the way, they stopped at a cheap store and bought themselves a new pair of jeans each, and a couple of sweatshirts. The bill came to £72. Their clothes were already feeling horribly dirty; and, anyway, Jack pointed out, they deserved a treat.

'Is there anyone you want to call?' asked Tara as they walked from the store.

Her voice struck Jack as distant, unconnected from the present moment, as though she were drifting off to some other place of which he had no knowledge. 'I already called Symonds,' he replied flatly.

'A personal call,' she continued. 'Someone you want to re-assure, tell them you are still all right?'

Jack shook his head. There was, he realised, no one. 'My parents are dead, you know that,' he replied testily. 'Who would I call?'

'Some friends, perhaps,' she said quietly. 'A girlfriend.'

He slipped his arm around her waist, letting it rest above her hips. 'No,' he answered evenly. 'It would be too risky.'

Tara smiled, and he asked her if she wanted lunch somewhere, but Tara shook her head; not enough time, she told him. Pick up a sandwich and get back to work. They now had less than forty-eight hours to figure out where the counterfeiting operation fitted into the picture. There was still work to be done.

Alan Lancer had spent two years as managing director of Arbex Internet Services in Birmingham, and this was the first time he had ever received a request for information from the special branch. It was the first time he had received any kind of a request from the police. And it had taken him by surprise.

The officer had explained that they were attempting to catch a pair of dangerous computer hackers, and Lancer had been only too happy to comply. Searching through the database for the last twenty-four hours was a simple matter. He issued the instructions to his technical staff, and within an hour of delivering the request the police had the name of the subscriber who had been using this system to hack into the Kizog network.

The Chairman had not been pleased when he heard the news. Late Wednesday afternoon, Fuller, Shane and Finer had gathered in his office to review the chase. 'It looks like they are smarter than we thought,' said the Chairman.

Reluctant though he was to do so, Shane had been forced to concede he had a point. The Arbex subscriber they were looking for turned out to be a Mr KH Reid, who gave an address in Amsterdam. A quick check with the Dutch police revealed that no such address existed. Tracking down the credit card number had revealed that Mr Reid lived in Enfield, south London. When contacted, he told the police he had never heard of Borrodin and Ling, and they believed him. 'Obviously a stolen credit card number,' concluded Shane. 'An old trick, mostly used by your minor criminal. Pick up one of the old-fashioned manual swipe receipts and you have the name and number and expiry date of the card. You can order pretty much anything over the phone with it. Usually you get caught within a few weeks.'

'We don't have a few weeks,' whispered the Chairman. 'We have two days.'

'I know,' replied Shane.

The next stage in the inquiry, he continued, was to track down the phone line they had been using to dial into the Arbex system. In theory that should lead them straight to Tara and Jack. The police had contacted British Telecom, instructing them to put an instant trace on the call coming into Arbex. Fortunately it was connected to an electronic exchange, so everything should be stored in the databases. It took them about three hours to sort

238

through the computer records. Unfortunately, Shane was forced to concede once more, they appeared to have thought of that possibility as well. The calls were coming from Holland. His first thought had been that they had done a flit to the Continent, and were working from Amsterdam. That made no difference to him; it was as easy to finish them off there as here. But the calls seemed to be originating from the international operator's exchange outside the city. It was impossible they were camping out in that office. 'It seems they have been phreaking the phones,' Shane concluded reluctantly.

'Phreaking?' asked Finer.

'They have been messing with the phone system,' replied Shane. 'Playing with the electronic tones that route the calls around the world. It's a device hackers often use to get free calls, and our prey seem to have developed quite a taste for petty crime. The trouble is it also buggers up the trace. The computers get so confused they no longer know where the calls are coming from. They insist it is coming from the operator's office in Holland, which is why they aren't billing for it.'

The annoyance was clear in the creases on the Chairman's brow. 'You mean there is no way we can locate them?'

'Just one more possibility,' said Shane. 'The telecoms engineers have told the police that so long as the line is left open long enough, and if they have detected the phreaker, they should be able to trace the call back, at least to the exchange that is being messed with. That would give us the area where they are located.'

'And they can do that now?' asked the Chairman.

Shane shook his head. 'The line is closed right now,' he replied. 'But if they come back in, I think we can get a fix on them.'

The Chairman looked thoughtful. 'I suppose it depends on whether they have enough information yet,' he said.

Tara held the graph up before her, studying the way the lines moved. She had been poring over it at the hotel room desk for several minutes now, her face composed in an expression of perfect concentration. Eventually she passed it over to Jack. 'See something odd about this?' she asked.

Jack looked at the graph and shrugged.

'From about 1990 onwards,' she continued, 'if you add the legitimate sales from its drugs to the money it received from the government for research, the two figures stop giving you a hundred per cent.'

Jack looked at it again, more closely this time. 'You're right,' he replied.

'So from then on the company is receiving big slugs of money from somewhere else?'

'The counterfeiting operation,' Jack replied. 'They are bringing money in from there. That would be my guess.'

Tara nodded. 'Look at how the line for weapons research revenues starts shifting downwards,' she continued. 'Think about the wider context. From 1990 onwards the Cold War is over. Defence expenditure throughout the West starts to be scaled down. At the same time, our friends at Kizog see their sales falling. My guess is that after the demise of the old Soviet Union there was no longer such a demand for weapons research.'

Jack took up the theme. 'Which is very embarrassing for the company. They can hardly go to the shareholders and say they are no longer getting as much for their biological weapons. They have to find some way of plugging the hole in the revenue line. And quickly.'

'Hence the counterfeiting?'

'I guess so,' replied Jack.

'OK, it's a theory,' said Tara. 'But can we prove it?'

Jack paused for a moment, numerous possibilities running through his mind. 'I think so,' he said at last.

Tara looked at him closely. 'How?' she asked.

'It means going back inside. If we can trace how they're using the money from the counterfeiting operation to fill the gaps in

240

their revenues, then we'll have them. The proof that Symonds is looking for.'

A look of concern flashed across Tara's face. 'Is that safe?'

'Probably,' replied Jack confidently. 'If they were able to trace us through the Dutch connection they would have found us by now, and we would probably be dead. I think we have fooled them. It's safe.'

The Chairman was staring out of the plate-glass window, watching dusk fall on the offices and laboratories below. So close, he thought. So very close. They can't stop me now.

Finer walked up to the desk, perching on its side, looking up at the Chairman. He too glanced through the window at the complex below. Time to bail out? he wondered. Perhaps. Perhaps not. He would see which way events unfolded, and make his decision later. 'You wanted to see me,' he said.

'I thought you should see this.'

The Chairman turned away from the window, standing over the desk, and handed two sheets of paper across to his finance director.

Finer glanced down. It was a transcript of a phone conversation earlier that day between Jack Borrodin and Julian Symonds. He read the words slowly and carefully, chewing them over in his mind, weighing their consequences. Borrodin was clearly working for the other side now, and his raids on the company's databases must have yielded something. He had much of the story, although, clearly, not yet everything. Suddenly, Finer decided, they were starting to look like dangerous opponents.

'From the wiretap?' he asked casually.

The Chairman nodded. 'Symonds's phone has been bugged for some time,' he replied. 'Always useful to know what the opposition is doing.'

'They are close,' said Finer. 'Too close for comfort.'

The Chairman wiped his brow. 'Shane will deal with them,' he replied quietly. 'They aren't there yet. And there is still time.'

'Sure,' said Finer. 'Everything will be OK. Just so long as we don't blink.'

The Chairman leaned over the desk, fixing a piercing stare on Finer. 'I wanted you to know something, Ralph,' he said.

'Yes?' the finance director replied evenly.

'Taylor is a joke, a simple buffoon, a leg man, that's all.'

'I've always thought so,' replied Finer, wondering what Sir Kurt was getting at.

'I mean, if anything were to happen to me, you would be the man to take over,' continued the Chairman quietly. 'That is why I have always made sure you were involved in everything.'

TWENTY-FOUR

The trail had started late on Wednesday evening. Jack quietly left the hotel room, walked through the night for several blocks, and then slipped into a phone booth. He checked his pocket for change; there was more than £20 in coins. And he checked his watch. It was just after nine. The Turks and Caicos Islands were five hours behind London time; all the offices there should still be open.

After collecting the number from International Directory Enquiries, Jack slipped a series of coins into the machine and placed the call. On reaching the operator at the First National Bank he asked to be put through to account enquiries.

Jack gave his name to the enquiries office, and answered a series of questions to establish his identity as the sole share-holder in Nidorrob International Trading, a company registered on the island, with an account at this bank; the account Finer had set up to receive the money that came via Shane when he

243

was first dragged into the counterfeiting plot. Jack asked first for the balance of the account. After a few moments the answer came back: £250,000. How long had the money been in the account? Jack asked. Ten days came the reply. And from whom was the payment made? The clerk had to check the files, and whilst he was waiting Jack fed another series of coins into the phone.

'That payment was wired through from the account of HKS Pharmaceuticals Trading, a company registered in the British Virgin Islands,' replied the clerk.

'Thanks,' said Jack, scribbling the name down on a piece of paper. 'One more thing, can I put stock trades through this account?'

'Certainly, sir,' replied the clerk. 'We charge a one and a half per cent commission for non-advisory trades, plus a hundred US dollars for holding the stock certificates.'

'Use the entire £250,000 to buy put options in Kizog,' said Jack. 'They are traded on the London and New York futures markets. Just execute at best price when the market opens.'

'Certainly, sir,' replied the clerk. 'And when the trade is completed would you like me to contact you to advise on the price we dealt at?'

'Don't worry about that,' said Jack. 'I'll call you.'

He put the phone down, still wondering if the futures trade was the right move. He shrugged, and began walking back towards the hotel. Fuck it, he told himself. If I am going to gamble Symonds's money on defeating Kizog, I may as well throw my own into the pot. If this doesn't work out, it won't do me much good anyway.

On his return to the hotel, Jack lay down on the bed. His limbs ached and his head was throbbing, and he could feel the exhaustion catching up on him. He wanted to lift himself back to the desk, and get back to work on the computer. There was so little time left. But Tara told him to rest; he needed a few hours' sleep, she warned, or else he was in danger of collapse. Just give her the information, and she would spend the first part of the night rooting through the database for the evidence they needed. Reluctantly he conceded. They needed more material. And so far, he reflected, their excursions into the Kizog databases did not seem to have exposed them to any danger. The phreak was safe.

Shane was on to his second Styrofoam cup; the first was already bulging with cigarette ends, and had been cast into the bin. Stile had been dismissed for the night; the man was starting to get on Shane's nerves, and anyway, he didn't have the stomach for this kind of work.

As for Shane, he was doing just fine, or so he told himself. True, he admitted, the prey had proved harder to capture than he had expected. Amateurs they might be, but they had shown a streak of ruthless professionalism. The phreaking was good, he reflected. A nice touch. Their route into the network had made it look as if they would be easy to track, then turned out to be a feint. Very nice. They were playing for time, leading him astray. Understandable. Time was what they needed.

But they were getting closer, Shane decided. Much closer. So close that he could almost feel them. They had, he realised, riled him. So what? he told himself. He was now relishing the chase. And when the moment came to deal with them directly, it would not just be another violent chore. No. He would enjoy it.

He had mastered the basic elements of the detection program, and the consultants in the US were also standing by, keeping their chips alert for evidence of another intrusion. So long as they came into the system again, this time the company would be ready and waiting. The net was closing.

It was just after five in the morning, and Shane was catching a few moments' rest, when he was aroused by an icon flashing on the screen. The program had located another intrusion. Shane keyed in the instructions, and within moments, the answer came back that the hacking attempt was coming over the Internet from Arbex. Shane picked up the phone and spoke briefly to the tele- coms engineers who were standing by. The line was live again, he told them. The call was tracked.

It was time for them to start untangling the phreak.

Jack had woken up early, his body refreshed and his mind clearer. He drank a couple of cups of coffee in quick succession, and felt ready to get back to work again. The nerves that had started to fray his mind last night were easing. They were closer now, and with the nearness of the resolution, he found to his surprise that he felt calmer. Soon it would all be over.

Tara had done some good work over the past few hours. Getting into the database was one thing. Finding the information that you needed was something else. There were hundreds of thousands of files in there, many of them random garbage. It was like trying to find your way through a maze; a maze with thousands of twists and turns.

Jack was sure that his hunch was right. Kizog had to be shifting the money from the counterfeiting operation into the company somehow. And it had to be doing it through offshore accounts; that was the only way to maintain secrecy.

Tara had been sifting through files, looking at them, deciding whether they were relevant or not, downloading anything that might be of some use. She had been looking at the code words Jack had given her, zeroing in on the offshore accounts that they felt were relevant. It was exhausting work, and her mind was starting to soften and her eyes droop. Jack stood behind her, and rubbed the back of her neck. 'You get some sleep now,' he told her firmly.

She turned, stood, and kissed him gently on the lips. 'I think we are almost there,' she told him.

It was just after nine on Thursday morning when the call came through directly to Shane. Tossing his cigarette into a coffee cup, he reached for the phone, his pleasure growing as he listened to what the engineers had to say. 'Good work,' he muttered into the receiver. Putting the phone down, he took the lift up to the fifth floor. He checked first in the Chairman's office, but the old man was not in yet. He would speak to him later. Next he checked the finance director's office. Finer was already at work, had been for more than an hour, and Fuller was with him.

They appeared to be deep in conversation, but Shane could not hear what they were saying. He strode into the office, standing a couple of yards from the desk where Finer was sitting. 'Found them!' he barked. 'Trapped like flies.'

Finer looked surprised. 'Where are they?' he asked.

'Around Russell Square,' replied Shane briskly. 'Makes sense. Lots of cheap hotels. Plenty of tourists. Not many locals to notice you. One of the best areas in London to hide away.'

'We have an address?' asked Fuller anxiously.

Shane shook his head. 'The best the engineers could do is an exchange, the one that is being messed with. It covers all the numbers starting 317. They faxed through a map.'

He passed over a sheet of paper. Finer looked down at it. 'A large area.'

Shane shrugged. 'I reckon they will be staying in a hotel. Only simple way of getting accommodation at such short notice. And without having to give any sort of identification. They'll definitely be in a hotel.'

'How many in the area?' asked Fuller.

'Thirty or forty,' he answered quickly. 'Fifty maximum. No more than that.'

Fuller stood up and walked across to Shane. 'We'd better make a start then,' she said. 'If we are to find them by tomorrow morning.'

'I can handle this alone,' said Shane.

Finer looked up at him. 'I think she should come with you,' he said. 'There are two of them, and she is useful back-up. We don't want to take any risks at this stage. Time is too precious for any screw-ups.'

'Whatever,' snarled Shane. 'We are wasting time already.'

He turned away and strode from the room, Fuller following along behind him. In the doorway, Shane stopped, leant against the frame and cast Finer a bitter look. 'And there won't be any screw-ups,' he snapped.

It had taken Jack all morning, but at last he felt that he was making progress. He started by scanning through the database, looking for references in the accounts for payments into or out of offshore deposits. There were plenty of them, and many, no doubt, would be quite innocent. Like any multinational company, Kizog maintained an intricate network of offshore subsidiaries; they were used for insurance, for employee pension plans, and for inter-company transfers, usually to switch profits from high-tax to low-tax regimes. Jack had checked through twenty-five, discarding each as of no further interest, before he began to smell any leads.

The one advantage he had, he realised, was that these were internal company records; any accounts presented to the public or the tax authorities would doubtless show a quite different picture. These records were intended for internal use only, and depicted a much simpler portrait of the structure; they were not designed to deliberately confuse, as the public accounts often were.

HKS Pharmaceuticals, needless to say, was not listed anywhere as a subsidiary of Kizog. That would have been too simple. Kizog, however, did appear to have a trading relationship with the company. Jack found the link where he least expected it; within the asset ledger, inside the property portfolio. A close examination of the records revealed that for the past four years Kizog had been consistently selling off a stream of properties owned around the world, then leasing them back from the new owners at peppercorn rents. The profits on the property sales were then booked into the accounts as revenues. And the new owner of the properties, paying far more than any of the buildings was really worth, was HKS Pharmaceuticals.

Turning to the spreadsheet, Jack hurriedly keyed in the figures for the property disposals; beginning in 1990, the numbers rose rapidly each year, starting at just £50 million, and rising to £350 million in the final year. He compared the numbers to the short-fall in Kizog's government research revenues they had un-covered earlier. The match was perfect. The company was feeding money in from the counterfeiting operation to make up for the cash that was disappearing from its weapons research.

Tara was still lying in bed, catching up on the sleep she had missed. 'I think we have found the link,' Jack whispered in her ear.

She looked up drowsily. 'Proof?' she asked.

'Linking the company directly to the counterfeiting operation,' Jack replied, pleasure evident in his voice.

'Are you still on-line?' she asked anxiously.

Jack nodded.

'One more thing,' she continued. 'See if we can find out what happened to those scientists working on Ator.'

The Chairman was sitting alone in his office. On the desk-top, his terminal had switched to a Reuters feed, and a display of FTSE stock prices covered the screen. The market had fallen by twenty points already today, and most of the screen was red, indi-cating the stocks where prices had fallen. His eyes moved to the Kizog share price, marked by the abbreviation 'KZG.L'; the price was down by fourteen pence, the first time it had fallen in several days. Using the mouse, the Chairman clicked on the asterix next to the stock price. Instantly, the story Reuters was carrying flashed up on to the screen.

KIZOG FALLS ON FUTURES TRADES
London: 11:32 GMT: Shares in the British pharmaceuticals giant Kizog were under pressure this morning
ahead of the conclusion of its contested take-over of Swiss
rival Ocher due to be resolved tomorrow (Friday). Futures
traders reported that a heavy put order from an overseas
investor had prompted market makers to shift prices

downwards. Analysts said, however, that Kizog was still expected to win the bid, and attributed the futures sales to investors covering positions after the heavy gains in the Kizog share price in recent weeks.

The Chairman clicked off the story, and the screen returned to the FTSE index. Kizog was now down sixteen pence. On the other side of the desk, the phone was ringing. The Chairman picked it up and was told by his secretary that Simon Morrison was on the line. He told her to put him through. 'Anything serious on the futures market?' the Chairman asked at once.

'We don't believe so,' replied Morrison. 'We haven't been able to identify the seller. Whoever it is, they are trading offshore, so it will be impossible to establish their identity. We don't think it's anything serious. There is only two or three hundred thousand being traded. Someone taking a wild punt that the bid is going to fail. They're wasting their money.'

'Fine, fine,' said the Chairman. 'What else?'

'One matter of some urgency has cropped up,' said Morrison edgily. 'The Bank of England want a meeting tomorrow morning.'

The Chairman paused. 'The Bank?' he replied at length. 'Why?'

'Apparently Zurich Financial requested it,' said Morrison. 'A last-ditch bid by Ocher to stop the bid, I believe. They wouldn't give any details, but we have to see the Deputy Governor at ten. I'm afraid we'll have to be there.'

The Chairman sighed. 'Then we'd better go.'

'Is there anything we haven't thought of that Ocher could dredge up?' asked Morrison. 'It is best to be prepared for these occasions.'

The Chairman paused. 'Nothing at all,' he replied calmly. 'Absolutely nothing.'

Jack could feel Tara's presence behind him, and could just hear her sipping on her coffee, but he was too engrossed in the information scrolling across his terminal to turn to face her.

At her suggestion, he had started rooting through the databases to see what he could discover about the three scientists who had died whilst investigating the origins of Ator. He had shut down the accounting records, certain that he would find nothing there. For a moment he had been lost where to look next. He tried calling up the directories but there were hundreds of them; how many documents Kizog kept stored on its mainframes it was impossible to say, but it could run into millions. The solution turned out to be simpler than he could have imagined. He keyed up a word search, and tapped the name Hans Gerter into the terminal. After seven minutes of searching, the computer replied that it had one document containing that name. 'Read,' typed Jack. 'Access denied,' responded the machine. 'Shit,' Jack muttered under his breath.

Leaning over his shoulder, Tara's fingers moved across the keyboard, tapping in a line of code she had used earlier to break through the firewall. Within moments they found themselves back in the same directory. 'Read,' Jack keyed into the machine once more. This time the document sprang to life. Tara rested against the back of the chair whilst they both read.

E-mail: from the office of Dr Peter Scott to the office of the Chairman: secure system: access restricted: time delivered: 14:03: 28/6/93
I have learnt that a researcher from Roche called Hans Gerter is to deliver a paper at a symposium on Ator next month, where he will argue that the virus might have its origins as a biological weapon. I don't believe that he has any direct evidence of this, but is merely working backwards from the impact of the disease and from its transmission mechanism. Obviously as research into the virus intensifies, this view is likely to gain wider currency. It is important that we move forward in resolving this problem.

Jack scrolled forward, searching to see if he could find a reply.

251

E-mail: from the office of the Chairman to the office of Dr
Peter Scott: secure system: access restricted: time
delivered: 16:10: 28/6/93
Message received and implications understood. Rest
assured, this matter is being dealt with urgently.

Tara stepped back from the screen. 'They murdered them,' she
said quietly.

TWENTY-FIVE

Julian Symonds paced anxiously around his ornate office on the seventeenth floor of the bank's London headquarters. He glanced at his watch. Already it was almost eleven, and so far there was no word from Borrodin. For the first time, doubts about the wisdom of his defence were starting to creep into his mind. There was no dishonour in watching your client be defeated by a wall of money. But this had the makings of a fiasco.

Arranging the meeting with the Bank of England had not been easy. At first their officials had been dismissive, suggesting that he present a written dossier of his evidence first. There was no time for that, he knew. A phone call to the Ocher chairman in Basle had triggered their change of heart; he had called his foreign minister, who had called the ambassador in London, who had submitted a direct, though confidential, request that the meeting be convened.

We're pressing the right buttons, thought Symonds. But can

they deliver? If not, my reputation will be finished.

His thoughts were interrupted by the sound of his intercom. 'I have a Mr Borrodin on the line,' announced his secretary.

Symonds grabbed the phone. 'Ten o'clock tomorrow morning,' he said instantly. 'At the Bank of England with the Deputy Governor. And let's hope to God that what you have is convincing.'

'It will be,' Jack replied calmly.

'It has to be proof, not conjecture,' said Symonds anxiously.

'It is proof,' replied Jack. 'Virtually.'

'Virtually isn't good enough.'

'Then I need one thing from you.'

Symonds sounded suspicious. 'What?' he asked.

'The bonds,' replied Jack. 'I need to know who is buying the bonds Kizog is issuing as part of its funding of the bid.'

'The usual people, I imagine,' said Symonds. 'Insurance companies, fund managers, wealthy investors. All the people who buy corporate bonds.'

'Get a list,' said Jack. 'I'm sure your people are capable of finding out who the buyers are. The ultimate owners. It may turn out to be crucial.'

'May I ask why?' asked Symonds.

'I'm working on it,' answered Jack.

Once again Symonds wondered why he was trusting someone who appeared so elusive.

'What's the price of October Kizog puts?' asked Jack.

Symonds checked on his Reuters screen. 'Eighteen pence,' he answered.

Jack made a quick mental calculation. The futures contract would enable him to sell Kizog shares at 670 pence and each right cost eighteen pence, meaning he would start making a profit as soon as the price went below 652 pence. He was sure it was going a lot lower than that. 'Start buying,' he told Symonds.

'There has already been some activity in Kizog options,' said Symonds.

'People are getting cold feet, I suppose,' said Jack innocently.

'I'll see you tomorrow,' said Symonds warmly.

'Fine,' answered Jack. 'And watch out for yourself over the next twenty-three hours. They can deal very roughly with anyone who gets in the way.'

Jack put down the phone, glanced along the street, and turned out of the phone box. He began walking the couple of blocks back to the hotel by himself. The streets were familiar, yet somehow different; as if seen through other eyes. His perspective had changed, and it struck him for the first time that this might be the last day he would spend in London for some time. Perhaps for ever. Would he be saddened to leave it all behind? It was hard to know. For the moment, he was just sure that he would be glad to put the events of the past few weeks behind him.

It was up to Symonds now.

The silver-grey Mercedes pulled up outside the Thistle Hotel, just off Southampton Row. Shane climbed out, clunking the door behind him, and fed a couple of pounds into the parking meter. Fuller trailed along behind him as he walked into the lobby of the hotel.

Shane doubted that they would be here. It was just a little too smart for their needs. The service would be too good; too many receptionists, too many bellhops and too many chambermaids to grow suspicious of the couple with all the computer equipment, who hardly ever went out. No. If he was in their shoes, this would not be the sort of place he would choose. Somewhere a little more down-at-heel would be his preference. There was no way of knowing what sort of mistakes they might be making, yet, from everything he had seen over the past few days, he suspected they would do the smart thing. Still, the only way to find them was to start at the beginning of the map and work his way through to the other side.

He would trap them, he thought to himself with a smile, as a spider traps a fly; slowly, methodically and for a living.

Patiently, Shane waited behind the Japanese tourist who, in

255

faltering English, and amid helpful smiles and bows from the receptionist, was trying to check into his room. He glanced down at the girl behind the desk, introduced himself, introduced Fuller, and flashed a police badge; it was a fake, but good enough to fool the untrained eye. When she asked how she could help, Shane produced pictures of Tara and Jack. Were they staying in their hotel, he wanted to know?

The girl shook her head, and said no, she had not seen them. She checked with her colleagues, and they too could not recall seeing either of them. Paid cash, probably, explained Shane. Stayed in their room most of the time. The girl shook her head again. No, nobody like that staying here, she said with obvious relief. Sorry.

Shane and Fuller thanked her for her help. He tucked the photographs back into his pocket and crossed the Thistle off his list. Together, they began walking down the street. Another thirty to go, he thought.

As Jack shut the hotel door behind him, he saw Tara at the computer, tapping away at the keyboard. He walked silently across the floor, standing behind her, running his hands through her short, uneven hair. With the palms of his hands he massaged her back. Below, he could see her hands slow down on the keyboard. She turned her neck, and their eyes met. For the first time Jack felt he could detect something different in her expression; a warmth and an eagerness that had not been there before. Desire, he decided. He leant forward and kissed her, their lips meeting, and in that moment Jack could feel his fears and anxieties dissolving.

'Tomorrow at ten o'clock,' he said.

Tara checked her watch. 'Twenty-two hours,' she said. 'I think we can survive until then.'

'Let's hope so,' replied Jack.

Tara had been spending the day typing up the results of their investigations into a neat, single document, straightforward enough to be understood by the bankers and officials for whom it was intended. Jack sat down at the desk, and began scrolling through her work, making occasional amendments as he went through it.

SUMMARY:
Kizog has since the middle of the 1960s been systematically researching biological weapons on behalf of various Western governments. It was paid for this work through the health budgets of the governments involved. The company provided perfect cover for biological warfare research because:
- it had ready access to a pool of biochemical research talent.
- the expenditure did not have to be disclosed to the public as it might have been in a normal military research establishment.
- the research would be unknown to the Soviet Union, and therefore would not be a target for infiltration by agents.

At its peak, this research was worth £300 million a year to Kizog, most of it pure profit.

As well as researching the weapons, Kizog also tested them in the Third World, usually in local wars, to establish data on battlefield effectiveness. The testing was organised through a network of pharmaceutical counterfeiting operations in the Third World which provided cover for manufacturing and delivery of the weapons.

One of the weapons developed by Kizog was Ator, the virus, which was extensively tested in Third World wars. It was based on leprosy, and developed from work originally done by a Dr Josef Zmitt, a defector from the Czech Republic, who had earlier worked on Soviet biological weapons programmes. As a result of battlefield testing of the virus in localised wars during the early 1980s, the Ator virus seeped into the general population, becoming a major health hazard by the early 1990s. Some biochemists working in the field had already started to suspect that Ator might be a military virus, but those closest to establishing the truth were assassinated by agents working for the company.

From 1990, military revenues to Kizog started to fall dramatically. The company began a programme of normalising its activities, which involved transplanting the counterfeiting operation to the West to replace revenues lost from the military work. Money from the counterfeiting operation was channelled into Kizog via a series of offshore property transactions. At the same time the company decided to release a vaccine for Ator, which had been developed simultaneously along with the virus. For this purpose an outsider was brought in, to make it appear that the virus was of Soviet design, and to obscure the fact that Kizog had possessed a vaccine all along. The takeover of Ocher was designed as the last phase of the normalisation process. Afterwards the reorganisation of the merged companies would allow both the biological weapons and the counterfeiting operations to be wound down. Mr Borrodin and Ms Ling would be held responsible for those activities, absolving the company of any blame.

'You left out the best part,' said Jack.

'We can't prove it yet,' replied Tara. 'Until we have evidence, we should forget it.'

The lobby of the New Bloomsbury Hotel was bare and sparse. By the desk were a pile of leaflets for musicals and plays, and the tourist attractions. The one receptionist was a man in his forties, with thinning hair, and a pallid complexion. He was sitting down, reading a book laid out flat on the desk.

His eyes glanced upwards at the man and woman standing in front of him. He did not recognise them. They were not guests.

258

A couple looking for a room for the night, most likely, he thought, although they had no baggage. In the car, perhaps.

Shane took out his badge, and flashed it at the receptionist. He pulled the photographs from his pocket, and put them in front of the man. His lines were well-rehearsed by now, and were delivered in a slow, mechanical tone. This was the ninth hotel they had visited so far today.

The receptionist shook his head. No, he said, he could not recall seeing them. They were definitely not guests here. Shane asked if the other staff might have seen them, but the man said he was the only person on duty tonight. He knew who was occupying all twenty rooms, and this couple was not amongst them.

Shane thanked him and left. He and Fuller stepped out into the street. Darkness was now falling, and Shane checked the map under the light of the hotel porch. They had covered about a third of the area so far. He glanced at his watch. It was just after seven. 'Plenty of time still,' he reassured Fuller.

It had seemed the most natural thing in the world. By early evening Jack and Tara had finished the dossier, checked through it a dozen times, and printed out five copies. Each was stapled together. The supporting evidence had been neatly marked up, leaving an easy trail for anyone to follow, and packed up in the sports bag, ready to be stowed away. Everything was ready.

Jack had left Tara alone whilst he slipped outside to pick up a couple of pizzas from the Pizza Hut around the corner. Along the way he dropped into the off-licence and bought a bottle of wine. If this was to turn out to be their last night together, he reflected, they might as well enjoy it.

On his return, he found her sitting on the floor. She had showered already, her legs were crossed and she appeared deep in thought. Jack sat next to her, uncorked the bottle of Australian chardonnay, and poured it into two tumblers he had retrieved from the bathroom. He opened the boxes, and they ate the pizza

259

with their fingers. Throughout the meal they joked about the orange furniture in the hotel room, the cardboard taste of the pizza, and the temperature of the wine. Both of them studiously avoided the one thing that was preying on their minds: tomorrow.

'You knew all along that Kizog was involved in Ator, didn't you?' asked Jack suddenly. 'Why did you ever get involved?'

Tara put down the pizza in her hand, and looked up at him. 'I suspected,' she replied. 'That's why I agreed to take the job. But I didn't know.'

'I'd have run a mile,' said Jack.

Tara turned her eyes to one side. 'I was obsessed,' she answered. 'After David died, I had to find out why. This seemed the most obvious course to follow. I'm only sorry that you became involved.'

Jack lay down on the floor, resting his head on her lap. 'They've been planning to set me up for years,' he said softly. 'I can see that now. Since before they posted me to Thailand.'

Casually, she slipped her fingers into his short hair, running her palms across his scalp. 'I'm glad you're here,' she said softly. 'I would hate to be doing this alone.'

When the food was finished, they sat with their backs to the bed, finishing the wine, and still talking and laughing. Jack would be unable to recall the exact moment later, but he could feel them drawing closer. They shared more than just fear now; they shared hopes as well. Hopes, Jack reflected, of being together.

He leant across and kissed her. Her lips fell towards him, hungrily, biting at his neck, and his hands started to roam across her body. He took her in his arms, and they drifted lazily towards the bed, collapsing on to the mattress still wrapped up in each other. His mouth ran across her face and neck, nuzzling her with kisses. She responded warmly, tugging him closer to her. She seemed different somehow. Her hair was gone, and without it the shape of her features had changed. Her body was unfamiliar. But he was intoxicated all the same. He lifted her T-shirt above her arms, and ran his tongue along her nipples, feeling them stiffen

260

beneath his lips. He ran his arms along her back, kneading her soft flesh between his palms. Jack was aware that this might well be the last time he made love in a long time. Perhaps for ever. He was glad it was her.

There was a passion and intimacy to her that Jack found enthralling. Though it was their first time together, there was none of the fumbling uncertainty he would have expected for a sexual début. It had been a long courtship – too long, perhaps, Jack found himself thinking – and they were already used to one another. Tenderly, he kissed her eyelids, and felt himself disappearing into her body. He could feel her, wrapping her legs around him, smothering him with her passion, and, in his mind, he could picture them, far way, somewhere hazy and exotic. In those instants, he felt afterwards, both of them had forgotten everything.

When it was over, he cradled her in his arms, feeling the warmth of her breath on his chest. Jack lay beside her, wondering about the other man, the one who had led her into this quest, the one who was now dead. Does she still love him? he asked himself. Or does she love me?

The receptionist studied the pictures carefully. This was the twenty-sixth hotel Shane and Fuller had visited, and they were by now just going through the motions. They knew they would get there eventually, but each visit held no sense of anticipation.

'I'm not sure,' he replied.

Shane's eyes darted upwards, scrutinising the man. 'They might have changed their haircuts, or disguised themselves in some way,' he said.

'With shorter hair, yes,' the man continued hesitantly. 'I think it might be them.'

'Plenty of computer equipment in their room?'

The man nodded. 'I thought they must be IBM salesmen, or something, they brought in so much stuff,' he smiled. 'And they insisted on a direct-dial phone. Paid extra for it. In cash.'

Shane slapped his hand down on the desk. 'It's them,' he muttered. 'How long are they here for?'

'Since Monday,' said the receptionist. 'Room 302. They paid in advance until Friday.'

Shane took the photographs back, thanked the man, and, with Fuller, walked towards the back of the dingy, poorly lit lobby. 'They're here,' he said.

Fuller could see his jaw harden as he mouthed the words. 'You want to deal with them now?' she said.

Shane shook his head. 'This is central London,' he said. 'You can't just walk into a hotel room and start blasting people away. Creates a nasty atmosphere.'

'Later,' suggested Fuller.

'Yes,' replied Shane. 'Let them rest. We know they are coming out. And I know how to deal with them in the morning.'

TWENTY-SIX

The sleek, blue, chauffeur-driven Daimler had turned in from
the M25 and was heading towards the City. Inside, a glass par-
tition separated the driver from the Chairman and his finance
director, and the shaded windows protected them from the early
morning sunshine. The Chairman was flicking through the
morning's papers, reading the financial pages; they were all
predicting an easy victory for Kizog when the deadline for
acceptances of its offer by Ocher shareholders passed at noon
today. The Chairman savoured every word, and smiled discreetly to himself as he read. 'The merged company will be
dominant within its industry, and will be one of the most powerful private corporations in the world,' said the *Telegraph*. Quite
so, he thought to himself. And more than anything else, it will
be mine.

For the first time in days the Chairman felt composed and
relaxed. He had spoken to Shane late last night and learnt that

263

the last obstacle had been trapped. Soon they would be dealt with. And by noon, everything would be perfectly in place. He would enjoy lunch today. There would be much to celebrate.

He checked his watch. It was just after nine. Plenty of time. Picking up the mobile phone, he keyed in the number of the one person he wanted to speak to. After two rings, Shane answered. 'Is it done yet?'

'Not yet,' replied Shane. 'They haven't come down yet. But they will soon. They don't have much time left if they are to make that meeting.'

'Let me know when you have them.'

'Right.'

Shane folded the mobile back into his pocket. He had booked a couple of rooms at the hotel; it was unlikely that Tara and Jack would try to move in the night, but he didn't want to take any chances. He had sent Fuller off the get some sleep, while he waited in the lobby, sitting on one of the sofas, keeping his eyes firmly peeled on the staircase and the lift. At three, Fuller had come downstairs, and he had slipped upstairs to get some sleep. By five-thirty, refreshed and feeling fit, he had come back down, sipping on a series of coffees, and smoking his way through half a packet of cigarettes, whilst he watched and waited. There were no Camels in the hotel machine, so he had switched to Rothmans. Apart from that he felt fine. Just fine.

Jack woke first. He looked at his watch and saw that it was just after seven-thirty. No hurry, he thought. There was plenty of time. He reached out across the bed, feeling her body, warm and comforting and asleep. His kisses woke her, and her eyes opened slowly. She greeted him with a smile, and tugged him close to her body. For ten minutes they just lay there, holding on to one another, reluctant to let go, enjoying a few brief moments of security.

Rising from the bed, Jack showered, and ordered some breakfast. Whilst Tara was washing, he drank a coffee and read once more through the dossier they had prepared. He felt good. The work was convincing. The evidence was all there. And there should be nothing that could go wrong now. For the first time in weeks, he was starting to feel calm and composed. By lunchtime today, he reflected, all of this would be over. They would be free. They would be rich. And they would be together.

Tara joined him, and they ate breakfast together. Just before nine, they dressed, and Tara started applying a few light touches of make-up to her face; it was an important meeting, she decided, and, despite the state of her hair, she would do her best to look good.

'How do you feel?' asked Jack.

'Positive,' Tara replied. 'I think we can win.'

Jack nodded, grateful for her confidence and her company. 'I'll go down and pay the bill,' he said. 'Wait ten minutes and then follow me. I'll meet you at the front door. If, for any reason, you don't see me there, then make your way straight to the bank. Don't try to look for me.'

He squeezed the top of her shoulder, noticing the worried look in her eyes. 'I'll come with you,' she insisted.

'No,' Jack replied. 'It is safer this way. We have come so far – we don't want to take any chances now.'

Holding her tight between his arms, Jack kissed her firmly on the lips, lingering for a moment as her tongue flickered seductively across his. Without looking back, he collected their two bags, and headed downstairs towards the lobby.

Shane spotted him at once. He lifted a newspaper up to hide himself, and whispered to Fuller to do the same. From the corner of his eye, he tracked Jack coming down the stairs, and walking up to the receptionist. He noted that Jack was alone, and presumed Tara would be joining him in a moment. He would wait. He wanted them both together; if just one of them escaped, they could still pose a threat.

Retrieving the mobile phone from his pocket, Shane dialled the number. 'Relax,' he whispered into the receiver as soon as it was answered. 'I have them in front of me. Everything will be taken care of.'

'Quite so,' replied the Chairman.

The Daimler was on the edges of the City now, held up in a traffic jam caused by one of the roadblocks that monitored all the vehicles coming into the Square Mile. The Chairman turned to Finer, a wide smile creasing up his face. 'They have them,' he whispered. 'We can enjoy this meeting.'

Finer nodded and said that was good. He had always believed, he pointed out, that everything would work out fine.

Glancing at her watch, Tara noted that there was another four minutes to go before she should make her way downstairs. Sitting on the edge of the bed, she could feel her pulse quickening. She looked at her watch again. Three and a half minutes. She could still smell him in the room, and in that moment she realised she just wanted to be by his side.

The receptionist gave Jack a wary look as he approached the desk. Looking in his file, careful to betray no sign of nerves, the man fished out the bill. The room had been paid for in advance, but there were service charges to settle. There were, naturally, no call charges; the blue box had ensured that none of the calls they had made had been billed to this number. The total for meals and drinks came to £140. Jack handed over the notes, and told the receptionist that he was not worried about the receipt. The man took the money, relieved, and a little surprised, that they had dealt with their bill before being arrested. He certainly had no desire to warn them; he would prefer they were off the premises before anything happened.

Jack collected the two bags, holding them both in one hand. He glanced at his watch. Three minutes, he noted. He walked towards the door, deciding that he would stand unobtrusively on the pavement, his back turned to anyone passing by.

Behind him, Shane and Fuller folded down their newspapers, stood up, and followed him at a brisk pace through the glass

266

doors. Shane stood behind Jack, easing the pistol from his pocket, and jabbing it hard into his back.

Jack's head spun round. He could see Shane's face, hard and unyielding, and he could just see the gun jabbing into him. Most of all he could feel it, a hard wedge of metal pressed deep into his flesh. 'Don't think for a moment that I won't kill you in the street,' said Shane. 'No one will stop me. All these people will flee. And I'll be long gone by the time anyone calls the police.'

The tone of his voice was steely and cold; it betrayed no nerves or doubt. Instinctively, Jack felt that he was telling the truth. The man would kill him, here and now, if he had to.

'Where's the girl,' snapped Shane.

Jack shifted his head, twisting his neck around to look Shane in the eye. 'She's already gone,' he said, hoping to mask the fear in his voice. 'Yesterday.'

Shane pushed him against the wall, the gun wedging hard into his back. 'Bollocks,' he muttered. 'You never did have the stomach for this kind of work.'

'You can do what you like to me,' said Jack. 'Tara has all the evidence. She'll deliver it anyway.'

'Let's just wait and see,' said Shane.

Upstairs, Tara checked her watch once more. It was, she decided, time to go. Taking a deep breath, she checked herself in the mirror. Running her hands through her hair, she rearranged the fringe. Grow it long again, she decided. And never let Jack cut it again. The guy had no idea what he was doing.

Tara looked around the room one last time, checking that they had left nothing behind. She would not miss that shade of orange, she decided to herself. Five days had been long enough. And, smiling at the thought, she switched off the light and walked downstairs.

Walking slowly into the lobby, she cast her eyes carefully through the murky room. There were two Orientals at the desk, and a pair of backpackers sitting in the lobby, poring over a map and a train timetable. No sign of Jack. Tara cast her eyes up towards the door. She could see the sunlight streaming on to the street, and an endless parade of tourists and office workers walking by. But no sign of him.

Hesitantly, she walked towards the door. She glanced nervously through the glass, before pushing it open, and stepping out on to the pavement. She glanced first to her right, scanning the road for some sign of him. Inside, she could feel her heart sinking as she realised he was nowhere to be seen.

'Go, Tara,' shouted Jack. 'Just move.'

Spinning hard on her heels, she turned. Five yards away, she could see him. His face was turned into the wall, and a rough-looking man with a leather trench coat was leaning hard into him. A woman stood next to them, her eyes darting anxiously down the street. 'Jack,' she whispered.

'Run, my darling, run,' Jack shouted.

Beneath her, her feet froze. Tara looked at the man again, then at Jack, and then at the woman walking towards her. Fuller grabbed her by the arm, twisting it hard behind her back. Tara could feel a streak of pain twisting through her veins. Fuller pulled tighter, leading her towards Shane.

Lifting the gun briefly from Jack's back, he flashed it towards Tara. 'Do what you're told or the cunt gets it,' he snarled.

Shane pushed the gun back into Jack, and took Tara's arm. 'Walk,' he said.

Silently, he pushed them across the road, and into the NCP carpark on the other side of the street. Shane had noticed the place last night, and decided it was the perfect spot. Fuller opened the door, and the four of them walked through, heaving them down the damp-stained, concrete steps. They went down one, two, three, and then four flights, emerging through the door on the fifth floor. Deep underground, at the lowest level of the car-park, the light was dim and sullen, and only a few cars were scattered through the empty concrete cavern.

Shane pushed them hard, shoving both Tara and Jack towards

the furthest corner. He threw them against a wall, beneath a thin strip of neon that cast a pale and ebbing light down on the blackened, exhaust-stained concrete. Walking three paces back, he stood away from them, his eyes fixed upon them in a malevolent, unforgiving stare.

'Crappy haircuts,' he muttered.

Jack could feel Tara gripping his back. Shane was standing no more than three feet away from them now, his legs slightly apart. He was holding the gun in his hand, and pointing it directly at Jack.

'Strictly amateur,' he continued. 'A real give-away. If I see someone with a haircut as shit as that, I know at once they are running from something. Get a decent haircut if you want to change your appearance. Not that anyone looks for haircuts. It's the eyes that people search for. If you really want to escape, use contact lenses to change the colour of your eyes. That really throws people off the trail.'

'We are amateurs,' answered Jack. 'You knew that all along.'

'And amateurs get burnt,' said Shane.

'We have the evidence,' interrupted Tara. 'We have downloaded it to a safe place. It doesn't matter what you do to us. The evidence will still be there.'

Shane took two paces forward, standing inches from them, and ran the barrel of the gun down the side of Tara's cheek. 'Don't try and get smart with me, Madame Wong,' he said roughly, leaning so close she could smell the nicotine on his breath. 'We're not here to play games. So you *have* downloaded this data. Big fucking deal. I can trace the number the modem has dialled, and then I'll go and destroy the computer you have transferred it to. End of fucking problem. And don't waste your breath with talk about some plan to make sure the information is transferred to the authorities. Just remember one thing. We are the fucking authorities.'

He paused and took one step back. 'Not very reassuring is it?' he said. From his pocket Shane fished out two strips of black cloth. 'Always carry these with me,' he said. 'Be prepared. The mark of a professional.'

'You wanted us dead from the beginning?' said Tara angrily.

'Chat, chat, chat,' answered Shane. 'Listen, doll, nobody is interested in your opinion.'

'I have a right to know,' said Tara.

Shane shrugged. 'So you say,' he replied. 'Personally, I don't like to talk while I am working. Ruins the concentration. Very sloppy.'

He handed a blindfold to Jack. 'Put this around her eyes,' he said. 'It will make things easier for everyone.'

Jack did as he was told. The will to resist had left him now, drained as soon as he saw Shane's face under the neon light. He knew what the man was like. He had seen him kill in cold blood, for trivial reasons, and with no sign of remorse. Resistance was now useless, and, strange though it seemed to him, too much of an effort. They had tried to escape from the clutches of these people. Nobody could say they had not done their best. They had come very close. And they had failed. Better to accept their fate calmly and with dignity.

He took the black cloth from Shane, and held it across Tara's eyes. He could feel her heart beating, hard and sudden, and her brow was moist from perspiration. He kissed her gently on the ear. Better the gun than the knife, he thought.

His hands trembled as he tied the cloth, his fingers fumbling with the knot. He wanted to say something to her, to find some words for the moment, but his mind was blank, emptied of all emotions apart from a lingering, melancholy terror.

The knot tied, Shane stretched out a hand towards him. Jack took the cloth and held it for a moment in his hands.

'Blindfold yourself,' said Shane.

Jack turned to look at Fuller but her expression betrayed neither sympathy nor concern.

She had nothing to say, and her eyes turned away to avoid all contact with his. Jack took the cloth and raised it to his face, covering his eyes with the mask, and tying a firm knot around the back of his head. His knees and his arms were shaking now.

270

Jack waited for a moment, his vision gone, already lost in the darkness. Silence. He felt the sharp tap of steel against the side of his skull. 'Kneel,' said Shane. 'Both of you.'

He could feel his knees buckle beneath him, only too happy to give way, and his body collapsed beneath him. He readjusted himself, and he could feel the cold concrete on his knees as he knelt on the floor. His head was bowed and he was wondering whether to pray. His whole body was shaking now, his manner, he knew, cowardly and undignified, but his limbs had long since escaped his control.

'Closing time,' muttered Shane.

Jack reached out into the darkness, and found her hand. She too was searching for him, and he grabbed it gratefully, holding on to her, desperate to spend these last few moments in her embrace. He could feel her squeezing his palm so tight the blood was draining from his fingers.

He heard the first shot, a loud, sharp retort, echoing around the room. Her first, he thought. He gripped her hand tighter still, desperate to maintain contact while he waited for the second shot. Through the skin, he could feel her veins in her wrist still throbbing.

TWENTY-SEVEN

The Deputy Governor of the Bank of England sat behind the ornate wooden desk in his office on the third floor of the stately Threadneedle Street building. Jonathan Donaldson was new to the job; his predecessor had resigned suddenly amid the wreckage of a sex scandal, and he had been drafted in from the CBI to fill his place. In all honesty, he would admit to himself, his inexperience was a liability; the economics was straightforward enough, but central banking was still an arcane science to him, and City regulation was not something to which he brought any depth of experience. Never mind, he told himself. He would learn.

On the problems that confronted him this morning, he had had to take advice from his staff. Ocher's bankers had requested an urgent meeting with the Bank, to present what they claimed were serious irregularities with the process of the bid. Donaldson's staff advised that any such requests were not usually granted, but since the Bank was the ultimate arbiter in matters of take-over regulation, it was natural that they should turn to Threadneedle Street with their complaints. After the Swiss Embassy in London has insisted the meeting go ahead, there had been little choice but to let it proceed.

No hint had been given as to the nature of their complaint; protocol did not require that they give advance notice of the matters they were going to raise. Inquiries among the supervisory staff at the Bank had not indicated there was anything unusual about the bidding process; they saw no obvious evidence of concert parties, or share support operations, or any of the other wild antics corporate financiers could devise when mounting a hostile take-over. So far as they could tell, everything was being done strictly by the book.

Still, reflected Donaldson, there was no way of knowing what might happen. Ocher were clearly taking the matter seriously, and Julian Symonds, he knew, was a banker of the old school; if he wanted a meeting it would not be on some frivolous matter. The request that the Swiss ambassador be present at the meeting, however, puzzled him. He had checked with his staff, and, though it was most unusual, they could think of no reason why the ambassador should not be present. Consultation with officials at the Foreign Office had established that it would be a diplomatic slight to refuse the request; Switzerland, after all, was a friendly European country, they pointed out. And so the request was duly granted; the ambassador would be there as an observer, although not as a participant.

Donaldson was still suspicious, and, despite playing everything back through his mind, could not track down any significant reason for the meeting. Obviously the take-over of a major Swiss corporation by a British rival was a matter of concern to the Swiss government, and they had a legitimate interest in seeing that fair play was observed. But the Bank could surely be trusted to ensure that all sides were treated equitably? True, he conceded to himself, standards in the City had slipped in the past ten years. But surely no one would doubt the integrity of the Bank?

Donaldson checked the clock on the wall and saw that he had half an hour to go. He returned to the papers on his desk; briefing papers prepared by his staff that set out the main issues involved in Kizog's bid for Ocher. He might not know what was going on yet, he decided, but he would at least be well prepared.

A mile and a half away, the blue Daimler pulled up outside the gleaming City headquarters of Kizog's merchant bank. The Chairman and his finance director climbed out of the car and walked inside the plush lobby. They found Morrison and two of his assistants waiting for them. Morrison stood to attention, and the Chairman shook his hand warmly. A sly smile was playing across his face. 'It looks like being a good morning,' said the Chairman cheerfully.

'I hope so,' replied Morrison. 'I certainly hope so.'

'How are the acceptances going?'

'Most of the small shareholders have returned their forms, and most are taking our offer,' answered Morrison. 'But they of course only account for about twenty per cent of the stock. It is the big fund managers who really matter.'

'And which way are they going?'

'They never make the final move until the last moment. It is not unheard of for a counter-offer to be tabled even in the final hours, so they have nothing to lose by waiting until eleven or so. After eleven we'll see a procession of bikers rolling up here with the papers. Then we can start counting. Our latest intelligence is that we'll get between sixty-five and seventy-five per cent of the stock. We should have a final tally by around three this afternoon.'

'Fine, fine,' said the Chairman.

'There is a lot more activity on the options market this morning,' Morrison continued, his tone betraying his anxiety. 'Some serious money is taking up sell options in Kizog stock. Someone is betting big that we are going to lose.'

The Chairman raised his eyebrows and peered directly into Morrison's eyes. 'Then they are going to get badly hurt,' he said firmly.

274

Morrison looked away, glancing at his watch, and pointing out that they should be making a move. Together with the Chairman he climbed into the waiting Daimler, sitting in the front seat whilst his two assistants joined Finer, climbing into the Jaguar that was following along behind.

The car slid smoothly through the City traffic towards the Bank. Morrison sat next to the Chairman. His mood was sombre, and an air of concern hung around him; a marked contrast to the serene confidence of the Chairman. 'The Bank told me the Swiss ambassador had requested attendance at this meeting,' he said.

'And will he be there?' asked the Chairman.

'They were surprised that he asked to attend, but the Bank felt they had no choice but to accede,' said Morrison.

'I don't suppose it matters,' replied the Chairman breezily.

'It indicates a certain seriousness, Sir Kurt,' continued Morrison. 'I can't imagine the people at Zurich Financial would want to involve their government unless they had something really serious to raise. It would be embarrassing for them.'

The Chairman turned to look at his banker. Despite his many years of experience, the force of the term 'embarrassment' in the City had never ceased to amaze him; surely these people realised that adult life involved an endless appetite for humility. What did he care if they were embarrassed? 'I have a strong feeling that this meeting will turn out to be a non-event,' he replied. 'Everything has been taken care of. The Swiss are just clutching at straws. Bad losers the lot of them. All we need to do is go through the motions, and then get back to counting those acceptances. By this afternoon I will have my victory and you your fee.'

Morrison simply nodded; long years of experience had taught him to accept the word of his clients. Privately he was not so sure this would be as simple as the Chairman liked to suppose, but for now he would keep his feelings to himself.

The Daimler drew up outside the front gates of the Bank at seven minutes to ten. Outside the two great bronze doors was the discreet sign: 'No admittance, except on business'. The party climbed out of the cars, and went through the doors. To either side of them were the doormen, dressed in the distinctive livery of the Bank: red waistcoats, pink tailcoats and top hats. They explained their business at the desk, and were told that Mr Donaldson would meet them in the first-floor committee room usually reserved for audiences with the Deputy Governor. A doorman escorted them through the magnificent marbled lobby, and led them up one flight of stairs.

A marble fireplace and the clock above it dominated the room. The windows looked out on to the garden court below, and down the centre of the room was a long wooden table. The Chairman sat down, and the rest took their cues from him, seating themselves around the table. It was still three minutes to ten, and they were the first to arrive.

Julian Symonds entered the room at one minute to ten. He was accompanied by the Swiss ambassador, Dieter Helms, a tall, elegant man wearing a well-cut double-breasted suit, with horn-rimmed glasses covering his eyes. Two assistants from his bank followed Symonds into the room, plus a legal adviser. Symonds and Morrison were already well-acquainted, and the two men shook hands. Symonds introduced Helms, first to Morrison and then to the Chairman, who welcomed him with a firm handshake and a broad smile. Symonds's eyes were scanning anxiously around the room. There was no sign of Tara and Jack and he had not heard from them since yesterday morning. Once again, he was starting to wonder where they were.

It was ten o'clock, and the chimes of St Paul's could be heard from several streets away. With the precise timing on which he prided himself, Donaldson entered the room. He was flanked by two members of his staff, experts in financial regulation and take-over law, there to advise him on any decisions that might have to be made this morning.

He walked through he room, shaking hands with each person in turn. They greeted him warmly and with a hint of deference; people, Donaldson had noted, were still impressed by the dignity and tradition of the Bank, even if much of it was a fiction these

276

days. He sat down at the head of the table, and indicated, simply through the inflection of his eyebrows, that the meeting was called to order. Along the length of the table, the rest of the party also sat, the Kizog and Ocher camps taking up opposite sides, facing each other, for the first time since the bid began, over four feet of fine oak. Donaldson cleared his throat. 'I believe there are certain matters you wished to raise this morning, Mr Symonds.'

'Indeed there are,' replied Symonds calmly. 'We believe there are serious irregularities in the way Kizog conducts its business and in the way it is financing this bid. Once these matters are fully explained, I feel sure the Bank will agree that the bid should be immediately suspended, and inquiries should begin into Kizog's activities.'

'We are most happy to hear you out, Mr Symonds,' responded Donaldson. 'Please explain your concerns.'

Symonds glanced across the table. The expressions there struck him as strangely confident and serene; there were no signs of nerves in their eyes. Two possibilities, he decided; either they have no idea how much Tara and Jack have discovered; or they are aware, and know something I don't. He could feel a trace of moisture on his brow as he realised the second possibility was the more likely explanation.

'If you will forgive me, Deputy Governor,' Symonds explained. 'I am waiting for two more people with a role to play in these events to arrive. Perhaps we could wait just a few more minutes before we begin.'

'If you wish,' replied Donaldson crisply.

A tense silence fell over the room. To his side Symonds could see the clock on the wall. It was already seven minutes past ten. He had posted a man at the door to keep watch for Tara and Jack, and instructed him to make sure they arrived in the committee room the instant they showed up at the Bank. He had told his office to put any calls he received from them straight through to this room. If there were any problems, he could be contacted on his mobile. But there was still no sign of them.

Where are they? he wondered, with growing apprehension.

Across the room, Symonds could hear the slow tapping of the Chairman's fingernails against the wooden table-top. 'May I remind you, Deputy Governor, that this bid closes at twelve,' he said. 'Anxious though I am to hear and defend myself against these allegations, time is pressing.'

'I understand your concerns, Sir Kurt,' replied Donaldson. 'You may be sure the Bank has no desire to interfere in these matters.'

'Without evidence and explanation, there is no basis in law or precedent for holding up this take-over,' said Morrison. 'Indeed, were there to be any delay we would have to consider our legal position.'

He left the words hanging in the air. The threat was clear enough, Symonds decided; Morrison was telling the Deputy Governor the Bank could be sued at any moment. He glanced across at Donaldson, and could tell from the frown upon his face that the Deputy Governor was not pleased.

'If you wish us to consider this matter, Mr Symonds,' said Donaldson. 'I suggest you proceed immediately.'

Symonds reddened visibly. 'A few more moments, sir,' he said, summoning every inner reserve of humility he had.

The Chairman glanced upwards. 'I must insist we start immediately,' he said acidly. 'I do hope Mr Symonds has not gathered us here unnecessarily. That would be very embarrassing.'

TWENTY-EIGHT

He heard only the sound of a gasp, and the crash of a body falling against the concrete. After that, silence; an eerie stillness, whilst he waited to feel the cold steel of the gun against his skull, and the impact of the bullet as it shattered through his mind. Blackness still engulfed him, and his shirt was clinging to his skin, drenched in the sweat running off his back.

Jack waited in the darkness, his body unable to move, his mind unable to think. He could feel Tara's hand clutching him, jabbing at his wrist. She is checking that I am still alive, he thought. And then, with painful and uncomprehending slowness, the truth slithered through the scrambled nerve endings cluttering his mind.

Both of us are still alive.

With difficulty, he disentangled his hand from Tara's clutches. She seemed reluctant to let him go. Reaching for his blindfold, he struggled with the knots. His hands were numb, and it took

279

several minutes to untangle the cloth that he had bound so tightly around his face.

The lights were still dim, but seemed harsh after the darkness he had escaped. Jack rubbed his eyes, adjusting his vision to the glow of the damp neon. He could see nothing in front of him, apart from the silent, inert row of cars. He looked first to his right. At Tara. She too was struggling to untie the knots on her blindfold.

Still kneeling, Jack slowly and nervously turned his head. His eyes fixed first on Shane. The man was lying about three yards away, slumped on the ground, his head pressing hard against the concrete floor, blood trickling from a wound in the back of his skull. Jack listened carefully. He could just hear the drip of the blood against the concrete. Apart from that, silence. He could detect no sign that the man was breathing.

Jack's gaze moved on. He looked up at Fuller. She was standing with her arms stretched out before her, her posture motionless, her expression disinterested; in the grip of her hands he could see a gun.

The weapon was still directed at Shane's dead body.

Fuller took two steps forward, and shoved her flat shoes into the body, kicking Shane over. His head rolled into the pool of blood, streaking his blond hair with crimson. Fuller knelt down, picked up his wrist, and held it in her hand. 'Dead,' she said calmly.

Tara had shaken free her blindfold. She laid it to her side, stood up, and walked across to Jack, holding him by the hand and helping him to his feet. She turned to face Fuller. 'You shot him?' she said.

To Jack her voice sounded fractured and hoarse, as though she was suffering from a bad cold. Fuller met her gaze and nodded. 'You got my e-mail,' she said.

Jack's mind was still shattered by the emotions of the last few minutes, and he was having trouble thinking straight, but he could recall the message he had received just before they had escaped arrest together; it had puzzled him for the past few days, yet he had assumed that it was just a way of making it easier for Kizog to destroy them. 'Who are you working for?' he asked.

Fuller reflected on the question for a moment, as if she were having trouble deciding how much to tell them. 'You have assumed that everyone at Kizog is on the same side?' she asked.

'So far, yes,' replied Jack.

'Probably incorrect,' said Fuller. 'Think about who benefits if you make your meeting.'

Jack was about to speak, but Fuller stopped him. 'There is no time to talk,' she said. 'It is almost ten, and you have to hurry. Do what you have to do.'

Jack collected the bags, still on the ground where they had left them, took Tara by the arm, and together they ran up the concrete steps, emerging blinking into the sunlight on the street. His head was still spinning, and Jack could feel the dampness of the sweat on his forehead. Never mind why she did it, he thought to himself. We are still here. Alive. And we still have time.

Fuller slipped quietly away. Jack could see her walk down the street, a slow saunter in her step, looking to all the world like a woman who was heading out for some Friday morning shopping.

He hailed a cab, asking the driver to take them first to St Pancras station, and then on to the Bank of England. Five minutes later, the cab pulled up in the forecourt of the station. Jack left Tara in the taxi whilst he walked inside the building. He went straight to the left-luggage lockers, placed one of his two bags inside a compartment, fed in some coins, and locked up. Slipping the key into his back pocket, he walked back to the cab. He told the driver to head for the Bank. As fast as possible.

Tara and Jack completed the ride in silence. Both of them, Jack suspected, were too bewildered by everything that had happened to speak yet. Never mind, he decided. There would be time to make sense of it later.

The cab pulled up outside the Bank at seventeen minutes past ten. Jack climbed out and paid the driver. Tara, carrying their sports bag, followed him on to the street. At once a young man in a suit and carrying a mobile phone rushed up to them. 'Thank Christ you're here,' he said. 'We were starting to worry about whether you would make it.'

He led them inside the foyer of the building. The footmen, plumed in their red and pink finery, looked distastefully at the jeans and sweatshirts of the couple walking in, and Jack could tell from the expressions on their faces that they were about to eject them. Brushing past the footmen, their new companion walked straight to the desk. 'Late arrivals for the meeting in the Deputy Governor's office,' he barked. 'We're almost out of time. It's very urgent.'

The man behind the desk issued three visitors' passes, and, scooping them up, the suit flashed them at the guards, took hold of Tara's arm and led them towards the stairs. 'This way,' he said.

Along the strip of corridor, Jack tried to slow his pace, breathing deeply, trying to compose himself for the minutes ahead.

Inside the meeting room, a silence was still hanging in the air. Symonds had refused to begin until his party was complete, and the Deputy Governor had given him until ten-thirty. After that, he had warned, the matter would be regarded as closed. The Chairman, meanwhile, was sitting back with the complacent air of a man with better things to do with his time. As each minute ticked slowly away, Symonds noticed that his expression became more and more peaceful.

The door swung open. Into the committee room the suit ushered Jack and Tara. Immediately all the eyes around the room swivelled towards them, following every inflection of their muscles as they walked down the length of the table, stopping next to Symonds, calmly pulling out a chair each and sitting down.

Jack noticed the Chairman first. The pupils of his eyes were suddenly wider; he tracked their movements through the room with a mixture of fear, surprise and disgust. The tapping of his fingernails on the table-top had suddenly ceased, and his shoulders appeared to have slumped. Jack looked straight through him. 'Sorry to keep you waiting, Sir Kurt,' he said sharply. 'We were held up for a few minutes.'

282

Symonds cleared his throat, glancing over their scruffy clothes, and his nose twitched slightly as he noticed the sweat still soaking through Jack's shirt. 'Deputy Governor,' he began. 'Allow me to introduce Mr Jack Borrodin and Miss Tara Ling.'

Jack glanced up the table at the man upon whose mercy he would throw himself. His expression was hard to read: part puzzled, part angry, part intrigued. This is it, Jack told himself.

Donaldson was aware of who these two young people were. He knew the names, and he knew what they were accused of, and he was far from sure they should be in the Deputy Governor's meeting room. 'Correct me if I am wrong,' he said carefully. 'But these two people have arrest warrants issued against them.'

Jack interrupted. 'All we ask is that you listen to what we have to say. If we do not convince you of our innocence then we are happy for you to turn us over to the authorities.'

To his side Jack could hear a palm slapping on the table-top. 'This is an outrage!' said Morrison, his tone filled with professional anger. 'I do not think we can be expected to hear any claims made by known fugitives.'

At the end of the table the Swiss ambassador raised a hand. Looking directly at Donaldson, he spoke slowly and clearly. 'My government would consider it a great courtesy if you would listen to what these people have to say.'

Jack looked again towards the Deputy Governor. He seemed deep in thought, and he was whispering something to one of his two advisers. 'Please go ahead,' he said. 'We will hear you out.'

Tara stood up. From the sports bag Jack had dumped on the floor she pulled out the five copies of the document they had prepared. With a winning smile she placed one neatly in front of the Deputy Governor. Walking around the room, she gave one to Morrison, one to the Chairman, one to the ambassador, and one to Symonds. Completing the circuit she sat back down next to Jack.

The moment was due, Jack reflected. In the next few minutes their fate would be decided. He scanned the room, trying to penetrate the minds of the men reading the document laid out before them. His eyes rested first on Donaldson. The Deputy Governor was concentrating hard on the few sheets of paper, racing through the words. A frown was playing across his forehead. Further down the table, Jack noticed, the Chairman was gripping the sheets between his hands, his face reddening as he scrolled through the pages; whether it was the result of anger or embarrassment, Jack could not tell. Finer was leaning over his shoulder reading at the same time; his eyes betrayed a certain glee, a sense of anticipation that Jack found puzzling. He glanced across at Morrison. His expression was clear enough; he looked like a man about to surrender to a funk.

Jack tapped Symonds on the arm. 'A word,' he said.

Symonds looked across at Donaldson. 'Will you excuse us for a moment, Deputy Governor?'

Donaldson waved a hand that seemed to signify he did not mind where they were right now. Jack stood up and walked towards the door. Symonds followed, shutting the door behind them, and the two men were alone in the corridor. 'We have the evidence,' started Jack. 'But not here.'

'Where?' asked Symonds anxiously.

'When I know that the options have been bought in our name, and transport arranged, then you get the papers.'

'Impossible,' started Symonds. 'The bid closes at twelve.'

'All I need is a fax guaranteeing the account has been set up and the options bought,' Jack replied. 'It'll only take a few minutes. Make the call now.'

Symonds took the mobile phone from his pocket and began dialling. Connected instantly, he whispered the instructions to his assistant back at the bank. 'Done,' he said. Together they walked back into the room and sat down. Jack leant across to Tara. 'OK,' he whispered. 'We're rich.'

He looked up around the room. Donaldson was nearing the end of the document, and as he finished the last page he sat back in his chair, a thoughtful expression on his face. 'Do we have any proof?' he asked.

'We can prove every word,' said Tara.

'But you don't have it here,' said Donaldson.

Symonds looked up. 'I believe we can have all the documentary evidence you need within an hour,' he said. 'Your staff can then examine it, and then form your own judgement on how solid our allegations are.'

Across the table Jack could see Morrison and the Chairman whispering to one another. 'I must protest,' said Morrison. 'To start with, Kizog entirely rejects all the arguments contained in this document. Secondly, all of these claims would be matters for the criminal courts. They will have to be dealt with in due course. But until guilt or innocence is proven the Bank has no business holding up the bid. That should proceed. In stopping it the Bank would be acting beyond its powers and could certainly expect legal challenge.'

A thin smile had returned to the Chairman's lips. Still manœuvring, thought Jack. Still hoping to escape, perhaps. Or simply unaware of the calamity that was about to overcome him. Denial or optimism? It was hard to tell.

Donaldson had consulted with his legal expert, and returned his gaze to the table. He directed his remarks at Symonds. 'I think Mr Morrison may be right,' he said. 'Serious though these matters may be, they pertain to breaches of the criminal law, not to breaches of the take-over code. I fear if we acted we might be ruled to be acting outside of our jurisdiction.'

Jack looked across the table. 'May I direct your attention to the last page, sir,' he said.

Donaldson turned to the relevant page of the document. 'Perhaps you could explain?' he said.

'It says that money is being channelled into Kizog via HKS Pharmaceuticals, which is a deposit point for money collected through counterfeiting operations.'

'I see,' said Donaldson.

'If we could prove that HKS was also funding the bid,' continued Jack, 'that in effect the bid was being financed by laundered criminal money, that would be a breach of take-over rules, and the Bank could intervene.'

285

At his side, the legal expert whispered something in Donaldson's ear. 'True,' replied the Deputy Governor.

Jack turned to Symonds. 'You found out who was buying the bonds?' he asked quietly.

Symonds nodded. He reached beneath the desk and pulled up his attaché case. For a moment Jack held his breath. If his hunch was wrong, they were done for. The waters would close above them. The bid would proceed. And they would be left to fend for themselves.

From the look of relief on Symonds's face, Jack knew he had been right. Out of his case Symonds pulled a sheaf of documents, laying them out on the table in front of him. 'Working out who has been buying the bonds Kizog issued was of course far from easy,' he began. 'We had to trace the orders through a string of registrars and nominee accounts. But we have been able to establish that the ultimate beneficiary of a substantial portion of the bond issue is HKS Pharmaceuticals. You should also note, Deputy Governor, that the bonds have warrants attached, meaning that the board can, if it chooses, convert them into equity at a later date. Meaning, of course, that HKS would, if the board took that route, end up owning a controlling interest in Kizog.'

Of course, thought Jack, the last piece of the jigsaw. The warrants would allow the Chairman to use the counterfeiting money to buy a controlling stake in Kizog. He would not only run the company; he would own it as well. It was so simple, he started wondering why he hadn't realised earlier. Everything fitted together.

Donaldson and his two advisers were studying the documents and charts Symonds had pushed across the table. From their expressions, Jack suspected they were satisfied with what they saw laid out before them. Across the table, he could see defeat written across the faces of the three men. Morrison was wiping his brow, his features creased up in humility; he was deciding whether it was time to sacrifice his client, Jack decided. Finer was peering down at the ground, avoiding eye contact with anyone. And the Chairman was leaning forward, the lines on his face suddenly deeper and craggier, his hands laid out flat on the table. He seemed to have aged a decade in the last few minutes.

He shot a look of pure hatred at Jack. 'What happened to Shane?' he muttered.

Jack shrugged, and allowed a playful smile to cross his lips. 'Mr Shane has been downsized,' he replied.

Donaldson ignored the conversation. 'Do you have anything to say about this, Sir Kurt?'

'Not until I consult my lawyers,' said the Chairman wearily.

'I'm sure that will be necessary,' replied the Deputy Governor sharply. 'In the meantime, Mr Symonds, you may inform your client that the Bank is this morning suspending the bid pending further inquiries. Off the record, you may tell them it is not likely to be allowed to proceed.'

A smile broke out on Symonds's face. He took out his mobile, preparing to put a call through to Basle. Across the room Jack could see a secretary entering. She stopped, whispering in the ear of the Deputy Governor, who directed her towards Jack. Walking silently down the length of the table, she put a fax in front of him. Jack glanced down. He recognised the Zurich Financial logo and he scanned the details; two million had been deposited in their joint account, and the money spent on Kizog put options. The bank, it pointed out, would be charging £383 a day in interest on the loan.

Jack folded the fax away, and leant across to Tara. 'It's done,' he said. He took the key from his back pocket, and pushed it across the table to Symonds. 'Locker 342. St Pancras left luggage,' he said. Symonds passed the key to his assistant, instructing him to retrieve it. Immediately.

Jack took Tara by the arm and stood up. Together they began walking towards the door. As they passed Donaldson, they stopped and looked down. 'Are we free to go?' asked Jack.

The Deputy Governor shrugged. 'Search me!' he replied. Then he smiled. 'I doubt that a man of my age would have much chance of stopping you. Good luck.'

Together they started walking down the corridor, their arms bound tightly round one another. As they neared the steps, they heard a discreet cough behind them. Jack turned, and saw the Swiss ambassador walking along the corridor towards them.

'My driver is returning to Zurich this afternoon,' said Helms. 'By private diplomatic plane.'

Jack nodded.

'You would like to accompany him?'

Jack nodded again.

'The blue Mercedes, outside,' said Helms. 'There are first-class tickets booked in your name on the Swissair flight to Bangkok, with onward connections to Vietnam.'

Jack turned, walking up to the ambassador, shaking his outstretched hand. 'Thank you,' he replied.

'I believe you may soon come into some substantial sums of money,' the ambassador continued with a knowing smile. 'The banks in my country are very safe, and very discreet. You would be well looked after.'

Taking Tara by the arm, Jack guided her into the Mercedes. Without a word, the driver pulled away from the kerb, heading west through the mid-morning City traffic towards Heathrow. Sitting back in the deep leather seats he tugged Tara close to him, kissing her softly on the brow. He could see a tear trickling down her face. 'We made it,' he whispered in her ear.

They completed the drive largely in silence, both of them too exhausted, their nerves too strained, for either of them to speak. Arriving at the airport, the driver escorted them to the first-class Swissair lounge. 'Your plane will be ready within an hour,' he told them.

In the corner of the room Jack spotted a Reuters terminal and, instinctively, he walked towards it. Casting his eyes through the list of FTSE stocks, he clicked on KZG L. A story appeared instantly on the screen.

KIZOG BID FOR OCHER SUSPENDED
London: 12:06 GMT: The Bank of England said this
morning that it was suspending the bid made by Kizog for
its Swiss rival Ocher pending investigation of various

irregularities. The Bank declined to comment on what the irregularities consisted of, but senior sources said it was unlikely that the bid would now be allowed to proceed. The bid had been scheduled to close at noon today, and Kizog was widely expected to emerge as the victor.

Kizog shares collapsed on the news, and are currently trading down 224p. Analysts were caught out by the sudden suspension of the bid, and are speculating that financial problems have emerged at the company. 'It is a very confused situation,' said one. 'The market is trading on zero information.' Meanwhile, the price of Kizog put options, the scene of significant turbulence in the last forty-eight hours, has soared. October puts are currently priced at 238p. 'Someone has made a killing,' said one trader.

Jack could feel Tara's arm slipping around his waist as he completed the story. He turned and smiled. 'What do you want to do now?' she asked.

'Shower,' replied Jack. 'And then take a long holiday. A very long holiday.'

She rested her head against his shoulder. 'Sounds good,' she said softly.

Jack gripped her close to him. 'So long as you come too,' he replied.

EPILOGUE

The machine spun endlessly around, the drum rotating to an even beat, as the chemicals inside were mixed to perfection. It connected to a compressor, from which emerged a steady flow of small, circular yellow pills, each one exactly three millimetres in diameter. Jack plucked one from the line, standing next to the row of Vietnamese packaging workers, and held it between his thumb and his forefinger. Perfect, he thought to himself. Grasping the pill in his fist, he walked slowly down the line. The second machine had just been installed, doubling the capacity of the small factory on the outskirts of Saigon. The orders had been booked, and with this extra plant the company would start making money.

Tara had been absolutely right, he decided. Vietnam was emerging fast, and the country felt fresh and young and ambitious. He was happier here than he had been anywhere.

After exchanging a few words with his foreman, Jack

walked through the rest of the factory, and into the distribution centre, keen to check that the day's deliveries had been made on schedule.

He was standing among the shelves when he caught sight of her standing in the cramped foyer, his pulse quickened and his jaw slackened. As it had done in the past, a riff started strumming through Jack's mind. Get down on my knees.

'It's been so long,' said Layla.

Jack allowed a warm smile to cross his face as he leant across to kiss her lightly on the cheek. Without quite knowing why, he realised he was pleased to see her.

'Ralph is waiting outside,' she continued. 'Is it all right if he comes in?'

Jack shrugged. Why not? he thought. We are safe here. And a lot of time has passed.

Finer emerged from the Mercedes parked on the forecourt, and walked hesitantly towards the factory. He shook Jack stiffly by the hand; his expression, Jack noted, seemed cloaked in uncertainty.

He led them back through the factory, and towards the laboratory. Inside, Tara, flanked by her two assistants, bent over her microscope. He patted her on the back, pointing towards Layla and Finer. 'Unexpected visitors,' he said.

Tara stood up, standing close to Jack, and eyeing them warily. 'What brings you to Saigon?' she said, her tone polite but cool.

'Business,' replied Finer. 'Possible joint ventures. And to see you.'

The man looked older now, his jowls heavier, his eyes surrounded by bags, and his face craggier. Burdened down, thought Jack. 'What happened?' he asked.

Finer rested his arms on the lab bench, and took a sip from the cup of Chinese tea that had just been brought in by the secretary. 'Let's put it this way,' he began. 'Not everyone at the company was following the same agenda. You probably guessed Fuller was working with me. There were clues after all. She sent you a message to escape. And I routed the money to you via HKS. It would have been easy to route the money through a shell company. Unless I wanted to make it easy for you to collect the evidence.'

'And after we left?' asked Jack.

'It was all quite hairy that morning,' Finer replied. 'The Chairman was losing it badly by then. The Bank told him the bid had to be dropped. It was either that, or they would call it off and make sure he went to jail for fraud. He had no choice really. A statement was made that afternoon. A few weeks later the Chairman resigned. There was no great surprise in the City. After the fiasco over the bid the share price had sunk like a stone. It came down by almost three pounds. Anyone who had bought some put options would have made a fortune.' He smiled at Jack. 'They brought in Sir Charles Betts, who used to be a junior minister in the Ministry of Defence, as the new chairman. A few weeks later Taylor resigned as chief executive. We got a new public affairs director as well. The company's image had, after all, taken quite a battering. Scott went. He took early retirement. And I was made the new chief executive. It was the only choice really. There has to be some continuity at the company. Business carries on.'

'That was the plan all along, right?' said Jack. 'You wanted the Chairman to fail, so that you could take his place. That's why you made it easy for us.'

'I never had much faith in his strategy,' replied Finer. 'It was all too complex. At some point it was all bound to unravel. Perhaps now, perhaps later. But eventually. It was different during the Cold War. We were just working for certain people in the defence establishment, and we had their backing. Sir Kurt had the support of the old guard, but he was basically blackmailing them, threatening to reveal what had taken place. That was not, in my judgement, a sustainable relationship. Sooner or later they were going to throw us to the wolves.'

'So you decided to jump ship?' said Jack.

'It seemed the best thing to do,' replied Finer. 'Plus I didn't like what was happening to you.'

'But if we hadn't succeeded,' countered Jack, 'no one would

have known you were helping us.'

'It's a cold world,' said Finer. 'People mainly look after themselves.' He paused, taking another sip of his tea. 'Anyway, I wanted you to know there have been some changes at the Ministry of Defence. Several senior officials took early retirement. And all investigations into Ator have been quietly dropped. If you wanted to return home it would be quite safe.'

Jack shook his head, holding Tara close to him, and Layla noted the gold wedding ring on her finger. 'We are quite happy here, thanks,' he replied. Shaking hands with Finer, he led him back through the factory, out on to the forecourt, and watched as Finer climbed back into the waiting car.

Layla hesitated for a moment, standing at his side, looking up into his eyes. 'It isn't nearly so much fun without you around,' she said.

Jack smiled. 'When this company gets a bit bigger, I'll offer you a job. We need someone to get the rumour-mill grinding,' he replied. 'What's your title now, anyway?'

She turned to face him, her eyes sparkling. 'Special assistant to the Chairman,' she answered.

Jack reached across and squeezed her arm. 'Well,' he said. 'Watch out for yourself.'